Praise for 'Revealing the Revolution'

"Subtly challenges the reader to think about the wider debate enveloping artificial intelligence."
Christen Civiletto, *Green City Savior*

"A fascinating and unique story that combines the thrill and camaraderie of a sports book with the danger and intrigue of conspiracy thrillers through a high-tech sci-fi concept."
Mary Fan, *Jane Colt series*

"An intriguing premise that should appeal to fans of The Hunger Games."
Adam Bender, *Divided We Fall*

"The characters are witty, the scenes creative, interesting and larger than life."
Amanda Masters, *reviewer at Nerd Girl Official*

"*Revealing the Revolution* is an enjoyable tale of futuristic sports which romance fans as well as young adult readers will want to add to their collection by a fresh new author."
Cheri Feih, *Goodreads reviewer*

Praise for 'Chasing the Underground'

"Sotzek is an incredible and daring author who isn't afraid to go for the big and bold idea. ... the story is full of adventure, danger, and intrigue and was definitely an edge of your seat page turner "

Amanda Masters, *reviewer at Nerd Girl Official*

"*Chasing the Underground* is an exciting novel that takes a lot of the plot lines from the first novel (*Revealing the Revolution*) and expands on them artfully."

Edward Edmonds, *Goodreads reviewer*

"The storytelling is fantastic. Maria is a brilliant female character, and I adore how she takes her own agency back when those with authority try to shut her down. This series is absolutely worth the time investment. Very highly recommended.

Asher Syed, *Readers' Favorite reviewer*

THE AIM CHRONICLES

Revealing the Revolution

Chasing the Underground

Finding the Impossible

FINDING THE IMPOSSIBLE

FINDING THE IMPOSSIBLE

N.M. SOTZEK

Published by N.M. Sotzek Publishing
Kitchener, Ontario, Canada
nsotzek.wix.com/nmsotzek

Finding the Impossible

First printing 2026

Cover design by JB Centeno
Publisher logo design by Becky Allen

ISBN 978-0-9937895-4-0 (paperback)
ISBN 978-0-9937895-5-7 (ebook)

To all of those who believed in me and this story.
This is for you.

CHAPTER 1

Sand whipped in the air in weak twisters. The group of twelve men squinted as the grit flew into their face while they drove through the small village; their helmets were no use against the sharp grains. One of the men looked at the people as they drove by. Most wore blank stares – the look of a people ravaged by war. Others, he noticed, wore cautious smiles. It was good to know that even after all that had happened between the two countries, some were willing to reconcile and willing to look beyond the past.

"It's no fanfare, but I'll take this over gunfire any day," another man shouted from the driver's seat of the large military vehicle. An American flag was proudly stitched to his shoulder, along with the other men in the convoy.

The first man grinned, loosening the grip on his rifle. Mistake number one. "McMurphy, I'd take your sister over gunfire."

The rest of the men howled, as Captain McMurphy swung to hit him over the back of the head. "What did we say about my sister, Collins? You sick-" He stopped the vehicle as a small object rolled across the road in front of them. He squinted for less than a second before he put the vehicle into reverse.

"IED!" he screamed as the device exploded, sending a blast of fire and metal out around it. The shock shattered the windshield, and they shielded their faces. Collins grabbed his rifle and leapt from the vehicle, followed close behind by his men. His ears rang from the explosion. Gunshots echoed against the buildings, and the villagers scattered, but the sound was muffled by the ringing in his head. Their screams were drowned out by the sounds of the invisible machine guns. Two more explosions erupted from the building next to the soldiers.

Collins pointed up ahead on the road. "Get to cover!" he yelled, and pointed to his sniper. "Rupert, get up into this building. Find where the shots are coming from, and take them out." He watched as the soldier ran into a building beside them, his assault rifle poised in front of him as he ran.

A group of men ran out in front of Collins and the remaining soldiers, each wielding a rifle. They shouted in Pashto, and wore the uniform of a group they thought had been disbanded years ago.

Collins did not need to be fluent in Pashto to know what the word on the chest of their uniform read: Mjahdan. He was about to fire on the men when two tigers walked out from behind the men.

"That's cute," another soldier commented. The name Reese was printed on the right side of his chest. "They have pets."

One of the Mjahdan men fell to the ground. A dot of red on his forehead showed where the bullet went in. Before the insurgents could respond, Collins pulled the trigger. The rifle shook in his steady arms as he fired. He dove to the side as they began to fire back. He turned his face as one of his men whipped around from the force of a bullet, blood spraying from his neck as he fell.

Collins propped his rifle where he lay on the ground, and fired three more rounds. His bullets met their targets perfectly. Looking around, two more of his men were down. One twitched as his blood poured out from his gut. *Where's Rupert?*

A resonating roar caused everyone to turn their heads. Collins' jaw dropped when he saw the animal standing over the mangled body of its owner. "Some pet," he muttered, and shot the animal.

His eyes widened when the animal simply shook itself, as though repelling the bullet. It roared at him in protest, and continued to tear at the dead man's flesh. He looked around, and saw another tiger lunge toward a soldier.

McMurphy ran towards Collins and lay next to him on the ground. "Why would they use animals in an ambush? This is insane," he continued to yell over the screams of both soldier and insurgent, and the roar of the wild animals. He aimed his rifle, and planted a bullet in three more enemies. At least in the confusion, they had a chance of killing every last one of them.

But the animals moved away from the free meal of their masters, turning their attention to the villagers peering from windows. As if rehearsed, they ruthlessly attacked whatever moved. Collins watched as two ran into a building, and gurgled screams echoed from the walls.

"Come on," McMurphy grunted, grabbing his second-in-command. He pushed himself up and ran after the fleeing insurgents. They all stopped suddenly when they were approached by another tiger.

Collins opened fire, emptying his magazine on those in front of him, both human and animal. The human targets fell to the ground, and the animals...

McMurphy swore as they watched the body of the tiger vibrate and bubble, flowing into an opaque-white gel. The gel mixed with the reddened sand in front of them. A group of fleeing villagers ran past the two soldiers, pushing them to the side. He watched as limbs of a uniformed man fell from a window in the building across from them; the building Rupert had used as his perch.

Collins fell back against the blood-washed wall of the building, clutching his rifle against his chest. He had never seen anything like this before. It had been years since he witnessed a massacre, but nothing ever at this speed or with these...things.

Around him, bodies of children were tossed on the ground like ragdolls. Blood was smeared along walls, doorways, and the street. Limbs of his men, and villagers, were scattered up and down the sandy road. It was only now that the pungent smell of burning flesh, emptied bowels and stomachs, and death reached his nose. He nearly heaved. Eyes wide with a soldier's fear, he turned to McMurphy.

"What the hell is going on?"

CHAPTER 2

Two weeks later...

"Do you have to go?"

She grinned and looked up at him as she slipped her boots on. "You have training tomorrow, and I have to get back to Kingston."

He pouted and pulled her back to him. "But, but, but, I don't wanna."

Maria laughed as she reached up to plant a soft kiss on his lips. "You, Ryan Hampton, don't want to train with your team? The second team in the country? I find that very hard to believe, my dear." She squealed as he picked her up and walked her back to his living room. "Ryan, seriously! It's a long drive back."

"There are these things," Ryan started, tossing her down onto the couch, "called planes. They fly up in the air, and take you places faster than a car."

She bit her lip as he kissed her neck. "But I have my work Jeep. I can't leave it here for civilians to tamper with." She raised a playful eyebrow as he sat up, but it turned into a look of concern when Ryan's smile disappeared. "What's wrong?" When he shook his head, she thought for a moment. "Do you actually not want to go to training? I know it's going to be cold this week, but you'll get some great scans up north. You can even beat Cam in scans again."

He shrugged and fell down beside her on the large couch. "It's not that. I'm worried about Cam."

"Why? He's been doing great since he's been back on the team. I haven't seen him like this since, well, since I met him."

"He's not used to this lifestyle, I guess."

She quirked her lips up into a smile. "What? Famous and still a nice guy? You seem to handle it fine." She too lost her smile as she thought it over.

For the first five years Cam was in the Canadian Scanning Tournament, he was a superstar. He treated others as though they weren't worth his time. He got any girl he wanted simply by telling them his name Maria. But when he quit after his daughter with Maria was stillborn, he changed. They all had. And then two years ago happened.

"Do you think he'll backslide?" Ryan asked. "You know him better than I do."

After a year of not speaking or seeing each other, Cam and Maria had grown close once again, despite her relationship with his team-mate.

"I don't think so." Maria sighed and propped herself up onto her elbows. "The CST is his life now. You guys came so close to winning last year, closer than ever. He's not going to give up now without the Underground to distract him. If you guys win this coming season, I can see him retiring. You know Cam. Always has to leave on a high note." Her eyes met his. "Did Rick and Owen talk to you guys?"

He nodded. "Owen's retiring."

"It's not like we didn't see it coming. He made the comment two years ago that he'd be retiring soon, near the time I'm finished my service. He's been off the team before, and he hated it, but his stats are dropping. It's better to leave on a high since there's more fanfare that way," she said with a grin. She looked at the clock on the end table before looking back at Ryan. "How about we go out for dinner? I'll leave early in the morning, but that means leaving before you wake up."

Ryan's forehead wrinkled with another pout. "You don't want to stay in?" They saw each other so infrequently now, with him travelling around the county for the tournament, and her travelling to various military bases. It was only during the off-season they were able to spend significant time alone together.

"We don't normally get the chance to go out anywhere other than fast food places lately." She stood up and held her hand out. "Let's treat ourselves for once."

He couldn't argue with that.

It had been a long time since they had gone to a restaurant, a high-end restaurant at that. Normally, Ryan was swarmed by photographers, which was a strange feeling for Maria. None had been around in a while but Maria wasn't one to complain about that. She knew now how Cam must have felt after he quit. It was strange at first, being ignored and invisible. But she had come to relish it. Most days.

They made their way out from the restaurant after their meal, but Maria was pushed to the side as they reached the entrance. She was about to say something when she saw who it was, and her eyes widened. "Cam?"

He turned to her and moved away from the door. "Hey, sorry about that." Cam nodded at Ryan as a greeting.

"What are you doing here?" she asked. She looked around before she finally noticed the embarrassment on his face. "Were you stood up?"

"I felt like going out for a nice dinner. Is that not allowed?" he growled, which earned a sharp look from her. Despite being a 'nice guy' now, he still had his darker moments.

"You actually asked that woman out?" Ryan asked incredulously.

Maria looked back and forth between them. "What woman?"

Cam shrugged, and shot a frustrated look at Ryan. "No one. Just someone I met at the bar with the guys." He opened the door, and let them walk out in front of him. Standing on the sidewalk was better than standing in everyone's way in the lobby.

"She was terrible," Ryan finished for him. "She didn't even follow Scanning."

"She wasn't that bad. It was nice to talk to someone about something other than Scanning."

"She's never even used an AIM before."

"Neither had you when you were signed onto the team, but that didn't really stop us, did it?"

Ryan laughed. "You weren't trying to get a date." He paused as he looked at Maria briefly. "Not all of you, at least."

"There's your problem, Tylar," Maria teased, stepping between them to ease the tension. "She didn't know you are *the* Cam Tylar, of Revolution. You need to go to a Sports Bar-"

"We were at one."

"-and find a woman who worships you."

Cam smiled lightly. The irony hit him smack in the face. He had found her, and lost her. "Not as easy as it used to be, when I could just tell a woman she was going home with me, and they'd follow."

She snorted. "You did not do that." Her eyes lowered when he raised an eyebrow at her. "Okay, but clearly those women didn't work out. Besides, since when are you defined by being in a relationship? When did this new Cam come in? You don't have time for a relationship. And before you give me a look, if you weren't looking for one, you wouldn't have picked this restaurant. You would have cooked for her, burned it on purpose, ordered pizza, and kept her there for the night if you wanted anything else. I know you, Cameron, whether you like it or not."

Maria paused for a moment as she looked him over. He had changed so much in the last three years. Had it already been that long? Afraid of either commitment or being hurt, it took the death of Maria's father for him to consider being in a relationship. Now he stood before her as a man readily seeking an actual relationship. Three years too late...

He stared at her, and it was nearly a glare. He turned his look to Ryan. "Control your woman, would you?"

"If you couldn't, do you think I can?" Ryan asked with a laugh. He opened his mouth to continue his jest when he was cut off by Maria's phone ringing.

Maria winced apologetically and answered it. "Lieutenant Kier." She listened on the other end, and her eyes widened after a moment. She swore and looked at Ryan as she continued to listen. "How many? ... I'm in Waterloo...can I get *where*?" She nodded as though the person on the other end could see.

Her eyes closed tight and her breathing quickened, heart pounding. She could feel the sand hitting her face in the wind, hear the sound of the tiger ripping through Rebecca's flesh. Her eyes flew open when she felt a hand on her arm. She took a deep breath and nodded to Cam, his face lined with knowing concern.

"Sorry, sir. Yes, thirty minutes." She hung up the phone and swore loudly. She apologized to a woman leading a young boy by the hand. She swore again under her breath as she looked around frantically. "I have to go."

Ryan grabbed her hand as she tried to walk away. "Wait, what? You're leaving in the morning, I thought."

"They're sending a chopper for me. I have to get to the hospital. It's the closest helipad."

Cam stepped forward again, the concern only deepening. "Maria, what's going on?"

She shook her head and she turned to look at him. She wore the face of a soldier now, no longer the jesting ex-girlfriend. But behind it all was the torrent of terror. "I...I can't. It's classified." It was two years ago all over again, when the two of them had been in the middle of an Underground war. She was trying to convince herself that it was not happening again. "Good luck at your training. I'm okay, I promise."

"I'll drive you," Ryan said, nodding to Cam as he walked her back to his truck.

Cam watched as they drove away and he swore. Things were never simple with her.

Maria was thankful she always kept a spare change of clothes and uniform in Ryan's truck. Just over two years of dating had taught her to always be prepared, especially when they lived in different cities. Though she hadn't prepared to leave her vehicle there.

As Ryan pulled up to Grand River Hospital, Maria finished lacing her boots. The helicopter was already waiting for her on the pad. She leaned over and placed a kiss on Ryan's lips.

"Sorry we had to cut this short."

"You could've just said you didn't want to spend the night. You didn't need to get the military involved."

She smiled before she kissed him again. She would never get tired of that feeling. "I'll see you after your training."

* * *

Maria saluted her superiors as she was escorted into the briefing room. It had seemed like a quick flight to Ottawa, but knew it had been an eternity to everyone else. As she entered the room, she eyed the occupants as was her usual routine. Always needed to salute to someone. She saluted her base commander, but left it at that. She eyed the two other men in the room, both wearing American army uniforms.

"Lieutenant Kier," Colonel Padmore said. With a nod, the four soldiers sat around the boardroom table. They allowed Maria to sit facing the wall of hologram screens which glowed faintly in stand-by mode. "Were you able to read through any of the report on your flight?"

She nodded, once again eyeing the two soldiers to her right from the corner of her eye. "Some, sir."

"Lieutenant, this is Major Collins and Captain McMurphy, American army. Collins was the one who wrote the report."

"Which, for the record," Collins interrupted, "is only a partial report." His voice was deep, and strong. But Maria imagined a slight crack in it. He looked at Padmore before he continued.

"Two weeks ago, my platoon engaged an insurgent group. We had tracked them to an area in northern Afghanistan." Suddenly, the screen came to life with a topographical map of the area mentioned.

Maria leaned forward to look at the location of the flashing dot. "I thought insurgent militias were all in the south, now."

"This one is a branch of a larger one based out of the south," Collins replied sharply.

She looked at him quickly with a frown, not appreciating the tone. But she had finally figured out the conversion and he was, unfortunately, her superior. "Your platoon should have had no problem, then."

"Which was what we thought." He paused. "We went into it with hopes high, and guns blazing."

The good ol' American way.

"Lieutenant Kier, have you seen what a Bengal tiger can do to human flesh?"

Her breath caught in her throat. Her face hardened once more. "Not a real one, no." When he didn't immediately continue, her eyes narrowed and she looked him square in the face. "What exactly happened out there, Major Collins?"

"We thought they were using animals as weapons. When the tigers began attacking their own masters, we laughed. Until we shot one, and it turned into a puddle of gel."

Maria's heart stopped. She stood quickly, the chair turning over with the momentum. "This is bull. We got all of them," she yelled, setting aside any and all decorum. "I went through every record of sale to militaries around the world. Rogues are gone. They've all been destroyed."

"Except for four," Collins said. His voice remained unchanged by her outburst, but a small cringe of his eye told Maria he had put his hope in it all being a bad dream. "Turns out if you're a militia group, no weapons dealer wants to put any transaction on paper."

McMurphy slid forward in his metal seat. "Lieutenant, your commander told us you were the only one in the military who has experience with these AIMs. Rogue AIMs, you called them." His voice was not as deep, but more compassionate than she expected.

He continued. "You've seen what these things can do, and you know their potential. The militia we had engaged, Mjahdan, has been in contact with our government and the McCarthy Group. They're under the impression they were knowingly given faulty equipment. They've been appeased temporarily with the promise of the updated AIMs."

Problem solved.

"But some genius over there managed to reprogram their old AIMs with highly classified military tactics," he continued. "These AIMs are now missing, running wild somewhere in the Afghan desert killing who knows how many people."

She swore. "They want the old AIMs back."

"Yes."

She looked at her commander and she felt her heart sink. She was going back.

"You will accompany McMurphy and Collins who will be leading a section out to find the rogues," Padmore explained. "With your knowledge of animals and rogues, we're hoping you'll be able to give a general trajectory of their travels. If rogues act as real animals, then we're going to need to know where they'd go."

"They act like robots acting like real animals," she said. "They're highly trained weapons which now have animal instincts. Satellite imaging hasn't worked finding them?"

"They have shielding activated," McMurphy offered. "It's one of the reasons we didn't realize they were there in the first place. Any of heat or electrical signals are also blocked. They're essentially invisible, except face to face."

Maria shook her head in disbelief. "No matter what, this will not end well, sir," she addressed Padmore. "How many of us?"

"Thirteen. Collins will lead the section with you as second-in-command. Your team will need a programmer, and the civilians will pair up with you as part of the fireteams."

She laughed. "Sir, no offense, but the programmers Cohner McCarthy has will be useless."

"We need someone else who has experience with rogues. You have the contact of the programmer from your previous report, correct?"

Just when she thought her heart could sink no lower. "I do, sir."

He nodded sharply and stood. "Bring your person in for briefing, and we'll go through the evaluations."

"Sir, I don't think-"

"Kier, Mjahdan is one step away from declaring war on the United States and Canada."

Maria paused, kicking herself inwardly. Well, it was her turn now. He had brought her into messes before. It had almost gotten her killed two years earlier. She wasn't sure she wanted that form of revenge. Finally, she replied, "he'll be here by the end of the week."

CHAPTER 3

"Up! Up!" Rick yelled into his AIRC, watching as his AIM in the form of the peregrine falcon struggled to fly up in the strong November winds. He smiled as the AIM finally reached the optimal altitude.

"It's not ready, Rick," Cam warned him as he kept a careful eye on his team-mate's robot. "It'll default."

"It'll be fine."

Ryan laughed. "Cam, I think he's trying to imitate you with your stupid stunts. Rick, seriously, it's not ready. Even I can see that. You can't force it."

Rick raised his eyebrows in disbelief. "You're turning on me?"

"I never said-"

"Hey, excuse me?" Cam interrupted. "Stupid stunts? It was my *stupid stunts* that got us full scores for every challenge, or did you forget that?" He couldn't help but grin at the rookie. Ryan wasn't such a rookie anymore, he supposed. He had been on the team for three seasons now, and had earned himself a solid spot on the team, and in their group dynamic. Of course, Ryan's relationship with Maria had made that spot tense at first, but Cam smiled and nodded his way through it. Most of the time.

"Rick, just try it and let them say they told you so," Owen said with a sigh, already tired of his team's antics.

Rick looked at his father, and captain, and his eyes narrowed. "You're telling me that you want Cam to be right?"

Owen shrugged with a grin. "Well, he claims to be right all the time. You have to make it true sometimes."

He let out a deep breath and looked back up at his floundering AIM. Looking at it now, he could tell his team-mates were right. What was with him? He hadn't felt like this since he started in the Canadian Scanning Tournament thirteen years earlier.

Rick wanted to show off, and for what? Or whom? It was his team. They all knew his skill, and knew he was good at his job. He had even survived a season, or at least a partial season, as captain. The great schism, he liked to call it in his head. When Cam and Maria had left the team.

"Okay," Rick called out through his AIRC. "Go aerodynamic, and come back down. When you're a kilometre from the ground, spread your wings and fan your tail to-" He stopped when he could no longer see his AIM. As he had been speaking, the robot followed his commands perfectly. It pulled its wings in close to its body and began the nearly supersonic descent that made the peregrine falcon famous...before the force made the robot ripple and lost its animal form.

Cam clapped the man on the back with a smug smile. "Told you it would default. Now you get to go look for it in the forest. Have fun with that."

Rick rolled his eyes and zipped up his sweater. It had become cooler with the sun setting earlier each day. It was nearing sundown now. He had just wanted to get one new move in with his AIM by the end of the day. "Every time your AIM defaulted back to its gel, I always went with you."

"That's because you're the better man." Cam gave Rick his signature smile before he began to fiddle with his AIRC, looking busy.

One more week. That was all there was until they stopped training for the winter. Every November, CST team Revolution trained for nearly a month. The colder weather allowed them to train in harsher climates. It had been a mild year until a few days earlier, and the team had woken up to centimetres of snow on their tents, which meant they would shorten their training. Rick had wanted to get as much training done as possible. Since Cam's return to the team two years earlier, Rick had noticed his own skills were diminishing and he was losing his connection with his AIM.

He knew Cam and his AIM almost seemed to be friends, and he felt he had had that once with his own AIM. But he was neglecting the very core of what it meant to be a Scanner. He had let that relationship fall to the wayside, and he had focused on simply getting good scores at each challenge. He didn't train, or scan, as much as he used to. But he was determined to turn that around this year and start fresh. If that meant turning into the arrogant side of Cam Tylar...well, maybe he wouldn't let it get that far. Not yet, at least.

Owen watched as his son started off for the woods, and he shot a look towards Cam as if that would send the younger athlete out with him. But Cam was stubborn. He supposed it wasn't a big deal for Rick to go off on his own. He very rarely got lost, especially with the GPS system in his AIRC.

"Okay guys," Owen called out to Cam and Ryan. "Let's call it quits for the day." When both nodded in agreement, he smiled. Two years ago, Ryan would not have even dared to speak the way he had today. He had been so timid, wanting to keep the peace. And he never wanted to show off. And Cam? The more interviews he had, the better. And no one had better get in his way of becoming the best Scanner. But when his and Maria's daughter died, Owen supposed all of them had changed. Cam had even quit Revolution, one of the top five CST teams. It would have been career suicide if he hadn't come back a year later from... Owen cringed just thinking about it.

How Cam had been part of the Underground for so long was beyond him. The black market of AIMs, creating illegal AIMs and importing exotic animals. He shut his eyes briefly in an attempt to push the thoughts away. Cam and Maria had both tried to convince him that the Underground did something completely different, that the AIMs they used now by the enforcement of CST officials – and the government – had somehow come into creation because of Cam. But the decision to let Cam back on the team had not been a difficult one. Having Maria's endorsement helped, especially when they had all found out she had been part of the team that had changed the McCarthy Company, or rather, the

McCarthy Group as it was now known. *A new name for a brighter future,* he thought to himself, imitating the commercials that had flooded every TV station for nearly six months.

Whatever Cam had done was behind him. As long as having him on the team was legal and wouldn't get any of them disqualified or black marked, Owen would take him back in a heartbeat. It wasn't quite the way everything happened, he remembered as he ran a hand through his now completely silver hair. They had said no, originally, to having Cam back on the team. But of course, that decision hadn't held for very long.

The Revolution captain looked at the youngest athlete. Ryan Hampton. They had all thought he would be the new *Cam Tylar*. In a way, they were right. It had been good for Ryan, Owen noted, that Cam had quit when he had. Ryan had been given enough instruction and guidance from both Maria and Cam before they left that he was able to continue their thoughts and put it towards his training. If the two had left at the end of the season, Owen wasn't sure how far Ryan would have gone to train. But they left only a month into the season, which gave the rookie even more time to become acquainted with his AIM. And it gave Rick and Ryan some more time to work together without the pressure of the season.

And then he had to go and start dating Maria Kier. She never let him think of her as a daughter, and he could barely get away with scolding her as a father would. But he understood. She had been extremely close with her own father before he died from a series of heart attacks. That had been a rough season for everyone, and her first season on the team.

After seeing the two in a relationship, and seeing the roller coaster that it truly was, everyone had warned Ryan against it. Owen had to admit that it seemed to be going well. Much better than with Cam. It helped, he supposed, that they weren't working together. But it must be hard to have Maria away all the time. At least Rick's wife, Brittney, was in one place with their children for him to visit when he could. Now that Maria was a soldier – still a strange thought to all of them, except Cam for some reason – she was constantly on the move. Who knew where she would be from one minute to the next.

"Hey, old man!"

Owen turned around to Ryan with an angry grumble. Old man… "You better be careful, kid. You're turning too much into Cam."

"We've been trying to get your attention," Ryan replied with an apologetic tone. "It's the only way to get your attention sometimes."

He laughed. It was true. He knew that this would be his last year on the team. His heart, body, and mind just weren't in it anymore the way it used to be. "What were you trying to say?"

"Rick called through the AIRC. Said he'd be doing some scanning in there for a while. I was gonna join him." Ryan glanced towards Cam who didn't seem to have any objections. "Just wanted to let you know before you send out a search party again."

"Excuse me, but you were actually lost that time, and you needed the search party."

"I had a GPS."

Owen paused. "Well, you didn't use it." He waved his arms. "Go on, then. Make sure Rick doesn't fall out of a tree or something." He watched as the youngest player ran off into the forest, followed by his AIM in the form of a porcupine. Owen held back a laugh as the large rodent waddled along in an attempt to keep up with its owner, grunting and chirping after him. A kingfisher landed on his shoulder and looked at him expectantly. He smiled and walked back towards their campsite with Cam close behind. He looked over his shoulder, and his eyebrows furrowed with concern.

"Kid, you okay?"

"I'm a kid now, am I?" Cam said with a small smile.

Owen laughed. "You're always going to be a kid to me. Seriously. You've been pretty quiet all week. Anything bothering you?"

Cam shrugged. He stumbled as his AIM ran just in front of his feet in the form of a golden retriever. He swore under his breath as he caught his balance. "No more than usual. Just trying to figure out how to prepare for the season." He paused. "Owen, have you ever wondered if you've reached your peak?"

He laughed again. "I know I've reached it. I'm not a young man anymore." He looked his team-mate over and shrugged. "There's nowhere to go above perfect."

"Says you," Cam joked. "I've been above perfect my entire life."

"You're not the one who should be joking about that anymore," Owen warned.

Cam remained quiet as they arrived back to their campsite. He sat himself down onto his camping chair and turned his attention down to his AIM who now lay at his feet.

Owen watched him for a moment. "Ryan still hasn't heard from Maria?"

He shifted in his seat and folded his arms across his chest. "It's not a big deal. It's only been a few days. She goes away like that pretty often. He should be used to it."

"Are you?"

Cam looked over at Owen with his eyes narrowed. "She's not my girlfriend to worry about."

"She's still your friend. You're allowed to worry about her." When Cam looked away quickly, almost with a huff, Owen's interest was piqued. "Or are you fighting with her again?"

"We'd have to talk to fight."

Owen rolled his wrist, urging Cam to continue. "So, you're not talking?" When it was clear Cam wasn't going to offer anything on his own, for once, he continued to prod. "Is it not working out? Being friends?"

"It's fine for me and her." He sighed when he realized that Owen wasn't planning on letting it go. "It's not as easy for Ryan. He has a lot to deal with, our history, and Lucy. He seems to think if we're around each other for too long, something's going to spark up again."

"Well, he's allowed to think that."

"Not when we've told him we're done. There's no going back to how things used to be."

Owen put a hand on Cam's shoulder. "Cam, that's what he's worried about. There's no going back, but there is going forward."

Cam shrugged his captain's hand away. "For once, can we focus on AIMs rather than my love life? I'm fine seeing Maria and

Ryan together. I'm fine on my own. I don't need to be that guy who needs to sleep with a different girl every night. Let me just be a Scanner."

But Owen knew Cam never was, and never would be, *just* a Scanner.

Cam looked up from the fire Owen had built when he heard voices travelling through the dark. He couldn't help but smile when he heard Rick and Ryan laugh about something. Their voices were too muffled to make out what the joke had been.

"That took them a while," Owen commented as the two other members of Revolution finally came within the light of the fire. "Did it take you that long to find your AIM, Rick?"

"You're too funny, Dad. I can't imagine why mom doesn't like your sense of humour," Rick answered flatly. To a stranger, his normal tone of voice would indicate constant misery, or at least boredom. But his family and team-mates knew that was just how he was. Owen at least gave him credit for developing intonation recently. It was better than nothing.

"Get anything good?" Cam asked, pushing through any beginning of an argument. The father-son pair were generally even-tempered, but one could never be too careful.

"Yeah!" Ryan answered happily. No-one could ever say that Ryan was not a genuinely happy guy. He sat down next to Cam and showed him his AIRC. "Got a better porcupine, which would've been awesome for the tournament. And we found a few foxes that hadn't woken up yet. I like this guy," he said, pointing out the snowshoe hare he had scanned last.

Cam swore as he pulled the AIRC into his hands. He flipped through the stats, and he shook his head in disbelief. "What a waste. This is an awesome scan. Can't even use it."

Ryan grinned proudly. "No, but I can use it to train. Train with the best, and everything else is a piece of cake."

"So, you *have* been listening." Cam laughed as he handed back the device. "Good job. Guess we know who's going to have top scanning points this season."

His face flushed and he pocketed his AIRC. "Thanks. If we can't be top overall, I'd rather have that." He had gotten better with his self-esteem, but that didn't mean he was any better at accepting compliments.

"Well, hopefully this training session will help. You've been pretty good the last two seasons." Cam looked over at Rick. "Did you get anything good?"

"Not really. *Someone* took the best scans for himself."

He laughed. "If Ryan got something, it was because he worked for it and deserved it." How words could work on so many different levels. But Ryan remained silent, looking down at his console. So much for his self-esteem boost. Attempt number three. "Owen, what's the plan for the rest of the training time? Weather network said a pretty massive storm is coming in a few days."

Owen nodded. He moved his chair closer to the fire. Its flames licked the air in all directions as the wind tossed it around. "We'll tough it out as long as possible, but we'll probably only be here for another week at the most. It may be fine weather back home in Kitchener, or Elmira," he added for Ryan, "but if the weather gets really bad up here, the roads will close and we'll be stuck here in the boonies for even longer. The closest hotel, or motel, is down in Cochrane."

Cam's eyes rolled up slightly as he tried to think back. "Wasn't there one closer that we passed?"

"Last year, yeah. It's closed now."

He leaned back in his chair with a shrug. "I still think we should have tried to train more in the snow. We've never really done that before, and every year we have at least one or two challenges in snowy conditions. It'll be good not only for our AIMs, but for us, too. If we need to run in snow, we better train for that."

"Running in sand is pretty similar," Rick noted.

"Only if the sand is up to your knees," Cam replied, to which Rick acknowledged with a nod.

"Well," Owen continued, "it's too late to add it to the schedule now. None of us are really prepared for that. Maybe in January, when the snow is here fully and we can get the supplies we need. But for now, we go when the weather kicks us down south."

Cam cringed as a gust of wind attacked the team. "I'm about ready to get into the tent. I wouldn't mind the RV right about now. This is getting pretty ridiculous.

All of a sudden, the four looked up as the trees began to move and shudder at the top. A *whomp whomp whomp* sounded above. A helicopter came over the tops of the trees and hovered above the clearing before he began to descend.

The team stood from their chairs and shielded their eyes against the leaves and debris the chopper's blades threw at them. They looked at each other incredulously.

"What the hell is going on?" Rick yelled to the others as the helicopter neared the ground.

It hovered for a moment, and that was when in the faint light the chopper gave off they noticed the markings in paint. It was a military helicopter. It finally settled on the ground, but the blades continued to turn. Rick, Owen, and Cam all turned to Ryan, though he didn't seem to know any more about it than them. He shook his head as if to answer their silent questions when two figures jumped out from the helicopter and made their way towards them.

"How much further?" Cam asked as his AIM ran alongside him.

"Not much-" But they stopped abruptly. Just ahead of them was a small group of people. Confused, Cam and his AIM approached the group to see what was going on. He pushed his way through the crowd to see the end of the path. A cliff. He looked down what turned out to be an extremely high cliff overlooking the bay.

"There wasn't something we missed?" Cam looked at his AIRC, examining the map for the hundredth time.

"The signal for the continuation of the course is on the other side of the bay," his AIM replied. "We could potentially trek through the forest and make our way around to the other side, but there is no path from what I have seen."

Cam swore. "That would take-" He swore again when someone shoved him out of the way. "Watch it," he growled and watched as a young woman looked down over the cliff. He didn't recognize her, but there were a lot of amateurs at the Open World

Tournament. "It would take too long to go around," he continued to his AIM. But his eyes stayed on her.

"Cameron?"

But he dismissed his AIM with a wave.

The woman, not much older than Cam if she was even his age, took off her pack and her shoes, putting them into the bag. Her AIM vibrated and shifted until it took the form of a pelican. She stood and the AIM grabbed the bag with its talons and began to fly over the bay.

Cam watched with interest as she walked through the group, back a few yards and then turned back to face them.

"Move!" she yelled, and ran at a full sprint through the now parted mass and leapt off the side of the cliff.

Cam swore and rushed to the side in time to watch her enter the water and, after a brief moment, return to the surface where the pelican sat on the water, waiting. His eyes were wide. "Who is she? What team is she on?"

His AIM was silent for a moment. A rare occasion. "I do not know. She is not a registered Scanner."

"You've got to be kidding me. She's not on a team?" He laughed and jabbed his own AIRC, transforming his AIM into an eagle. "Well, I've never shied away from a water challenge before." He shook his head. "I need to find out who she is."

"And then?"

"I'm going to marry her."

Cam immediately recognized Maria's figure. How could he not? Even in the dark – and in her fatigues – he still knew her. He glanced briefly at the taller man beside her, a very angry looking soldier. Not that most of them didn't look angry.

"So nice of you to join us, Maria," Cam joked. "You're a little late for training. I guess your friend can participate, too. If he's used an AIM, he's already ahead of where Ryan was when he started with us."

"Very funny," she replied in a similar tone to Rick's. "You're pretty hard to find when you turn your tracking off on your AIRC."

He grinned. "With my ego and big head, I shouldn't be too hard to find."

"You'd think." Maria stepped towards him and handed him a data pad. "We'd like to have a meeting with you first thing in the morning."

Cam glanced at his team-mates before he looked at the data pad in his hands. "I'm in the middle of training."

"Believe me, this is a meeting you want to be part of."

"And who's 'we'?"

Maria paused. "The Canadian and American Armed Forces."

If the helicopter didn't do it, that got the team's attention.

Rick's jaw nearly dropped. "Please tell me Cam isn't on the most wanted list. One year. Just one year where nothing happens. It's not a lot to ask."

"You had two years of that," Maria responded with a small smile. "Things must be working out better without a woman on the team." And they all knew that struck a chord. No one hid their feelings about working with a woman. When she joined the team, they hadn't let her participate in a challenge until the end of the first month, and only because they couldn't afford the penalty of attempting with only three players.

But Cam was still processing what she had said. The last time he had worked with the military... "What is this about, Maria?"

"Just read the report."

"Maria, I'm serious. If this is about two years ago-"

"Just read it, Lucas," she said forcefully. Quietly she added, "please. Believe me, I don't want to be the one asking you to do this."

He avoided everyone's eyes for a moment before he nodded. "Where is this meeting?"

"Ottawa. A chopper will pick you up at six tomorrow morning. Bring everything you have. I don't know how long we'll need you, and I doubt you guys will be up here long with the weather that's coming your way." When Cam nodded, she returned it and turned to leave. She glanced at Ryan, and the look on his face nearly broke her heart. With the meetings she'd had all week, there had been no chance to even try to contact him.

It killed her knowing that she was hurting him with her silence, and now showing up wanting to see Cam wasn't making it any better. She gave him a soft smile which he attempted to return, but she could see the pain behind it. She would never be able to share her life with him. She had realized this after the events with the Underground, but she hadn't had the heart to do anything about it. Maria cared about him, maybe even loved him, and she didn't want to be without him. But what was she supposed to do? She was going back to Afghanistan. And that was all she knew. She sent a glance to Rick and Owen and decided she would need to spend some time with them before she left.

Revolution watched as Maria re-entered the helicopter with the other soldier, and waited to speak until it was far enough away they didn't feel the effects of the blade. Rick looked at Cam with a raised eyebrow. "Why would both militaries want to meet with you?"

"He probably can't talk about it," Ryan muttered before he sat back down in his camping chair.

Cam let out a sigh. He and Maria still hadn't told anyone exactly what had happened between the Underground and the McCarthys, and he doubt they ever would...or could. "I have no idea, honestly."

Owen gestured towards the pad. "What's in it?"

He shrugged and booted up the data pad, flipping through a few screens. His face turned red and he felt his heart race. He swore and nearly tossed it away. "Something they have no right to have."

CHAPTER 4

The next morning, Cam finished packing up his tent by the time anyone else woke up. Unfortunately, Ryan was the first one. Cam avoided his eyes as he continued to pack, but when the younger man sat down outside his own tent, Cam let out a sigh and walked over to him. "You have to believe me; I have no idea what any of this is about. And you know it isn't her personally wanting a meeting with me."

"I know," Ryan said simply. He watched as Cam carried on with his packing until he finally leaned forward in his chair. "You know, it wouldn't be so bad if you both didn't keep trying to reassure me. I know nothing's going on between you two, but the more often you both say nothing's happening, the more it feels like you're covering up something. I get you're not over her, and that's fine. But she's finally over you, Cam. I'm sorry, but it took a long time for her to get to the point she could actually say that and believe it for herself. I want to be your friend, but being your friend and her boyfriend isn't working out and I'm going to choose her if you make me."

Cam stopped, listening to what he had to say. He wanted to laugh at how ridiculous it sounded. But Ryan was right.

"I'm not going to make you choose." He looked up into the nearly-winter sky when the faint thump of helicopter blades broke the forest silence. "I am over her, you know. But she is female, and I tend to flirt with females whether I like it or not."

"You don't flirt with Brittany."

Cam rubbed his jaw with a grin. "When you punch the way Rick does, I'll stop flirting with Maria."

"Well I'd hope it wouldn't come to that." Ryan looked up at Cam with a curious grin. "Did he seriously punch you?"

"I made the mistake of flirting with her when Rick wasn't around, and I guess it was making her confused. I guess she assumed that Rick was giving the impression she was...willing to try new things. Obviously, it made her uncomfortable, and Rick and I were at a bar when she called him to talk. He hasn't drunk the same way since."

Ryan couldn't help but laugh. "That would've been something to see."

"Yeah, I bet."

Owen and Rick exited from their tents as the sound of the helicopter grew louder. Cam picked up his duffle bags, waiting for the helicopter to land. Owen stood next to him and put a hand on his shoulder. "Everything'll be fine. At least you won't have to deal with the drive back to Kitchener with all of us. You get to fly in a nice helicopter."

Cam laughed. "You've clearly never been in a helicopter before."

Owen's face suddenly turned serious. "Just don't say or do anything stupid. I don't want to find out my star player is in jail for contempt or something. Whatever is in that datapad Maria gave you made you pretty angry last night." Cam stiffened under his grip, and so he kept his hand in place. "Remember that they obviously need you for something, and if both militaries need you...you have to look past whatever they're holding against you."

"I don't think this is necessarily blackmail," Cam said as the chopper finally landed. "I think this is going to be a guilt trip."

"And you don't think that's blackmail?" Owen gave a small smile. "I'm sure Rick would beg to differ with you on that one. I don't know if Brittany knows the difference."

Cam copied his captain's smile and he turned to the rest of his team. "This should be good for you guys. It'll give you some extra time and maybe with it you can get up to my level finally."

"And on that note," Rick said with a slight roll of his eyes. "Have a safe trip. Don't fall out."

Cam looked at Ryan who simply nodded. It was time. A soldier came out to meet him.

"Cam Tylar, I'm Captain McMurphy. Are you ready to go?" a tall man said in a somewhat gruff voice, most likely made that way by the wind of the chopper's blades.

"I don't think I have a choice."

The soldier shot him a quick grin. "Trust me, you have a choice now. After the meeting, you may not think so."

Cam followed him onto the helicopter, trying to remember the last time he had been on one. It had most likely been one of his first years in the Underground, when Dr. Henk Baxter had more people in the military on his side. Things had changed drastically over the years and they had indeed gone fully Underground.

That had been about the time he had quit Revolution and gone full time with his work with the AIM scientist, unknowingly finishing the work of his deadbeat father. Cam shut his eyes briefly. No, not deadbeat. He had left his family to save them. Then he died. No matter what the man ended up being to Cam, he had finally visited the man's grave. Maria had gone with him, neither telling Ryan about the trip.

He looked out through the small window as they were lifted into the air, and watched as his team-mates grew smaller, until they nearly disappeared behind them. That always seemed to be the way.

He looked at the pilot before he turned his attention to Captain McMurphy sitting across from him. "So, who exactly am I meeting with?" he asked through the headset the pilot gave him.

"You'll meet them when we arrive."

Cam rolled his eyes. "Yes, I assumed that much. I had hoped to prepare myself."

"You won't be able to prepare yourself for what we're going to tell you."

"You'd be surprised," Cam muttered.

* * *

"What do you think all of that was about?" Rick asked as his team, what was left of it, moved back into the forest for more training with their AIMs.

"I have a feeling it has to do with whatever he did when he was in the Underground," Owen replied, trying to cut back his annoyance with the situation. He knew Cam's work had been important, but Owen wasn't sure it would ever sit well with him.

Ryan kicked at the ground in front of him as he walked. "Whatever it is, no one's going to tell us, because that's what happens now."

Rick looked at the young man with a raised eyebrow. "Where did that come from?"

He shrugged. "No one ever talks about what happened two years ago. No one asks, and no one offers anything. Maria nearly got killed. But that's all she would tell me. She didn't tell me who did it, why, or how Cam was even involved in something with the military. She lied to me about even being with Cam."

"I don't think her job allows for her to be very open with people," Owen said softly in an attempt to calm him down.

"That doesn't mean she can lie to me about ex-boyfriends living with her in a safe-house. And then there were more injuries. Cam was shot, too. Did he tell any of you that?"

Owen thought back. "Saw a scar on his side, but that's about it." He stopped and turned to his team-mate. "Look, Ryan. If you have problems with Maria, or if you're having trouble trusting her, then you need to tell her, not us. If you can't handle the fact that she can't tell you what happened, then you need to make a decision and tell her that, too.

"We all want to know what happened because it brought Cam back into the spotlight. But if it means that it requires silence for some reason, his being back, then I'll take it. As long as they're both safe and alive, that's all I care about. Going a year not knowing whether that was true or not was torture." He nodded towards him. "And how are we supposed to feel that you had been in contact with Maria, dated her, while we had no idea what had even happened to her?"

Ryan looked down. "She asked me not to. She wasn't ready, yet."

"Then maybe she's still not ready." Owen thought for a moment. "Do you think Eric had anything to do with what happened?" he asked. It had been a question on everyone's mind. Eric Thompson, the newest member of Revolution and promising athlete, quit suddenly in the middle of the season, and in the middle of the...whatever was happening with the Underground and the military.

Ryan shrugged, but then he thought for a moment as well. He had never made any connections, but now as he went back over the events, some things began to fall into place. "Cam and Maria came to speak to him that once, which was how our relationship was found out. And then I had confided some things to Eric about Maria. She got really upset with me, because I wasn't...well, I'm still not supposed to talk to anyone about her or what she does. But I did with him. Maybe he wasn't a very trustworthy guy after all."

Rick shook his head. "Doesn't sound like it. I remember that day. It definitely looked like they were ganging up on him. I knew it sounded wrong when Cam said his old sponsors were after Eric. Eric was good, but he was nowhere near the level Cam was. It would've been nice to have another sponsor, though. You never really realize how much we depend on the money from our sponsors."

"Or flights," Owen added. "I can't remember the last time I paid to fly on a plane."

Rick and Owen continued to discuss the various vacations they've been able to take, and began to plan their next family vacation. But Ryan remained quiet. What Owen said resonated with him. Maybe Maria really wasn't ready to share with him. The hardest part was knowing that there was someone she could share with.

With a sigh, Ryan turned his attention to his AIM. He smiled at it when the robot, in the form of the fox from the night before, rubbed up against his leg like a cat. He was glad he had chosen to use his old AIM to train with for this session. The new AIMs they had released were superior in their training abilities and response time, that he had hardly needed to train it at all. Sometimes it was nice to work with something familiar.

* * *

Cam surveyed his surroundings as he was led from the helicopter and across the small airfield. He followed the captain into a large building, like one of the main administrative buildings of the base at Ottawa. He felt his body tense as he was led down the bright hallways. The last time he had been in this type of environment was with Maria in Kingston where they learned that her C.O had been involved in the attack which nearly took her life. Cam saw the home she had lived in while they were apart. He saw the bullet holes in the wall, and the blood on the floor. He saw her face and the fear in her eyes when she looked at the closet where her attacker had hidden for three hours. Cam was sure he would never have fond memories of the military. No matter what they did to save his life there would always be that other side.

As the captain led him around yet another corner, another soldier joined them but remained silent. Thankfully Cam was led into a room with a large table in the middle. All the walls, he noticed, were set up with projection tech. Likely used for surround maps. He saw Maria standing in a line with other soldiers but he refused to meet her gaze.

"Thank you for meeting with us on such short notice." The soldier in the middle spoke first and offered his hand to Cam, which was taken reluctantly. "I'm Colonel Padmore. You've already met Captain McMurphy. This is Major Collins. Both are United States Army. And I assume Lieutenant Kier needs no introduction."

Cam nodded to the rather gruff looking soldier before he looked back to the colonel. He paused, and when the senior officer did as well, he couldn't hold it anymore. He slammed the datapad down on the table, and finally met Maria's gaze.

"What the hell is this? If you think for one second I'm going to be blackmailed by you just because you're the military, send in the firing squad."

"Cam," Maria tried to interrupt.

"No," he said, and pointed at her. "After what they did to you, you think I would trust any of them?" Cam thought for a moment. "And either you're in on it, or they're screwing you over, too. I don't know which is worse," he added softly.

"Mr. Tylar, no one is blackmailing you," the colonel began to explain.

"Then explain why this data pad has all my records and research from when I was in the Underground? How did you even get any of this? These are my personal research files."

The colonel allowed Collins to step forward and answer. "Dr. Baxter and Ms. Rodriguez both wanted to help and they provided most of your research. I'm no scientist, or Scanner, so can you give us a quick summary of your work?"

Cam glanced at Maria, still unsure of what was going on. When she gave him a small nod, he answered Collins. "I was creating a new computer program and code to use with the new AIM substance."

"What was its purpose?"

"Is."

Collins raised an eyebrow. "Excuse me?"

"What *is* its purpose? It's being used now in the AIM update. It's to ensure no communication errors between the chip and the AIRC, or the substance."

"Cam, just tell them," Maria said finally when the room remained silent.

Collins lifted a hand. "No, I think I get what he's saying." He slid a file folder across the table to Cam and motioned towards it. "Your code was making sure this wouldn't happen?"

Cam opened the folder and his eyes widened. He closed the folder quickly and covered his face.

The soldier took the folder back and took out the photographs. He looked at the disfigured corpses, barely recognizable as human, and he too shut his eyes for a moment. "Kier, what was the term you used for them?"

"Rogues," Cam interrupted. "When an AIM's chip malfunctions and disconnects from the AIRC, it's called a rogue AIM." He removed his hands from his face and looked straight at the soldier. But a thought hit him, and he looked at Maria. She had been deployed to Afghanistan two years earlier, and her partner had been killed by a rogue AIM.

But that photo...they were Afghan who were killed. Not soldiers. They were innocent civilians. Now she was seeing this photo again. He remembered how haunted she had been by what had happened. Ryan had mentioned to him that she still screamed at night. "They've been dealt with, though. I don't know how I can help you. I can try to get them back connected with the AIRC, but you wouldn't want to use them again anyway, since there's a higher risk they'll go rogue again."

"Apparently they haven't all been dealt with." Collins nodded to himself. "Have you heard of Mjahdan?"

"No, I haven't. You don't hear about much of what's going on over there on the news."

"We'd like to keep it that way. Apparently, your friend Trevor McCarthy sold them AIMs when there were large weapons deals going through. And like most weapons dealers, he made sure this was all under the table. No records. Nothing. There aren't even any records of the AIMs ever being manufactured. No serial codes on the chips, even," Collins continued.

"Let's get one thing straight. Trevor McCarthy is not my friend," Cam said forcefully. "I do not work for, or with, the McCarthys and I never will. They use my research, and I make sure they don't screw it up. End of story." But Cam caught on, and he let out a frustrated sigh. "No records means they weren't able to give them updated AIMs. So they went rogue. Going to tell me how this involves both militaries?"

"They believe they were knowingly given faulty units. They're angry, and threatening war."

Cam shrugged and leaned back in his chair. "So, give them new ones, talk about how much better they are for destroying Western culture, and they'll be happy."

"We want you to come with us to Afghanistan."

His face blanked and he looked at Maria, whose eyes locked with his. "You want me…to go to the Middle East?" He forced out a laugh. "Seems like a waste of time to fly me all the way out there. All I need is half an hour to reboot the AIMs, set up the new ones. Piece of cake."

Collins gave a dark grin. "Well, we have to find them first."

"What?"

"They're missing."

Cam swore. "They couldn't contain them?"

"Would you like to see the photos again? I'd like to know how you'd contain rogue AIMs in the form of a Bengal tiger."

"Always be prepared with a second AIM," Cam replied, returning the soldier's tone. "Change it into something strong, but not as big as the tiger, so it's not bait, but not a direct threat. Keep it entertained until you get the programming fixed and it's under control again."

Colonel Padmore nodded and finally stepped forward. "Which is what we'll need you to do for us."

"After you find them, you mean?"

The colonel paused. "We'll need you for that, as well. The GPS units in them have been deactivated. All we have is a trail of blood."

Cam looked between the soldiers. "If you need them tracked, you need a hunter on your team, someone who knows how animals behave."

"We both know these aren't ordinary animals," Padmore said slowly. "We're trying to limit the people who are sent over, and we'd still need to send you."

Cam thought for a moment. "So, what is it exactly that you're asking me to do?"

Maria was the one to step forward now. But Cam saw the look on her face. No matter what mask she wore, or how thick her soldier skin was now, he could still read her like a book. And she was broken. "We're putting together a team to find and neutralize the AIMs, replace them, and get the hell back home. We'd like you to lead the team of programmers and scientists. They'll be coming from the McCarthy Group mostly. I'll be leading the Canadian military escort that will be with you. We'll be the ones in contact with Mjahdan, and will have any resources you may need. Cam, I...we need to warn you...that this may take a while, and there's a chance it will cut into the season."

"I hardly think a stupid game is more important than war," Collins snapped.

"He's not a soldier," Maria yelled. "And you're not a Scanner. We all have our priorities. If he doesn't want to go, we'll find someone else."

"You said there's no one better."

She paused. "There isn't." A quick glance to Cam.

Cam stood up slowly, and the movement caught her attention. "When do we leave?"

Maria shut her eyes as she felt her heart break. They both knew she would never forgive herself.

Maria waited outside the meeting room for the rest of the soldiers to leave. They had given Cam the rest of his instructions and expectations while she had excused herself with some talk about contacting another AIMOT. She leaned against the wall, and let her head fall back. What had she done? They needed the best, and he was that after all. But it was Cam. And this was a suicide mission. He wasn't a soldier. He was a Scanner. Is a Scanner. One of the top Scanners in the country, and now compared with those in the States, he was topping those, too.

She stood to attention when the door opened and she watched the Colonel and McMurphy escort Cam out of the room. She stepped forward quickly. "I can show him out. I want to talk to him briefly about his team, and make sure they have plans set in motion." When she noticed Collins, she stared hard at him. "The world still goes around as people die. It's nothing new."

She stood where she was as the others left her and Cam, walking back to wherever they were needed at the moment.

Cam glanced at her, trying to get a good look at her face. "Well, that was…eye opening. I can see why you haven't talked to Ryan since you've left."

"Please don't go."

His eyes narrowed in confusion. "What?"

"Don't go," Maria pleaded. "Tell them you've changed your mind. We can use anyone. Hell, I've even managed to get an AIM under control. We can get you in remotely, give you access to the AIRC. You don't need to be in Afghanistan."

He looked at her straight on now. "You're going to Afghanistan, right?"

She nodded. "Yes. Obviously."

"Then I'm going."

"Lucas…"

"If I'm the best there is, then that means it'll be done the best way with me there. The best way is the quickest way. If me being there means you get home quicker, then I'm going." He looked her over. "You didn't tell them how bad your episodes are, did you?"

She glanced around to see if anyone was listening. "I'd be discharged. I'm not about to let them do this mission without me, especially now that you're going."

"Then there's no way I'm not going. Especially if it means taking care of more rogues."

Maria ran a hand over her smoothed back hair. "There's no end date for this mission."

"Yeah, I know." They were silent for a moment. "What are you going to tell Ryan?"

She let out a sigh as she shrugged. "I have no idea. What am I supposed to tell him? I haven't been able to tell him much. Now it's going to look worse now that you're coming too."

"Tell him we're running away together to some exotic place," he said with a grin.

Maria smiled softly. "We did that once, remember?"

"I do." He gripped her upper arm gently. "It'll be okay."

She shook her head and looked back into the room. "You saw those photos..."

He nodded and followed her gaze, keeping his hand on her arm. "This can't be easy for you, after what happened to Rebecca." He always wondered if she had even told Ryan her name. He knew she didn't tell him why she screamed at night. He also knew she didn't tell Ryan that every time Cam had fallen asleep at her place since, she hadn't screamed in her sleep.

"It'll be good for me to be part of this. It'll finally give me closure," Maria said slowly. "I've been wondering what else there was, what else there could possibly be to ruin everything I have now. I knew there was something else waiting to happen, another way Trevor could kick us all the way from prison. And this is it. This is his way of making sure his madness just...keeps hurting, and killing. He has to keep in control, even when he's lost all of it."

Cam smiled softly and stepped closer to her. "Hey, we're in control now. Well, maybe not of those AIMs, but we will be. And we'll get home safely, and everything will be fine."

"Famous last words."

Maria watched as the helicopter carried Cam away. As soon as it was out of sight, she returned back to the building and went in search of the colonel. She found him after a few moments in a temporary office with Collins and McMurphy. She had no negative opinion about McMurphy. He actually seemed to be a decent man, and from what she heard, a more than decent soldier. The decorations on his chest were a good indication of that. She glanced down at the strips of fabric across hers, and she frowned. She knew that some were earned in ways she never expected.

Collins, on the other hand, needed to work on his...well, entire personality. He was rude, rough, arrogant...all the things Cam used to be. But Maria had looked through that folder. She had seen the recorded footage. She knew that Collins was suffering from PTSD. Maybe not as severe as she had, but it was enough to make her wonder what he had been like before the rogue AIMs killed half his unit.

Maria rapped her knuckles against the door, and saluted when her superior noticed her presence.

"Kier, yes, come in. At ease," he added, when she remained stiff near the door. "So, that was Cam Tylar."

"Yes, sir."

Colonel Padmore nodded. "Not really what I expected."

"If we have to protect that guy, we've got our work cut out for us," Collins muttered with a laugh.

Maria shot him a glare. "Cam can hold his own. It'll be the rest of the civilians we're bringing in, if you're even used to protecting people. Maybe all you know to do is shoot people." Of all people, she should know the worst things to say, and she did. But she had the habit of still saying it.

"Kier," the Colonel warned.

"You think you even know what you're talking about, *Kier*?" Collins growled as he stepped towards her. "You think you can even imagine watching an animal tear apart your colleagues, and be able to do nothing about it?"

She took a step towards him and looked straight up at him, feeling his disgusting breath on her face. "No, I can't. When a rogue AIM killed my partner in front of me, I shot it four times before it defaulted. And when I got shot twice trying to stop Trevor McCarthy from selling more faulty AIMs, I got him put in prison. When Cam nearly lost his career because of what he did for the world, I got it back for him. Maybe you know what it's like to be helpless...but I don't."

"Lieutenant Kier, that will be enough," the Colonel said softly. He knew, rather, all the Canadian soldiers at the base knew what Maria had gone through to be where she was at the moment.

"Helpless," she continued softly, "is not knowing there's an assassin in your closet for the last three hours, and then finding out your commanding officer was the one who ordered the hit because you knew too much. AIMs are different from humans, Collins. Even rogue, they can be controlled. Humans are unpredictable, and malicious. They're the ones to fear. Remember that it was a man who continued to sell these robots, knowing full well what would happen to them." Maria finally turned to the Colonel. "Please dismiss me, sir. I have a lot of preparation to do."

"You're dismissed, along with Captain McMurphy. You'll both need to approve the soldiers used in this mission. You'll know who we'll need on our side, Kier, and he'll know which of the U.S Army he'll need."

Maria nodded and left the room along with McMurphy. She glanced up at him as they walked down the hall to yet another meeting room. He seemed nice enough, but there was something about him that made her wonder if he was hurting just as much as Collins seemed to be.

CHAPTER 5

McMurphy walked with his hands behind his back, and he leaned down to Maria. "Remind me to not get on your bad side," he said with a wry grin.

She gave him a small smile. "So, what's your story?" she asked as they sat down around a table with a glass top. Maria touched a panel on the corner and it lit up with a map of Afghanistan.

"What do you mean?" he asked, involving himself with the map. He slid two fingers along the side of the map, and a list of names scrolled up. "I don't have a story."

"What really happened out there?"

He smiled sadly. "You show me yours, I show you mine." He looked back down at the screen. "You seem to have a pretty interesting one yourself."

She shrugged. "Not much more to it. My C.O was working for Trevor McCarthy who happened to be killing a bunch of people. After my battle buddy was killed when I was deployed in Afghanistan, I wrote up the report describing the rogues. Trevor found out, ordered the hit, so I teamed up with the Underground to stop him."

"And this Cam Tylar worked in the Underground?"

Maria gave him a small smile. "You don't watch sports, do you?" When he shook his head, she continued. "Cam and I were both on a Scanning team together."

McMurphy laughed. "You were a Scanner? That would explain why you had his back about priorities."

"You'd be surprised the priorities a Scanner has." Maria leaned forward to look at the list McMurphy had pulled up. She cringed inwardly, remembering a similar list she had used two years earlier, determining who was a threat and who was a target. Unfortunately, she had been the latter. "Four programmers should be enough, including Cam and whoever he chooses as his second. What he'll likely do is have them controlling AIMs to corner and subdue the rogues while he defaults them. My team of AIMOTs will need to support them with our AIMs. They won't be as strong as the rogues, but the military tactical training should be an advantage. Do you have any idea what Mjahdan used to train their AIMs?"

He shook his head and pointed to a place on the map. The contour lines indicated a medium-sized mountain directly north of it. "This is their main training facility, or at least it was. In the past, we've gone to help them train their AIMs, so they likely use the same tactics we gave them. This was only about ten years ago, and when they weren't a militia. The ones we're dealing with used to be a branch of the Afghan army. Obviously, that didn't work out so well. We have no idea what AIMs they're using now, which is what's going to make this more difficult for Cam."

"Who are you going to need?" Maria nodded towards the list. "I don't recognize any AIMOTs on there."

"You wouldn't. We have a different branch for the AIM trainers and technicians." McMurphy tapped on one of the names and a picture of a male soldier appeared on top of the map in an overlay. Next to his picture was his military profile which showed his rank, decorations and merits, and his record of missions and deployments. It was a rather long list and Maria shook her head. "Three out of the last four wars. He must've seen it all...except for rogues."

"Shepero is a good guy. After Collins, he's one of few I'd trust my life with. We'll be more the brunt force of the mission. All the soldiers will have to be on high alert to make sure the civilians get back alive."

Maria felt her entire body tense. "Civilians shouldn't even be out there with us. Cam was right. He can disable them remotely.

It's unnecessary for so many lives to be risked for this, people who haven't trained for this and haven't devoted their life to protecting their country."

"No, but from what I saw of Cam, he has." When he noticed her tension, he looked at her fully. "Is this going to be a conflict of interest?"

She shook her head. "No, it's fine."

"It doesn't look it. He may be the best man for the job, but if it's going to detract from your abilities-"

"Then I'm not a good enough soldier."

"Maria?"

It was very rare for a soldier to use the first name of another soldier. She wasn't sure how she felt about it. She felt...naked, almost, and exposed. But it was nice, to hear her name for once. "We dated when we were on the team together. That's not an issue. I just don't like civilians in combat." Maria saw him nod and she raised a questioning eyebrow. "You still haven't shown me yours. And what's the deal with Collins?"

McMurphy pointed to another area of the map and spread his fingers against the glass, zooming in to show a small village. "We had heard Mjahdan was using this village as a rally point for weapons deals. We were hoping to ambush them and catch them off guard. They caught wind of our plans and were waiting for us, with their AIMs. All of a sudden...their AIMs started to attack anything that moved, including their owners. We thought, stupidly, that they were using real animals. Until we tried to shoot one and it wouldn't go down." He stopped and simply stared at the village which Maria now knew held no life. "We lost a lot of good people in only an hour. Very little of that was due to Mjahdan directly."

"And Collins?"

"He was leading the patrol."

"He's looking out for his guys," she commented softly. "I can understand that. As long as he stays off my peoples' back. There's no way I'm going to trust him with the programmers or my soldiers if he's only looking after his own, and favouring soldiers over civilians."

"He won't."

"Good," Maria said firmly. "I guess this is our team, once we get a finalized list with the names of our programmers."

McMurphy leaned back in his seat but kept his eyes on the map. "Any idea where the AIMs may have gone?"

She shrugged and surveyed the map. They were in the form of tigers. From what she understood, they had had quite the feast in the village and then had moved north, which would not make sense to a normal tiger. "Well, they seem to be moving north, up to the mountains, but if they were to get hungry again, or thirsty, they should be going east into Pakistan. It also depends on the migration of animals there currently. I don't know much about Middle Eastern migration patterns, but Cam would have some resources into that.

"It wouldn't hurt to get in touch with the bordering countries and get them involved at least in communications and open those lines in case we need to use them." When he nodded, she copied him and stood. "We'll be able to get into more details when we have more information, and can give better goals. Are you guys going back to the States until the deployment?"

"Yes," he stood as well. "Need to get some things together. Say goodbye."

"It doesn't get easier with time, does it?"

"It's never easy saying goodbye."

Later that evening as Maria sat in the commercial plane, she was glad to be back in her regular civilian clothing. She hated flying in her uniform. She didn't mind the looks. She was used to that from being part of the CST. But it was too stiff, too blatant that she was a soldier. Sometimes it was nice to blend in. She let out a sigh and let herself sink into the seat all the way, or at least as much as an economy class seat would allow. She smiled lightly at her AIM sitting in the seat next to her, in her favourite form of a cat. Maria didn't have a favourite breed, and tended to change that often, but the feline form was simply a comfort to her, the same way Cam felt comforted and protected by a golden retriever.

"I guess I should call Ryan," Maria said to it.

"Would you like a reminder?" the robotic voice asked as an automatic response.

With another sigh, she replied, "sure." She had grown accustomed to Cam's sentient AIM. She had enjoyed having full conversations with a robot, now that she knew she could. It was a nice relief from speaking to soldiers, and Scanners all the time. Maria thought ahead to what she would say to Ryan, and to her old team-mates.

What could she say? It wasn't as though she was going to war. In a way, this was worse. She wasn't at liberty to mention details of the mission, nor could she give an end date. But not giving a deadline would give them warning flags, and she couldn't have that. Maria didn't feel comfortable lying about when they'd be back...they...her and Cam. Both of them together in Afghanistan. How was she going to justify to them his being part of the mission as well? How was she going to justify it with herself?

"Distress signal found," Maria's AIM called out over the sound of the waves.

She turned her wrist, making sure to keep hold of her AIM in the form of a dolphin. There on her AIRC was, in fact, a distress signal. "From another player? The emergency teams will help the person."

There was a pause. "Negative. Distress signal is short wave, not linking to satellite communication."

"Can you boost the signal for them?"

Another pause. "Yes. Emergency teams are not located within an acceptable distance to the source of the signal."

Maria swore. "Whoever's in trouble is off course." She looked ahead. She had lost time at the last obstacle. She went from being in the front of the pack to near the middle. She had foolishly let her dad talk her into signing up for the Open Tournament, but she had to place here. Despite being open to all levels of athletes, Maria knew she was competing mostly against professional Scanners. The sooner this was over, the sooner she could go to Basic training and start her own career. And get away from her mother.

The distress signal continued to flash on the screen of her AIRC. She swore again. "Let's go. Change course."

"Plotting new target."

Maria didn't see anything at first when they arrived on shore. After a moment the head of a dog popped up from behind a sand dune. 'What the…'

The dog barked and loped towards them, circled them, and then ran back to the sand dune.

With a quick glance at her own AIM, she followed the dog. She swore once more when she reached the sand dune. A young man, probably her own age, lay on the sand. His wet blond hair stuck to his forehead. He wasn't breathing.

In a quick fluid motion Maria changed her AIM into the form of a bird and dropped to her knees beside the man. She immediately started compressions on his chest. "Go. Find some officials. Emergency team. Anyone who can help. Give them our coordinates. Tell them…" She paused her command to breathe into the man's mouth. "Twenty-year-old male, unresponsive." Maria looked him over as she continued compressions. "Minor head lac, potential concussion. Go."

She didn't need to look up to know that her AIM had left. "Come on…" She moved from compressions to breathing, the dog laying beside the man watching every move. After another few compressions, Maria felt his body twitch, then convulse.

The man began to cough and she rolled him to his side to help clear the water from his lungs. When he was done, he rolled onto his back, breathing deep. His eyes fluttered open and he began to look around.

"What happened?"

Maria leaned forward. "Does anything hurt?"

"That didn't answer my question," he said with a grunt and began to sit up.

"No, no. Lay down," she said and gently got him back onto the sand. "I got a distress signal. I thought it was from a player." The dog beside them seemed much more subdued than before. "From your AIM, I guess. Thought it was a real dog."

"Trained it well." He swatted her hand away when she felt around the small cut on the side of his head. "That hurts."

"Anything else?"

He looked at her for a moment silently. "It's you."

Maria raised an eyebrow. "Excuse me?"

"You jumped off that cliff yesterday. That was awesome."

She held back a smile and began to rummage through her bag. "Do you know what day it is?"

"I know the date, where I was born, my name. I don't, however, know yours."

Maria looked down at him incredulously. "Are you seriously hitting on me right now?" When he gave her a grin, she rolled her eyes and pulled out her first aid kit. "Maria."

"Just Maria?"

"Kier."

"Cam Tylar."

She hesitated for a moment. Then continued pulling out a small sewing kit and antiseptic. "From Revolution."

"You're a fan?"

"I know some teams."

"So that's a yes?" He swore when she poured a small amount of antiseptic on his cut. "What the hell?"

Maria held up her sterilized needle and thread. "A gash like that is going to get infected. I've sent my AIM to get help, but you're pretty far off course and I don't want to risk it. Or, in a language you understand, your face won't be as pretty if I don't stitch it up."

Cam grinned again. "You think my face is pretty?"

"I'd bite down on something if I were you."

"So why haven't I heard of you before?" Cam was sitting up now, allowed only after he convinced Maria he wasn't going to pass out.

"Why would you have heard of me? You grew up in Kitchener. I'm from Owen Sound."

He gestured around him. "You're here. My AIM couldn't even find you in the Scanning database."

"That's because I'm not a Scanner."

"Never even on a Tiny Tikes team? Or a Junior?" He swore and laughed when she shook her head. "You've got to be kidding me. So, what, you just thought one day 'Hey, I'm bored. Being beautiful isn't enough. I have to try this Open Tournament thing'."

Maria rolled her eyes. "Does that ever work on anyone?"

"You tell me."

"Cut the crap, Cam." She stared him in the eyes. "I'm not buying it."

He looked away finally and stayed silent for a good while. "My mom died a few months ago."

Maria looked at him quickly, her eyes open wide in surprise. "Cam, I'm so sorry. I had no idea."

Cam shrugged and ran his hands through the sand. "The guys helped me keep it quiet for the most part."

"What about your dad?"

"Left when I was five. I was even named after him. Cameron is my middle name. I'm Lucas Cameron Tylar." He paused and looked back at her. "I've...actually never told anyone that before."

"What I said before-"

"You were right," Cam interrupted. "I'm alone. It used to be just me and my mom. She was my biggest fan. Then the cancer...who I am on TV, in challenges, that's the guy I need to be to get where I want to go. My stupid comments...I'm sorry. You saved my life, Maria." When she shrugged, he shook his head and put a hand on her arm. "I'm serious. Thank you. The rest of the people out here, they're all trying to win. I don't know how long I would have lasted if you didn't come."

Maria gave him a small smile. "No one gets left behind."

"What?"

"Something my dad taught me. He's in the army. Whether we're all competing against each other or not, I wasn't going to keep going knowing that someone was in trouble."

Cam absently stroked his AIM's fur. "That explains it. You're an army brat."

"Explains what?"

"Let's go back to before I made an ass of myself. Why are you here?"

She sighed. "My dad made me a deal. He'd fast track me in Basic for officer training if I gave Scanning a chance. I wasn't about to commit to a full season so this was our compromise."

"And?"

"And... it's fine." She laughed when he gave her a pointed look. "Okay, it's pretty cool."

He scooted closer to her and held his hand out. "Okay, how about you make a deal with me, then? You do one season in the Juniors. Then you can join the army or Basic or whatever. Deal?"

She thought for a moment but then shook his hand. "Deal."

Maria sat in her car outside Ryan's apartment building a few days later. She had been happy he moved out from his parents' farmhouse, but he knew he missed being in the country. But this was a good thing, and he had been able to be part of more CST events. And it allowed his parents to accept his being away so often for the tournament. She leaned her head against the steering wheel briefly before she took in a deep breath and went into the building. It had been nice having her own set of keys, but this...this was likely the last time she would use them.

Out of courtesy, she knocked on his door before she let herself in. "Honey, I'm home," Maria called out in a jokingly sing-song voice. She laughed when he ran up to her and grabbed her in a tight embrace. "Ryan, I'm so sorry I couldn't-" but she was interrupted by his lips pressing against hers. She let herself melt into him until he pulled away. She felt the reluctance, and she smiled. "I missed you too."

"Hi."

"Hi."

She smiled again softly as they moved into his living room. Maria looked around and resisted the urge to roll her eyes. Why did men refuse to decorate? The walls had remained bare, and everything was very Spartan. It made sense, to not have much since he was only home for half the year, but for the other half it would be nice to have it feel like a home. "Sorry I didn't give much notice."

"No, it's fine," Ryan said with a shake of his head. "We only got back yesterday. Without Cam there we didn't really want to do too much training. We can do individual training any time, but we really needed to do team training."

Maria glanced away. She and Cam had agreed to meet with the team the next day to talk about their joint deployment, and the possibility that he wouldn't be competing this season, or at least not for the beginning. "Since when has Cam enjoyed the team training?"

"Apparently it's a recent thing," Ryan said with a shrug. "I don't think any of us are going to complain any time soon." He gave a laugh and pulled her down onto the couch with him, giving her a quick kiss on the cheek.

She bit the inside of her lip and turned her body to face him on the couch. "Ryan, I need to tell you something."

Ryan looked at her, suddenly feeling his high crash and burn. "What's wrong?"

She took a deep breath, and knew she would need to rip the band-aid sooner rather than later. "The meeting I had in Ottawa…" She paused. "I'm being re-deployed to Afghanistan."

His face paled, and he swore his heart clenched and stopped beating altogether. "You're…you're being deployed."

Maria nodded slowly, and it took all she had in her to not break down. "I…yeah."

They were both silent for a few moments. Ryan continued to hold Maria's hands from when he had led her to the couch. "When?" he asked quietly.

"Two weeks." Before he could respond, she continued quickly. "But I'm only here in Kitchener for another week. We have some training and organizing before we actually fly out, but I'll be able to call before I leave. I won't be able to visit, though."

"Okay." Ryan took in a deep breath and forced a smile. "You're a soldier. This is what happens with soldiers. When something happens, you have to go. I knew that. I was prepared for that."

"I wasn't."

Ryan smiled and pulled Maria in. He closed his eyes as he took in her scent. How long was it going to be until he could hold her like this again? He thought back to anything he had seen on the news that should have triggered something, but he realized that things had been settled in Afghanistan for years. "How long are you going for?"

Maria pulled away slowly, and slid her hands from his grip. "That's something else I needed to talk to you about. I…I have no idea. They're thinking it'll be for a few months, but we're not sure what we're going to find when we get there. Once we're in Afghanistan, we should have a better idea," she lied. She hated herself for it, but it had to be done. "We honestly have no idea. Once we're there and see what we're dealing with, it could be years."

"Well, there's a reason the internet was created," he replied with a half-hearted smile. That's all he felt he had right then: half of a heart.

She shook her head. "I won't have any access. I won't be at a base. We could go months or years without talking." Maria finally met his gaze, and she allowed him to see the tears which had filled her eyes. "None of this is fair to you, Ryan. I have no idea when I'll be back."

"We'll play it by ear, then."

She shook her head harder this time. "Ryan, you don't get it."

"Then help me. Talk to me, Maria."

"I might not be coming back."

Ryan stopped, then. "Is there a war going on we don't know about?"

She hesitated, trying not to tell him too much. "That's what we're going to find out, and we're going to try to stop it. With me gone for who knows how long…Ryan, I can't have you stuck here, waiting for months or years, for someone who might not be coming back. If something does happen to me over there-"

"It won't."

"I'd be dead for nearly four months before anyone back here in Canada would know. Especially since you're not my next of kin."

He stared at her then, his eyes wide. Nothing had ever been so final like that. Not between them, at least.

Maria gently took one of his hands again. "I don't want to leave you behind like that. I don't want you wondering about a girlfriend, and I can't be wondering about my boyfriend back home. I need to make sure I'm all there, so I can come back and be all here."

He moved away from her then, slipping out of her grasp. "Are you breaking up with me?"

"I don't want to. Ryan, I care so much about you, and all of this has been…it's been amazing." Her lips quivered as she finally let her tears fall. "Believe me," she started as her voice cracked. "Breaking up with you is the last thing I want to do, but I can't have you wondering about a girlfriend, worrying about whether or not she's dead."

"Breaking up isn't going to make me stop worrying about you."

She shook her head, flinging tears from side to side. "I can't do it, Ryan. I can't leave you like this. I need a clean break. Please let me do this. Please," she pleaded, barely getting her last word out before her voice broke out into sobs. "I can't…"

Ryan wiped his face and held her again. "It's okay," he said, whether he believed it or not. He shut his eyes and leaned his head against hers as she sobbed against his chest. After a year of wanting to be with her, and after finally dating her…it all came to this. "When you get back," he forced out, trying to keep his voice steady. "When you get back, it'll be like you never left."

"Don't." She gripped his shirt and pressed herself further against him. "Don't do that. Don't wait around, thinking I'm coming back. We're breaking up, Cam. This has to be it."

His body tensed, and one arm dropped slightly. "Ryan."

She sniffled and looked up at him. "Wha-" but then she heard what she had said. "Ryan. Oh God, no. Ryan."

"You said his name," he said quietly.

"Ryan, no."

"You said his name."

"It was a mistake." Maria wiped her face and tried to pull Ryan back to her as pulled away. "I just saw him, and it was a mistake."

"You're breaking up with me, and you said his name."

"This has nothing to do with him." But nothing was going to make it any better. Maybe it was better this way, after all. Maybe now he wouldn't think about her as much. Maybe it would be easier for him to think about her a little less each day she was gone. Maybe killing him would have been less painful.

"When are you telling the others you're going?"

She shut her eyes against his harsh and cold tone. "Tomorrow. I was going to talk to you about coming along to your meeting."

He shrugged. "Well, you better, I guess." He looked at her, and his face automatically softened. "Are we going to tell them…about us?"

"We probably should. Or you can tell them alone, if you want. I don't think it'd necessarily be appropriate to announce right after I say I'm leaving. If they ask, I'll let you decide what to say." She was thankful that he wasn't one to hit with low remarks. She knew what she would say, if the roles were reversed. And if it wasn't him. She never wanted to hurt him. He didn't deserve that. But the name had just slipped out, like a typo that can't be erased.

"Do you want to tell him?"

"Ryan, come on…"

He shook his head, and she realized he hadn't meant anything by it. "I just meant since you're closer with him."

She thought for a moment. "No. He's your team-mate. It would make sense to come from you first. I'll still talk to him about it. Probably cry some more, and make him uncomfortable." She smiled softly. "That never really worked with you. You're always so steadfast when I cry. Always know what to do."

He returned the smile, but said nothing. Sometimes, there was just nothing that could be said.

CHAPTER 6

Rick looked over at Maria curiously as they sat in his father's family room. His mother had made herself scarce, shopping with Brittany and the kids. He smiled, thinking about his son and his infant daughter. After Maria and Cam's daughter was stillborn, he had been wary about telling them he was expecting a daughter. But they had been fine, and Cam had even been a big help to him and Brittany. Rick wasn't sure if Maria knew how much Cam had helped out with Susannah, watching her, and even doing some errands for them.

Cam had told him Maria shared the ultrasounds with him, and the recording of Lucy's heartbeat, but that had been it. Maria hadn't even looked too pregnant to have even had a hand on her swollen belly. He looked around at the rest of his team, and he suddenly felt the changes of the past three years. So much had happened, and they had each changed so drastically. Now, he knew, things were going to change once more.

"Last time you sat in on a meeting, Cam had some pretty rough news for us," Owen said. "Is it your turn now?" he laughed. When Maria glanced at Ryan slowly, his smile faded. "Maria?"

"I'm leaving in two weeks for Afghanistan," she said simply.

There was the band-aid.

The room seemed to stop breathing. All except Cam.

"I'm going up to Ottawa for the first stage of the mission, and then next week we fly out," Maria continued. She let out a deep breath and she looked at Ryan once again. "I couldn't tell you everything last night." Her eyes flickered towards Cam.

Cam shifted in his seat as he looked at his team-mates with mixed emotions. What was he supposed to say to them? This was going to be the last time he would· see them. Owen, as much as Cam had tried to fight it, had been the only father figure he had known and moderately accepted. And Rick was the brother he never had. Just when he was starting to get along with Ryan...his life turns into some sort of science-fiction movie, and he's sent away.

"Remember how I was part of the Underground?" he started hesitantly.

"Were we supposed to forget?" Owen said, holding back his true remark.

Cam shoved past it. He had to. "The military found out about the work I was doing there...and they've asked me to go to Afghanistan, too."

Now the room seemed to be void of all oxygen.

Ryan's head whipped towards Maria. "You knew about this last night?"

"Cam had to be the one to tell you, not me," she answered quietly.

Rick shook his head as though it would help him to take in the information. "Okay, wait a minute...you're both going to Afghanistan?"

"Yes," Maria answered. "We're hiring him as a contractor to work with some AIMs he dealt with in the Underground. Unfortunately, he's the only one we could go to. Believe me, I want him on this mission even less than you."

Owen nodded slowly. He had had multiple friends and even a few family members go over for the wars over the last decade. "What does this mean for the season?"

"It means," Maria started, "that you should be looking for someone to take his place. We have no idea how long this mission is going to be. When we get there, we'll know more. But the safest bet is to have someone on standby in case he isn't back in time for the beginning of the season."

Owen stood and began to pace around the room. Maria took the chance to look at Cam slowly, but his face was blank. Everything was sinking in harder, now. It was so much easier the first time she was deployed. She hadn't been speaking to anyone other than Ryan, and she had an end-date for her first deployment, and scheduled home visits. This was different. No one liked it.

"We'll pull someone from the roster, now that we actually have one," Owen said finally.

"This can't be happening..." Rick said, his voice trailing off as he shook his head with disbelief.

Owen sat down next to Cam, but refrained from touching him. His normal gesture would have been to put a hand on his shoulder, but that didn't seem like it would be enough. Nothing would be. "Anyone on the roster you think would do a good job until you get back?"

Cam let out a short laugh. "Could anyone do as good a job?"

"Probably not," he admitted with a smile. "But you did help pick some of those guys, and you were technically the one who found Maria, so you have a good eye at least."

Maria looked up at that, her head cocked to the side. "What are you talking about?"

Cam looked away as Owen began to answer. "He put your name in to be part of the team when he saw you in the Open. You knew that."

"No." She turned to Cam. "No, I didn't know that."

Rick looked between Cam and Maria and thought for a moment. "Yeah. We went to a few of your challenges after that, once you actually joined a junior team."

"So, we're going to Afghanistan," Cam said suddenly. "We can focus on that."

"You were the reason they were interested in me," Maria stated simply.

Owen looked at her dead-on. "He got our attention put on you. We would have found you eventually. He just jump-started things."

She nodded slowly, unconvinced. "Well, he's right anyway. We're leaving, so it's good for you to figure out a replacement."

"Until he gets back," Rick added.

"Right." Her eyes met Cam's. "Until he gets back."

The team was silent for most of the afternoon, only speaking when something about the season came across their mind. But the thought of two of their own going to war, or going to whatever it was that was happening over there, was too heavy to be moved by the CST. Maria was thankful for that. Mindless chatter or small talk had its time and place. She wondered if they would hate her if they found out she had been the one to bring Cam onto her team.

"I should head out," Maria said finally, and quite reluctantly. "I have a lot to get done before I go up to Ottawa, and I only have a few days now."

"I should probably go, too," Cam said. "Do you…" He looked at his team. "Could you guys check on the house while I'm gone? I haven't really finished up the barn yet, and who knows what this winter's going to do to it. Some of the tarp came down yesterday from the roof."

Rick nodded with a reassuring smile. "Don't worry. We'll use your place to host our loud and annoying meetings and training sessions."

Cam laughed. "Feel free to finish the barn reno while I'm gone."

He shook his head and grabbed Cam in a fierce hug. "You finish it when you get back."

Cam nodded into the man's shoulder but pushed him away quickly. He had never cried in front of the guys, and he was not about to start that today. "We'll see."

While Owen had his turn with Cam, Rick moved on to Maria, embracing her a bit more gently. "You take care of yourself. And Cam."

"I'll try."

"I mean it," he said softly. "With his mouth, he'll get shot by one of your own before anyone else gets a chance to do it."

She laughed. He was right. Although Cam had gotten better with his attitude, how he had acted during the first meeting had not been a good foreshadowing of how things were going to be. "Like I said, I'll try. But Cam can hold his own. I think you'd be surprised."

"I probably would be." Rick smiled and put a hand on the side of her head, cupping her face. "Please stay safe." When she nodded, he kissed the top of her head. "Good." He looked at Ryan and made way for him to get to the two.

"I'll go outside with them," Ryan said, the first thing he had said in quite a while. He let Cam and Maria head out the door first. He took a deep breath before following them out into the frigid November air. He and Maria stayed near the porch while Cam wandered a few steps away towards the driveway.

Ryan turned to face Maria, who was avoiding his gaze while still turned towards him. "Hey," he said softly, and placed his hands on her arms, gripping them gently. "It'll be fine. We're all about adaptability, aren't we?"

Maria smiled at that. Looking back over the last three years, and even further beyond that in some instances, Revolution had needed to adapt to the various obstacles life and the world had put before them. Even the small, seemingly insignificant things needed to be worked around. Her break-up with Cam. Owen's heart attack. Ryan's signing. The stillbirth. The breaking up of the team. All of it had required them to adapt, and change. And change they had.

"We've adapted pretty well, haven't we?" Maria answered in a quiet voice.

Ryan dropped his head slightly. "We'll get there." He continued to look down at her. "Can I…?" When she nodded, he pulled her close against him and pressed his lips against hers. He wanted to hold back, and how he tried to keep it together, but when she parted her lips just so slightly, he put everything he had into that last kiss. His arms wrapped around her waist, holding her tight until he thought he would squeeze the breath right out from her lungs.

After too short a time, he pulled away as slowly as he could, trying to feel her as long as possible. Ryan kept his eyes closed for a moment longer before he looked down into hers. He couldn't help but smile, albeit a sad and tortured smile. "Just come home." She nodded, and he resisted the urge to kiss her again. There was no way he was going to replace that kiss. "I love you," he whispered.

Maria smiled and took in a deep breath. He had said it before. It had been in his sleep, but it had still counted. She opened her mouth, but was stopped by Ryan before she could get a word out.

"Don't," he said with a smile. That same lopsided smile she had first seen when they were looking for Owen's replacement, when Cam had stormed out of the boardroom insistent on the fact that they had no need for a fourth player. "You don't have to. It's okay. Just come home."

She nodded and backed away, and finally turned towards her car. She looked over her shoulder and saw Cam and Ryan shake hands. There would be nothing more than that, she knew. Even if they wanted to show their emotions, or express their concern for the other, with Maria in the middle they would never be anything more than friends who got together on rare occasions. But when Cam seemed to be speaking to Ryan in a hushed tone, Maria's eyebrow went up curiously. *Last minute advice for the season?*

Maria waited until Ryan went back inside, and Cam walked towards her. "Well, that went relatively well." When Cam shrugged, she stepped in front of him, blocking his way to his car. "Was that true? Did you actually get them to sign me?"

He let out a frustrated sigh and tried to walk past her. "Does it matter? It was seven years ago. I barely remember how we met."

Maria stood dumbstruck. "If you hate me so much for dragging you into this, you could've just said so."

Cam shut his eyes, and she knew he regretted his words. "I don't hate you. And I remember how we met." He looked at her then. "Yes, I put their attention on you. After the Open Tournament, I kept tabs on you. I wanted to see if you'd actually follow through and join a Junior team. As soon as you did, I made sure to keep up with your stats. I watched a few of your challenges on TV while the guys were around, and just made a few comments here and there about your technique. I said I was interested in seeing the junior challenge in Owen Sound when we were there, and they saw you on their own." He shrugged. "I just mentioned that if we were to ever have a woman on the team, you'd be the one who could handle us."

"Why?"

His gaze never faltered. “I wanted to be around you. After what we went through, what you did for me, how could I not? Maria, you were such a good athlete.”

She smiled, but it faded when he began to laugh. “What?” She realized it after it was too late.

“You’re blushing.”

“Shut it.” Maria unlocked her car quickly. “I’ll see you in Ottawa.” She jumped when Cam’s car horn honked. She turned to see his AIM as that same golden retriever standing on the wheel of his car. She heard it bark faintly through the windshield, and she smiled. “Can I say hi before you go?”

“You better,” Cam muttered. “He’s been complaining that you don’t come around anymore.”

“He? What happened there?”

He shrugged as he opened his door. “The ‘she’ phase didn’t last long. He believes it’s because he identified with me for so long, that he thinks himself as male.”

Maria smiled and knelt down as the AIM jumped from the car and pranced around her feet, jumping down as if ready for her to throw a stick. “Hey you! What about when you’re in a female form of an animal?”

Cam groaned at the way his AIM was behaving. “He’s made me try to scan only male animals.”

“L.J. tells me you do not like the farmhouse,” the AIM ‘spoke.’ “But I knew it was because of your relationship with Ryan.”

She smiled and pet the robot, calming it down enough to stay in one place. “I’ve been busy. And I also don’t like dog hair all over me,” she joked. “I really need to get going.”

“You are not going to be with Ryan tonight?” it asked, cocking its head to the side as a real dog would.

Maria noticed Cam look at her, and assumed he had the same question in mind. “No. We had our goodbyes already. I can’t handle much more.” She stood and wiped the dust from the driveway off her knees. “I’ll see you later.”

“Maria,” Cam said, stopping her as she began to turn back to her car. He hesitated a moment too long, and he shook his head. “See you in Ottawa.” He looked down at his AIM and pointed towards the car. "Let's go. If you had opposable thumbs, I'd be getting you to clean the car."

"Perhaps you should invest in a primate scan," the AIM replied as it jumped back into the car.

Maria smiled as the two continued to bicker. She wondered if the AIM would continue to do so while they were in Afghanistan, or if it would remain pretending it was a regular AIM. She got into her car, and began to drive to the hotel she booked for the night. The others on the mission were bound to find out about his AIM. There was likely going to be a good reason for the AIM, and for Cam, to reveal its sentience. But for now, she would leave that up to Cam. She let out a deep breath as she pulled away from Owen's home. She just had to get through the night.

Cam sighed as he let himself fall down onto his living room couch. He held the TV remote in his hand, but did nothing with it other than point it at the TV.

His AIM jumped up onto the couch beside him, despite being told numerous times that that particular form shed too much. "You were rather quiet in the vehicle on the drive home. Did the meeting not go well?"

"As well as it can when you tell the only family you have that you're going to Afghanistan." Cam looked at the robot. He had known for a long time that he had stopped thinking of his AIM as a robot, and more like a friend. "I never asked what you thought, if you even wanted to go. I can bring another AIM to assist me. This doesn't have to be dangerous for both of us."

The AIM lay down across Cam's lap with a snort. "L.J., I will never leave your side. When you have more children, I will never leave their side."

Cam gripped the fur of the canine form. "Even when bullets are flying?"

"Especially then." Both remained silent for a few moments. "Are you afraid?"

Cam thought for a moment. Was he? He was technically going to war. He would be in the middle of the desert, hunting dangerous AIMs. Other than the setting, it didn't seem to be much different from what he had done in the Underground.

"I don't think so. Not yet, at least," he finally answered.

"Well, you let me know when you have figured out your emotions," the AIM responded as it yawned and let its head fall back onto his lap.

He smiled and rubbed the top of its head. "I can't be afraid with my fierce AIM at my side." He shoved it playfully when it wouldn't reply. "Don't even try to pretend to sleep. You're sentient, but you're still a robot. Robots don't sleep."

"Sometimes I wish I could. Not that I could around you. You have developed quite the habit of snoring and speaking in your sleep."

"I have not!" Cam said defensively. "And if I have-"

"It is because you do not have anyone to shove you awake when you begin to make those horrifying noises."

Cam paused. "Did I really snore when I was dating Maria?"

"She would not let you."

He laughed and covered his face. "Good thing noise never woke her up." He turned his head when there was a knock on his front door. The sound was muffled by the sound of the wind rattling the shutters on the farmhouse's windows, and the creaking of the tree branches. Cam waited until he heard the knock again to make sure it was made by a human rather than nature.

"A late-night visitor?" his AIM inquired curiously, and jumped down from the couch. "I thought you had no need for those any longer, unless you have been hiding something from me."

Cam rolled his eyes as he moved to the front of the farmhouse. He looked around the room for a brief moment with a small smile. He had worked so hard to restore the house. After he and his mother had left it, no one had taken much care of it until he had bought it two years earlier. His team had helped him bring it back to a livable condition, but there was still a lot of work to do. There was always something to do, it seemed.

He opened the door, and an eyebrow rose with concern. "Maria?"

She smiled lightly. "Hey." She winced as a blast of wind pushed against her and the house, whipping her hair around her face. "Mind if I come in?" She stepped in when he moved out of the way, and she slipped her shoes and coat off quickly. "Man, winter's coming fast. What happened to our mild winters?"

"At least we don't have any snow yet," Cam noted as he followed her into the living room, where she made herself at home. He held back a smile at the thought. "What's going on? I thought you had work to do."

"I do." She paused. "I did. I got most of it done. I can't do much here. Most of it is back in Kingston and Ottawa, but...I didn't want to leave Kitchener yet. Or I guess Elmira, since I found my way up here."

Cam motioned towards a wine bottle had placed on the end table earlier that evening. When Maria nodded, he made his way to the kitchen to grab her a glass. He hadn't felt the need to open the bottle yet since getting home and so it had sat in his living room. There hadn't been a reason. Until now, at least.

He handed her the glass, and began to open the bottle. "So, is there any special reason for your visit, or am I just lucky to see you twice in the same day?" He paused. "Does Ryan know you're here?"

Maria held out her glass as he readied to pour. "We broke up yesterday."

Cam continued to pour, seemingly unfazed. "I'm sorry."

She looked up at him with a roll of her eyes. "No you're not. You already knew."

He nodded as he sat down with his now full glass of wine. "Yeah, he told me earlier. We hung out for a bit after the meeting. How are you?" Cam watched her down the entire glass. "That good?"

Maria shrugged. "I don't know. I'm upset, obviously. Break-ups aren't fun. I just...I couldn't go to Afghanistan and leave him behind, worrying about a girlfriend. A friend is one thing, but a significant other is something completely different. I couldn't have handled it. You saw what we're up against. There'd be no way I could concentrate on both at the same time. I could barely handle dating you and the tournament at once."

"You were pretty good at both," Cam said as he finally took a drink from his glass.

She was quiet for a few moments. She smiled when his AIM bumped against her legs.

"Sure. You don't jump up on her lap," Cam muttered. A thought occurred to him. "What will happen with your work while you're gone? You were working with that psychologist?"

"Oh, I've done most of my part already. I was able to train two AIMs to sense a PTSD episode and finished the training manual. Dr. Kerrigan will fine tune it and write a report about the two I've already trained. They've been with their partners for...seven months now." Maria let a small smile appear on her lips. After her first deployment, she began working on using AIMs as a form of therapy animal for veterans. "I hope all of this will end up helping people. Even if it only helps one person, it'll be worth it."

Maria began to stroke the AIM mindlessly. She let out a heavy sigh before she turned her attention to Cam again. "I'm sorry for the way I've treated you the past few years."

"What do you mean?"

"I shouldn't have pushed you away like I did. I should have just told Ryan to get over his insecurities. You're my best friend, Cam," she added softly. "And you didn't deserve to be pushed to the side like you didn't mean anything to me."

Cam let his shoulders drop quickly and he set his glass on the coffee table. "He meant more, and that's fine. That's how it should've been. I was fine with giving you guys your space. He wasn't comfortable with me being around all the time, and I needed to respect that. I didn't like being away from you, but I saw you with him. I saw how happy you were. I'm sorry you broke up." When she looked at him, he nodded as if to reaffirm what he had said. "I am."

"Thanks. I'm still sorry. More because I feel like we lost out on a lot of time. We barely got to catch up after…everything."

Cam didn't respond, and she knew she had hit a nerve. She had hidden her pregnancy from him, and he had missed out on all the firsts. She had kept something so important and intimate from him that he would never get back. And since then, she still had to hide things from him. They weren't able to share their grief. They weren't even able to patch things up between them, because Ryan had already come in the middle by that point. Cam had kept his distance for Ryan's sake, but it meant they never had any time alone to even mention Lucy, or the incident with Trevor McCarthy. They had both lost friends in that time, friends neither of them realized they had.

"Did you ever get to go to Jack's funeral?" Maria asked quietly.

He shook his head. "No. There would've been too many questions. I guess you didn't?"

"I went to the CST memorial with Ryan, but it probably wasn't the same. He wasn't well-liked by any athlete I know of." She took in a deep breath and covered her face. "I knew it couldn't be over. It couldn't just end so nicely with the bad guy in jail."

"He's up for parole, you know."

Maria's hands dropped along with her jaw. "You're kidding me. How did you find that out?"

"Henk. I guess he's pretty close with Cohner now. Cohner's going to make sure the parole doesn't go through."

She shook her head in disbelief. "He was convicted as a terrorist, and he's up for parole. What's wrong with that country?"

Cam gave her a crooked grin. "Do you really have to ask?"

Maria rolled her eyes and copied his smile. "Guess not." She let herself sink deeper into the full cushions of the couch and she looked around. "You've done a really good job with the place, Cam." She sat up quickly after she thought for a moment. "I haven't seen it since you finished the kitchen, or the upstairs, for that matter."

He raised an eyebrow with yet another mischievous grin. "Upstairs, huh? I remember you being much more forward than that. Just can't come out and say it?" When she looked away, he continued quickly. "Sorry. Old habit."

"No wonder he didn't like us being around each other with you talking like that. I don't really think he liked the reminders that we've slept together. I don't really like the reminders either."

Cam glanced down at his AIM. He had changed, he reminded himself. In the past, he would have made a snide remark, or said something before she could hurt him even more. Hurt before you get hurt. "Was it that terrible, compared to him?"

"Cam, we fought all the time," she answered. "And fought, and screamed."

"And loved each other."

She froze, hearing the words again. It was different this time. It had never been said in the past tense before. "Yeah. There's that." Maria closed her eyes as a tight pain came across her chest. She let out a soft cry and stood up quickly.

"You okay?" Cam asked and stood up beside her, his face turned down towards her with concern.

"Uh, yeah. I just…maybe just some water," she managed to get out. What were the signs again? Tingling of the left arm? Or was it the right? Blurred vision, slurred speech? She only had the chest pain. And the shortness of breath. There was the blurred vision now. "Oh, God…"

He stepped towards her and wiped her face free of the tears. "Maria, what's going on? Is this Ryan, or Afghanistan?"

Right, tears. "Just some water."

Cam hesitated, watching her for a brief moment before he moved back into the kitchen.

"She does not need water," his AIM said from behind him.

"Probably not, but she asked for it," he replied as he turned on the tap and filled a glass. Her panic attacks were all different, and as far as he knew he had seen them all. This was just a minor one, thankfully.

"The past tense."

"What?" But then he stopped. He turned off the tap slowly, the glass overflowing in his hand. He emptied it and set it down on the counter. He strode down the hallway and back to the living room.

Maria finished wiping the tears from her face. "I'm so sorry," she called out before he made it back to the room. "I have no idea what that was." She forced out a smile when he re-appeared, without water. "You forgot it. You had one job."

Ignoring her, he continued walking, took her face in his hands, and pressed his mouth against hers hungrily. He felt her tense for a brief second before she slowly copied his hunger. It had been years since he had been able to kiss her, to hold her in his arms, and feel her body against his. Nearly three and a half years since he had had her. Now, having her like this again, it felt like she had never left.

*   *   *

"Maria, stop." Cam reached out and grabbed her arm, pulling her back towards him. "What the hell was that?"

"What?" she asked, exasperated. "What do you want me to say?"

He glanced around, making sure they were alone in the hotel hallway. "I get one-night stands, but we both know that's not what happened last night. Not with us. And I'm not used to waking up expecting to see someone next to me. I'm also not used to expecting it, but waking up alone."

"Last night was a mistake." She winced when she saw his face flinch, a hurt in his eyes.

"Don't even try to pull that crap. Last night was a long time coming, and we both know it."

Maria slipped her arm from his light grip. "Cam, you're my team-mate. I've worked so hard to get where I am, and I can't screw that up. You've been a superstar since your first challenge. I'm still a novelty. And now I'm sleeping with my team-mate? With Cam Tylar?" She shook her head and took a step back. "And how will it look once they actually get me in a challenge?"

Cam narrowed his eyes. "First of all, I'm good at keeping secrets. We don't have to be public. Second, you're a damn good athlete. But you're telling me that you worked hard? I've been working towards where I am since I was five years old. This is all I've wanted. Then there's you. One shot at the World Open, get in the top twenty. Then signed onto a Junior team."

"Cam."

"You were on that team less than a year when we started scouting you," he continued. "Sleeping with me isn't going to hold you back. Don't use that as an excuse."

She looked up at him and let him step towards her and put his hands on her arms. Kissing him for the first time the night before, sleeping with him, finally acting on nearly a year's worth of tension...it was the first thing that made sense in so long.

"Rick and Owen will hate this."

He gave her a half grin and kissed her. "Let them."

Maria woke the following morning slowly, but kept her eyes closed to shield them from the cruel morning rays. She allowed herself to enjoy the feel of the down comforter, and the wonderfully soft mattress. It had been years since she slept this well. She smiled lightly and her eyes opened as she felt lips on the back of her neck.

"Good morning," came the soft greeting.

She rolled onto her back and turned her head. "Good morning indeed."

Cam grinned and kissed her bare shoulder. "Good morning," he said again after a moment.

She laughed. "You said that already."

"Right." He brushed the hair from her face and glanced at her forehead. The scar from her meeting with Trevor McCarthy was still visible, and it tore his heart. "Do you want to talk more about what happened with Ryan?"

She shook her head and moved in closer to him, resting her head on his shoulder. "No. I want you to make me breakfast."

Cam looked at her, his forehead lined with marks of seriousness. "Why me?"

"Because you don't have a chef on staff."

"Why did you really come over last night? Why are you here? Before, I would have thought it was for my skill set." He grinned, but only briefly. "But it's different now. What's going on? I know you're upset about breaking up with Ryan, but what happened last night had nothing to do with him. That much I know. If I hadn't initiated it, you would have."

She sighed and moved back to her side of the bed. "Can we just keep this as a good morning?"

"Maria."

She was quiet for a moment, and Cam was about to ask her again when she began. "We're going to Afghanistan."

"I know. I was there when they asked me to go, remember? When you asked me to go."

"Ryan and I broke up because I don't want him worrying about me."

He shrugged. He propped himself up on his side with his elbow, facing her. "He'll still worry about you. That won't change."

She let out a frustrated sigh. "You don't get it. There's no end date for this mission."

"I know."

"Would you listen to me?" Maria's voice rose, which earned her a harsh look from Cam. She ignored it and continued. "They have no idea how long this mission is going to take. It could be a week; it could be years." She paused. "Cam, they're not expecting any of us to survive our meeting with Mjahdan. The AIMs aren't what's making this mission dangerous."

Cam's eyebrows furrowed as he thought. "So, you slept with me because you think you're going to die? Or I'm going to die?"

"I broke up with Ryan because if I didn't, he'd wait nearly four months before finding out I'm dead, and he'll have to say his girlfriend was killed. I came over last night because I realized that if either of us dies over there, the other will be there too, and I wanted that."

He said nothing as he leaned forward and placed a gentle kiss on her forehead. "What do you want for breakfast?" he asked finally.

She looked at the clock on the bedside table and groaned. "Something quick. I have to get to Ottawa early. Rehearsal for tomorrow."

"Rehearsal?"

"Today's the tenth."

"Get ready," Cam said as he sat up. He threw the covers away before he stood and grabbed his clothes from the floor. "I'll have breakfast done for when you're downstairs." He paused before he put his shirt on, catching Maria's stare. With a grin, he threw his shirt at her before heading downstairs to the kitchen.

Maria came down the stairs after her shower to the smell of eggs and bacon. A smile came over her face as she rounded into the kitchen. She laughed when she saw her breakfast all ready to go, wrapped up.

"A breakfast burrito?" she said with a laugh.

He shrugged, still shirtless, and leaned against the counter. "It was quick, and you can take it to go. If you want," he added.

She nodded but stayed in the doorway. "Now it really does feel like the first time. No idea what to say."

"You just broke up with Ryan," Cam replied. "It's fine."

Maria shook her head and stepped into the kitchen. "That wasn't rebound, or 'I'm sad I broke up with my boyfriend' sex. That was 'I need one more time before I die'. You always think there's going to be time, more time. But what if there isn't?"

He didn't answer, but picked up her breakfast and handed it to her. "I'll come up tomorrow, and I'll get my Second to meet us in a few days."

She nodded, taking the hint, and walked with him to the front door. She paused as she put her hand on the doorknob, and turned back towards him. "I broke up with him because I'm leaving. Just because you're coming too..."

Cam rolled his eyes with a smile. "I didn't think last night meant we're back together, or magically fixed all of our problems."

"I'm just saying...just saying that if we both come back alive, we can talk then. If that's even something you want to talk about." She closed her eyes as he kissed her in response, and her body flushed with the memory of last night. "I'll see you tomorrow," she whispered.

He closed the door behind her and went back to the kitchen where his AIM was sitting. He shot a glance at it before he began to clean the breakfast dishes. "What?"

"Next time, would you terribly mind warning me before you do that again? I am no longer accustomed to the sounds produced."

Cam grinned, grabbing a frying pan he had let cool already. After so much time, everything still felt the same. He could say it all he wanted, that he didn't want to be with her. But every time he said it, he knew it was a lie. His grin faded as he thought of their mission. Even the idea of an 'afterward' conversation was overshadowed by the possibility of something going wrong in Afghanistan.

He hadn't taken into consideration the terrorist group. He had focused so much on dealing with the AIMs that he had forgotten that he would also have to deal with humans. And a rogue human was infinitely worse than dealing with a rogue AIM. Part of him regretted his choice for a Second programmer. He supposed Maria felt the same way about bringing him into the mission. Now, they would both carry the same guilt, on top of any they each already carried. After so much time, everything was still the same.

CHAPTER 7

Cam stood amidst the crowd in Ottawa gathered around the cenotaph. Veterans had marched in already, led by the music of bagpipes, but he had missed that. He hadn't been to the ceremony in years, since the first year he was dating Maria, and they went to support her dad. A month earlier, he had returned from his time fighting in the war, the last war Canada had been in. For now.

After a few minutes of looking around as active soldiers marched into the square, he saw her. Maria was standing in formation with a group of AIMOTs, all paired with their AIMs in the form of a German Shepherd, the standard form of a military AIM.

He admired the strength she embodied today of all days. It was never easy for her, always crying within the first few notes of the song 'In Flanders Field.' Not today. She was a soldier today. What had she been yesterday? He shook his head as if to shake away the recent memory of their tryst. She was a soldier. The night before, it had been difficult to see that. When she was a Scanner, it had been hard for Revolution to believe she was raised as an army brat. But seeing her in this element, among soldiers and the ceremony, Cam realized that this was her place. In one week, that place would take her to Afghanistan. And his place as a Scanner, somehow that too would bring him to Afghanistan. He switched his attention to the mayor who began to recite a poem.

"They shall grow not old, as we that are left grow old:
Age shall not weary them, nor the years condemn;

At the going down of the sun, and in the morning;
We will remember them."

As the mayor finished the poem, a blood red poppy proudly pinned to his lapel, the church bells nearby began to strike the hour. The soldiers along the front of the ceremony area around the cenotaph, and those scattered among the crowd saluted, their hand raised to touch just above their right eye in a rehearsed and precise movement. No matter the generation, no matter the war, or where the battle was fought whether it was on foreign or domestic soil, the soldiers were all the same to Cam. They all shared in the values, the ideals, the nightmares, and the hope. And the salute, honouring those fallen and active.

Cam was jolted by the sound of gun fire, a single shot as the bell tower struck for the eleventh time. The crowd bowed their heads as the soldiers continued their salute. Two minutes later, another gunshot. Once again, he was jolted not by the sound of the guns, but by the blare of the trumpet sounding out the lament. He looked up to watch Maria's face. How far she had come. Both of them. Was he now a soldier too? Listening to the trumpeter's lament, he knew that next year on the eleventh of November, he would know for sure.

It wasn't until the end of the song that he realized he had already been in a kind of war. He had gone to war with Trevor McCarthy, and he had lost comrades. First Mark, and then Jack in the final moments. Countless others in the Underground were killed, people he barely knew. Was he not already a soldier of a different kind? A veteran of a secret war?

His AIM had asked him if he was afraid of his upcoming mission. He knew the answer now. He was terrified; not of dying, but what it would mean to be part of this type of war. He was terrified of what it would do to him. What it would do, and what it had done, to her. He had contemplated on his entire drive to the nation's capital calling the person he had chosen and telling him to forget the whole thing. Cam now understood why Maria told Ryan so little about her job. It was the same reason he had told her so little about what he had done in the Underground. The more information someone had, the more danger they were in. It was almost as if they were bringing a child into a corrupt, and lethal world, knowing they would die minute later. It wasn't fair to the child. Nothing was fair anymore.

The school choir commissioned by the legion began the powerful musical rendition of the famous Canadian poem. He was not used to this version, but he sang it in his head along with the choir, and it surprised him to realize that the words now took on a new meaning. Suddenly, his eyes met with Maria's. While she put on a brave face of a soldier, Cam knew her better. He could see the torment in her eyes, the painful memories flashing in her mind of her first deployment overseas. Now she was returning to the desert along with a small group of civilians and soldiers, and no one knew if they were coming back.

"It was a good ceremony," Padmore said later that afternoon. The four soldiers sat in a meeting room, going over the decisions that would could cost the lives of thirteen people.

"What was that song called?" McMurphy asked.

"In Flanders Fields," Maria answered with surprise. "You've never heard of it before?"

"It's Canadian," Padmore reminded her. "They celebrate Veteran's Day. We have Remembrance Day."

"When you're over there," Collins started as though he hadn't been listening. "Your focus is on your next target. You're thinking about surviving, and the lives of the soldiers at your side. At night, you think about whether or not you'll wake up, if you can even get to sleep. But you're not thinking about the mothers and fathers you left behind, or about the siblings. You forget how real war is even to the people who've never held a gun."

"Imagine that," Maria snapped. "Civilians feeling upset about war. Who would've guessed?"

"That's not what I meant."

"No. You just meant that unless you're a soldier, you don't know what the real world is like." When he didn't argue, she rolled her eyes. "My point. There are different kinds of wars, and different kinds of soldiers. Look at this," she said, tapping the tabletop until a list of names slid across, with an empty line of question marks at the bottom. "Four civilians who will be a veteran without being a soldier, if they survive. I think the civilians in those villages know more about the 'real world' than even most soldiers."

"Do you have a problem with authority, Lieutenant Kier?" Collins asked. "Because you'll remember that I'm your superior. You can have say over the scientists, but in the end, I will make the final calls."

Maria looked at Padmore, but she knew she'd get little support from him. Collins was right. Although she hated the idea, Collins was in charge. She was just the liaison. "So, who are you guys bringing to the table?"

McMurphy cleared his throat, warning Collins to let the topic be dropped, and he began to answer. "Sergeant Major Shepero, our communications officer. We'll rely on him to communicate with home base, and in case we split into smaller units, each other." A face and profile of the soldier appeared on the wall before them. McMurphy had already showed her this particular soldier, and Maria figured him to be a good judge of character, so she trusted his decision with this man.

"Next we have-"

"Colonel," Collins interrupted. "Do we need four civilians on this mission?"

Maria was the last person to want civilians around gunfire, but even she knew when they were needed. She rolled her eyes discreetly, but allowed the senior officer to answer.

"These two were specifically chosen by the General upon evaluations and recommendations made by Cohner McCarthy and Dr. Henk Baxter. Cameron-"

"Cam," Maria interrupted.

He hesitated, not happy with the interruption, but continued. "Cam Tylar is our main programmer. Whomever he chose to be his Second programmer will undergo the same evaluation. Cam has already approved this list. So, to answer your question, Major Collins, yes, we need four civilians."

She looked at the list of civilians again. "Do they have assignments, yet?"

"They'll be given in Afghanistan when they undergo their physical training," Padmore answered. "Any word from Cam about his Second?"

She shook her head. "He mentioned they would both be here tomorrow but other than that, I have no other details. He likes surprises. But you can trust him to get the job done. He'll do what he needs to in order to finish."

"Just make sure he does."

Maria slammed her phone down for the third time. He was late. Cam had refused the pick-up, claiming he would come with his Second at noon. It was three o'clock. And there had been silence. She saw him at the ceremony, so she knew he made it safely into town. So, she let herself become angry. Being angry, Maria had found, was easier on the heart than worrying. Had he changed his mind? No. He wouldn't have done that, especially without telling her.

"Lieutenant, your programmer showed up."

Maria looked up at Collins when she heard his deep voice in her doorway, but then looked around him to follow his gaze. She let out a frustrated breath as she watched Cam walk towards her temporary office on the base. Her eyebrows lowered as she noticed Ryan walking behind him. His eyes scrolled over his surroundings as he walked. She walked from behind her desk as they entered, and she glanced towards Collins. With a quick and unnecessary salute in her direction, he left.

She stared at Cam, her arms folded over her chest. She glanced down at her arms for a brief moment, looking at the digitized fatigue pattern of her uniform. "What is he doing here?"

"I found my Second," he stated simply.

"He has no experience with rogue AIMs," Maria replied as she finally turned to Ryan to study his face, which he kept turned towards Cam. There was a hesitation on his face, a slight wince, and concern in his eyes. He did not want to be there. At least, not in this dynamic, and not so soon after breaking up with Maria.

Cam handed Maria an AIRC. "His AIM is half rogue."

Her head swung back to Cam as she took the electronic device. "Excuse me?"

"It's been like that since I got it," Ryan offered quietly. "It obeys me, but there are times I feel like it struggles. I don't know, but it has conversations with me too. Always has. It's shy, though, so I never had to worry about it speaking up in front of other people."

"Half rogue, half sentient?" Maria asked as she looked through the programming on Ryan's AIRC, looking for what she had learned were rogue markers in the code.

"That's what it looks like. I've been working with Ryan for a while to keep it under control," Cam added, watching her face closely.

Her eyes flashed coldly to him. "You mean after the challenge in Toronto?"

All three paused. Three years earlier, when they had all been team-mates, they had failed for the first time at a challenge. It had been a month-end challenge, and Ryan's AIM went rogue. Cam had later fixed it, but for a short time, the AIM had been dangerous.

Maria handed the AIRC back to Cam. "Find someone else."

"What? Why?"

"Ryan's AIM went rogue before. If it's been struggling to keep control and in contact with the AIRC, then it's a danger and a liability. He should have gotten rid of this when the new AIM model was distributed. This is the kind of thing that's illegal now." She shot a look to Ryan. He had promised her when they first met that he would stay away from the previously illegal Underground. Now it seemed as though he was exactly like Cam had once been.

"I did get a new one. I don't use this in challenges anymore," Ryan answered somewhat harshly. He very rarely raised his voice, especially with Maria, but no one was going to take his AIM away from him. No one.

"That's not the point, Ryan. These things are dangerous. Just being around it..." They stared at each other. She knew how attached he was to his AIM, how hard it had been to get the upgrade. She let out a short breath and thought she saw him relax ever so slightly. "I won't make you get rid of the AIM, but you're still not coming. Leave your AIM with Cam, but you're staying here."

"It doesn't like other people using it," Ryan argued.

"Exactly my point! It shouldn't care who uses it!"

"We need him, Maria," Cam said emphatically. "We need another sentient AIM to work with mine, and to predict the movements of these other AIMs."

"Can you promise me it won't go rogue?"

He paused. "No."

"Then it's too dangerous to bring with us."

"I think I'd know better than you what a dangerous AIM is," Cam spat angrily, immediately regretting it.

Maria froze, her eyes glaring into Cam's. "Really? You've seen what a dangerous AIM can do, have you? You've seen a rogue AIM kill an armed soldier? You've seen a rogue AIM get shot at with a military rifle and still survive? You've seen a rogue AIM decimate the population of a village? You think because you saw a few photographs you know what it's like to watch it happen?" She paused as Cam's face hardened. Neither would give in.

"Let me get one thing straight right now, because when we get to Afghanistan, this needs to be understood." She moved towards him until she was inches from his face. "I am not your ex-girlfriend. I am not your ex-team-mate. I am a soldier in the Canadian Forces. In fact, I'm the soldier in charge of this mission. Ryan's AIM is a danger to the success of the mission, and a danger to the lives of those I'm protecting. I am not going to let your pride start a war between three countries. Ryan and his AIM are not part of this mission. Have I made myself clear?"

The two stood in the office, staring at each other while Ryan stood back from the tension. Finally, Cam swore as he looked away. He looked at Ryan silently, before his eyes slid down to the ground where the AIM in question stood in the form of a small mouse. "What if I trained it?"

She tilted her head. "What do you mean?"

"What if my AIM worked with it? They're both sentient, in some way. My AIM can work with it, and I can work on the programming."

"Would that take away the threat of it going rogue?"

"I don't know."

Ryan stepped forward, and the mouse ran up his leg to crawl into the safety of the pocket of Ryan's hoodie. "Wait, I don't want my AIM changed. I like it the way it is."

"You shouldn't even still have it!" Maria's tone surprised both Ryan and herself. They'd never spoken to each other like this before. "You have no idea what these things are capable of. You're lucky I'm not confiscating it now." She looked back at Cam when Ryan turned away, his face flushed with either anger or embarrassment. "Do you think you can do it?"

"I can try. I am Cam Tylar, after all."

"No. You're Lucas Tylar." Their eyes met. "You have one week. If it's not trained by then, we leave without your Second." She watched him nod as he turned for the door. "Ryan? Can I talk to you?"

Ryan looked at Cam with a nod. He closed the door behind Cam and turned to Maria. "Look, I didn't think this was going to be a big deal. Cam didn't even really tell me what was going on. He just said I could help."

"Is that why you want to go? You want to help?"

He shrugged, and forced back a smile. "Partly. I think I'd be more excited about being over there, and the animals I could scan."

She groaned. "Ryan, this isn't a game."

"I know." He was suddenly sombre.

"You could get killed." When he paused, she shook her head and took a step towards him. "I can't send you over there with a potentially dangerous AIM. I can't...I can't send you over there where you could get killed. The thought of you dying over there scares the hell out of me."

"But you're okay with Cam going over?"

"No, I'm not, but we need him whether I like it or not. I refuse to have both of you die."

Ryan stepped forward and nearly took her in his arms, but she stepped back to keep the distance. "No one's going to die. For all you know, it could be the easiest mission in military history."

"If Cam can get your AIM stable and under control, and if you pass all of your evaluations, then – and only then – can you go. Let Cam do what he needs to with your AIM. He's just trying to help."

"I know." He stepped away and towards the door. "I'll see you later."

She closed her eyes as he left, and Collins re-entered the office. "So that's who's going to help Tylar? He doesn't look like he could handle Afghanistan."

"He probably can't."

Collins eyed Maria for a moment, before he motioned with his head down the hallway. "You know him?"

"Yeah. He was on the team with me and Cam. Well, he's still on the team. They both are."

Collins groaned. "Great. More athletes."

"Look at it this way." Maria grinned, and nearly laughed. "They're at least as fit as us, trust me on that. The other two scientists work in a lab all day. I think you'll find you like the athletes."

He groaned once more, and this time she did let out a laugh. "If it makes you feel any better," she continued, "if they get through the physical screening, we'll at least be able to protect them without too much difficulty. They won't be too much dead weight." She grabbed her bag from where the chair she had dropped it on that morning and shut off the lights, forcing herself and Collins from the room. "Let me know when Cam and Ryan are finished processing."

As she walked out of the building and to the parking lot, she worked hard to control her breathing. How dare he? How dare Cam bring Ryan into this? She froze as she realized something. He had met with Ryan after the team meeting. That was before they had slept together. Maria swore under her breath. She unlocked her car and flung her bag onto the passenger seat. She nearly kicked her AIM getting in, not noticing it jumping in before her. He knew that Ryan was going to be part of the mission, and he had still slept with her. Well, it was going to be a nice chat the next time she saw him.

Ryan looked at Cam and watched as he made up his bunk. They had been given a room for the night on the base. There was no point having a hotel for one night before their physicals, and whatever else the army was going to put them through.

"Maybe this was a mistake," Ryan said. He rolled onto his back and stared up at the grey ceiling. "I'm a Scanner. I have no business being here."

"You have just as much business as I do," Cam replied, finishing the last tuck of the sheet under the mattress. His AIM jumped up onto the bed before he could even move. "Why do you insist on the bed?" he yelled. "Every time!"

"Simply because I can," his AIM responded as happily as a robot could, and lay down. "Not as comfortable as ours. But it shall be satisfactory."

"Mine. My bed," Cam corrected.

Ryan turned back onto his side to look at Cam and his AIM. "I don't think I've ever noticed your AIM act like that before."

"Well, there's no point hiding it around anyone here," he said. "It's his sentience we're going to need in Afghanistan."

"His?"

Cam grinned. "Long story."

"Have you named him?"

Cam rolled his eyes and fell back onto his bed. His AIM looked up at Ryan and began to wag its tail.

"Cameron refuses to give me a name, although I do not mind. Most of the names he has attempted to use have been most unsatisfactory, and actually rather unpleasant."

"They haven't been that bad," Cam said in defense.

"Pal? Spike? Fluffy?"

"I was six."

"Teen."

Cam rolled away, putting his back to the robot. "Whatever. Name yourself."

Ryan laughed. "Fluffy?"

"I was offended by that name," the AIM said. "I believe he was saying that the fur in that animal form made me look fat."

He laughed again and was silent for a moment. He watched Cam's AIM shift on the bed, crowding Cam but there were no complaints. He took a deep breath, and decided to take a chance. He was going to need to take a risk every day on the mission, so there was no reason to not start now.

"Has Maria told you what happened the last time she was deployed?"

Cam sighed and sat up. He took a moment before facing Ryan. "I think we need to agree to not talk about Maria while we're here, or overseas. She was right. During the mission, neither of us is her ex-boyfriend, and neither of us is her old team-mate."

Ryan nodded slightly. "Then...can I talk about my ex?"

He paused. "What do you want to talk about?"

"She stopped seeing her counsellor."

That got Cam's attention. "When?"

"A few months ago. She said she didn't need to anymore. But...she's still so reserved. She doesn't share anything, and I know she can't but she needs to be sharing with someone."

Cam looked away. "I don't know what to tell you. I can't say if she has or hasn't. I'm sure she has colleagues she shares with."

"I'm just saying-"

"Ryan, seriously, just stop. Maria is not the same woman you met on Revolution."

"I know."

"Then you know that her closing herself up, not sharing, not happy, that has nothing to do with you."

Ryan slouched against the wall. "How does her unhappiness not have anything to do with me?"

"She has Post Traumatic Stress Disorder. She's depressed, Ryan. That has nothing to do with you, or me." Cam lay back down and put an arm under his head. "Even if you want to blame me. Go ahead. But you might also want to keep it quiet we both dated her. This isn't the place to air that laundry. All they know is that we were all on the same team together."

"Your relationship was kind of put in the spotlight with...what happened," Ryan said. He hadn't spoken Lucy's name once, and hadn't really said the word 'daughter' either, not to either of them.

Cam shifted his shoulders. "The Canadians know, but the two American soldiers I met barely know a thing about Scanning." He looked at Ryan from the corner of his eyes. "Get some sleep. This is probably the last full night of sleep you'll get."

Ryan got under the covers, and turned out the light with the switch over his bed. He felt his AIM at the foot of his bed, and he nearly smiled but it was hard. There had been so many secrets when he had joined Revolution. The secrets just kept coming.

CHAPTER 8

One week later, Cam was led into Maria's office, and the door was closed behind him. He looked at her and folded his arms across his chest.

She stood and held her hand out, and he placed Ryan's AIRC into it. "Well?"

"I didn't have to change much. I put a type of restraint in the code, so it should be more stable without affecting the personality of the AIM. Mine's been working with it, too," he answered. "He's worked with the more animal side of the AIM, basically training it the way we would but instead of training it to act like an animal, it trained it to act like a robot."

"Is there a chance his AIM could go rogue while we're there?" Maria asked simply.

Cam hesitated. "Only because it's still one of the original AIMs, but," he added quickly, "but the chance is extremely low. It has the same chance now as my own AIM going rogue, and I trust him with my life. And yours."

Maria crossed her arms across her body and stared at him. She could still say no. She could still send Ryan back home, despite the processing and training he'd gone through already. He could stay safe, and away from her. "Did he complete the training?"

"We both have."

She nodded. She had already been told he passed every test, with only a few concerns of his rehabilitation back into civilian life.

"Fine." She stepped towards him and jabbed a finger into his chest. "If absolutely anything happens to him-"

"It's on me, I get it."

"No," Maria snapped. "It's on me." She stepped around him and began to open the door.

He pushed it back closed and stepped between her and the door. "I'm not going to let you blame yourself if something happens to him."

"Now you're telling me what to feel?"

"Yes," he said, standing as close to her as he could handle. "Because I know you. I know how you take on the weight of the world for yourself, even when you have someone in front of you desperately trying to share the burden." He lowered his voice, his eyes still matched with hers. "Whatever happens out there, I'm right there with you."

"Get out of my office," Maria said softly, and pulled the door open. "You all have homework to do."

He looked at her for a moment before giving her a mock salute. "Yes, ma'am," he said and left her alone.

'Scan Complete' flashed on Rick's screen, and he laughed. "Man, this is a great one. Look at these stats." He showed the screen to Cam who sat next to him at the base of a tree. They had been scanning for a few hours now, and the mid-August humidity was starting to make it only slightly uncomfortable. When Rick saw the distant look on Cam's face, he had a feeling it was about to become more uncomfortable. "You there?"

Cam nodded and absently stroked the fur of his AIM, once again in the form of a golden retriever. "I think...I think I screwed up." He risked a glance at his team-mate, but thought better. "Don't worry about it. This is weird."

"Yeah." Rick shifted on the dirt. "But maybe you need to...talk?"

"We don't talk."

"We can start?"

He hesitated, weighing his options. Desperation won. "I've been seeing someone. A few months now."

Rick laughed. "Here I was thinking this would be bad. You could've told me earlier. What's the problem? She's not good enough in bed anymore?"

"She's incredible. Everything about her. She's amazing."

"I still don't see a problem."

Cam picked up a clump of dirt and tossed it in the dark. "She broke it off, said she needed a relationship. A future."

"You're not the relationship type. Commitment and intimacy? They're not really your thing."

He was silent for a moment. "That's what I said. The thing is...I don't think that's true anymore. I mean," he swore and dug his heel into the ground. "I want to be the relationship type. I want to be that for her. I think I'm in love with her."

Rick swore, surprising both himself and Cam. He watched his team-mate's face for a moment. "Cam, the only things I've known you to love was your mom and winning. If you think there's even a chance you love her, then I don't know why you're sitting here."

"I still have a job to do." Cam returned Rick's look and laughed. "How do I even be a boyfriend?"

"I'm sure you'll figure it out. You don't need to be anything but yourself."

"No, I don't. But I want to be more than I already am."

Rick whistled. "Cam Tylar is gone, that's for sure."

Cam smiled lightly. "Did I ever tell you my first name is actually Lucas?"

Ryan hunched over his tray of food, looking around. He sat at the far end of a long row of tables as the soldiers on the base ate their lunch. He had been trying to think of ways he would be able to survive this atmosphere for long periods of time, but he knew he was a Scanner. He knew that this new world Maria was in, it wasn't his. He felt his body relax when he saw Cam come into the mess hall. He didn't wave, but let Cam find him on his own. He waited for Cam to sit down next to him, and looked at him expectantly.

"Well?"

"You're coming, but she's not happy."

He nodded and looked back at his food. "I'm starting to understand why."

Cam watched as his team-mate shoved his food around the plate with his fork. Ever since Ryan was given all the information about the mission, and shown the photographs, he hadn't spoken much. "When I worked in the Underground, before we really knew how to stabilize rogues, I had to go up against two grizzlies."

"I think two grizzlies are a bit different than four Bengal tigers with military training."

"I was alone."

Ryan nodded as if the story was finished, but glanced at Cam. "What'd you do?"

"Survived."

He nodded again and turned back to his food. "Well, it's a good thing we're used to working together, and our AIMs."

"I didn't choose you for your good looks." Cam nudged him with his elbow. "We're a good team, when I actually decide to work with other people. I got your back, Hampton. I need to know you have mine."

Ryan looked at Cam now, forgetting his meal. "I do. I got your back." If only that was what they needed.

As the soldiers, and Ryan, finished their lunch, the main doors to the room opened. Before Cam could see who it was, the soldiers all stood in unison and saluted. Cam looked at Ryan and with a shrug, both stood but refrained from saluting.

"At ease," rang out a strong male voice. Cam recognized it as Padmore. "Tylar, Hampton. Come with me."

The two hesitated, looking around quickly to make sure there weren't soldiers with the same names. Cam wondered what they did in those circumstances. Before the Colonel could yell again, they moved quickly to the door. As soon as they rounded the soldiers, Maria came into view as well, standing next to Padmore.

"Lieutenant Kier will bring you to finish your registration," he explained. "The other two programmers will arrive this evening. And you head out tomorrow." When they nodded, he turned his attention to the rest of the room. "As you were," Padmore called out, and left.

Maria jerked her head. "This way."

Cam and Ryan followed as she led them down a maze of hallways neither had really seen before. While Cam made a mental note of where he was going, Ryan simply concentrated on following the soldier ahead of him. It was easier to think of her that way, than to think of her as Maria. If he did, he saw a Scanner. He saw the girl, woman, who got along so well with his parents, and doted on his siblings. She was Kier now.

Maria led them through a doorway and into what seemed to be a locker room. She opened two lockers and from the first she pulled out a pile of meticulously folded clothes. Heavy black boots sat on top. She handed the package to Cam before giving Ryan an identical one.

"Civilians don't typically wear uniforms when they're contracted by us, but they don't usually go into combat, either," she explained. "Try them on tonight, make sure they fit. You have two pairs of clothes, one pair of boots, that's it, so learn how to take care of them."

She reached into each locker again, and paused. After a moment, she pulled out two silver-balled chains. "Your dog tags." Maria held back a sigh. "These don't leave your body for any reason. If someone holds a gun to your head, trying to get you to take it off, you let them shoot you because they're gonna do it anyway."

They each took their own, and Ryan looked his over. "They're that important?"

"Yes. They're used to identify you in case your body or face is too torn up," Maria answered seriously.

Cam set his clothes down and fastened the chain around his neck. "And if someone takes it off me?"

She hesitated before answering. She stared at him with his tags around his neck and resting against his chest. "For you guys, if the chain detaches, we get a warning at the base that the connectors have separated and we know you've been compromised." She nodded. "That's it then. You each have a list of what you can bring. The rest will be left here for when we get back."

"At least you said 'when'," Ryan said quietly. He still held the necklace in his hand along with the clothing. He wanted to hold off changing his identity as long as possible.

Maria glanced away. "Make sure you get some sleep. Wake up call is three A.M." She turned to leave, but stopped and looked at them again. "Thank you both, for serving your country." She left quickly before either could say a word.

Cam picked up his uniform. He paused as if he wanted to say something. He looked down at the tags against his chest, and silently left the locker room with Ryan close behind. Sometimes there was just nothing that could be said.

Ryan and Cam stood in the hangar with the two other programmers. They had barely spoken, and no one seemed interested in conversation. Ryan looked around nervously. He took a look at the female scientist from the McCarthy Group. She had red hair, which she kept in a ponytail. He wondered if she would be made to wear it in a bun as he usually saw Maria in.

The man seemed to be much older, likely in his forties, Ryan guessed. But if he was there, he was physically able to do whatever needed to be done in the desert. He winced and rubbed his shoulder. He had thought he was physically fit, being an athlete, but they had been made to do some pretty rough obstacles. Most of the time they were shown manoeuvres which were to protect them. They were told to hide rather than engage the enemy. That was for the soldiers to do.

The sound of heavy boots echoed from the far end of the hangar, and the group turned to see two lines of soldiers come towards them. Ryan held back a smile when he recognized Maria at the front, next to Major Collins. He still thought it was strange that everyone referred to each other by their last name. He had seen it in movies, but he hadn't thought that was how it was actually done. Despite seeing Maria in this element, Ryan still had a hard time seeing her as a soldier. He had only ever really known her as a Scanner. He had never seen her at her workplace before. Her uniform seemed like it was just a costume instead of something which now defined her.

Maria held her face as stoic as possible as she neared the group of scientists. She still wasn't sure what their exact titles were. Cam was the programmer. She knew that much. Ryan...his assistant? He didn't have much knowledge of the programming, just how to handle the rogue AIMs. Handler? That would be good enough. She would have to get to know the others to figure out their skills, if they had any. As she passed the group of civilians, she looked each in the eye, keeping her face blank as best she could. When she saw Ryan's face darken, she knew she had done a good enough job.

The soldiers stopped suddenly, and Maria and Collins turned towards the civilians. She took in a deep breath. It all began now. "It's a fourteen-hour flight, so if you have problems flying, I suggest you take something now. Let's move," she said and led the group onto the open cargo ramp of the transport plane in front of them. She watched as the soldiers all expertly stowed their bags beneath the seats and strapped themselves in, while the civilians stood on the plane, not knowing what to do. But then she noticed Cam copying the soldiers. She watched as he stowed his bags in the same way, and sat down a few spots away from one of the soldiers.

"Hurry up, pick a seat, and sit down," she called out as she chose a seat near Cam. The ramp of the plane hummed to life and began to rise, which encouraged the two scientists and Ryan to sit down hurriedly. They sat across from Maria, along with McMurphy and three of his soldiers.

The plane began to rumble with the sound of the engines coming to life, and Maria felt her body tense. Her breathing became shallow, and already she began to sweat. She closed her eyes as the plane started to taxi down the runway, and her hands curled into fists on her knees. The last time she had flown this long…

"Hey, you okay?"

She opened her eyes when she heard Ryan's voice, and saw that he was looking at her. A quick glance around at the other soldiers, and they were stealing glances at him. She remained silent, and simply closed her eyes again. She was afraid of what would happen if she opened her mouth.

The soldier next to Ryan leaned over slightly. "There are some questions you don't ask," he whispered.

"I've flown with her before," Ryan replied, just as quietly although he wasn't sure why. "She's fine on planes."

"Ryan," Cam said from across the plane, a bit too harsh. "Enough."

He looked at Maria, and saw her eyes still closed. "But..."

"Look around," the soldier said, still patiently explaining. "Return flights are never easy flights."

Maria wasn't the only one. Both Collins and McMurphy were on edge, although showing different symptoms. Cam had been the first to notice. And he noticed now when she opened her eyes, just a sliver, and looked at him. He knew. She would have jumped out of the plane while it was over the Atlantic Ocean if he and Ryan hadn't been on the plane. This was going to be a long flight.

Eight hours. It had only been eight hours. Maria looked around. The two scientists were sleeping, and had been since take-off. Ryan was doing something on his AIRC. His AIM suddenly changed from the German Shepherd they had been advised to use to a grey squirrel. The AIM climbed up Ryan's leg and sat on his knee, rather happily, she noticed. How had she not noticed it before? Ryan had made such a big deal about her keeping secrets from him – national security secrets, mind you – and he had been keeping a massive secret about his AIM from her. It was her job to not tell him everything, and he knew that. He also knew that his AIM was different, and he should have done something about it earlier.

She looked to her left at Cam, two seats over. And him. He brought Ryan into this. She couldn't decide if she was more upset about the fact that he had chosen Ryan, or that he had known Ryan was coming, listened to her talk about the break-up, and then slept with her. She wasn't sure it mattered.

"It couldn't have killed the budget to have an in-flight movie," Collins said.

It took her a moment to realize that he had been speaking to her. She looked at him quickly. "What?"

"It's been eight hours, and no one's even really said a word," he answered. "A movie might've been nice."

Maria rolled her eyes, but grinned. "Depends on the movie. My first time over, I wanted to kill myself it was so bad."

Collins gave her a small smile only a soldier could give, one which understood that joking about death was something much more. "How long were you over?"

"Three months," she replied and quickly looked away.

"That's it?"

"It doesn't take long. You?"

"Two and a half years."

"That's it?" she mocked.

He shrugged. "Long enough for the people back home to forget about me."

She looked across at Ryan. "Count it as a blessing. Trust me, it's easier."

Cam woke up with a start. He felt the plane turning, angled in the sky. He wished he could see outside. It would have made the flight a bit more bearable. Halfway through the flight most of the soldiers had begun to talk and joke around. During those hours, Cam had felt somewhat excited to be going to Afghanistan. Thinking about it, when else would he have the chance to go? There wouldn't be an Open Tournament in the country for another decade or so at the earliest, and he had no real reason to travel to the Middle East. During those hours, he had tried to convince himself that he was excited to go, excited for the challenge. But reality hit him as suddenly as consciousness: he was going to war.

The plane began to descend, and Cam noticed everyone tense. No matter the progressions in other technology, landing was still the most dangerous part of flying. The wheels bounced against the runway, and Cam gripped the armrests. Finally, there was touchdown, and the plane began to slow. After a few moments of taxiing, the transport plane came to a stop.

Everyone gathered their belongings, and Cam watched as Maria, along with the other soldiers, swung a rifle over her shoulder and across her back. Their eyes met for a moment. She broke away first, looking at Collins when the ramp began to lower. The group of thirteen gathered at the entrance. Cam winced as rays of the bright desert sun made their way into the plane, and he was immediately hit with the intense heat and sand-filled air.

The soldiers saluted as an older soldier stepped up onto the ramp. If Collins was the highest-ranking soldier on the plane, judging from the stripes on this man's uniform, Cam realized he must be in charge of the base. What rank that was, he had no idea. "Ladies and gentlemen," the soldier boomed. "Welcome to Kandahar. For some of you," he paused and nodded to a few of them. "Welcome back."

"These will be your quarters for the next few days before you continue on," the Kandahar Base Commander explained as he led the group through a row of what looked like cabins. "Two people each, so Kier and Collins will deal with that." He continued on, not slowing his pace or checking behind him to make sure everyone was keeping up. Thankfully, they were.

"Get your food over here," continued the tour guide as he pointed to an open pavilion. "And our hospital is behind it, not that you guys will need it before you move on. Main building is to your right, and that's where you'll be spending most of your time."

"Colonel Reynolds," Maria said, taking a quick step to move to his side. "I'll need a list of all soldiers we'll be in communication with, and our liaison at the base."

"It'll be ready for your briefing with the unit." He stopped abruptly, which the soldiers seemed to be prepared for, but the civilians nearly walked into the person ahead of them. "I'll leave you to it."

The soldiers all saluted and he turned away and into the main building. Collins turned around to face the group.

"Alright, listen up!" he yelled, projecting his voice to get their attention. "When I call your name, go where I tell you. Get some sleep and get back here in four hours. Go inside, and you'll find the room we'll be using. No questions. Shepero, Filsinger, number one. Strong, Lim, number two. Ellis, Johnson, number three. Hanks, McMurphy number four. Tylar, Hampton, number five, Kier, Travato, number six. I'm in number seven."

Ryan looked around as the group dispersed. He jolted into motion when he saw Cam start to walk, and he followed him. "You have any idea where we're going?"

"Following orders." Cam nodded towards where they had passed their accommodations. "They had numbers on them. Reynolds said that'd be where we're sleeping, and we're in pairs. I made the connection." He stopped and turned to Ryan. "Believe me, I know this is overwhelming. You're not the only one out of your element. So just…open your eyes. I don't really like people yelling at me."

Ryan grinned. "Oh no? But it gives you a chance to yell back."

He rolled his eyes and swung his duffle bag around, hitting Ryan on the back. "Come on." They walked back to the cabins. Cam looked around as they walked, taking in the surroundings. Soldiers, both on and off duty strolled around. Some were sitting at tables, playing cards. Others, sitting next to the ones losing money, were cleaning their weapons. Perfect harmony.

"Did you think it'd be this hot?" Ryan asked. His eyes were narrowed into a squint as they reached their cabin.

"I had no idea what to expect." He saw Maria sitting on the step in front of their door. "Locked out?" he asked.

"We switched cabins," she said as she stood. "Just thought I'd let you know before you walked in on us."

"Disobeying orders already, Kier?" Cam joked. "Here I was thinking I'd be the troublemaker."

She didn't respond but turned around. "Don't be late," she warned.

"Wait," Ryan said, looking at the cabin Maria had abandoned to them. "What's wrong with the other cabin?"

She didn't turn around. "It's where I stayed last time." And the door closed behind her.

Cam dropped his bag onto the ground and rummaged through it. "Hey, do me a favour?" He stood again and handed Ryan the duffle bag. "Take this in for me? I'm going to take a look around." He slipped his sunglasses over his eyes and turned back towards the eating pavilion without waiting for Ryan's response.

He looked down at his AIM which had followed him quietly, and obediently, the entire time. "Do you think you should pretend while we're here, or just act...like yourself?"

"Will it cause problems for you back home, or here, if I act like myself?" it replied.

"I think your personality is the least of my problems while I'm over here," Cam muttered. He shoved his hands into the deep pockets of the uniform pants. The boots were heavy, and felt awkward on his feet. He felt like he was simply stomping around, ready to squish tiny humans. He looked around as he walked. He grimaced as a gust of wind picked up the sand and threw it into his face. Cam stopped when he got to the pavilion and sat down on one of the benches.

Only a few soldiers paid any attention to him as he sat, but a few eyed him a little longer. The soldiers on the base had been told to expect some civilians, but hadn't been told what they were doing there. Cam noticed a soldier lean over towards another and nodded in his direction.

"I wonder," his AIM started, "how many soldiers share Maria's affections for civilians on military property, or in combat."

When the soldiers stood and began to make their way over to him, Cam replied, "I guess we're going to find out."

The first soldier stopped in front of him and folded his arms over his chest. Cam noticed a small Canadian flag on his shoulder. "Hey. You're one of the civilians?"

"Well, I'm not a soldier," he answered. He really needed to work on his attitude.

"You're a Scanner," the second soldier said. "CST?"

Cam grinned. "Yeah, that's right."

The first soldier shoved his friend and swore. "You're Cam Tylar. What the heck are you doing as a civilian here?"

He shrugged and leaned back casually against the table. "Guess I'm just that good you guys need my help with something."

"You gonna be back in Canada for the season?" he asked, and his voice changed. "Did they replace you again?"

Cam shook his head with a laugh. "You can't replace me. I don't plan on being here that long, but just in case, they have a temp lined up to keep my spot warm."

The soldiers sat down with him. "Be honest with us. Where did you go? You dropped off the radar for an entire year. You keep saying in interviews that you were finding yourself, whatever that means, but that's bull."

He paused and studied the faces of the soldiers sitting with him. "Is this your first time in Afghanistan?" When they glanced at each other and shook their head, he continued. "After your first deployment, did you need time away from…everything?"

The second soldier nodded and looked down at his arms resting on the table. "Had a pretty hard time being around people back home."

"Well, instead of dealing with it, I ran away from people because it was easier than figuring out how to be around them again." All three nodded their heads slowly, and Cam found himself realizing why Maria fit in so well with the soldiers. They were all veterans of something.

Maria looked up as Cam came into the room. She checked her watch and saw that he was ten minutes early, which was strange for him. It was a nice change, but still strange. "Couldn't sleep?"

"Didn't need to," he said with a shrug and sat down near the back of the lecture-style room.

"I hear you made some friends already." When he shrugged again, she rolled her eyes. "What, now you're not talking to me? I'm the one who's supposed to be upset with you."

"I'm just sitting here, waiting." He paused. "Doing okay so far?"

"It's hell, but I have to be here, so I'm making it work."

He nodded. It was all she would likely say on the subject, knowing her. He grinned and bobbed his head towards the door. "You have some fans on the base, too."

Maria groaned. "Don't remind me. When I was in Basic, a few guys had the picture, and I still come across it every now and then when I check out other facilities."

Cam laughed. When Maria first joined Revolution, she had posed for a photoshoot modelling very little clothing. It was an athletic swimwear line, and the team had approved it, but it had haunted her ever since. No one seemed to care that he had been posing with her, or they didn't seem to remember. He smiled at the memory. It had been fun after the shoot, at least.

She looked away quickly when she realized what he was thinking about. Thankfully, the other soldiers began to trickle in along with the civilians. Her bunkmate, Sarah, had fallen asleep right away so she hadn't had the chance to speak to her at all. It was going to be interesting, being the only two females on the mission. It would be bad enough being the only female soldier. It had only happened to her once before, and it had not been a pleasant experience.

When McMurphy stepped in, she moved to the side to share the front. She counted the group quickly. Thirteen. They were ready.

"Hello, *team*," McMurphy started. "I know none of us have really had the chance to be introduced, but that will come in a few moments. For now, you'll need to know me, Captain McMurphy, United States Army, and Lieutenant Kier, Canadian Armed Forces. We will be leading this mission, so it's best you get to know our faces. For the civilians, you will refer to us as either McMurphy, Kier, or sir and ma'am, even for those who know us personally." He shot a glance at Maria quickly before continuing.

"You should have all had an introduction as to what we're dealing with, so I'll be able to skip all of that." The lights dimmed, and the wall behind Maria and McMurphy lit up. They stepped to the side so the others could see the map. A red dot began to pulse in the lower part of the wall, and he pointed to it. "Five weeks ago, four AIMs went rogue in this village, killing most of its inhabitants, soldiers, and their insurgent handlers. From there, they have been seen in three other towns heading north." Three more red dots began to pulse, each a staggered distance north from the other.

"Our two programmers, Cam Tylar and Ryan Hampton, will work on a progression map to give us details of where our next move will be. We can assume they'll continue moving north for now. Once we track down these AIMs, we will engage them, stabilize them, and bring them to a pre-arranged rendezvous point with the insurgents." A fourth dot began to pulse in the northwest region of Afghanistan.

"Here," he said, and pointed to the dot. "This is where we will return their AIMs, briefly. It's the job of our programmer to communicate to them the dangers of the outdated AIM, and the benefits of the new version. If necessary, I will step in. The United Nations has been informed of the transaction, and they have already affirmed that the Afghan government and the militia group will receive international pressure to destroy their old AIMs and take the new one without complaint." He paused for a moment. "Any questions?"

A hand shot up. Maria recognized him as one of the American soldiers. "What do we do if we are engaged by the enemy prior to arriving at the drop-off point?"

"Protect the civilians at all costs," McMurphy answered confidently. "Return fire if necessary, but our main objective is not to disband the group but to find the AIMs, and protecting the civilians is how we're going to do it."

Another hand went up. Another American. "Who will be the translator in the villages?"

"Major Collins will translate all communication between us and anyone we meet on the way in order to gain more information. For the women we find, Kier will speak to them privately, as is their culture. No man is to approach an Afghan woman. Is that understood?" When the room nodded, he nodded as well. "Good. We will be in Kandahar for one week for the programmers to create our projection, and for the civilians to receive their basic training. In the event that we become engaged and it is a life-or-death situation, the civilians are given clearance to fire if fired at. You will each be assigned a weapon which you will be trained to use properly." He looked at Collins with a nod, before switching positions.

"During this mission," Collins began, "we will stay with joint-force protocol. For the civilians, that doesn't mean much to you, but it helps to keep the politics from our respective countries under control and we focus on the completion of the mission. We have the same goal in mind, and that's what we need to remember. Each one of us plays a specific role. Civilians, get ready to take some notes. Our squad, or for the few Canadians, our section will consist of two assault groups, each with two fire teams.

"Fireteam one in the first assault group consists of myself as Alpha, and Sergeant Major Shepero as Bravo, who is our comm." When the soldier's name was said, he raised a hand briefly. "He'll be the one who will be our liaison between the base and our unit. He'll also be in communication with our contact in Mjahdan. Fireteam two consists of Charlie, First Lieutenant Hanks is our sniper. In the event that we are engaged with Mjahdan, he'll be our best weapon. Hanks, during this mission, Kier has rank and you'll treat her as you will myself and McMurphy." When the soldier nodded, he continued.

"Delta is Staff Sergeant Filsinger as our logistics specialist. He'll be working closely with our programmers on the field. Private Johnson is Echo, and our American version of an AIM Operations Technician." Collins looked at Maria. "Hopefully he'll be of use to you guys."

She nodded and stepped forward. "Assault group two will consist of Captain McMurphy as Alpha in fireteam one. Corporal Strong is Bravo, and Corporal Ellis is Charlie of fireteam two. They are both highly trained AIMOTs who will be giving support to the programmers once the rogues have been found and engaged. Ellis will handle the transportation of the AIMs in their default form. Strong is also our trained medic, so I suggest you all play nice with him. I'll bring up the rear as Delta as the second in command for this mission.

"As for the civilians, we have Ms. Sarah Travato, and Mr. Peter Lim. Both will be engaging the rogues. Once the rogues have been stabilized, they will assess their ability to be reactivated or neutralized, but not until we have word from Mjahdan. Mr. Ryan Hampton is our junior programmer, and Mr. Cam Tylar is the senior. When it comes to the rogues, he will make the calls. If something is too dangerous in his eyes, we back out and try again. Soldiers, we get the civilians to the AIMs. Once we're there, that's their territory, and they pull rank unless it breaches protocol or international laws."

"Each civilian," Maria continued, "will be paired with a soldier for their safety. As you will not be directly engaging the enemy, you will not be officially assigned a fireteam, but an individual soldier. Tylar with Collins, Hampton with me, Travato with Johnson, and Lim with Strong. With the exception of Collins, each of these soldiers has a background with AIMs and we will support you in any way we can."

Maria stepped back and allowed McMurphy to stand once more. "For those interested, this is a highly classified mission, which is why so many high-ranking officers are leading rather than a Sergeant. I don't want to hear any complaining about how a Corporal is part of a small section like this. Tylar, Hampton, stay for a moment. The rest of you are dismissed."

Cam and Ryan remained seated while the rest of the group made their way out of the room. All that was left was Maria and the two main American soldiers. Cam shifted forward in his seat. "It would've been nice to know you wanted us to map the area before we got here," he shot.

"Currently," Collins replied, "you're on a need-to-know basis."

"And currently, I need to know everything the minute you find it." He stood and walked towards the man. "You want me to do my best out here, out of my element? Fine. But you better give me the tools with which to do it. You want those AIMs, I'll find them for you. You want them safe? I'll do that to. But from now on, this isn't a need-to-know situation."

Collins stepped forward to stare Cam in the eye. The two were the same height, which made the standoff that much more intense. After a moment, the door opened and an Afghan soldier came in. He stopped suddenly when he saw Cam and Collins staring at each other. Neither moved, or flinched.

When she realized Collins wasn't going to speak to him, Maria sighed and addressed the other soldier. "*What do you want?*" she asked in Pashto.

"Mjahdan have been in contact. They want to know your plan to retrieve their AIMs."

"Two days."

The soldier shook his head. "They won't be happy with that answer."

"They can get in line." Maria glanced at Collins before looking back at the other soldier. "Knock next time. Is that understood?" He nodded and quickly left.

She turned back to Cam and Collins who had now both stopped their stand-off. She looked at Collins with a nod. "This is going to be more time sensitive than I hoped."

Ryan stood finally and took a few steps towards them. It seemed that Maria had kept quite a bit from him. When she had found the time to learn a new language, he had no idea. "What was all that about?"

"Mjahdan apparently want to be in contact with us the entire way," Collins answered. "They want to know what our plan is. Lieutenant Kier here said you'd have a plan ready in two days."

Cam nodded and looked at Ryan. "It'll be done." He shot a glare at Collins. "As long as you keep the information line flowing." He looked at Maria with a small smile. "Thanks for giving us a bit of extra time. We'll try to make the map pretty for them."

She rolled her eyes. "Just get to work."

"Yes, ma'am."

CHAPTER 9

Maria sat down in the pavilion next to the soldier she recognized as Shepero. She gave him a small smile and held out her hand. "Maria Kier."

He returned the smile with a laugh and shook her proffered hand. "Chad Shepero. And I know who you are. I'm a sports fan." She groaned and stared at the food in front of her. "It's been three years, and people still ask for my autograph."

"In the States," he explained, "there aren't many females in the top teams, so my daughter watches the Canadian Scanning Tournament. Even went to a few challenges in Windsor. I'm from Michigan, so it was a nice day trip for the family."

She smiled. She had heard it before. What a great thing it was, her being on a top team and being female. It was usually followed with 'when do you find time for a family?' And the awkward 'oh, you don't have a family yet?' So much for equality. She had only been twenty-one when she quit Scanning. That was nowhere near old enough to be thinking of a family. She glanced up as Cam sat down along with the other civilians across from them. Bad timing.

"How about you?" Shepero asked. "Any kids?"

"I thought you said you're a sports fan," she said and strategically filled her mouth with the salad she had sitting in front of her.

He laughed. "I watch the AST mostly; it's my daughter who watches you."

Maria looked at Cam as she chewed, buying time. They hadn't talked about what they would say to people about Lucy while they were there, or their history. She hadn't done that with Ryan, either. For those who knew them, that was one thing. They wouldn't bring it up. But for this? Soldiers trying to get to know each other, and what's waiting for them back home. He gave a small nod. He had talked about it on national television. He was okay with it.

"So, no kids then?" Shepero offered.

Before Maria could respond now that her mouth was empty, Collins and McMurphy joined then, Collins letting himself fall onto the bench. He let out a sarcastic laugh. "Not surprising. You don't seem like the motherly-type."

She took in a deep breath angrily. "Why's that?"

He shrugged. He reached in front of her and grabbed a handful of Shepero's fries. "Just doesn't seem like it fits you. Can't imagine a kid with you."

"Then I guess it's a good thing my daughter died," she shot at him. She grabbed her AIRC and stood. Without another word, she turned and strode back to the cabins.

"This is why you don't ask personal questions," Collins said as he shifted over to sit beside Shepero. "We're just here to do a job and survive."

"Or maybe you could be less of an ass," Cam snapped.

He rolled his eyes. "If I said the same thing to a man, he wouldn't act like that."

Cam stood. "My daughter died too, and the only reason I'm not storming away is because it's different for men when their kid dies before they even knew they were going to be a dad. And the only reason I'm not pummelling your sorry ass right now is because I'm not entirely sure you wouldn't use a weapon against me."

Collins stood once more, but McMurphy stepped between them. "God help us if this is how it's going to be the entire time," McMurphy yelled. "Sit back down, both of you. And Collins, you of all people should know not to talk about this."

Collins shoved his partner away, and smoothed his uniform. He turned his attention to the civilians and jabbed a thumb towards the hospital. "Physicals in half an hour. Tomorrow your training begins. Tylar, Hampton, you better be working on that projection map tonight."

Ryan spoke up finally. "We have it figured out already. Just need to plot the coordinates. And add some sparkles."

When Collins strode away, Cam sat back down beside Ryan. After a moment, he let out a laugh. "Since when do you talk like that?"

"He's an ass."

Cam laughed again. "And since when do you talk like that? You've barely been around them, and you're already talking like a soldier."

"Collins was wrong," Ryan said.

"About what?" McMurphy asked. "He's usually wrong, but what're you talking about?"

"They can get you in trouble, but most of the time it's the personal questions that can save things. If they're answered. And giving people your personal information doesn't make you vulnerable. It makes you real."

An hour later, Ryan found himself waiting with the rest of the civilians in the hospital. Most of them had shown up late for their physicals, but so had the doctor. Technically, the doctor and nurses were in the hospital, but a hummer had shown up with four badly injured soldiers, and of course they took priority. The other two seemed to be rather impatient, or nervous. Everyone was out of their element here.

When he thought about the two being from the McCarthy Group, he had thought it was pretty neat to be sitting with people who worked for the company which produced AIMs. But on the other hand, for all he knew their only connection to the McCarthys was the Underground, like Cam. He decided he would take the chance to find out.

He smiled at the young woman he guessed to be around Cam's age, not much older than Ryan himself. "Hi, I'm Ryan."

"Sarah," she answered, returning his smile hesitantly. Being around rough soldiers was definitely taking a toll on most of them.

No one seemed to know how to act. Except Cam. Ryan remembered Sarah being called out with Maria for the cabin assignment. Travato was her last name.

"So, what do you do? You actually work for the McCarthy Group?"

She nodded. "Yeah, I'm in charge of inspections. Every AIM that goes out to the public is inspected three times, and I analyse each report before we send them out."

"How long have you been doing that?"

Sarah glanced at Cam briefly. "Technically I've had this position for six years, but it...changed, dramatically, two years ago. It's much more involved than it used to be."

"For good reason," Cam added. "Now you see why."

Sarah said nothing, but looked down at her feet which seemed fascinating in the large boots.

The older man looked at Cam with a harsh look in his eyes. "Are you going to have this grudge against us the entire time?"

"I have a hard time believing so few of you guys knew what Trevor was doing, or knew that the old AIMs went rogue," Cam said, fighting hard to keep his voice down. "Sarah was the quality control inspector. She should've seen the problems in the coding and substance long before any of this happened.

"Well, who trained her the first time?" he snapped. "You think Trevor wanted her to know what to look for? Hell, I didn't even know about any of this."

Cam rolled his eyes. "Peter, you worked in the lab. You all thought Henk's work was done. None of you bothered to even test it out through progression samples, which I find amazing for a group of scientists. I managed to get a new one up and running in five years."

"I'm sorry we all didn't have Lucas Tylar for a father," Peter snapped back. He turned away when Cam went silent.

Ryan shifted uncomfortably in his seat. "So...you're Peter, then." He paused. "I'm starting to get the feeling I'm the only one who doesn't know anyone here. All three of you know each other?"

Peter nodded. "Mostly. Sarah works in quality control, like she said. I work mainly in the lab. I do a similar job. I test each unit of AIM substance to ensure it's connecting with its chip and AIRC.

Like Sarah, my job changed two years ago with the introduction of the updated AIMs."

"And you all know Cam...how?"

"I trained them," Cam answered.

Ryan looked at Cam, his face lined with confusion. "What do you mean, you trained them? What exactly did you do in the Underground?"

Peter laughed and finally returned his gaze back to Cam. "You never told your own team-mate?" He looked at Ryan. "He pretty much created the new AIMs. Dr. Baxter created the substance, and Mr. Hotshot over here came up with the programming to go with it, and put together the chip. He came in and trained Sarah, showing her what to look for and what can happen if she messes up. He showed me the same thing, although Dr. Baxter did quite a bit more with me on the more scientific aspects of it."

"Peter Lim?" a female nurse stepped into the waiting room. "Sorry you guys have been waiting so long. We're ready for you, Peter."

The man saluted to the others and followed the nurse down the hall.

Ryan looked down at his lap before looking at his team-mate. "And you couldn't tell us that, why?"

Cam shrugged. "After doing it for so long in the Underground, I wasn't about to out myself to the public. I let Henk, Dr. Baxter, take the credit so I could continue my career in Scanning. Even with it being legal now, there's still a stigma, and I was done with it. I was stupid enough to think it wouldn't follow me. But it chased me all the way here to this hell hole."

He nodded. "And your dad? What does he have to do with your work in the Underground?"

Cam sighed. "You ask a lot of questions."

"You might as well tell him," Sarah said. "Isn't it better for people to know personal information?" Ryan had said that, and while Cam had agreed, it wasn't necessarily true for him. Maybe now was the time to air everything.

"He helped create them, but started his own work. Without even knowing it, I was finishing my dad's research, which Henk saw as a sign or something. The prodigal son returns."

Ryan nodded slowly. Things began to make sense, at least. Cam's AIM, how he had gotten it so early, and how he had such a natural skill with the robots. "You were named after him."

"Yeah. Hated it as a kid, so I went by my middle name." Cam paused and stared at the ground.

When Cam didn't continue, Ryan followed his gaze but couldn't understand what he was looking at. "What?"

Cam pointed. "Is that your AIM?"

Ryan looked again at the penguin waddling awkwardly on the tiled floor. "Oh. Yeah." He shrugged when Cam continued to stare. "Is there a problem?"

"I guess not."

"Okay then."

He nodded and looked around. He shot a glance at Sarah when he heard her giggling. With a sigh, he looked back at Ryan. "You know we're in a desert?"

"No one's going to expect a penguin to be trained in the desert."

"Cam Tylar," the nurse called out with a smile. "We're ready for you."

Cam stood with a grin. He walked towards her and eyed her. "No you're not."

She rolled her eyes as she led him down the hall.

Sarah and Ryan watched him go, but Sarah soon turned her attention back. "I heard rumours."

"We all hear rumours at some point."

"About Cam."

Ryan shrugged. "Like I said, we all do at some point."

"When Maria said her daughter died, and Cam too, it was their daughter together. Right?" When Ryan nodded, she sat back in the chair. "Is he always like this? I don't think I saw this much attitude when he was training us in Boston. I mean, you see things on TV but you never think that's how they really are."

He thought for a moment. The Cam he had met had been arrogant, self-important, and easily angered. Everything seemed to set him off. But that had been after a break-up. When he had been alone with Cam, things seemed okay. Cam had helped to train him with his AIM, and he had been patient, and almost even fun to be around. Over the past two years since his return to Scanning, Cam had been more a team player than a solitary athlete. He did more interviews together rather than on his own.

He finally shrugged. "I guess there's more to Cam than we know." He supposed there was more to all of them than even they knew about themselves. "Do you have any idea what the training is going to be like tomorrow?"

"Not a clue. I thought we already went through our training," Sarah answered thoughtfully.

"Apparently not. I guess it makes sense, though. They need to know we can hold our own, that we won't be that much of a liability. I figured we'd have more, but McMurphy did say that we were each getting a weapon. I'm not sure how I feel about that."

Sarah shrugged. "I think I'd feel better holding one than not. I'd feel even better holding one and knowing how to use it."

Ryan smiled, remembering when he had first gotten to know Maria. She had hated the idea that he had been hunting for sport. His smile faded when he thought about her job now. Now she was the one hunting. Maybe not necessarily for sport, but he knew she had had to use her weapons. He still had no idea if she had killed a person. He wasn't sure he wanted to know.

Ryan sat hunched over maps of migration patterns for various animals of the area, while Cam studied video footage of the rogue AIMs. They had muted it after the first few seconds of carnage. Ryan trailed his finger up along the paper, following a dotted line. If the AIMs were acting like real animals, they'd be hungry, and if they were hungry, they would look for food. The problem was that they were only acting like real animals. They hadn't necessarily been taught how to fend for themselves in the wild. They had been trained to complete military missions.

"If they have any residual memory from the original scan," Ryan started, "they should be moving without a set pattern. This area is all dependent on the weather and where there's food. If there's a drought, they need to find somewhere with water."

Cam brought up a map on the table-top screen and pointed to an area in the northeast. "As far as anyone knows, there's still an active group of...Mjahdan, or however you say it, in this area. My thinking is that the military training is still active in their chips, and that's what they're using as their animal instincts. It's like salmon. They were programmed to return there, so as animals, they think it's a safe area where they've found food before."

"If that's what they were trained to do," Ryan thought out loud, "why wouldn't they just wait for them to get back?"

Cam pointed at the screen on the wall on which the silent videos were still playing. "I'm sure they don't want a huge trail of death and destruction to follow the AIMs. And we still need to stabilize them. If they just wait, they'd be killed too."

"So now we figure out how to cut them off."

He nodded and sat down next to Ryan. "Well, we at least have a projection. Tracking them down is only the first part of this. If these guys want to use the AIMs again, we need to rework them so the data can be extracted from them. They've been rogue so long I don't even know if it's possible. In the meantime, we'll get the strategists to figure out how to cut them off. They're not necessarily animals, in this regard. They're the enemy. We figured out where they'll be, and when." Cam sat back in the chair. "Now they get to actually figure out how to get there safely."

Ryan looked over the map once more and shook his head. "This seemed too easy."

"Yep."

He looked at Cam slowly. "That's never a good thing."

"Nope."

He paused. "Someone wants us to find those AIMs."

Cam nodded. "My guess is that there are more than four AIMs they want us to deal with."

Ryan studied the map again. "We're not going to be back for the season."

"No. We're not."

Maria strode in front of the group of civilians. Her eyes passed over them as she moved. The two from the McCarthy Group barely paid attention to her scrutinizing eyes. Ryan seemed to be no better. She glanced at Collins with a wry grin. "They do know what a line is, I hope," she muttered, making sure to be heard by the civilians.

Collins smiled. "They're civilians after all."

"Alright guys, listen up! Does anyone know how to use a gun?" When all the civilians raised a hand, including Ryan, she raised an eyebrow. "Has anyone ever used one?" Sarah's hand went down. "Has anyone ever used one and hit their target successfully?" All hands but Peter and Cam's lowered.

"Thank you, Mr. Tylar, for volunteering to teach your colleagues how to shoot a gun." She knew they had a better chance with Lim teaching them, or any of the soldiers, but she had to make a point. To whom, she wasn't quite sure yet. Her head lowered slightly and she addressed the civilians. "You have two days to get acquainted with the weapons. Anyone who can't hit a target directly will be staying here in Kandahar, and on the next flight back to North America."

"They were chosen specifically by the General to help on this mission, Loo-tenant," Collins commented before the group dispersed, emphasizing the American pronunciation of her rank.

"And they were put into my care. Their job is not just to find the AIMs, but shoot if shot at. If they can't do that, then they're no good out here. Coming here not knowing how to shoot is like coming here not knowing how to use an AIM."

Collins glanced at Ryan quickly before facing Maria. "From what I hear, you've dealt with that situation before."

Her eyes narrowed. Now was not the time for him to finally know something about her background. "No one's life was at stake. You can't do your job here, you're dead." She stepped towards him, prodding him in the chest with her finger. "If I say they don't come, they don't, and I'll deal with the General when we complete this mission. Is that clear?"

He stepped forward, pushing her hand against him. "You may be leading this mission, but you'll remember that I am your superior, Kier. Is that clear?"

"Kier!" a breathless voice came from behind them.

Without turning, she called out, "what do you want?"

"Your physical. You missed it yesterday."

With her eyes ablaze, she turned on her heel, and dismissed her unit as she followed the medic to the hospital.

"You worried us when you didn't show up," the nurse said as she went over Maria's chart. "We thought you were avoiding us. And after all we've been through." She smiled at her hesitantly. "How are things going?"

She shrugged. "I'm back here, aren't I?" She nodded towards the young woman. "You didn't tell me you were coming back either."

"It was a last-minute thing. They offered me a position here for the next three years, and I'm a trauma nurse. I was going crazy being cooped up at the Kingston base with nothing bigger than...well, your case two years ago." The nurse smiled. "I know it was terrible, but it was the most excitement the base has had in a long time. Other than the CO being put in jail. And you putting him there."

Maria rolled up her sleeve and waited for the woman to take the blood sample. "Did you do the physicals for the civilians?"

"Yep. They all check out. Pretty fit group you got yourself."

She paused as the needle broke her skin. "Anything you want to ask?"

"No, why?"

Maria looked around awkwardly. "Cam...and Ryan?"

The nurse swore, and nearly shifted the needle while it was still in Maria's arm. "I didn't even make the connection! They're both here? What the hell is that about?"

"The world hates me. Didn't you know that?"

The nurse picked up a clipboard and looked at Maria seriously. "You stopped going to your appointments."

"I couldn't talk about it anymore. I just...I needed the break. I was getting worse talking about it so constantly. She wouldn't let me just bring it up naturally."

"Talking about your PTSD doesn't come naturally, Maria," she said softly. "She has to keep bringing it up. Especially when you're a suicide risk." Maria instinctively covered her arms as the nurse surveyed the first few questions and made a few check marks.

"When you get back to Canada, promise me you'll start going again."

Maria sighed. "I'll probably have to after this."

"Not going so well?"

"Panic attack on the way over."

She nodded. "We see that pretty often with repeat soldiers, especially those Stop-Lossed."

Maria glanced away. She couldn't imagine what it would be like to think she was going home, only to find out she would have to stay for another tour...with no chance of going home in between.

The medic chuckled as she went through the standard questionnaire. "I'm supposed to ask you if there's a chance you're pregnant, but I think we can skip that one. I know your history."

Maria simply smiled politely. The quicker they went through the questions, the quicker she could make sure the civilians weren't blowing each other up. She trusted Cam, but to train them all with weapons? Hopefully Collins hadn't left them alone. She nearly shook her head at the thought. She was going to need to get used to relying on these soldiers she barely knew. It wasn't her strong suit, but she would need to learn to adapt. They all would.

Maria watched as the group of civilians stood in formation later that day. She was impressed, but only barely. She knew that Cam and Ryan would have little trouble with the physical training, but how was she supposed to send back those who could not handle the pressure? There was more to this mission than being able to run and shoot. No one seemed sure what to expect with this mission. But Sarah Travato was another story. She seemed physically fit, but there was something about her. Skittish was perhaps the right word, but Maria wasn't sure.

She stood next to Filsinger and watched as Ellis ran them through another set of training exercises. "What do you think?"

He looked at her briefly before turning his attention back to the civilians. "About them? In general?"

"To start."

Filsinger paused. "For what we're meant to do? I think they're in pretty good shape, and not just physically. I think they all know what's at stake, and I think they each have personal motivations to have this mission completed as quickly as possible." He turned to her. "And with as few casualties as possible."

"Any concerns?" She watched Ryan and Cam work with Sarah as she struggled slightly with an obstacle, working well together as always. Well, perhaps not always but recently at least.

"I'd have to get to know them a bit more, or get into their files deeper to know what makes them tick. One concern is that I don't know whether or not they're all willing to do what it takes to get this mission completed. You know this is not going to be an easy mission, even for the soldiers. We're on a tight schedule with limited resources. That's already a pretty bad start. "

Maria nodded and held back a smile when the group was able to finish the task under the allotted time. They would go through simulations similar to this every day until their dress rehearsal, and as of yet no one was quite sure what that would be like. "So, what do we need to make this a success?"

"From the looks of it, we already have him." Filsinger motioned towards Cam. "Have you told him? I heard he's requested to be taken off the need-to-know basis list."

"There's still the element of security. He was right, though. He works best with all of the facts, so we're giving him everything we have."

"Everything?"

She turned her attention away from the civilians to fully face her fellow soldier. "I'm not going to pretend that even I know everything, but we're going to tell him what we can while keeping the rest of us safe. The problem with a mission like this is you never really know who knows what. I'm apparently second-in-command here, but I know it's really Collins and McMurphy running the show. I have authority only because of my experience."

"Are you afraid for them?"

Maria took in a deep breath and held it momentarily while she considered her answer. "Every minute."

Cam watched as one of the American soldiers, Filsinger, went over the different parts of the rifles each one of them had been assigned. He looked down at the weapon in his hands, feeling the weight of it. He had never used something so big. A hand gun was all he really knew, and none of that had been good memories. Not much had changed in the world of weapons, not really, when Cam thought about it. Sure, there were new models of guns and rifles, but they were all the same. You still aimed, pulled the trigger, and ended a life. He was jolted back to reality by the popping sound of a rifle being fired. He looked forward at the target which had been set up. It hadn't been hit. He noticed Sarah pulling up her weapon with a frown.

Filsinger motioned towards Cam. "Tylar, you're supposed to be the only civilian who's shot a gun. I'm not sure where I put Lim. He's not quite a civilian because he's supposed to have experience. But can you at least aim?"

He glanced at the three other civilians. With a sigh, he pulled the rifle up, securing the butt of the rifle into his shoulder. He looked through the sight, and after a brief moment he let out a breath and pulled the trigger.

The soldier grinned, looking at the target which was now pierced in the centre. "Not bad. How long have you been shooting?"

Cam relaxed and let the rifle hang at his side. "I don't."

Taking the hint, Filsinger continued to explain to the group how to properly use the sight on the rifle, how to aim, and how to stay calm. Cam allowed his mind to wander during the tutorial. He watched Ryan with interest.

He had tricked Ryan years ago into telling Maria he had been hunting, and what he had thought would turn into a fight or the beginning of hatred towards Ryan, Maria had convinced Ryan to never hunt again. Cam wondered if this counted, hunting AIMs. In any case, Cam knew Ryan had used a rifle before, but apparently he had not actually killed anything. Maybe he had told that to Maria. It was most likely the reason, or one reason, why he had easily given it up. It helped him sleep at night, at least.

"Just so you all know," Filsinger explained, "none of you are given clearance to actually shoot unless shot at. If you see a member of Mjahdan and find him to be a threat, you still cannot shoot. And even when you are shot at, your first thought needs to be how to get away safely. We are here as your backup. We have your back, and we will do everything we can to make sure nothing happens to you. In the event that eventually the soldiers are equal to civilians, this is when your knowledge of the rifle will come in handy. If you become compromised, you will need to know how to use this weapon, and this weapon alone."

Ryan turned the rifle over and looked at it as the soldier spoke. Cam noticed the man's hesitation even holding the weapon. He was likely thinking the same thing Cam had already thought: how many lives has this taken? How many lives am I willing to take?

Sarah put up her hand hesitantly, but put it back down. "Are we supposed to be able to hit the target perfectly? Because I can barely aim a basketball, let alone a gun. At least not the way Cam can."

"Even hitting somewhere close to an enemy is good enough. If they're startled, they won't be aiming properly either." He smiled. "Don't you worry your pretty head about it. We'll take care of you."

She nodded slowly. She brought her rifle up, aimed, and made an exact copy of Cam's bullet hole in the target. "Is that how you do it? Is that how you're planning on protecting my pretty head?"

Cam laughed. "Looks like the civilians aren't doing too badly." His laughter died slowly when he looked at Ryan. He remembered what the man had looked like when he had first seen his picture. Looking for a replacement for Owen had not been a good experience for Cam, and it was not something he had wanted to do, so he had left. Mostly. He had watched from the hall as Ryan's picture and stats were presented.

Ryan Hampton. Twenty years old when he was signed. Only twenty years old. He had looked so happy in the picture: a genuine smile, wavy brown hair. And he had been so excited to meet the team. Cam had no problem seeing why Maria fell for him. Ryan Hampton was a genuinely kind, and happy person. But that wasn't the man he was looking at now.

The light in his eyes was gone. The rare smiles he had given in their time in Afghanistan so far had been forced, and Cam had been able to see straight through them. The desert was killing him, and it would devour him before any member of Mjahdan came for them, or before a rogue AIM could maul his flesh. His soul was going, and seeing Maria work so well in this environment was making it crumble even faster. He had been helpful, Cam thought. More helpful than he would have thought. He had made the projection map nearly on his own, and had indeed added the promised sparkles in the form of time frames and destruction extrapolation charts.

He grimaced inwardly, thinking about the figures they had discovered. They would be able to find the AIMs within a month but in the meantime, the rogues would be causing mayhem to nearly thousands of people. And there was nothing they could do. Every moment that passed, someone was in danger. After realizing the final plan of Mjahdan, Cam and Ryan were beginning to see the true danger.

Filsinger put up a hand after allowing Peter and Sarah practice a few more times. "Hampton?"

Cam and Ryan's attention turned to the soldier slowly, both as if coming out from a dream. Ryan didn't respond, but simply stared at him.

"You need to know how to shoot." He laughed. "Kier says she'll send you back, but as much as we may not like civilians here, we need you guys. We also need you to know how to protect yourself for the worst-case scenario."

Ryan held the rifle just a bit tighter. "If this isn't worst case, I don't know how you guys do it."

Filsinger paused. "We think about one thing at a time, and what there is afterwards. My afterwards is going home to my family, and if learning how to shoot a gun makes that come faster, I'll do it gladly. If running after a stupid faulty robot gets me back home, I'm the first one out there."

"And if the only thing you want is here?"

The soldier smiled with a shrug. "Then you do what you need to do to make sure you both get home."

Ryan glanced at Cam before he aimed his rifle and pulled the trigger. Not a clean shot, but good enough. It may not get him home, but it would get him closer. That was all he needed.

Cam lay on his back on the bed of the cabin he shared with Ryan. His AIM lay across his stomach, thankfully in the small form of a chipmunk. They had each learned their lesson when he was a boy that the AIM should not be in a large canine form and try to show that form of affection.

"Did you know that civilians work in quite a few places here in Afghanistan on Canadian bases?" Ryan asked.

He looked over at him and saw him in the same position he was in, but his AIM was in the form of a turtle. He remembered when Ryan had scanned that animal. The first time he had taken Ryan out for some training. Turtles aren't necessarily a difficult animal to scan, but that particular turtle had been elusive. That was how they both agreed to tell the story, and no one would argue against them. "Do they?"

Ryan nodded, rubbing the back of his head against the pillow in the process. "Yeah. Drivers, technicians, interpreters. It's cheaper for them to hire civilians than train soldiers, pay their pension, and in some cases, for their schooling." When a knock sounded on their door, he sat up slowly, holding himself up with his elbows. "You want to get that?"

Cam groaned. "Sure thing, darling." He shot Ryan a grin as he got up from the bed, causing his AIM to tumble to the floor in the process. He paused, making sure the robot wasn't harmed, and opened the door. "Come to switch cabins again?"

Maria leaned against the door frame. "McMurphy gave your map and projections to our contact with the Mjahdan."

"And?" he asked as Ryan joined him at the door.

"They're not happy, but appeased for the moment." She glanced over her shoulder as if checking for eavesdroppers. Maria looked up suddenly as a fighter jet passed by overhead. She took a few steps backwards, going down the steps to follow the path. "I hope you guys got some good target practice in today."

When she turned to go, Cam went down and took hold of her elbow. "I meant it when I said that I need to know everything before going into something."

She looked up at him silently for a moment. Her eyes flickered behind him to where Ryan was standing in the doorway. "I know as much as you do."

"You need to say it."

Another pause.

"We're going to find those AIMs, save thousands of lives, and stop a war from starting. But we're not going home anytime soon."

CHAPTER 10

Maria stayed back as Filsinger went through trial shots with the civilians. She had to admit they impressed her. The rifles they used in the military were not difficult to use, but they had picked it up quickly, and their aim was quite impressive as well. She waited as Ryan took his shot. She hated what she saw now when she looked at him. Not as steely as a soldier, but she had never seen him hide his feelings before. He may as well have been an AIM for his lack of facial expression. A regular working AIM, at least.

Collins stepped to Maria and folded his arms across his chest, the stripes on his sleeve prominent in this position. "They've passed the only training needed for civilians on a combat mission. Some of them are better shots than my own men. Is your majesty pleased?"

She wondered when it would begin. If a woman tried to show authority, she was acting like royalty rather than someone who actually had power and rank. Which she did. "Who's the best shot?"

"Tylar and Travato."

She was not surprised to hear Cam's name. She motioned to Sarah. "Show me."

Sarah stepped forward and positioned her rifle. Before she could prepare and aim, Maria pulled out her handgun and shot at the woman. Sarah screamed, nearly dropping her weapon.

"Shoot!" Maria yelled as she shot again. She didn't wait for Sarah to aim again before she shot at her. All her shots missed her by inches, but she wasn't trying to hit her. She continued to shoot as Sarah visibly shook, the strap of the rifle swaying back and forth as she tried to keep it within her grip. Finally, Sarah got a round out, none of which hit the target.

"Kier, what the hell was that?" McMurphy yelled. He had been pretty patient with her. They all hated the thought of sending civilians into combat, but it was clear now that Maria had personal reasons.

"If they can't shoot while being shot at, then their training is no good," Maria replied using the same tone. "It's one thing to hit a target, even a moving target, with all the time in the world to set up the shot. It's another to know how to shoot under fire. That's the only reason they'll be shooting, is that correct?" When McMurphy remained silent, Cam stepped forward.

"Try it on me." Cam watched her face, watched her go through the various scenarios. He had seen her shots on Sarah. They were scare tactics. It was what the Mjahdan would use on them, at least until their AIMs were found, retrieved, and replaced. He had dealt with this before. When Maria nodded, he turned to face the target.

He brought his rifle up and took aim at the target, and waited. She sent the first shot. Cam turned on his heel and sent one back at her. He winced suddenly, feeling a pinch on his arm. He looked down to see a trail of blood going down towards his elbow, and the sleeve of his uniform was ripped. He swore as he pressed his hand against the wound. "You shot me."

"All's fair." After a brief hesitation, she slung her rifle over her back. "You shot at me, too."

"Our orders are to shoot if shot at. The target wasn't shooting me. That's not the enemy. The enemy is the guy with the gun. Take out the guy trying to take you down first."

Maria nodded. She turned to the rest of the civilians. "If someone is shooting at you, make sure they stop."

McMurphy held his tongue, his face turning red as he attempted to control his temper. "Tylar, go see the medic. Filsinger, go with him." He turned to Maria as the two headed to the hospital. "If you ever pull a stunt like that again-"

"You'll send me home? Make sure I stay in Afghanistan? I don't care," Maria said calmly. "I want to make sure the civilians know what they're getting into. I need to know they can handle it."

"You can't care this much, Kier."

"I have to."

He took a step closer towards her, ignoring the soldiers and civilians staring on. "You need to tell me if there's something more."

Maria hesitated. She knew the consequences. Relatives, spouses, significant others, they couldn't work on the same mission. They could be on the same base, but not part of the same unit. "Every single civilian was approved by the General, correct?"

"Yes."

"Then there's nothing more that matters if you don't already know."

McMurphy let out a deep breath. "We move out tomorrow. Wake-up call is at three A.M. Be packed and ready to go. Dismissed." He waited until the others left before turning back to Maria. "You knew he'd shoot you."

"I was proving a point. You can't trust that the person shooting at you is going to miss. He knew I was trying to scare them. Prepare them for the unexpected."

Collins took a quick step to keep pace with them. "You worked with him before, didn't you?"

How much would she tell them? Once they left the base, there'd be nothing they could do. They'd be stuck in the desert with little communication. If they found out then, they'd have no choice but to carry on with the mission.

"Yes. Cam, Ryan and I were all on the same team in the Canadian Scanning Tournament."

He nodded with satisfaction. "Good."

She raised an eyebrow. "Sir?"

"You already know how to work together, and trust each other. We need that, now most of all."

If only he knew.

*　　*　　*

"Revolution, you have ten minutes," a man wearing a small earpiece and holding a data pad reminded the team. As quickly as he had arrived, he left for the next team.

Owen barely had time to thank him as his team huddled around him. "We're good on the order? Just like other month-ends. Just play it the same."

"It's the last month-end," Maria muttered. "This isn't just any challenge."

"Which is why we'll play it the same. Don't let nerves get the best of us. Forget about the pressure. Just play." He stopped when Maria's phone interrupted.

Cam held back a laugh when she groaned, apologized, and answered.

"Hello?...yes...yes, he's my dad..."

That was when Cam watched her face carefully, straining to remember if her dad had been sent away. No. He had just returned from deployment. Three weeks earlier if he remembered correctly. Then Maria's face froze, her jaw partially open, her hand hovering in front of her mouth.

"How...when did he go in?....okay...no, I'll be there in an hour." She put her phone away with unsteady hands. "I have to go," she told her team.

"The challenge is in five minutes," Rick reminded her.

"I have to go," she repeated, her eyes looking around blankly.

"Maria, what happened?" Cam asked, ignoring Rick. She had all of his attention. She had all of him. He put his hands on her shoulders, and repeated the question.

She looked up at him as though she only just noticed him. "My dad's in the hospital. He had a heart attack. He's...he's in surgery."

Cam let go of her and picked up his pack. "Let's go then."

"Cam," Owen exclaimed in disbelief.

"No." Maria shook her head, clearing some of the fog. "Stay. Compete."

"It's your dad, Maria. You're not going alone."

She put a hand on his chest, holding him back. "You can take a handicap with three people. Please, compete." The determination on his face made her continue. "He'll still be in surgery when you finish. I'll be in Owen Sound. Just...win, okay?"

It was just a heart attack. So, Cam nodded and let the rest of his team pull him back to the starting area.

An hour and a half later, Revolution sat together in the waiting area of the surgical wing. While small, the hospital in Owen Sound was still a modern looking building. Cam appreciated that, at least. Sitting next to Maria it took most of his willpower to not hold her, comfort her. Her face was blank, staring down the hall the doctors seemed to be coming from to speak with other families.

It was taking too long. At this point, Rick and Owen seemed to realize it was worse than they thought. Probably glad Maria had left. They had won, best scores so far, even with the handicap.

Cam noticed Maria straighten, a look of relief on her face. He turned and saw a surgeon walking towards them.

"Maria Kier?" she affirmed, her face and voice both stoic and professional.

Cam stood when Maria stepped towards the surgeon, watching them carefully. Alex was a good man. He had been kind to Cam, even after finding out about his…knowledge...of Maria.

Maria swept her hair from her face. "How did it go? Is he awake yet?"

"Miss Kier, your father suffered a massive heart attack," she explained. "He was still in cardiac arrest when he arrived."

Maria nodded. "Yeah, I was told that on the phone."

The surgeon paused, and Cam took a small step forward. He knew that pause.

"During surgery, your father experienced two more attacks. Despite our best efforts, we were unable to resuscitate your father."

Rick and Owen sat forward, paying close attention now.

But Maria shook her head. "I...I don't understand. He was in surgery. He had a heart attack."

"I'm so sorry, Miss Kier. He's gone."

All at once the floor fell away. Without hesitation Cam was at her side, his arms around her, holding her steady. He held her tight against his body as she let out a desperate wail. He squeezed his eyes shut as though it would turn back time, as though he could will Alex to be alive again. For her. Anything for her.

He felt her legs go and he let her pull them both to a sitting position, his arms still around her in the only protection he could give her. Cam knew most people would say 'it's okay, you'll be okay.' But it's never true. He couldn't lie to her.

"Cam."

He looked down at her, her eyes already red and pleading with him.

"What do I do? I don't...I don't know..."

Ignoring the onlookers, he kissed the top of her head and looked her in the eyes. "You're not supposed to know, babe." He swept some hair from her face. "I'm...I'm so sorry, Maria."

"Cam."

He shook his head. "You don't have to say it yet."

"My..." She took a deep, shuddering breath. "My dad's dead."

Cam pulled her in close again and looked around. His eyes met with Rick, and the look they shared told him everything. They were officially outed, at least to Rick. But that was the least of his concerns.

"Some people from the hospital are going to speak with you shortly," Cam said gently. "About your dad. About a funeral home. They'll ask if you want to see him."

She struggled in his arms, panic setting in. "No...no, no, no. I can't do this. I can't." Maria looked up at him again. "I can't do this."

"You can," Cam responded forcefully. "You can. When my...when my mom died, I was alone. I wasn't as strong as you, but I did it. I promise you, Maria, you will not be alone. You can push me away, but I'm staying right here. Do you understand? I'm not going anywhere."

"There are six fundamental elements of a mission of this nature," McMurphy began. He stood in front of both civilians and soldiers in the small boardroom where they were to hold all of their meetings and discussions. "Simplicity, which is the limitation of our objectives. Ours is simple: stop a war before it begins. We will do this in two stages. The first, find the AIMs and stabilize them. The second, to bring the AIMs – old and new – to Mjahdan. That's it." He nodded to finalize his statement. "Do whatever you need to do to make those objectives personal. This is another element: purpose. You need absolute dedication to this mission, or it will fail. I don't care what it is, but make sure you're ready to die for it."

"As we've already discovered," McMurphy continued, "not everyone will have the same intel. This leads to the second component: security. This is not simply about making sure we have the proper defenses against our enemy. This is about making sure the intel we possess does not get into their hands. The less people who know, the better."

Collins interjected. "Not a single one of us has all of the information, and it's been planned that way. Complaints won't be taken seriously."

McMurphy let out a breath of frustration before he continued. "The civilians have been practicing through training exercises, but soon we'll all be working together going through scenarios we may come across. In reality, we have no idea what's going to happen out there. All we can do is prepare for the worst, hence the repetition. Tylar has been training the other programmers how to distract a rogue AIM, but we have no idea what will happen. Let's just make sure we have a fighting chance.

"We will each of us be working closely not only with each other, but with our AIMs. It is this very technology that has us here in the first place and we need to make sure our partnership with them is strong before going into the field. The soldiers will need to work with the sentient AIMs to know how to predict their movements, and Tylar will train them to recognize aggressive tactics or behaviour from the rogues."

"Which shouldn't be too difficult to recognize," Cam added. "It usually looks like a lot of bragging and boasting. But it's when the animal is most vulnerable." He could not help but dare a glance in Collins' direction before turning his attention back to the front.

"Are we done with the peacocking?" McMurphy asked, and waited for a moment before the two nodded, both grumbling like children. "We need to be in and out of there as quickly as possible. Once we've actually begun, we need to find the AIMs before they can get to another village, stabilize them, and in a perfect world our hand-over would be the same day and we can all be on our way home after our debriefing sessions. A shorter mission allows us the chance to gain what we call relative superiority."

"The upper hand," Cam spoke once more.

McMurphy looked at him, surprised. "That's right, essentially. The quicker we gain it, the better the chance we'll succeed. The longer the mission drags on, the higher the likelihood that we'll lose it. And once that happens, it's hard to get back." He looked at the soldiers, his eyes piercing into him. "Let's make it our priority not to lose relative superiority."

"When do we gain that?" Cam asked.

Maria was surprised, but that seemed to be her constant state as she watched Cam and Ryan in the desert. She had not thought they would adapt as well as they had so far, and it seemed now that Cam had actually paid attention and done his homework before they arrived. "What do you mean?"

He looked at her. "Do we have an idea when we'll get it? What that point is in the mission?"

From the corner of her eye Maria noticed Collins sharp stare and she bit the inside of her cheek. "We already have it."

"Which brings us to our next point," McMurphy added, bringing the attention back to him. "Surprise."

Cam caught up with Maria after the meeting. "Maria." He sighed. "Kier," he added when she seemed to ignore him. He picked up the pace and grabbed her elbow, pulling her around. "What was that back there?"

"What was what?" she asked. "That was a meeting. You've been to them before. Maybe with a different topic, but at least we didn't yell at each other during this one," she said with a weak smile.

"Is this part of that need-to-know basis you guys are so in love with?" he snapped.

"It's not like that, Cam," she said with a sigh.

"Then what was that about?" Cam stepped closer to her and lowered her voice. "McMurphy can go on all he wants about the mission, and its purpose, and how we're supposed to make it personal, but it's a little hard when my purpose doesn't seem to be talking to me."

"Your purpose can't be a person."

"It'll be whatever the hell I want it to be. You know why I accepted this, why I agreed to come. My being here gets you home quicker. That's my purpose. Finding those AIMs, getting them to Mjahdan is what will get you home. That's what I'm fighting for. But I can't do that if I don't know what's going on. I need to know if we have a chance, and here you are telling me we already have an advantage, that we already have this in the bag."

"We do, for the most part." Maria paused and glanced around. "We've held relative superiority for a while now. The longer we have it, the more likely we are to succeed. But..."

"But what?"

"Mjahdan will fight even harder to get it."

Cam raised an eyebrow. "And what is it?"

She looked up at him, pain on her face. "You."

After nearly two weeks of training and rehearsals, Ryan felt as though he knew a small amount of what to expect. He knew physically everything would be difficult, but training with such a large group and logistically trying to concentrate on both soldiers and AIMs had been challenging to say the least. Cam had it worst of all, trying to manage everything at once. Rehearsals have gone well, but in a controlled setting here on base that was to be expected.

Ryan looked around as he shovelled food into his mouth. He had no idea how long he would be able to eat this way, and was willing to take it for all its worth. Maria had shown him rations once, and he was not looking forward to eating any of it. At the thought of her, he realized he had not seen her since the meeting. Or Cam. He started when Sarah sat down next to him. "Hey," he said sheepishly, embarrassed at his reaction.

She laughed lightly. "If you jump at the sight of a woman sitting next to you, how are you going to be in a fire-fight?"

He shook his head and looked back down at his food. "Would I be convincing if I said I'd be fine?"

"No. I don't think any of us would be fine. Not even the soldiers, from the looks of things," she commented. She smiled when Peter joined them. "You haven't been here before, have you?"

Peter shook his head as he examined the food he had taken. The hesitant look on his face implied to the others that he may not have chosen wisely. Not that they had much of a choice. "Nah, mostly deployed in Asia, and a few times in Russia. Went from one climate to the other to test out a few pieces of technology." He nodded in remembrance. "Pretty interesting results."

Ryan looked up with interest. "Wait, you're ex-military?"

"I wasn't in long. I was testing out the AIMs in different climates, trying to find a common form for them to utilize in all climates."

"You didn't find one."

Peter smiled at Ryan's knowledge. "Of course not. Not a specific species, at least."

Ryan nodded as he chewed on his food. "A bird would be best. Doesn't matter which kind, really. Unless you're doing reconnaissance and need the AIM to blend in with the native animals."

"We did indeed decide on a bird."

"So why the German Shepherds?"

Peter tapped the side of his nose with a grin. "I was in the Air Force."

He smiled in understanding. For the first time, he actually understood something in this desert. He could see why Maria had done so well and advanced so far in such a short time. She had such a deep knowledge and understanding of animals and AIMs. He had no idea it would be like this. His smile disappeared as he continued to eat. The trouble was, he had no idea what would come next.

Maria sat over the projection map that evening, looking at their intended path over and over again. So far, the AIMs hadn't been meandering. They were moving in a straight line. She leaned forward more, something suddenly hitting her.

"May I join you?"

She jolted suddenly at the sound. She swung around quickly, surprised to hear and see Cam's AIM in the doorway. "What are you doing here? Shouldn't you be with Cam?"

"We are not glued together, nor am I bound to him." The AIM walked in, and leapt up onto the chair beside her.

Maria was surprised to see the AIM in the form of a German shepherd. Maybe Cam was preparing. If anything, he'd be preparing the AIM to be in this mode more often. At least it didn't shed as much.

"Do you know how a regular AIM thinks?" She asked it, or him. "I know you communicate with normal AIMs."

"Yes, I believe I do."

She nodded. "Do they have a connection with their owner?"

"The way Lucas and I are connected?"

"No." Maria paused, trying to think of the wording. "If they're stolen from their original owner, would they stay loyal to their owner, or simply follow the person who stole it."

"They would follow the person who stole it."

She nodded. "Like a form of leader and follower mentality?"

"Yes."

"Do you think they could be led by someone out there?"

"It is unlikely, but we could add it to the threat list."

"Let Cam and Ryan know. And maybe add in the possibility of one becoming the alpha. This may change our approach. Either way, we still leave in the morning, and should be in Ghazni by the evening."

The AIM was silent for a moment, still looking down at the map. "He knew that you would shoot him. He is thankful it was not the head."

"Does he think I hate him because of Ryan?"

"Do you?"

Maria paused. "No. I want to, but he's right. We need him, or I guess Cam needs him. They've worked together, and you've worked with his AIM, so it makes sense. Cam doesn't play well with others, so trying to get him used to working with someone new would take too much time. If Cam trusts Ryan, then we need him, whether I want him here or not."

The AIM turned and put a paw on Maria's hand. "I will do what I can to protect the three of you. I always liked you, you know."

She smiled. She remembered not feeling comfortable with the idea of a sentient AIM, mostly because all she had experienced were rogue AIMs. She had learned in the past few years just how special Cam's AIM truly was. "So you say. But I appreciate it." She thought back to the training, back to two years earlier. "Cam's a good shot."

"He is."

"But he missed."

"To miss, one must first attempt to aim," he replied.

She rolled the comment around in her head for a moment. Even after being shot, he still did what he could to protect her. "He knows I'm not being this way because I'm angry, right?"

"He is getting used to seeing you as a soldier. Ryan is not. He has barely spoken since our arrival. He will do the job well, but I do not think he will adjust if we return to Canada."

Maria nodded. "That's what I figured. Hopefully he'll snap somewhere down the road, snap back into it I mean. It's what happens most of the time."

The AIM jumped down from the chair and bumped up against her leg affectionately. "I will relay our discovery to Lucas and Ryan. Have a good sleep." It began to walk out from the room when it stopped and turned back to her. "Would you like me to stay with you for the night, so you can rest? Or is it only Lucas' presence that helps?"

She didn't know what it was, or why it was that way, but whenever she fell asleep at Cam's or even around him, her night terrors had stayed away. It was ironic to her, since most of the night terrors included him. "I'll be fine for the night. I've been okay."

He didn't call her out on her lie, which both knew it was. "Good night, Maria."

"Good night, Fluffy."

Cam groaned as they were woken mere hours after he had laid down on the bed. He had no idea the next time he would feel a mattress again. He knew he would miss it, which was saying something with the state of his current one. He looked around groggily and rubbed his face when he realized it was Collins waking him and Ryan.

"What the hell are you doing here?" he muttered, sliding out of the bed.

"We need to talk," Collins answered, and hit Ryan to wake him as well. "Both of you. You guys got Kier's message last night?"

"Yeah." Cam grabbed his uniform and began to change quickly. "We're coming. Meet at the Humvees?" When Collins nodded and left, he hit Ryan who simply rolled over when the soldier hit him. "Get up. We need to add to our contingencies."

"But the sparkles," Ryan said, his voice muffled by the pillow.

"We need more." He sat down on the bed to pull his boots on. "I can't believe we didn't see it before."

"You are used to working on a team of four," his AIM spoke up. "When have you won a challenge on your own."

Cam opened his mouth, but paused as he thought back. "Sarnia, Ryan's first season."

"You solved the problem, that is correct. But it was Maria and Ryan who completed it," he reminded him. "You must remember that."

Despite the fact that the sun had yet to rise, Cam put on his hat, the only thing they were given with the camouflage pattern. He smacked Ryan again. "Come on. We need to figure out the new plan." He waited a moment to see if Ryan would stir. He folded his arms across his chest. "Let me tell you about the first time Maria and I slept together-"

Ryan bolted up. "Stop. I'm going. I'm up."

McMurphy nodded in greeting to the two as they joined the three soldiers. "What are your thoughts?"

"We go ahead like we said," Cam said simply. "If they're being led, they're not as dangerous as we thought they were. Tigers are extremely territorial creatures. They'd never hunt, or live, together. If one tiger encroaches on another's hunting grounds, there's a fight," he explained. "But they're working together. They're not acting like animals. Not completely at least.

They're still reacting to something, whether it's a beacon of sorts or their training. The training is programmed on a chip it shouldn't be able to access in their rogue form."

Cam took a moment to look at Maria. He had seen her in uniform, and was used to that by now, but this morning she was in full attire. Along with her jacket and pants, she wore her helmet with the strap already fastened under her chin. The other two had kept theirs undone for the moment. She was also wearing her vest which he assumed was already loaded with rounds of ammunition. For nearly the first time, he wasn't able to tell it was her from her figure. She was barely recognizable by her face, too.

Collins nodded as he leaned back against the Humvee. "Which means this is going to be more tactical than scientific."

"Yes," Cam agreed. For once. "My concern is whether they're actually rogue."

"You're saying the AIMs killed my men on command?"

"I'm saying they may be half rogue, and have been stabilized. Either that, or we're dealing with something even more dangerous."

Maria glanced at Ryan briefly. "It's possible that they have some residual memory of working as part of a tactical team, rather than the instincts of the scan. The animals used for military scans aren't usually wild animals, and I'd bet anything that when Trevor sold them the AIMs that he threw in the scan too."

"We would have trained them with that scan," McMurphy said, affirming Maria's thoughts. "So, it's a possibility."

"But the greater possibility," Ryan finally spoke up. "Is that we're walking into an ambush. It's a test." He looked at the others for confirmation. "They want to see if we can do what we say we can. They want to see..." His voice trailed off as he turned to Cam. He kept his thoughts unspoken, but it was a shared thought. They wanted to see who would step up and fix the rogues. The question was what they would do once they saw.

McMurphy was silent for a moment. He looked at Collins. "Do we tell the others?"

"No," answered Maria, before Collins even had a chance. "We stick to the original plan, but keep the base up to date with absolutely every move we make, and Mjahdan. It'd be nice to disband the S.O.Bs once and for all, and this might be our chance to do it."

"For once," Collins said with a grin. "I think we're on the same page."

Cam looked off to the horizon, waiting for the sun to show its face. "As soon as we head out, I want to send out three AIMs as recon. They should go past Ghazni to give us an idea of what's out there. Maybe find any other trails the rogues travelled on. It's possible that they're not even travelling together, that they just happen to each get to the same town at the same time. It could explain the intensity they have when they attack. They all know where the food is, so to speak, so they're more aggressive once actually in the same territory. While it might be an ambush, I really think part of it is residual programming. I've seen it before."

"We'll go ahead as planned," McMurphy affirmed. "Once we get results from the recon, we'll have a better idea, and from there we'll continue on to the villages in the path of destruction. If there are any survivors, we'll hopefully be able to get more information on what the AIMs were doing."

He looked around as the rest of the unit began to gather around the Humvee. He gave a small nod to them and jabbed his thumb behind him to the vehicles. "Four per vehicle. Kier, Tylar, Hanks, and Strong. Up front. Collins, Ellis, Shepero, Travato, next," he began calling out names, and each began to head for their vehicles, each soldier knowing who would drive as if rehearsed.

Maria hung back a moment when Ryan was assigned to the last Humvee. She held onto his elbow as the others dispersed. "You gonna be okay at the back?"

Ryan looked around and gently pulled his arm from her grip. "Is there one vehicle better than the others?"

She shrugged. "Out of four? The third is usually pretty good. Not too windy."

He forced a small smile. "Then I'm okay."

"I need to be sure that you are." When he paused, she stepped closer towards him. "Ryan, we haven't left yet. There's still a flight back to Canada."

Ryan shook his head and started for the last vehicle in the caravan. "I'm as okay with this as you are. You can't fault me for that."

No, she couldn't. With a sigh, she jogged up to the leader vehicle and jumped in the back as the engine roared to life. She sat beside Cam, with Strong driving and Hanks as the navigator. "Can you get us to Ghazni in one piece, Corporal?"

He laughed. "I'll see what I can do, Lieutenant. I warn you, as the driver, I have full control over the radio."

Maria groaned. "Isn't this mission going to be bad enough? Hanks, you have permission to shoot if he even tries to play Country." She smiled when there was laughter in the front seats. She glanced at Cam beside her and quickly let go of the smile. She looked out the bullet-proof glass as they pulled out of the base in Kandahar. Her hand closed into a fist as the desert highway stretched ahead of them. A wet nose nudged her fist and she looked down to see Cam's AIM beside her in place of her own. She couldn't help but smile at the gesture. But she felt so heavy, so weighed down by the uniform she wore.

"Kier?" Strong called back to her as he led the caravan to Ghazni. "How free am I to speak?"

She glanced at Hanks. She did not know this soldier, but McMurphy seemed to like him more than Collins did...which made him want to like him immediately. "Freely."

He looked over his shoulder briefly to look at the two behind him before turning his attention back to the road. "Are you guys just going to focus on the mission? Because I have to admit, I'm just waiting for things to hit the fan, if you know what I mean."

"We'll be fine," Maria answered. There were few people who didn't know about her past relationship with Cam, or about the daughter they had together. Strong had worked with her on the base in Kingston, so he had a better idea than Ellis, and he was likely the only one who also knew about Ryan. It would come out sooner than later.

"Yeah, because you've been fine so far, haven't you?" Cam muttered.

"You brought him."

"I had to," he yelled, although the volume of his voice did not seem inappropriate in the loud vehicle as it crunched the sand and rock beneath its tires. "And you brought me, remember?" When she didn't reply, he looked away.

A few moments passed in silence, other than the sound of the tires and the engine. Finally, Hanks turned in his seat. "Collins and McMurphy…they don't know about you two, do they?" Maria shook her head and Hanks continued. "No offense, Lieutenant, but I hope things never do hit the fan. Not out here."

But she knew it would eventually, and it wouldn't be between her and Cam. And it wouldn't just be the fan. It would be a flock of geese getting sucked into a plane's engine. And they were the geese.

Ryan looked out the window of the last vehicle as they made their way to Ghazni. The city was slightly off the path he and Cam had projected, but it would be their last stop at a military base before going on. They would be able to gather more information here, and the soldiers were hoping to speak with people who had survived the last village attack. Thinking about speaking with the villagers only reminded him of how little he knew about Maria.

How had she learned an entire language without him knowing? Although, he had to admit that she was the only female soldier on the team. She may not be entirely fluent, but she was the only one who could speak to female Afghans. He frowned. No, he had heard her speak Arabic. Pashto, he corrected himself. That had sounded pretty fluent to him.

"You gonna be okay, Hampton?"

Ryan looked forward at Johnson who was in the passenger seat ahead of him. "I've never really been outside of Canada before, other than a trip down to Michigan with my family when I was younger."

Johnson laughed. "Quite a culture shock for you, then."

"You could say that," he muttered.

"Hey, I wouldn't be worried out here. It's not like we haven't worked with civilians before," the soldier said with a smile. "And you're paired up with Kier. She's a pretty awesome shot, from what I saw in training last week."

McMurphy let out a laugh. "No offense, Hampton, but you weren't supposed to be paired with her. I had to give Tylar over to Collins. It'd be a conflict of interest. But Johnson's right. From what I've seen in her file, she'll take care of you."

Ryan remained silent, and he shut his eyes tight. How could he ask them to stop talking? He held in the urge to scream at them, to find a way to go back to when he knew nothing about what Maria did, or who she knew. The resentment he had allowed to build the last three years had disappeared. How desperately he wanted to go back to not knowing who she truly was. Even now he barely knew, but he had no desire to see it first-hand.

Cam sighed. Five and a half hours, and the only conversation had been in the front seats. Maria hadn't so much as looked at him for long, or rather in his direction. He leaned over towards her. "I need to know you have my back out there."

She looked at him with a raised eyebrow. "What are you talking about?"

"I know you're not happy with me. I can't tell if it's because I brought Ryan, or if it's because I slept with you knowing my plan was to bring him along," he said, which caused the front seats to go quiet suddenly. "I don't know what the hell Mjahdan has in store for us, but whatever it is, I need to know I'm going into it with my back covered." When she remained silent, he leaned closer. "Maria."

"I have your back," she said quickly and turned to him. "I always have." Maria looked away just as quickly. "But technically, Collins has your back." She let herself smile softly. "But I'm going to assume he's not the person you'd necessarily choose if you had your pick."

"No, not really."

"Twenty minutes, Kier," Strong called from the driver's seat.

Maria nodded and pulled out her AIRC from her pocket. "Okay, let's get the AIMs out."

Cam copied her motions and looked at his AIM. "You'll have to keep them in line. I trust you to be the leader."

"Will Ryan's AIM be coming as well?" he asked in response.

Cam hesitated. "Yeah. We can't afford to not send it out with you. Work with it a bit more. It might have a bit more insight. Something tells me the internal conflict those rogues have are more like what's going on in the chip of Ryan's AIM."

"Internal conflict?" Maria asked. "You make them sound like they're nearly human."

He motioned towards his AIM. "Other than a weird substance as a body, is there much that makes this guy different than me?"

"Well," she started and looked at her AIRC to avoid his gaze. "You both have an attitude, and lack tact. So, I'd say you two are pretty similar."

Cam rolled his eyes with a grin. "Ha ha. You're hilarious, you know that?" He shook his head when she shot him a wide smile. "On my count?"

Maria stood and opened the hatch above their heads. She pulled herself through to the gun house and made room for Cam. She winced as sand was blown into her face by the speed of the Humvee. She pulled her bandana up from her neck and around her mouth. She knelt and turned around to face the vehicles behind them. She waved her arm and held up two fingers. After a moment, she saw Johnson pop up to the top of the last Humvee in the caravan. When he signalled back, she turned to look at Cam.

"Are you ready?" she yelled over the wind.

He motioned to his AIM, already in the form of a Barbary Falcon. "Talk to him." He looked at the stats for the scan and he shook his head with disappointment. "If I had been here on any of type of business, I would have had a field trip. I can't imagine scanning this guy in the wild." He turned his attention to his AIM. "You know to give us updates every hour, or when you see something notable."

"Yes, Lucas," it responded through the AIRC. "You have trained me in the form of a Peregrine falcon. This scan is quite similar, and the hunting patterns are similar to that of other falcons I have been in. We will remain staggered to give the illusion of hunting." It flapped its wings and hopped slightly as some air caught it unexpectedly. "Time?" When Cam nodded, it pushed itself up with its legs, its wings folding and bending as it flapped, bringing its body up into the air quickly and with ease.

Cam watched in awe as the AIM flew up high into the air, flapping its wings quickly to get lift. "Have you ever seen anything like it?"

Maria smiled as she looked at Cam. For a moment, both of them could forget they were sitting in the gun housing of a Humvee in the middle of the Afghan desert. For a moment, they were Scanners again, admiring nature and its creatures. "We'll have a bit of down time at Pearson. I'm sure you and Ryan could slip away to do some scanning."

He shook his head as if coming out from a trance. "No. We have to keep our AIRCs committed to the recon. Even in the down time..." His voice trailed off and he looked at Maria. "Do you think they'll wait for us to find their AIMs?"

She nodded and looked at her AIRC, readying her own AIM to be sent up. "They have to. We'll make the switch. They'll give us time to report back to Kandahar, and then all we can do is wait. You have to be sure you can get this done, Cam."

"I quit Revolution to put my entire focus on making sure rogues became a thing of the past. I need to see this through, Maria. I need to be here."

She didn't respond. Instead, she jabbed the screen of her AIRC with her thumb, and her AIM transformed smoothly into another Barbary falcon and followed Cam's AIM up into the air. She sat back and watched it climb into the sky.

Cam watched her for a moment, trying to keep his eyes open with the sand blowing into his face. "Can I ask you a question?"

"Depends what it is."

He hesitated. "When the heck did you learn to speak Pashto?"

She laughed. "I started when I was first deployed. My dad knew a bit as well from his time here, so I already knew some basic phrases."

"I never knew that," he said as quietly as he could and still be heard over the sound of the Humvee.

"There's a lot you still don't know about me."

The look Maria gave him made him want to…he didn't know what. There was so much going on now he barely knew how to feel, or react. Before he could make up his mind, she turned away to watch Johnson's AIM fly up into the air. He looked ahead and saw what looked like a settlement in the distance. "That's where we're going?"

She turned around and after taking a brief moment to examine the surroundings, she nodded. "Yeah. Forward Operating Base Pearson. We'll be able to get more support and supplies here before we head out tomorrow." She leaned back against the barrier as if enjoying the ride. "You have it pretty good, you know. My first week here, I had already been out on two overnight patrols."

"Did you get shot?"

"No."

He pointed at his arm which was wrapped in bandages beneath his uniform. "Well, my first week here, I got shot by my ex-girlfriend."

She laughed. "Okay, we're even."

"Oh no we're not. Because not only do I have to work with her, but her most recent ex-boyfriend. You shot me, Maria. I definitely have had a worse experience here, in the same amount of time."

"Excuse me? I'm here with two of my ex-boyfriends. One of which is the father of my child."

He grinned. "I'm equal with you there, so I'm still ahead." When she had to stop to think, he couldn't help but laugh. "You can try to beat me, but won't because you shot me."

"I had to."

"Why?"

She lost her smile, and her face turned back to stone. Ever the soldier, closing up her emotions. "You're Cam Tylar. You're too good for your own good." She cleared her throat. "Besides, I didn't want people to think I was playing favourites, or that I will."

"People meaning Ryan?"

"He's not doing well out here."

Cam shook his head and leaned back against the barrier, his shoulder pressed up against hers. "No, he's not. It's not helping that the three of us are here. Are you going to tell him what happened?"

"I haven't decided. Definitely not here, at least." She watched as he looked at the desert as they flew through it on the highway, the base coming closer on the horizon. He had always been so intense with everything he did. Even if it was something small, like doing the dishes, he put the same intensity into it as he would a CST challenge. She had ignored the intensity he put into their relationship, into keeping her safe, into loving her. "What happened…I don't think should happen again."

"I thought that was a conversation for after. But that's fine," he replied without looking at her.

When she realized he wasn't going to continue, she spoke again. "I'm not saying I didn't enjoy it, I just-"

"You already explained yourself, Maria. If you're regretting it, then you need to deal with that on your own. I don't regret, so I'm not going to say anything to try to make you feel better."

"I don't regret it."

He let out a heavy sigh and finally looked down at her. "Then what is it?" he asked impatiently.

Normally she would have fought back. She didn't deserve that tone, and she would have fought back which, of course, which have made him retaliate and it would continue from there. But they did need to work together, and despite her anger and whatever else she was feeling, they couldn't afford that.

"I didn't…expect to want to have an 'after' conversation. But right now, I need us to pretend it didn't mean anything so we can concentrate on the mission without being distracted."

And normally, he would have snapped at her, lied to her, choosing anything to hurt her. But all he could do was nod his head. Sometimes, there were no words.

Maria's radio crackled to life suddenly. "Number four stopping," McMurphy called. "Got something wrong with a tire."

She swore but Collins responded before she could. "Keep going. We're within walking distance."

"Is there an active mechanic among us?"

"No."

"Then we're stopping."

Maria let out a frustrated sigh. They were so close to the safety of those walls. Not even a full six hours into their mission, they already have something break down? And Ryan's vehicle, too. Well, at least it was just the tire.

Ryan looked around out through the windows. He saw what he assumed to be the base up ahead. "I don't think it'd hurt to go to the base and check it out."

Johnson opened his door and hopped out. "It won't hurt now. You any good with vehicles?"

He shrugged, but smiled lightly. "Actually, I'm not bad." He slid out after Johnson and they walked to the back of the Humvee. Ryan knelt down to look at the tire well. He waved his hand in front of his face in an attempt to settle the dust. "I don't see anything, but it definitely felt like it was something in this tire."

Johnson took a step back to give Ryan some room, and to not block his light. "It's double-wheeled. Maybe something got stuck between."

Ryan nodded and laughed. "As long as he doesn't start driving, I can keep my arm." He reached in and felt around the large tire. It wouldn't have hurt to keep driving. If something was stuck, the worst it could do was scrape up the tire well, which Ryan figured was pretty durable. Suddenly he felt something wedged between the tires. He wrapped his hand around something metallic and his heart stopped. He fingered it, trying to determine its shape.

He looked over his shoulder to the soldier. "Uh, Johnson? It's metallic."

Johnson pulled Ryan away and slid himself under the vehicle to get a better look. He laughed, and a moment later, he came out from under the body with a piece of scrap metal. "Debris."

Ryan nearly swore when he saw the harmless piece of metal in the soldier's hand. "Maybe next time, I'll just stay inside the car."

He laughed. "Probably best." Johnson pushed on the button for his radio and stepped sideways to get a clear view of the first vehicle. "We're all good. Just debris." He waved his arm and took another step to the side to look for their return signal. When he saw the wave, he threw the piece of metal off the side of the road so no one else would kick it up into their tires.

Ryan brought his arms up in front of his face before he was thrown against the side of the armoured vehicle. The metal had fallen on a landmine. He slumped to the ground as ringing filled his ears. Dust and dirt formed a cloud in the air, backlit with flames. Suddenly, he felt arms around him, pulling him up. He saw Collins' face, and his mouth was moving, but Ryan heard nothing. He let the soldier pull him into the Humvee and barely felt it roar to life and fly after the others as the world went black.

CHAPTER 11

The Humvees rolled through the gate of FOB Pearson, surrounded on both sides by concrete walls and barbed wire toppings as they passed by. When they came to a stop, Maria swung her legs over the barrier and jumped down to the ground, followed closely by Cam. She ran to the back of the convoy as Collins stepped out with Filsinger carrying Ryan. His face and clothes were covered in dirt and soot, the arms of his uniform burnt black.

She held back a sob as they shoved past her. "What the hell happened back there?" She started after them when someone grabbed her elbow. She swore and twirled around to McMurphy. "What the hell was that?"

McMurphy swore, punching the driver's door. "Johnson triggered it with the debris. Landmine."

She mimicked his curse as she started after the soldiers carrying Ryan when another hand grabbed her elbow. She wrenched it away when a quick glance over her shoulder showed Cam behind her. "Don't," she snapped before heading to the small hospital.

Cam watched as she jogged away and wiped his face as if it would wipe away the last ten minutes. Ellis came up beside him and he simply shook his head at the soldier. "Just like that...first day off-base, and we've already lost one." He swore. "They can't even kill us face-to-face; they have to use landmines and IEDs."

Ellis put a hand on his shoulder, patting it. "It doesn't get any easier, losing guys."

Mark's face flashed in Cam's mind, his dead eyes staring at him. And Jack. The idiot had let himself get killed because he had thought Maria... "I'm not new to death. Cowardice, yes."

"We do the same thing, sending in missiles," Ellis noted. "The actual shooting comes after."

"Something to look forward to."

Hours later, Maria was allowed to see Ryan. She stood next to the bed once the doctor had explained what he had done. No surgery, not really. There had been no shrapnel, thankfully, but Ryan's arms had suffered second degree burns, and a small sliver of his face had caught some debris. He had been lucky. She stared down at him for what seemed to be forever, watching him sleep. Maria did not look forward to when he woke up, the pain he would be in from the burns. It could have been worse. He could have been Johnson.

Maria looked up from Ryan when movement caught her attention. Her eyes narrowed as Cam stepped forward.

"Is he awake yet?" Cam asked softly.

"No. No thanks to you," she growled. Even through her anger she could see the hurt on his face.

"I didn't plant the landmine. He's my friend, too. I almost...I've lost enough friends," Cam replied in defense.

Her face flushed and she swore. "You brought him here. You brought him."

His face reflected hers, his anger mirroring hers as it usually did. "You're seriously blaming me? And if something happened to me, how much would you hate yourself for bringing me?"

Maria threw off her jacket and thrust out her arms towards him. The pale skin was side up, marked with jagged scars, and Cam couldn't help but notice some were still healing. "That's how much I hate myself."

Cam stared at her. He knew she had stopped going to counselling, but he hadn't noticed... And when they had slept together, her arms hadn't been high priority. He hadn't noticed. "Maria..." he said finally.

"Just go away." She sank into a nearby chair and resumed her watch over Ryan, falling dead to the world outside her bubble. She looked him over, watching his chest rise and fall slowly, deeply. They had finished cleaning up his uniform, or had given him a new one to wear once he woke. Maria had not paid much attention.

The blood she saw, she convinced herself most of it was Johnson's. Had Ryan noticed before he went unconscious? He had grown up on a farm. Blood was not something new, but she doubted he had even had another person's blood on him. Growing up on a farm doesn't prepare you to see death in that way. Nothing does.

Maria barely noticed when McMurphy put his hand on her shoulder and addressed her.

"We're going out to...retrieve Johnson. Strong's AIM is surveying the area for the next twelve hours. Ellis' will take over at that point. If there's absolutely anything suspicious, they're going to let us know and we'll deal with it."

She looked at McMurphy after a moment. Ryan was breathing. His arms and face were torn up, but it was more than could be said about Private Ian Johnson. "I'm sorry."

"He was a good kid," McMurphy said with a small nod. "Get some rest, do what you need to do before we head out again. Hampton'll be fine." He turned to leave. "I'll keep an eye on Ryan when he wakes up. Make him talk, about anything. I know how dangerous it is to let him go quiet."

When he left, she punched the wall, barely feeling the blood rush to her knuckles. She took in deep breaths, holding back the hysteria she knew was building. It was one soldier. But it could have been Ryan. At least it wasn't him. His chest continued to move up and down. As many times as she would tell herself, Maria knew it would never bring back a young man who had sworn to protect his country.

It was seven days before the medic at Pearson admitted Ryan was well enough to leave with the rest of them. Physically, at least. Strong took over his care, and had already tended to changing the bandages on Ryan's arms. Ryan had gotten away without needing a skin graft, but he had been kept heavily sedated for nearly the entire week.

Cam sat with Ryan in a large tent the day before they were scheduled to continue on their mission. The base was much smaller than the one in Kandahar, and looked as though it was a temporary base if one ignored the concrete walls, which he learned could be put up in less than three hours. The buildings were large tents which kept out the sun, but not the heat. He had given up trying to look good constantly. It happened without trying, of course, but he ignored the sweat underneath his clothes. He looked at his team-mate who was studying the map. He had been cleaned up, and the uniform hid the bandages on his arms, but Cam knew he was far from alright.

“I was thinking of finding another path, rather than a direct approach,” Cam said, and trailed his finger along the paper map. Apparently digital tables weren’t something they had in bases such as this. “I talked to McMurphy about interception, and he thinks it’s possible to get ahead of the pack, once we can confirm their location.”

The two looked up when Maria, McMurphy, and Collins stepped into the tent. They nodded and sat down with them. He had not spoken to Maria since the incident, not for a lack of trying. Seeing Ryan awake and moving around seemed to have made her open to the idea of being around Cam again. Even so, he avoided looking in her direction.

“We’ve gathered more information about active Mjahdan sites,” Collins said. He grabbed a red pen and made small Xs. “In the last two hours, Strong’s AIM has recorded small cells of insurgents. It seems the IED was planted the day before we got there.”

“Our AIMs never reported anything,” Cam replied slowly.

“Because they were sent on a specific trajectory, while Strong’s is on a basic recon around the base,” Collins answered.

“Should we be widening their area?”

Collins shook his head. “No. We need them going ahead of us. Maybe one can switch to a basic recon maneuver, and we’ll send another one up for it too, to keep our bases covered.”

"But we have a problem now," McMurphy continued. "We need to stay clear of these areas." He pointed to one X in particular. "This one isn't going to be easy. They've taken over one of the villages we need to investigate. They typically don't stay in one place for long and they should be gone by the time we get there, but coming from another approach should be considered."

Cam nodded. "Ryan and I were actually just discussing that."

"Good. I'll make sure Filsinger stops by to give you guys some help with the tactical side of this. This was all supposed to be dealt with before we even got here, but things happen and we need to adapt. I'm sure you're both used to doing that in your own line of work."

When the soldiers turned to leave, Ryan looked up at them. "What happened to him?"

Collins and McMurphy paused, but Maria sat back down. The counsellor on the base had attempted to talk to Ryan about Johnson but he had remained silent, staring off into space. This was the first time most of them had heard him speak, except for Cam. "He will be brought back to Kandahar," she explained gently. "They'll have a memorial for him. Then he'll be brought back to the States for the autopsy, and in a month or so after the investigation, his next of kin will be notified,"

"Investigation?"

"They need to be sure it was an enemy's IED, and not one of ours. We don't usually work with IEDs, and we'd never plant it where it was, but it still has to be done. Politics." When he nodded, Maria placed a hand on his briefly. She looked at Cam before leaving with the other soldiers.

Cam stayed silent for a minute, giving Ryan some time to think despite what everyone had said. Don't let him think. Keep talking. Keep trying to get him to talk. "We should be able to finish this up quickly. What do you say we do some scanning afterwards? Even within the walls of the base, we can see tons of wildlife, at least birds." Ryan was Revolution's top Scanner, in the literal sense of scanning. Cam had finally admitted that he couldn't be the top in all categories, and had encouraged Ryan with the skills he already had.

Ryan seemed to ignore him when he turned away. "Maria broke up with me because she didn't want me waiting months to find out she was dead. I think I'd rather wait the few months instead of seeing her die in front of me."

"Let's just finish the map, Ryan."

But he stood quickly, overturning his chair. "He's dead, Cam. He blew up, right in front of me. How can you be so calm?"

Cam paused, and took in a deep breath. "Two years ago, I was part of a shoot-out with Trevor McCarthy, and Jack. I watched Jack shoot an innocent bystander in the head, and watched Trevor do the same to Jack. That image never goes away. But I keep going, because I can't let that take control. And...I'm just glad you're okay."

Ryan stared at Cam. This was the first time anyone had even offered up any information about what had happened two years ago. He picked his chair back up, righted it, and sat down. No one had even explained why Trevor had stepped down, or what had landed him in jail. Everyone assumed it had been some form of embezzling scheme. At least Ryan had. But now it seemed to be much worse.

"Trevor McCarthy...killed Jack Tyson?"

"Trevor was afraid of his company being taken away from him. He was afraid of losing control. When I, and the rest of the Underground, told him that rogues would be appearing in the general public soon, he got scared." Cam spoke slowly, not only for Ryan's sake, but his own. He hadn't re-lived the events in a long time. "So, he tried to get rid of everyone who knew about rogue AIMs. And then one Canadian soldier wrote a report about her partner who had been killed by a rogue during her deployment. And he got even more scared, because now it was in another country, and in the military. He ordered a hit on her." He paused, waiting to see the realization on Ryan's face. "And that soldier got scared, and angry, and went to the Underground for answers. She came to me."

"He tried to have Maria killed."

"Yes."

Ryan continued to think for a while longer. "All this time, you two have been holding onto all of that."

"Yes."

He nodded slowly, his face softening and his body relaxed. "I liked the world better when I thought that all this death, and violence, was so far away from me. I saw a man blown up."

Cam didn't respond, but looked back down at the map. "You'll see me blow up at you if we don't get this figured out soon." He tried to smile, but there was no point. Not anymore.

Ryan thought for a moment. "How long have you known about what happened to Maria here the first time?"

"She told me when we were at the safe-house together. She had blamed me for the hit, but she realized it was because of what she knew, not that I was part of the Underground."

He nodded. "What happened to the American soldiers..."

"Maria saw happen to her partner," Cam finished.

"No wonder she can't sleep at night," Ryan muttered.

Cam's eyes moved over the map, and only briefly glanced up when Filsinger joined them. "Well, at least she hasn't shot you."

Maria stood outside, watching the sky in the late afternoon sun which burned into her face. Three dots appeared in the distance. Her AIM had reported they were returning shortly. They would be sent back out the next day when the section would go out and follow the new map Ryan and Cam had created. She had taken a look at it, and it wasn't much different from the original one they had given to Mjahdan. They would not be giving them the updated version. The soldiers couldn't be blamed for altering their path when obstacles got in the way. The course was different enough to keep themselves safe, but not too different to tip off the militia group.

She held her fist up as her AIM landed on it. It wasn't a real falcon, she knew of course, but while it was in the form of a particular animal, she would treat it that way. She couldn't help but smile, admiring the creature. It was a beautiful scan. One of her few regrets was not travelling more for scans, or at least to see animals in different regions of the world. She had found herself considering retiring when her service was over in two years, rather than continue on as a career soldier.

She had never thought she would retire, instead favouring what her father had done. Becoming a Scanner had put this plan on hold, and she had found she loved being an athlete. But then being here in the middle of the desert, she felt she made a difference. If she put aside what the desert was doing to her, if she ignored the death, it was an easy decision. Nothing else gave her the same feeling of achievement, not yet at least.

She watched as Cam's AIM landed down next to her and instantly began its transformation into a German shepherd. This part of its sentience bothered her, that it could change form at will, although it still needed to be programmed with the next scan beforehand. Thinking about it, it was a huge advantage to use in the tournament if Cam could use that feature during a challenge, which he certainly could not, even with the updated AIMs.

"Nothing to report at all?"

"Some tracks," his AIM answered. It seemed to have taken the leadership role, just as one of the rogues seemed to have done. She hoped. "No sign of the rogues, and we were unable to sense any of their frequencies. We scanned for any activity, in case they had not fully disconnected from the network."

"If Mjahdan is still in control, even partially, would they have their frequencies anywhere?" she asked.

"Yes, but I assume they will not be willing to give that information."

She sighed. "You assume correctly."

It pawed at her leg gently. "I am sorry about Private Johnson."

"Yeah, me too. Keep an eye on Ryan. I doubt that helped him being out here."

"I do not think it helped you being out here, either."

She opened her mouth to speak when she noticed Cam and Ryan walking towards her. She smiled when the AIM loped towards his friend and jumped on him, just as real dog would when its owner arrives home. "Did you guys get anything to eat?"

Cam looked at her warily. "I'm already missing the food in Kandahar."

"It doesn't get much better. Maybe we'll have to get you to cook something." She tried to smile at Ryan, but he was avoiding looking at...everything, it seemed, like he was waiting for something to jump out at him and finish him at any moment. She couldn't blame him. A siren blared once, and she spun around towards the gate. In a single motion, she threw her AIM up into the air and it flew towards the gate of the base and she began to run, followed closely by the two men, although Ryan hung back by a few paces.

The three joined a group of soldiers already near the front, and Maria pulled on McMurphy's sleeve when she found him. "Who is it?"

"We don't know," he answered, taking a second to look at Cam and Ryan. "It's a woman, but we think she might be bait."

Maria swore. "Have we sent out any scouts?"

He nodded. "Nothing's been found."

Cam stepped forward. "What do you mean, bait?"

McMurphy motioned towards the gate and the woman beyond it, standing in the middle of the road some distance away. "Terrorist groups, militias, usually use women and children to lure soldiers out from bases or out of vehicles. When we try to help them, or bring them back for medical attention, the insurgents detonate the bomb strapped to the women's chest."

"That's sick," Cam said and swore. "People actually still do that?"

"Seems like it."

Cam looked at Maria quickly when he noticed her take off her combat jacket, showing the green t-shirt underneath. "What are you doing?" He continued to watch as she failed to respond and instead took a scarf from one of the many pockets in her pants. "Maria?"

She continued to ignore him as she wrapped the scarf around her head, pinning it under her chin before she flipped the long end of the scarf over her head once more. As Cam watched her, he was surprised how much she looked like someone native to the area. Her skin tone was darker than his, but not quite as dark as Afghans. She could at least pass for Israeli or Lebanese with the headscarf, if nothing else.

"Open the gate," she said to McMurphy.

He only hesitated for a brief moment before he stepped to the side and held down the button for the gate. "Don't take any risks, out there, and check her before you bring her in, if you do."

When Maria took a step forward, Ryan grabbed her by the elbow and pulled her back. "Don't you dare."

She looked back at him with a hard look, but it disappeared, realizing what would be going through his head. Maria put a hand on his. "I'll be okay. I promise you."

"You better come back," he whispered.

She nodded as he let her go. He turned around as she began to slowly move out of the safety of the base. When the woman noticed her, she stopped and put her hands up. *"Salaam alaikum,"* she called out.

A faint voice called back, *"wa-alaikum salaam."*

Cam stepped beside McMurphy who had now been joined by Collins. "What are they saying?"

"Just hello," Collins replied, his eyes intent on Maria as she pulled her handgun from its holster, held it up, and placed it on the ground. He swore. "She's going to get killed if she keeps this up."

"Maria's always taken risks, but they're always calculated," Cam breathed. "She hung upside down from a two-inch wire in a challenge once just to finish a challenge."

"Walking up to someone potentially wearing a bomb is a bit different," Collins bit back.

"Not from where I'm standing." Cam copied Collins' stance, staring out after her. "Either way, she can die in front of me. And there's nothing I can do about it." He turned when Ryan grabbed his arm suddenly, but still with his back to the road and Maria. It had been different then, seeing her out on the wire. "She did die. In my mind, for just a second, when we were repelling." He spoke as though in a trance, his voice monotone with the memory.

He watched Maria reach the woman and she checked her for explosives. "Her rope snapped. And in my mind, I saw her body on the rocks below us." Both heads bobbed as they spoke to each other, headscarves waving and rippling in the wind. "Then I caught her. I can't catch her out here."

McMurphy looked at him from the corner of his eye, remembering what Maria had told him. He hadn't believed she had told him the entire story about them dating, but when she had shot Cam, he believed it a little more. "You two aren't dating anymore, right?"

That got Cam to look away from her, only briefly. "What?"

"She told me you two dated when she was on the team, but never mentioned if it was over. If there's any conflict of interest here-"

"There isn't," Cam answered quickly.

"I need to know you'll have my back as much as hers."

"Can't guarantee that. But I'm not going to let you die, if that's what you mean."

"You still haven't answered the question, Tylar," Collins muttered.

Another quick glance away. "Interested?"

"She's single," Ryan spoke up harshly over his shoulder. "Broke up with her boyfriend to come here."

Collins suddenly stepped forward as Maria began to come back to the base with the Afghan woman. He knew to keep his distance. "Is she clear?"

"Yes," Maria called out, and spoke softly to the woman. Whatever she spoke seemed to ease the woman who had been startled by Collins coming out. "She knows the man who put the IED that killed Johnson. She had tried to get here sooner, but..." Her voice trailed off when Collins could see the woman's black and blue face. "Her husband tried to keep her quiet. I'm going to take her to the clinic."

"Mjahdan?" Collins asked.

The woman turned, and rebelliously answered, *"ho."* Yes.

Collins swore. "Will she let me take her?"

Maria asked the woman, who thought for a moment before she nodded, eyeing Collins as though it would keep him at bay. She watched the two walk away before Ryan shoved her, causing her to stumble a few steps. "What the hell?"

"What the hell was that, Maria?" he yelled, moving to shove her again, but McMurphy stepped forward and swung his fist, connecting with Ryan's jaw.

"McMurphy!" Maria yelled and stood between the two men. "Are you children?"

"You are a civilian," McMurphy yelled, pointing a finger down at Ryan who hadn't tried to stand up again yet. "If you try to hit one of my soldiers again, I will send you back to Canada the same way Johnson is going. Is that understood?"

"McMurphy, stand down," Maria growled.

He turned to her, his face red. "Remember your rank, Lieutenant. Hampton, remember your place."

"Yes, sir," he muttered.

Maria waited until the soldier walked away before she held a hand out to Ryan to help him up. He ignored it and stood, rubbing his jaw. "What the hell was that, Ryan?"

"Forget it." He turned to leave, but she pulled him back.

"The wire. Niagara Falls," Cam hinted, watching the two.

She looked between the two and shook her head. "Ryan, I'm fine. Nothing happened."

"And all Johnson did was throw some debris," he yelled at her.

"Everything we do out here is a risk, Ryan. Every person we speak to is a potential killer. I swore an oath to put my life on the line, and that's what I did."

"I'm not going to watch you do it," Ryan said firmly and walked away.

She let out a heavy sigh and turned to Cam. "I can see why you never shared anything with me about the Underground. I don't think I would've acted much differently than him."

He shook his head and felt his face redden. "Don't you dare do something like that again," he whispered. "I watched you die once. I heard you die two years ago when Trevor shot you. Don't make me go through that again." Cam took a step away but stopped. "That was awesome, though. And you look nice in a hijab." He gave her a small smile and followed after Ryan.

She had to admit that no matter how stupid her risks, he had always been behind her. No matter what.

Ryan lay on the cot he had been assigned for the night. He had no idea how Maria could stand any of this. Everything was so rigid, and structured. One was told what to eat, when to eat it, and even how. And then after you were told where to sleep, when, and for how long. Of course there was also the constant threat of death, but there wasn't so much of that concern back home in Canada. How she could live with so little freedom was beyond him. How she could have chosen to keep this life above him, he didn't want to think about that. He heard heavy footfalls echo in the nearly empty barracks. When they stopped close to him, Ryan turned his head to see who was coming.

Collins stood beside him with his arms folded across his chest. "Come with me."

Not seeing any other choice, Ryan got up from the cot slowly and followed behind the soldier, his AIM close at his heels. After a few minutes, he took a quick half step to walk beside him. "Where exactly are we going?"

Collins stopped suddenly and turned. He handed his rifle to Ryan and pointed to a target a little distance away from them. "Shoot it."

Ryan backed up with a shake of his head. He already regretted following him. "I'm not really in the mood."

"Trust me, you are." He shoved the rifle at Ryan again. "Take it, and shoot the target."

He stared at the soldier for a moment, but let out a sigh when he realized he would not back down. What was it with Americans and wanting to shoot things all the time? Or was it soldiers? He took the rifle and positioned it against his shoulder as gently as he could. His arms were mostly healed, but the new skin was still soft and tender. He let out a breath and pulled the trigger. The bullet went through the outer edge of the target.

"Again."

"I really don't think-"

"Again."

Ryan brought the rifle up once more and aimed. "Shouldn't you start shooting at me, or something?" he muttered, and fired. This time, the bullet-hole was closer to the centre.

"Again."

The bullet went through the centre of the target.

Collins nodded. "Good." He walked towards the target and stood in front of it. He kept the majority of his body off to the side. "Again."

Ryan lowered the rifle. "Are you crazy?"

"Hit the target. Pretend it's someone holding me hostage. Hit the target."

He waited for a minute and looked around, looking for anyone to confirm Collins was crazy. It hit him then. What was he expecting to do out here? He wanted to stay safe, and wanted Maria to stay safe, but there were so many variables, it'd be impossible. He raised the rifle again quickly, and fired. It barely hit the target.

Collins waved his hand, calling him over. "Switch with me."

Right, because that wasn't a death sentence. He did it anyway, and felt his heart pound as Collins aimed the weapon at him. Well, in his general direction. Suddenly there was a shot fired, and Ryan jumped. He looked around to see where the shot came from as Collins made his way towards him.

"When we send soldiers out into the front lines to engage the enemy, or to investigate a potential threat," Collins explained patiently. "We are always watching that soldier. Every move made is seen. If there's something wrong, we take out the threat." He turned Ryan towards the building and pointed to the roof where Hanks was positioned on his belly with a sniper scope. "Don't think for one second that we didn't have less than two guns aimed at the woman Kier was talking to." He looked back at the target and motioned towards it with his head. "Want to keep shooting?"

Ryan paused, taking in what he had said. He nodded then. "Yeah."

Maria ducked her head down to Peter's bunk a while later. She had looked around the barracks but couldn't find Ryan anywhere. After his little outburst, she had wanted to give him some time to cool down, but when Cam said he hadn't seen him since then, she began to worry. Not that he had anywhere to run away to, but she needed to keep an eye on them. On all of them. "Hey, Peter, have you seen Ryan around anywhere?"

He looked up with a small grin. "Are you allowed to be referring to us by our first names?"

She laughed. "I was going to call you Lim, but it's weird calling Ryan by his last name when I know him personally, so…whatever. Have you?"

Peter shook his head. "No, not really. I saw him walking with Collins a few hours ago, but not since then. I don't really look around when I get food though. Sarah and I try to stick together and just avoid everyone. Seems to be the safest thing to do around here. I mean, I've been on military bases, but people don't seem to care I'm a veteran. I'm a civilian now. It was hard to get used to even when I was around civilians full time. It's pretty rough being around ex-colleagues. So, we just try to stay out of people's way."

Maria nodded. That was probably true. It was nice for the both of them to have someone else they knew there. In such a different environment, let alone culture and region, it helped psychologically, and most likely emotionally as well, to have some form of familiarity. She wondered if she was able to give that to Cam and Ryan. Ryan was finally seeing how different she was from who she was before. He was even learning more about Cam, which was probably making him less familiar. "Any idea what direction they were heading?"

"Sorry. I have-" Peter stopped short and pointed behind Maria. "There he is. Must've just got back."

She stood straight up and waited for Ryan to walk towards them, and his cot. He looked at Maria and gave her a small smile, which she returned. "Hey. I've been looking for you."

"I was with Collins. We were going over some stuff."

She glanced over her shoulder at Peter, who seemed to have forgotten their presence and returned to the book he had been reading before Maria's interruption. "Look, about earlier…"

Ryan shook his head and held up his hand to stop her. "I'm sorry I reacted like that. I've seen you take risks before. I'm just…not used to seeing you like this, and I reacted without thinking. I know you don't do things without planning it out first. If I'm going to be out here, and be out here with you, I need to trust that you know what you're doing and that if you take a risk, it's for a good reason."

She let out a sigh of relief. Maybe he was adapting better than she thought, or gave him credit for. She wasn't sure if that was a good thing. "I'm glad. And you're right. I need you, all of the civilians actually, to trust us. I know you're used to seeing me as a Scanner, so you probably don't think I know what I'm doing, but I do. I'm good at this job, Ryan."

"It's just so soon after Johnson..."

"I know. Believe me."

He nodded and leaned against the bunk bed support. "So, who was she?"

"The woman? Her husband is part of Mjahdan. A small chapter of them meet in their home, and she overheard them talking about placing a landmine outside the base to greet us when we came. She tried to get here sooner to warn the soldiers already here, but her husband found out what she was doing and took out his anger, trying to put her in her place. But today she had her sister cover for her and she came here. I didn't tell her it already took a life. She doesn't need that kind of guilt. With it off to the side, it was meant as a warning."

"What happens now with her?"

Maria thought for a moment. "She'll stay here for a while. Someone will probably bring her south to Kandahar, which will be far enough away that her husband may not look there. It's still a risk to keep her on a military base, especially with her ties to the militia group. We may be able to get her passage to either Canada or the States so she can start over."

"Like a witness protection program?"

"Exactly."

Ryan sat down on his cot and looked up at her. "How often does that actually happen?"

"More often than you'd think, but less than we'd like. It's mostly the reason why I learned Pashto. With me being in the front lines the majority of the time, I'm part of the FET, the Female Engagement Team, which McMurphy explained already."

"You could have told me you learned a new language," Ryan said quietly. "I don't think that was really a top-secret thing you did."

She sat down beside him. "No, it's not. I'm sorry. Honestly, most of the time it's just hard to talk about."

"I get that."

Maria looked at him, her eyebrow raised in slight disbelief. "Do you?" How could he have had such a turn around? She would never say that how she had treated him had been fair, but for him to understand why she had kept her secrets was beyond amazing, for her at least.

"I do. Do I like that you did it? No, but I understand it, and I'm sorry I pushed you so often. I understand sharing a little means sharing a lot, but if you had told me how bad your PTSD is and your triggers, I probably would've been more understanding."

"Being alive is a trigger."

He thought for a moment and scrunched his face like a child eating something disgusting. "I can't help you with that. You're going to have to deal with that trigger." When she looked away quickly, he placed a hand on her forearm gently, remembering when he brought her to the hospital. "You should get some rest."

Maria stood up and looked down at him. "Oh, I should? I'm fine with only a few hours' sleep."

"Yeah well, if you're going to risk your life again, I'd like to know you got a good night's rest."

She laughed and mock saluted him. "Yes, sir!"

Ryan groaned as someone pulled on his arm. He waved his arm sleepily in an attempt to shoo the person away. Suddenly he felt himself falling and his hands went in front of his face just in time to save it from hitting the floor. He opened his eyes and looked up to see Cam standing above him. "Wake-up call isn't for another hour."

"Maria set up a communications line with the team," Cam said quietly, not wanting to wake up the soldiers around them. "The video call starts in a few minutes."

He stood up quickly, his eyes bright with anticipation. "Seriously? Rick and Owen?"

"What did I say? Now come on."

The two walked quietly through the men's barracks to where Maria waited at the door. They continued to walk, following her down a hallway and into a computer room. It amazed Cam that he hadn't thought to try to contact people back home. He had wanted to talk to them, of course, but hadn't given thought to the possibility.

"Will they even be awake?" Ryan asked as they sat down around a computer.

"It's a nine-hour difference," Maria answered. "It'll only be eight o'clock for them, and the kids should be in bed so no distractions." She took a deep breath as she connected the call.

She had debated even being part of the video call. Maria hadn't spoken to, or seen, anyone from home the last time she was here simply because it was too difficult. But Cam and Ryan would benefit from it, and this was their last chance before they completed the mission. They needed the send-off, and she needed to see them happy.

"Just a few things before we connect," she said as she looked at the men. "Keep the conversation light. It sounds cliché, but talk about the weather, and the animals you've seen. They're already worrying about us as it is, they don't need to know about training, or Johnson, or anything like that."

Ryan's face darkened. "They're going to see my face and the bandage. I don't think they'd appreciate it if I lied about what happened, or if they found out I kept things from them."

"I got my dad to tell me how things really were one time during the war. It's something I can never un-hear. Cam can tell you I was out of the tournament for a week because all I could think about or imagine was him telling me about how he carried half the body of a soldier so that the body wouldn't be taken by the enemy. And I still remember seeing the bullet hole in the brim of my dad's helmet from when he said he wasn't paying attention." Maria shook her head. "It sucks knowing they're keeping something from you, but believe me when I say that I preferred the omission much more than those images. We do it out of love."

When Ryan had no response, Maria connected to the server. A brief moment later, the screen filled with Rick and Owen's smiling faces. They waved, nearly jumping out of their seats as if the computer could teleport them.

"You're all still in one piece!" Rick said with a laugh. "Good to know you guys haven't killed each other yet."

The three each put on a smile. From now on, each would be much more conscientious of the words they chose to speak. Cam glanced at Maria briefly and put a hand on his arm. "Not killed, per se."

Maria kicked his leg subtly, making sure to not make the gesture seen to Rick or Owen. She rolled her eyes. "You should see Cam with the soldiers. He barely listens to my orders."

Owen laughed. "Did you expect any different from him?"

"Not really, but I can always hope."

"You always were a dreamer." Owen looked at Ryan through the screen. He paused, and the three knew he was likely considering asking what had happened. The bandage on his forehead from the blast was at least clean. Instead, Owen put on a smile. "Are you keeping them from fighting?"

Ryan shrugged. "Think I could stop them? With the way Maria handles a gun, I'm not going to be the first one to step between them."

There was an awkward pause, and Maria sighed inwardly. Apparently neither knew how to keep conversations light, which was surprising for Ryan. "Speaking of which," she continued as though nothing deep had been said. "Rick, let Adam know that as soon as spring comes, I'm having a water-gun rematch with him. I'll never hear the end of it if I don't."

Rick laughed, picking the conversation back up. "He's not letting anyone hear the end of it. So, how's desert life for you guys?"

Cam shrugged. "Hot. There's sand. Think of Alberta, but instead of wheat fields it's just all sand."

"Sounds pretty nice."

He nodded, and his face lit up. "Oh, you have to see this." He turned to his AIRC, and after touching the screen a few times, his AIM transformed into the Barbary falcon. Cam held out his arm and the AIM flapped up onto it. "Isn't this guy amazing?"

Both Rick and Owen leaned towards the screen. "That's not a peregrine, is it?"

"Nope. A Barbary. A bit smaller than the peregrine, not as fast, but really easy to train and handle. Their hybrids produce fertile offspring, too, so I'd be interested to see if anyone picks up on that for Scanning."

Owen shook his head with disbelief. "Are you guys actually scanning while you're over there?"

Cam jabbed a thumb in Ryan's direction. "You do remember why we brought him onto the team, right?"

Owen laughed. "I suppose so. I'm glad you guys are doing okay out there."

He nodded. "Yeah. I have to admit that it's nice working with Maria again. Even if she thinks she's the boss."

"Cam, I am the boss," Maria interrupted with a grin. "I can get the Prime Minister on your case for not listening to me."

"You're going to tell on me?"

A faint crying came from the Canadian end, and Rick winced. "Sorry, guys. That's my cue. Susannah hasn't been sleeping too great lately."

"We should get going too," Maria said. "We'll see you guys when we get home."

"You just make sure we do," Owen said."

Maria gave him a wink. "I may leave Cam in a hole somewhere if he gets on my nerves."

"Well, I'll allow that."

"Thanks," Cam muttered. "It's nice to know I'm missed."

"You are," Owen said seriously.

He nodded. "I miss you guys too. Train hard. We'll be back soon."

CHAPTER 12

Maria strapped on her helmet as Collins stepped up next to her. She barely glanced at him as she addressed him. "Hampton will be in my vehicle from now on. Tylar will go in yours, McMurphy will go with Lim. I want you to bring up the rear."

"Whoever had the idea to bring him," he started, "should've thought twice. Hampton's clearly too attached to you. I thought you were only on the team together for a month."

She shrugged and slung her duffle bag over her shoulder. "We've been friends since, even if we weren't team-mates. If Tylar says he needs him, then he does. Whether he's attached to me doesn't matter. He'll do that job. Besides, he passed the psych-test. He's mentally fit to be here, so there shouldn't be an issue." Maria paused and turned to look at him. "But whatever you did with him yesterday, it worked. Thank you." She let out a small smile. "You might actually be human after all."

He rolled his eyes and walked by her. "We need this team to work together, and work with clear minds. That's all."

"Of course. You wouldn't want people to think that you actually wanted to make him feel better. That would just make you look weak, and not as manly," she mocked.

"When you were on Revolution, did you guys ever fight?"

Maria raised an eyebrow. "By 'you guys' who do you mean?"

"Any of you."

"Cam and I, mostly."

"How often?"

She thought for a moment. How often did they fight during the season? While they were dating, it hadn't been that often. They did manage to work together extremely well. It was more when they were in the 'off' phase of their vicious cycle. And their last season as a team had been horrendous, even with the addition of Ryan to the team. "That's a long answer," she said, as simply as possible.

"When you guys were fighting, how well did you work together?"

"I get your point."

Collins turned and looked at her. "No, I don't think you do. I don't know what it's been like with your units, if you guys were all lovey-dovey and everyone supports each other and buys each other Timbits, but where I'm from we need to make sure we're all on the same page. And it's hard. We don't do things to make the other person happy. We do it to keep the other person alive."

"I'm starting to get why you're single."

"Who said I am?"

She rolled her eyes once more and continued walking. "It's really not much of a surprise, Collins. Even if you were dating someone before your last tour, you're not anymore." She paused. "No relationship could survive that," she said quietly. "You come back too changed. You keep too much in, and push the other person away. You're too mad at the world for its ignorance, and you hate yourself too much because you can't enlighten anyone. No one had to tell me you're single, Collins. It's our line of work."

Collins caught up to her easily. "And isn't it magnificent?"

Maria looked over her shoulder to the sun rising up from the horizon. "Some mornings, it really is."

"Then the afternoon comes."

She laughed. "Keep talking and I may actually end up liking you."

"Should I shoot you?"

"I'll let you know," Maria said as they reached the rest of the section. It was unlike her to be the last to arrive, although technically she had been with Collins so they had both been last. After the video call with Rick and Owen, she had needed to take a moment to herself. Well, her AIM had been with her, but that didn't count. Had it been Cam's AIM, maybe it would have. This would be their last time in a place of moderate safety and support. From now on, they would be at the mercy of villagers, if they let them into the village.

They had all agreed that if the villagers were neutral towards them, they would play it safe and stay just outside the village limits for the nights they needed to stay there. If someone could go either way about another person's life, then clearly it was not a safe place. McMurphy had received good reports about the people in the area from the last time they were there. Things may have changed with the recent increase in Mjahdan activity, but they were hoping for the best.

"Alright guys," Collins shouted. "Change in the order. Tylar, car three. Hampton, car one. McMurphy, car two. Any complaints, bring it up with me and watch as I couldn't care less. Let's move out."

Cam walked past Maria. "Already sick of me?"

"That's exactly right," she said with a grin as she hopped into the first Humvee.

He copied her grin and got into the last vehicle. He didn't mind the change. He didn't need to be around her constantly. The only problem was…

Collins looked at Cam from the passenger seat. "Try not to be yourself. And try not to talk. I'd really rather not have you be my first kill on this mission."

This was going to be a long drive.

Ryan kept his eyes on his AIRC as the convoy travelled across the desert. They had all downloaded the projection map onto their consoles, and he was keeping an eye on it as they went. Hanks seemed to be a fine enough navigator, but it never hurt to have a second pair of eyes. If Scanning had taught him anything, it was that. And to keep a good partnership with your AIM. And to work with the strengths of each team member. It seemed Scanning had taught him more than he had thought.

"So, why Ghazni?" Ryan asked. "We have to go back south, so why go all the way to the FOB?"

Maria glanced away. "There were things we needed to do there," she said hesitantly.

"Such as?"

Strong looked over his shoulder briefly from the driver's seat. "Are they still on a 'need-to-know' basis?"

She thought for a moment. Cam had asked to be kept in the loop. Ryan hadn't. None of the other scientists really needed it. Ryan had made a huge shift in his attitude, but she wondered what would make him backslide. "It's up to Ryan if he really wants to know." She looked at him. "You know what information does. You can either go along at the level you've been, or you can go deeper and darker. And trust me, it's there."

Ryan returned her look. What did he want? After realizing that they likely weren't going to make it home, he had been surprisingly calm. Part of him thought that maybe it was a bad dream, that somehow, they would all make it out of there alive. Now 'all of them' excluded Johnson. "I want to know. I know enough now to never go back, so I might as well keep going forward."

Maria nodded to Hanks, who explained. "Ghazni is as close as we can get to their current active headquarters, or whatever they want to call it. We were trying to draw them out, see how worried and paranoid they are. Clearly, they're worried we're going to just try to disband them without living up to our end of the agreement. Johnson had to pay that price."

Ryan raised an eyebrow. It made logistical sense. One needed to know the mindset of the enemy before engaging. If they're going into it to the death, or as an act of honour, the enemy would be unpredictable. Which also meant they would make mistakes. However, if the enemy was planning on backstabbing, from either end, they would have numerous variables calculated and planned for. "I thought you weren't supposed to make deals with terrorists."

"We didn't," Maria answered. "We never actually agreed to their terms."

"What? Then who's to say they'll do what they said they would?"

She turned to him again. "They didn't say anything. They wanted us to get their AIMs back. That's all. They never said they would keep their distance, or spread the word that we're co-operating."

He nodded slowly after a moment. "They're not just scared. They're disorganized."

"They want their AIMs back," she said. "They need them. But they're not making sure we don't die first." She gave him a grim smile. "How many Scanners does it take to stabilize rogues, and give them back to their owner?"

Ryan's heart stopped for a moment. "One." When she remained silent, he paused for a moment. "Does Cam know?"

Maria looked at her colleagues, hoping to get some help from them. But they remained silent. Sometimes it was better to say things on one's own. "He has an idea. We're trying to come up with an exit strategy. Mjahdan know you guys need soldiers to get you to the AIMs, and to get the AIMs back to them. After that, anything is fair game. Our concern...is perhaps something we should all be discussing together. Hanks, what do you think?"

There was silence in the front seat again, but he turned around to look at the two in the back. "Well, they're going to need to know the exit plan, so they'll all need to know eventually. And I think we're going to need to work with all of our AIMs more, get them all working together rather than just partners. Camp tonight, and we'll see how it goes. We'll be there in about half an hour."

Ryan raised an eyebrow. "Half an hour? Is that the first point on the map?"

"No," Maria answered. "The second. We know the AIMs aren't likely to be here, but moved past it. We need to gather some more information first, especially from people who've seen them or know of people. This is the most likely place for refugees from the destroyed villages."

He nodded and looked back out the window. There were four programmers on the team, but only one who could stabilize the AIMs. How would Mjahdan know which one was doing the main work, and who was there as support? For some reason, it always seemed to come back to Cam, and constantly being compared to him. Ryan never thought the comparison would cost him his life, and he hoped it never would.

The convoy pulled into the village, staying near the edge. Despite the wars being over, there were still tensions that no one wanted to disturb. Collins gathered the section. "Tylar, you have a report from the recon?"

Cam bit his tongue as he began to make a smart remark back. For the entire ride, he had been forced to stay silent. Granted, it had been a relatively short drive, but he was partially convinced Maria hated him to have put him in the same vehicle as Collins.

"We already know the AIMs haven't been here, but there's been some activity just north of here. When we're finished getting whatever information you soldiers need, we'll head up there. I say we skip the next village and just go straight after the AIMs while we have an idea where they are. Or if there's a plan in place for an intervention, that would be preferred. Having them come to us is a lot easier to deal with, and will be more secure. That much, at least, I know."

"Has there been a visual?"

Once again, he bit his tongue. "Not yet, but-"

"Then we go ahead as planned."

"But there are embers."

Collins turned towards him. "Excuse me?"

"We can't be running after every ember we see," Maria said quickly before Collins could make a move.

Sarah put her arm up slowly. "What exactly is an ember?"

"It's a term we used in Scanning," Maria explained. "Most of our challenges were following markers, or scent trails of a sort. Think of it like this. When you have a fire that goes out, it doesn't die immediately. The flames go down, but then you're left with embers for a while. When you're looking for a scent trail, or in our case rogue AIMs, when they're attacking somewhere it's on fire. Maybe not literally, but it's there. Once they leave, they leave behind embers." She glanced at Cam briefly and bit back a smile when she saw him wink at her. "The problem is that embers last a long time. In our case, we can see the effect of attacks for weeks, sometimes months after the enemy's left. And with something as unpredictable as rogues, we can't be going at full steam ahead at the first sign of an ember. We still need information, and we still need to make up an alternate plan in case the embers turn into forest fires."

McMurphy stepped forward. "But we'll keep them in mind," he said to Cam. "Send out the AIMs again tonight. We'll give them a break tomorrow..It should be easier to track the rogues at night. Heat sensing should be easier."

"No, we talked about this. You even brought it up. The robots don't give off any heat," Cam added. "Not much, anyway. If you think our AIMs can pick something up during recon flights, that's fine, but I'm telling you it's a waste of time and energy. They're not living organisms and don't give off heat."

"But they should give off some sort of short-range electrical signature," Maria countered. "Even in stealth mode, at close enough range our AIMs will be able to pick up something. Once we're in range, however, means we're also close enough for them to attack."

When Cam acknowledged the fact, McMurphy nodded and turned his attention to the rest of the group. "Okay, just so everyone knows, this is a potentially sensitive area. We will be moving in our fireteams, and the civilians will go with their partners. We don't want to start anything while we're visiting.

"And that's exactly what we're doing here: visiting. We're not trying to find connections to Mjahdan, and we're not looking for a fight. We're looking for AIMs. Let's keep that in mind. A.S One, contact us if there's a female you need to speak with. In the meantime, take the east and keep in touch. If we are engaged, we give it back and get out. Let's move."

Cam grabbed Maria before she could move away. "You hate me, don't you?"

She smiled. "You have the privilege of being the top programmer, which means you need to be with the head of the mission. That happens to be Collins."

"You do realize that the rest of my team is in the second assault group?"

Her face fell and she took her arm from his grip. "Which means that we'll be the target, not you," she said seriously, and she watched as realization came across his face.

"Are you serious?"

"Kier, let's move!" McMurphy called out.

She began to walk away. "We'll talk about it later. Just..." She looked around. "Take it in while you can. You're not a soldier. Don't be afraid to be a bit of a tourist right now. You'll never see anything like this again." Maria gave him a small smile before she caught up with Ellis who had grouped up with Ryan and Sarah.

Cam watched as she left. Collins shoved him and he shot him a harsh look. "You make it easy to want to learn how to shoot better, you know?"

"That's the plan," Collins muttered as he let the group around the east part of the village.

He resisted the urge to grumble. He had grown up in the last three years, to the extent that others had commented on his new-found adulthood, despite the fact that he was now twenty-six. Most would still consider that to be a young adult age but with what he had been through, Cam knew that the number had nothing to do with how one acted. He became a father the moment he lost his child, and there wasn't a day that went by where he didn't think of her. He took in a deep breath as he walked beside Collins. He was not a soldier. He was still on his own mission, and technically contracted by the army, but did that mean he had to look at the country through their eyes?

Cam looked around as they walked down the sandy streets. The people hardly seemed to notice them. For the first time, he really paid attention to the conditions people lived in. He had a hard time considering it poverty, but now when he fully looked at the people, he began to appreciate what he had back home. Groups of men milled around at the sides of the street, talking emphatically with their hands in a language that Cam could barely recognize. He barely even learned French in school, and he had absolutely no ear for foreign sounds, nor did he have the desire to develop one. What struck him was the lack of women, anywhere. He thought for a moment and went against his better judgement and looked over at Collins beside him.

"How strict are they with their religion here?" he asked quietly, not knowing if anyone there spoke English. Like they had said before, they didn't need to make the tensions worse.

"It's not just a religion," Collins answered uncharacteristically patient, which unnerved Cam. "It's their culture. This is how it is over here. The women usually stay inside for most of the day unless they need to see someone, or get water. The men are the ones who travel, and buy things, and work. In some villages, I've seen women working the orchards as well, especially if it's family-owned."

"Seems a bit oppressive."

Collins shook his head. "Going outside is a lot of work. They stay covered outside, but in their own home they have more freedom, and safety. Think about the women back home. They go through even more work before they step outside, and when they do, they bring things along with them to make sure they stay looking the same all day. You're going to tell me that's not oppressive?"

"The only women I've seen get ready in the morning don't put that much effort into it, and knew they didn't need to just to look good. But I get where you're going." Cam stopped suddenly when he glanced at the window of one of the white-washed buildings. Collins had been right. A young woman peeked out from the side of the window, her hair showing. But what caught his attention was the bandage across half of her face.

"Hold up," he said and looked around. Cam noticed a group of three men nearby and he pointed in their direction. "Collins, find out who lives in this house."

"Why? What'd you see?"

He motioned with his head towards the window, but the woman had moved away. "A hunch."

Collins paused and eyed Cam. Nothing would ever make then get along, or like each other, but he had been forced to watch the athlete's challenges and he had to agree that he had good instincts. It also was not difficult to see that when the man gave up some of his arrogance, he worked very well on a team, and that was what was important to him at this point. "Give me some distance. We don't need them to think we're challenging them."

Cam watched as the soldier held his hands up, letting his rifle drop from them and slung around his shoulder as he made his way towards the men.

Before Collins reached them, the men turned towards him. *"You are an American soldier?"* the oldest asked.

"Yes, but I'm here with Canadians, as well."

"We don't help soldiers."

That answered the question of where they would sleep for the night. *"We have Canadian civilians with us, as well. We're looking for something very important to give back to your army. We don't want to fight."*

The man looked at his friends briefly, but said nothing to them. There was nothing he could say to them Collins wouldn't understand. *"What are you looking for?"*

"Information. Who lives in that home?"

He suddenly shook his head. *"Our government has no need to be here. You'd be safer if you leave."*

From where Cam stood, the conversation was not going the way it should be. A quick name was all that was needed, but Collins was pulling teeth. He looked down at where his AIM stood next to him. "What are the chances that we could be shot if I changed your form?"

The AIM paused, calculating. "By those men, none, as they do not have any firearms. However, I cannot see through walls and do not know how many are aimed at you currently."

"How stupid would it be to change your form right now?"

"Very."

"Okay then." Cam pulled out his AIRC as he walked towards the Afghan men and Collins. With a press on the touchscreen, his AIM swiftly morphed into the form of a Bengal tiger, which roared dramatically. He rolled his eyes. His AIM tended to be a drama queen, or whatever the robotic version of it was.

The men began to yell at Collins, backing away, and Collins turned on him. "What the hell are you doing?"

"Ask them if anyone's been hurt," Cam said as he stared at the men.

"Get that AIM out of here."

"Ask them!" he yelled.

Collins let out an angry breath and turned back to the men, relaying Cam's question.

Cam switched his AIM into the form of a squirrel and held it in his hands, showing it was under control and able to be dominated. "We're trying to help," he said, knowing the men couldn't understand, but he hoped the tone spoke more than the words.

The men looked at each other, and the one who had moved to the back now stepped forward and spoke to Collins. After a moment, Collins pulled out his AIRC. "Kier, we're going to need you over here. We have a female victim."

Maria stood in front of the house with the group and took off her helmet, quickly replacing it with a headscarf before the men could catch a glimpse of her. "How old is she?"

"Nineteen," Collins answered. "Her parents were killed, and her brother brought her here to live with their uncle. That's all they'd tell me."

"That's plenty. Where's her husband?"

Cam gave her strange look. "She's nineteen."

"Which means she's been of marrying age for about six years. If she's not married, then there's a reason. Either her family loves her and has given her a choice, or they've needed to keep the family secluded. Let's hope it's the first." She stepped to the doorway but stopped when Collins tried to follow her. "You know how this works."

"We're just staying outside the door. That's not breaking any custom."

"But it makes her feel like a prisoner," Maria replied. "Stay at the gate. You'll know if something's wrong." She glanced at Ryan, who had a much better composure than the day before. "In the meantime, Collins, go back around and see if you can find anyone else. Maybe the brother and get his side of things." She looked at Cam. "Be on standby. I'll translate what she says and hopefully it'll give you an idea how the rogues are working."

Maria paused and looked at Collins. "Do you think talking to her is going to have repercussions?"

He sighed and gave a small shrug. "We're going to have to take that chance."

With a nod she stepped into the house.

Maria smiled at the young woman who stood in the front hallway, which was actually part of the front room. She looked around quickly and put a hand on her head. *"Are then any men home?"* The girl shook her head, and Maria removed her scarf. *"My name is Maria."*

"Faizah."

"Faizah, I'm part of the Canadian Army. Do you mind if I ask you a few questions about what happened?" The girl's face scrunched as she attempted to hold back tears, and Maria reached out for her. *"I know it's hard, and I know you're scared. My team and I are trying to find the AIMs that did this to you, and I promise you when we do, we will stop them and make sure it never happens again."*

"They can't be stopped," the woman sobbed. *"They kill everything they see."*

"I know," Maria said soberly. *"They killed my friend in front of me. Faizah, they can be stopped. We have someone with us who has been doing just that for years."* When she began to calm down, Maria put a hand on her arm. *"I need you to tell me what happened. Take as much time as you need."*

The girl nodded but took a moment before she began. *"We heard screams. My father went to the door to check. He sent me and my brother to the roof, but I went back down to see."* She shook her head with disbelief. *"The tiger broke down the door so easily..."*

"There was only one?"

She nodded. *"There were others in the village, but they were crazed, going everywhere."*

"Did you feel like they were hunting you?"

Faizah thought for a moment before she shook her head. *"They were toying with us. It did this to me,"* she pointed to her face. *"Then it left. They were killing, that was all they did."*

Maria nodded and spoke into her radio, relaying to Cam what Faizah had said.

"Ask about how they left, if they all left together like a group or left when each was finished," he responded.

"Faizah, did you see them leave?"

She shook her head. *"My brother took me out of the village right away, hiding from the other tigers."*

"Where is your brother?"

"Working with my uncle."

"Is there anyone else here from your village?"

Faizah shook her head, and Maria took her hands. *"I know you're hurting. I'm so sorry for your loss. We will stop them. I promise you. My team and I will be staying for a few days to try to find out as much as we can about what the AIMs did in this area. If you can think of anything else, or if your brother knows anything, please send him to us."*

"You are very kind for a soldier."

She nodded and patted the woman's shoulder. *"I'm not a soldier right now. I'm a woman who is sharing your pain, and trying to help."*

"I thank you."

Maria replaced the headscarf and left the humble building. She raised her hands to show she was coming of her own accord. She strode straight towards Cam and McMurphy joined them. "I have no idea what the heck is going on. The AIMs aren't working together. They're not even hunting. She has no idea if the rogues left together or not, but it definitely seems they're heading to the same place and just happen to be hitting the same villages on the way."

Cam kept his eyes on the house. "They're starving. Or, they think they're starving. They're trying to hunt but they don't know how." He turned to McMurphy. "Have the others found the brother yet?"

"She said her brother is working with her uncle right now," Maria offered.

Collins added over the radio, "We'll be here for a few days, so we have some time."

Cam shook his head. "We need to find him today. I doubt they'll stay here much longer now that we've been asking questions."

"We'll do what we can," Maria answered. "McMurphy, bring him back to Collins. Ellis and I will continue on."

Cam watched as Maria left with her partner before he followed McMurphy. "You know we should be going after those AIMs as soon as possible. If we don't want any more people to die, you know that's what we have to do."

"But it's not that simple," he replied. "This isn't just about getting the rogues under control. There are more political aspects to this than we anticipated, and now we need to find out what's really motivating the rogues."

"I can tell you: a screwed-up chip, that's what. I know you guys know your military stuff, tactics and all that, and that's great. Good job," Cam said emphatically. "But I know AIMs, and I know rogues. They are going to get more violent, more unpredictable, and it's not going to end well for anyone. If they are being controlled by someone, we need to find that frequency and cut the ties. It'll make it a lot easier for me to do my job in stabilizing the units."

"I appreciate that," McMurphy said sincerely. "But we need to do things a certain way. Yes, people are going to die in the meantime, but going through this means more don't die in the long run. We can't be going into this head-on. I know your M.O and I realize it's what you do best. You get right in there, get it done and you get it done fast. But people's lives are at stake."

"I know."

"Then we need to take time to make sure that we're getting all the information so we don't want into a suicide mission."

Cam slowed his pace. "Isn't that what this already is?"

McMurphy stopped and looked at him finally. "Only if you go in expecting to die. And hopefully you're not, because you know your part of the job goes beyond four rogues."

Four hours later, and after no sign of Faizah's brother, or anyone else able – or willing – to help, the section returned to the vehicles with Maria trailing behind. Collins gathered them around.

"From the response we've received from the people in this village, we'll have to stick to the outskirts while we're staying. We'll set up camp here," Collins said, and with a final nod the soldiers immediately began to unpack equipment from the Humvees in a rehearsed fashion.

Ryan stood back for a moment before joining Filsinger and carried the other end of long poles he assumed would be used for a tent. He had tried to keep an open mind while they were walking around. The interruption of Maria's interrogation had given him a chance to observe their surroundings. He had the chance then to really look around at the buildings. He noticed that only a few of the homes had walls around them with an ornate gate. He assumed those were the wealthier families, but for the most part it seemed to be a preference.

Despite the white-washed walls, Ryan was entertained by the brightly-painted doors in the village. If he had been here under any other circumstances, he saw himself enjoying a visit to the area. Perhaps not Afghanistan with the political and military tensions, but maybe a more stable country such as Jordan. And although he logically knew he would see few camels, he was still disappointed to have not seen any animals other than goats and dogs.

"How many times have you been here, Filsinger?" he asked as they put up a large tent which would turn into their sleeping quarters. There was no room to be discreet anymore. Men and women would be in one, which Ryan didn't think would be a big deal. No one else seemed to mind either.

"I haven't," the soldier answered. "I've been posted in Germany the past two years. That's pretty much the extent of my time overseas."

Ryan pulled down on the canvas tarp, using his body weight to bring it down to the ground on his side. "How was that?"

Filsinger shrugged, but he smiled. "It was actually pretty awesome. The food's great, and it was easy to get home and visit my family. They came once, which was nice." He looked over his shoulder when someone turned on the radio. He laughed when the static cleared and Arabic music filled the camp. "Don't we have enough of that around us?"

"Leave it!" Maria called out. "We need some fun around here right now."

"Are you going to dance for us, Kier?" Ellis asked with a laugh.

"Maybe later, if you behave," she said and gave him a wink.

Ryan turned when Filsinger started to take off his jacket slowly, bouncing to the upbeat tempo of the music. He laughed when the coat was flung off. "Soldier turned stripper takes the stage."

"We prefer the term exotic dancer. And for your information, the tips are amazing," Filsinger said with a laugh and continued to dance. He shimmied over towards Shepero and motioned with his flailing hands for the soldier to join him, which he did with a laugh. Another combat jacket made its way to the ground.

After a few minutes of embarrassing and convulsive dancing, Collins stepped between them. "That's enough. No one wants to see you dancing like that." He grinned and threw off his jacket. "We all know I have the better body." He pushed the two soldiers away and lifted his shirt to cheers from the soldiers. "Oh, but wait," Collins said as he pulled out a piece of paper from his pocket. "What's this? It seems like someone may have a better body than me." He turned the paper around, but Maria knew what was on it before he made the gesture. "You sure you don't want to dance for us, Kier?"

"Not for you."

"I find it hard to believe you chose a uniform over this lovely little outfit," he jeered.

"Cut it out," Cam said, stepping forward finally.

Collins laughed and shrugged. "I'm just curious what made her go from being a swimsuit model to a soldier."

Cam pulled out his AIRC and swiped the screen a few times to show yet another photo. "There are plenty of athletes who pose for their sponsors. If you knew anything about the soldiers you were fighting beside, you'd know that."

He raised an eyebrow and looked around. "She's twenty-six, enlisted for barely three years, and she's already a Lieutenant," he hissed. "Some people work hard to earn their ranks, with their clothes on."

Cam rushed him, throwing his fist against the man's jaw. Collins grabbed his fist before it made contact and threw Cam around him with the momentum. Cam brought Collins down with him and managed to roll on top. Before he could land a swing, he was pulled off by two soldiers. "Let go of me," he growled.

Collins stood up and wiped the dust from his pants. "Yeah, let him go. Let's see what he can do."

"You make a good point, Collins," Maria shouted, turning the attention back to her. She took off her combat jacket and let it fall to the ground. "I made good money. Great money, actually. Better than your pay grade." She slipped off her shirt to show her sports bra which, while not as provocative as what she was used to wearing, still made the point. "I had photoshoots about once a month, and I see those photos still hanging in lockers around bases I travel to. And man were they fun."

She slipped the boots off, hiding the pain she felt when her bare feet hit the hot sand. Her pants came off next and she strode towards Collins. "You want to know how I got my rank?" she whispered to him, standing mere inches from him.

She stepped back suddenly, pointing his own handgun at his face. "Because I have more experience with an AIM than any Canadian soldier my age. Because I've trained harder than a soldier for the three years I was an athlete, in all climates. Because my father trained me to be a soldier from the age of five."

Her eyes narrowed. "And whether I'm in full uniform or wearing only a bikini, I still have better aim than you, and if shooting you wouldn't start an investigation from the American army, you'd already be on the ground. I've been the eye candy. I've been the one hired to a team based on looks rather than my skills. They learned their lesson. You better learn yours." She dropped the clip from his handgun and threw the weapon to the ground.

Cam watched Maria walk back towards her clothes and tug them back on her body. "For the record, Maria," he started. "Ryan was signed mostly for his looks. You at least had more skill than he did."

Maria turned to him and gave him a small appreciative smile before she went back to working on the tent they would use for the night.

McMurphy walked towards Collins who kicked his jacket. "What's your problem? Do you want to get yourself killed out here? Tylar's a civilian, but I'm pretty sure he could beat you any day, and Maria was right about her aim being better."

Collins turned to him quickly. "Maria? Since when are you on a first-name basis with her?"

McMurphy's eyes narrowed and he jabbed his index finger into the soldier's chest. "I'm on a first-name basis with all of them when they need it. Just because you have nothing to go home to, doesn't mean you can make the others feel the same way."

"Thanks for the pep-talk, Cap."

"I mean it," he said harshly. "Ease up. No one wants to be here, so stop acting like you're the only one hurt by these things we're hunting." McMurphy walked away before Collins could respond, and made his way to the centre of the camp area. "Hey guys, can we pull in again for a moment, with our clothes on this time?" He smiled lightly in an attempt to ease the tension.

Whether it worked, he didn't know. He doubted it, but tensions needed to be there, sometimes. "We'll stay just tonight, and head out to the next village tomorrow afternoon. With the rate the search is going, and with some of the information we've gathered so far, we have a few concerns that need to be addressed and shared. Now would be a good time to work with our AIMs, even if it's just one on one, but we need to make sure this team is unbreakable, feelings aside."

McMurphy looked at Maria who glanced away. He continued on. "Once the AIMs are found, we have no idea what Mjahdan plans on doing with them, or if they'll have any further use for the programmers. Our concern..." He paused, and tried to think of a way to speak without creating a panic. "Our concern is that they feel only one programmer is needed, either before or after the AIMs are found. That is why your safety is our top priority, and you can worry about tracking down the rogues," he added quickly. "We doubt it will come to this, but we also want to be prepared for a hostage situation. If they have more plans for their AIMs, they'll want to have access to the people who trained their new AIMs."

"You mean the person," Cam said slowly.

"We get in and out, and we do it quickly," the soldier answered.

Sarah took a hesitant step forward. "So, what you're saying is that we're all targets?"

"Yes. They won't understand the need for us to have four programmers, but I doubt they'll risk it if we do. If anything happens, it'll be after the exchange," McMurphy answered gently. "But we'll be ready for them."

"Seems like they've been staying a few steps ahead of us this entire time," Peter muttered. "We haven't even figured out why the rogues are moving the way they are."

"Actually," Cam said, stepping forward. "Ryan and I were talking, and their actions make sense. I don't think they're being controlled. From what the girl was telling Ma... Kier, the rogues aren't working together. Tigers are extremely territorial, and use exclusive hunting areas. If they're too close together, they go into a bit of a craze. Think of an angry, lonely man, who instead of lashing out at the person making him angry, he throws his anger at anyone close by." He shot a look at Collins before he continued. "They're in a craze, and instead of hunting, they kill everything around so the other tigers can't get to it first and have it as food. Then it moves on."

"The problem is that the tigers that were scanned are mostly domestic, and only know how to be around other tigers when they're not hunting," Ryan continued for Cam. "Which explains why they're travelling together. We know now they're not being controlled because they're fully rogue, which actually makes our job harder. If they were being controlled, even slightly, we'd be able to try to hack their AIRCs and disconnect them, making them easier to find and stabilize. Our earlier thought of them having residual programming seems to be panning out, but they don't seem to be using that when they attack which we can consider some form of blessing. Dealing with an animal, albeit starved and angry, is still better than a starved and angry robot with military training."

"We also know they're not even partially sentient because they're killing people," Cam said, taking back his turn.

"Isn't sentient the same thing?" Collins asked with a snarky tone.

Cam looked down at his AIM and grinned. He held his hands forward as if giving up the stage, and the AIM walked forward.

"A rogue AIM," it started, "is not hindered by the laws of robotics. However, a sentient AIM, you arrogant piece of flesh, is unfortunately limited to respecting humans. Physically, only. You have no intellectual, or emotional respect from me."

Collins, and the rest of the section, looked down at Cam's AIM with eyes wide. "What did you just say to me?"

The AIM looked back at Cam. "Must I repeat what I said, or will he understand the insult soon?"

"What the hell are you getting your AIM to say," Collins growled to Cam, who simply laughed.

"If I could control what he says, I'd have had a much better childhood," Cam said happily.

"Cameron has, in the past, attempted to control my speech patterns, but my sentience allows me to ignore him," the AIM continued. "And for the record, your treatment of your fellow soldiers is severely lacking. I understand why you were passed on your last promotion."

Collins looked at McMurphy quickly, anger blaring in his eyes.

"Your partner did not need to say anything," the AIM explained. "I have access to all military personnel records, which includes all misdemeanours. The records are not very secure, despite what your government believes. They are only lucky that there is no other sentient AI with my capabilities. And I will tell you now that the rogues will be the least of your concerns if you repeat any of those misdemeanours against anyone here."

"That's enough," Maria said. "I think he understands the difference now. Give him a break. He's learned a lot today." She glanced at Collins before she addressed the group. "Tomorrow, we need to find the brother, and I'd like to hear what the uncle has to say, as well. See if anyone else in the village took in someone from the attack site, then we'll move on. Let's just get through the night. Cam, Ryan, why don't you guys go through some exercises with everyone and their AIM. Get them working together. We need to rely on them as much as each other."

*　　　*　　　*

Ryan grimaced as he took his portion of dinner from Strong. Rather than an open flame, they had been able to cook over a mini stovetop, but Ryan was more than sure that it wouldn't make the food taste any better. He took a second plate and walked to where Collins sat at the edge of the camp. He sat down beside him and handed him the plate. "I talked them into putting extra salt on it in the hopes of making it taste like something."

Collins hesitated before he took the plate. "Here I was trying to watch my sodium intake." He looked at Ryan and watched him take the first few terrible bites. "Thanks."

Ryan offered a bit of the 'meat' to his AIM to sniff, and it immediately turned away from the offering. "Don't thank me," he muttered. "Really."

He laughed and began to eat. He held back a grimace. As bland as it was, Collins was used to the food. Fifteen years in service had given him the army palate. After so long, he had thought he had seen it all. He swore under his breath and threw his plate down.

"I told you not to thank me." When the soldier didn't respond, Ryan went back to his meal. "You're a lot like Cam. It's probably why you guys hate each other."

"The pep-talks have been great today," Collins muttered.

"He's not a bad guy. I wouldn't hate to be compared to him, not in the positive at least. He has a pretty tough shell to get through, but he's a good guy." Ryan waited for some form of reaction. Without one, he continued. "I'm sorry about your men. But harassing the people on your side isn't going to bring them back, or find the rogues any faster. And you can't be blaming other soldiers for their quick rank promotions just because you were passed over."

"Anything else?"

Ryan thought for a moment. "Cam's AIM freaks me out."

Collins let out a laugh. "Seriously! What the hell was that about?"

"I mean, it's cool, but it's almost like a person, listening. And it never sleeps, so it sees and hears everything." Ryan thought back, and realized something for the first time. He groaned, and covered his face.

"What's your problem?"

"It's not like Cam's always been single. It'd be like having someone watch you...all the time, everywhere, with everyone."

"I don't see the issue."

Ryan paused. "No, you probably wouldn't."

Cam whooped in triumph as his AIM landed gracefully from its dive. He grinned and turned to Ellis. "That's how it's done."

Ellis shook his head as he scrolled through the options on his AIRC. His own AIM had defaulted as it attempted the same maneuver. He chose the Barbary falcon scan and watched the opaque gel vibrate back into the bird. It ruffled its feathers as though filling out the skin before it hopped and flew up to the soldier. "You have to show me how you got it to dive like that."

He nodded and his AIM flew up once more. "I've trained him with other bird of prey scans, so we've done things similar to this in competitions back home. It's more acclimation than anything, getting them to do it over and over again. It's like a human fighter pilot, basically. Do enough G's and you're going to pass out. But get enough training and you can probably push through it until the pressure stops. Have your AIM work its way up to that speed, dive at a small angle and then increase it each time along with the height."

After a while, Shepero joined them, watching at first but then finally spoke up. "Is this actually helping? Doing the same thing over and over? How is a dive going to help us later?"

Cam smiled as Ellis' AIM did the dive perfectly alongside his own. "It's not just about the dive. The AIMs, they were synced. They worked off each other's signals, so now when they need to do something a bit more challenging, like perhaps distracting an angry Bengal tiger, they can do it with little commands from us. Their computer brains work faster than our measly human ones. They'll see the shifts in the rogues better than we will, minute shifts that could be the difference between life and death."

Shepero nodded and after a moment he pulled out his AIRC. "So, how do I do that dive?"

* * *

Sarah sat down on the cot next to Maria's and waited until it seemed to be a good time to speak. She was rubbing her feet with her eyes closed, and didn't want to startle her. "I can't believe you stripped down. I don't know if that's a step forward or back for feminism."

"It was a step back for my feet," Maria muttered.

She laughed. "You could've left your boots on."

"What, and mess with the ensemble?" Maria replied with a smile, finally opening her eyes.

"Collins is a jerk."

She shrugged. "He doesn't even know how to have fun normally anymore. I get that he's been through a lot in the army, but it's like he's never worked with a female soldier before."

"He hasn't."

Maria spun around on her cot as McMurphy walked in. "Seriously?"

"Not directly, at least. And not one younger than him." He smiled and looked around. He switched his bag with one already on a nearby cot and lay down. "You're a threat to him. Doesn't help that you look, and act, like his ex."

"Yeah well, he acts like mine."

McMurphy laughed. "They are so similar, I wonder if they even see it."

"Cam would kill us if we mentioned it to him," Maria said with a giggle. "They're both impossible. Literally impossible."

Sarah looked between the two. "He knows you used to date Cam?"

Maria nodded. "He figured there was something. So, he knows, my guys know, and Hanks does too. We used to date," she said pointedly. "End of story."

"You know, my wife used to belly dance. She was good."

She laughed and threw her dirty sock at his face. "I'm not dancing for you either, Kyle."

He screamed girlishly as the women laughed at him. "Oh, why not? I have two beautiful women here, and neither are going to dance?"

"Careful, McMurphy," she warned. "In a uniform, there are no genders."

He groaned. "You sound like the training videos."

"There are no races, or religions," she continued in a sing-song voice. "We are one body, under one oath to protect our nation. God bless America!" She finished with a dramatic salute.

"You're Canadian."

"Don't you people think it's the same thing?" She laughed.

"Obviously not. Only one can be the best country in the world."

"Ah yes, that. And again I say, God bless America."

CHAPTER 13

"Okay guys, let's finish this village and get moving by the afternoon," McMurphy called out as the section walked back into the village the next morning. He turned when Shepero caught up with him. "What, you don't want to work with Collins, now? Looks like he's scaring people away left and right."

"Just wanted to check in. Don't worry, I'm going, I'm going," Shepero muttered as Strong laughed at his back.

Strong held his gun firmly in his hands as they walked up the main street of the village. "Think they'll have left? The family from yesterday?"

He shrugged. "I guess we'll find out. I can't see them leaving, not when they have nowhere to go." When they came up to a crowd around Faizah's home, they stopped. McMurphy swore and called through his radio. "Keep the civilians away from the main street." He sighed. "And you don't need to ask about the brother, or the uncle. They're not talking." He swore again as he looked back at Faizah's body hanging by a rope around her neck attached to the top of the wall. "We'll take an hour, and then move on," he muttered as they continued on. No one was safe.

Shepero turned back to where he had left McMurphy and swore. He held it in, as usual. He couldn't show his hatred towards the people who killed the innocent young woman. He couldn't yell or scream at the people who simply stared at her body without even the thought of taking it down. He had to be culturally sensitive when it came to honour killings, so he couldn't even condemn the family for having absolutely no respect for a living human being, let alone their own blood relative. There was no way he could show just how glad he was to have a daughter who knew he loved her, and was willing to die for her honour rather than kill her for his own.

He had been able to separate work from his personal life for the longest time. When he was with his soldiers, he was a soldier first and foremost. When he was home, his main priority was his family. Shepero spoke differently with his soldiers than with his family, because they knew him as different people. But as he watched his daughter grow into the beautiful teenager she was, or pre-teen even though she hated the term, it was getting harder and harder for him to make jokes with the guys.

All he could think about was how he would want men to look at his daughter, how he would want them to treat her. And although he hadn't worked with her before, he respected Maria for her work in the Canadian Scanning Tournament, and even more now that she was a soldier. It meant so much to his daughter that Maria had joined the Canadian Armed Forces. It showed her that working hard can get you anywhere you wanted, no matter your background or gender.

He had never hidden the fact that athletes posed for their sponsors, and while he had to admit that Maria's photos always tended to be more on the provocative side, especially those with Cam, Shepero had let his daughter know about that side of the athletic world. What Cam had said had been true. Most models at that time were retired athletes, or athletes modelling on the side during the off-season. Athletic and toned were the new anorexic. Shepero had, however, made sure his daughter knew when it was, and wasn't, appropriate to wear what Maria had in her photos. And of course the when it wasn't appropriate was any time before his daughter turned forty. He smiled at the thought. She hadn't argued, yet.

"Captain," Ellis' voice came over the radio. "We should head out as soon as possible. It's starting to look like a riot starting. They're not a fan of us being here, it seems."

McMurphy looked around and finally noticed the anger-filled stares, and the small groups of men standing along the edge of the street. "They think we did it, or convinced her to do it. My guess is that the brother and uncle are long gone," he said to Strong. "Collins," he spoke into his radio. "What's the temp in your area?"

"Gettin' pretty hot over here," he returned. "Kier?"

"Looks good over here, for the moment. But it's not a bad idea to leave while we can," Maria responded. She was surprised, actually, that no one had targeted her yet. She had been the one to speak to Faizah. If anyone was to blame, it was her. But it had been obvious that she wasn't in charge. It was the men, and they would be the ones who would be punished, if the villagers got the chance.

"What's going on?" Ryan asked her.

"Most people here don't like soldiers. Even Canadian soldiers."

"But the girl you spoke to, shouldn't that have made things better? If she was safe, so are they kind of thing?"

"Faizah's dead," she said simply, and immediately regretted it.

"Which explains why he didn't want us around there," he said softly. "I'm sure I've seen worse than whatever happened to her."

"That's the spirit," she said with a small smile.

He didn't return the smile, but kept walking, picking up speed while they passed another group of people on the streets. "What are we even looking for?"

"It seems we've already found it," Ellis said.

Ryan glanced around. "What?"

"Help," he explained. "And any suspicious activity. We found both. Faizah was willing to help, and because of that, she was killed. And now no one seems to want us around. If that's not suspicious, I don't know what is."

"I don't get it," Ryan said. "Why wouldn't they just tell us everything they know about the rogues, if they've seen anything or not?"

"Most may not realize they're AIMs, since they thought AIMs can't hurt people. And who's going to believe we're looking for real tigers? They think we're hiding something. And if we're looking for AIMs owned by an Afghan militia, they're likely thinking we're going to start another war."

He nodded in understanding. “A no-win situation.”

“Exactly.”

Maria stopped suddenly and stared at the side of a wall covered with graffiti. One word in Arabic stood out to her. Her heart stopped. Suddenly she was back in Niagara Falls, falling down the side of the cliff. In an instant, her blood began to boil, but she pushed down the fear and seething rage starting to surface.

She pulled out her AIRC and took a photo of it. “Hey Collins, can you take a look at this and tell me what you think?” she called through the radio. After a brief second, the man swore through the static.

“Guys, we’re heading out now,” Collins called out. “Hanks, Filsinger, get there first and check out each vehicle. Make sure nothing’s been tampered with while we’ve been gone.”

Maria tugged on Ryan’s sleeve. “Let’s go.”

He pointed at the markings on the wall. “What does it say?”

“I said let’s go,” she hissed, pulling him away as she began to job back to where they had left the Humvees. She glanced over her shoulder at Ryan behind her, and Ellis right him.

Scanner.

They were being watched. But which one? “Tylar, Strong, send out your AIMs on intense recon in a fifty-kilometre sweep. I want to know about every single living thing they see, even if it’s a single ant. I want to know, and I want it done in the next hour.”

“Yes, ma’am,” came the response from both.

She looked up to see two falcons take to the sky, and she sent hers up with them. If they didn’t find the rogues, they would find the people watching them. At least they’d get a shot at one.

The section gathered a few minutes later back around the vehicles, as Hanks and Filsinger finished their inspection.

“All clear,” Hanks called out.

Collins nodded and took a few steps back, forcing the rest of them away. “Here goes.” He tapped an area on his AIRC and each vehicle roared to life safely. “Okay, let’s move. We’ll spend tonight at the next village and make our way out of it tomorrow evening. We can’t be risking this anymore.”

"And we don't accept invitations, either," McMurphy added. "We can't risk an ambush in the middle of the night. Any conversations we need to have with them, we make it out in public, that goes for you too, Kier."

"Yes, sir," she replied and pushed Ryan into the first Humvee of the convoy. She followed close behind as Strong and Hanks got into the front. "Tylar, any report yet?"

"It's only been five minutes."

"And I've seen a flock of birds fly overhead without a report."

"There was a flock of birds sighted."

"Knock it off," she growled into the radio. "I meant it when I said absolutely everything. We need to know if anything is out of place or startled. Animals will lead us to humans. You of all people should know that."

"I do," he replied.

"Then do what I asked."

Hanks turned around in his seat with a grin. "You guys used to date, right? You and Tylar?"

"Yeah."

"You guys trying the whole, 'let's be friends!' deal?" he asked in a sweet voice, laughing at the end. "We all know how that's going to end."

"At this rate, it'll end up with one of us dead."

"Exes can't be friends," Strong added. "They either part ways, or end up back together."

Maria glanced at Ryan quickly, but his face remained blank, too stoic for her liking. "Believe me, neither will happen. What's the report from your AIM?"

"There's some activity just south of the village we left," he answered professionally. Hanks was right, though. It had to be one of the two options, but in this case, with Maria, there were a few more variables. And he knew Maria would tell him once more to keep his eyes on the road and stay out of her personal life, but they needed something to keep them entertained. It was all they had out there in the desert: each other.

"Human activity?"

"They're checking it out, as far as I know. Looks like animals, but they could be AIMs. Ours are too far away to get a signal if they are in fact AIMs."

"Alright, keep on them, then. And since you two seem to be so interested in my personal life, I think it's only fair I show the same interest in you." Maria smiled sweetly and placed her hands on the sides of her face. "Hanks, tell us about yourself, other than how strapping you are."

He laughed and fluttered his eyelashes. "You flatter me." He shrugged and looked out the windshield. "Not much to know."

"When'd you enlist?"

"Ten years ago. Managed to steer clear of the wars, though, since they were just ending around there." He paused. "My brother was a marine. He died just at the end of the last war."

"I'm sorry," she commented.

He nodded before continuing. "We enlisted together, but he was always trying to get into the rougher side of the things, so obviously he had to be a Marine. He was a good one, too. But the Army suited me just fine. Worked my way up, specialized in distance shooting."

"I hear you're pretty good," Maria said. "I looked through your file. Won a few competitions, too."

"I know, I know. I'm very impressive." Hanks shifted in his seat and puffed out his chest. "And ever so important."

"Yes, you are," she laughed. "You're keeping us alive, which means you're my best friend."

"I'm not braiding your hair."

"It's too short to braid anyway."

He paused and gave her a grin. "So, best friend, huh?"

She rolled her eyes. "Don't make me confuse you with Collins."

"I keep hearing from women that a man in uniform is apparently extremely sexy," Strong chimed in. "But honestly, a woman in uniform does it for me. Maybe a skimpy one, but I'd take that over a bikini any day. At least until it came off. No offense, Kier. Sure, that was a hot picture, but a woman who can handle a weapon is pretty good too."

"We're still supposed to be hearing about Hanks," Maria muttered. "Cam modelled too, and I don't hear anything about that."

Ryan looked at Maria finally, his face still blank. "You know, I think I'm the only person in the world who's never seen any of these photos."

"What, you mean Kier didn't have them plastered all over her walls at home?" Strong asked.

Maria groaned. "I'll show you when we get home."

"Or Collins could show him. I guess he has a pile of them."

She groaned again. "Strong, can I give you a sub-mission?"

"Take back the photos he's likely using on himself?"

"I will shoot you. You know that, right?"

"Not while I'm driving you won't."

She grumbled under her breath. "As soon as you stop, then."

Two hours later, the section piled out from their convoy and assessed the area. Cam stood back as the soldiers did their initial observations. From the lack of farms around the border of the village, Cam concluded that this village was not as well-off as the first. Looking around, he noticed that windows were boarded up, and no one was idling around on the streets like last time. No children playing either. It was a village filled with scared people. And scared people meant they had seen, or heard, something. He stepped over towards Ellis. "Are we going to have to knock on doors?"

"Most likely, yeah," the soldier answered. "At least we know something happened here. Maybe they'll be a bit more willing to talk."

"And what if they're not scared from rogues, but from Mjahdan?"

He shrugged. "Either way, they have information we want and need."

Cam nodded in acknowledgement and he looked at Sarah. He had barely spoken to the other two programmers. There really hadn't been much to say, to anyone, outside of business talk. "How're you holding up?" he asked her. He hadn't needed to talk to her to see her fear when she kept so close to the soldiers.

"Same as any civilian would," she answered. She gave him a harsh look suddenly. "And don't ask that like you're not having a difficult time out here, either. You're not a soldier, Cam."

"I hadn't noticed."

"I was starting to think that."

He shot her a glare before taking a step back, allowing her to resume her closeness with her soldier partner. He had tried to keep everything so separate. He wasn't a Scanner out here. No, he wasn't a soldier, but he was on a military mission, and he needed to force himself to be in that mindset. Some people were better at it than others. He had hoped he wasn't part of the latter group.

McMurphy rounded up the section. "Same as before. We move in fireteams. We don't go into any houses. Any conversations we have, we have on the front step or out on the street. We keep our eyes open the entire time, and on each other. Any conversations with females will have to be around males, unfortunately, Kier, so do what you can. What happened with the recon?"

"There was a group of insurgents found," Maria reported. "Seems like they were part of their own scouting group, probably more concerned with the other guys watching us than anything. I kept Strong's AIM following to see if they'd lead us anywhere. They began moving north, like us, so we'll see what happens with that."

"Any concerns?"

"Not overly. We'll keep an eye on them. If they're watching us, might as well keep them entertained. Collins, maybe you could share some of the copies of my photos with them. I hear you have quite a few."

Collins stared at her. "I'm not one to share."

"Don't want your hand getting sore."

He shot her a smirk. "I can show you sore, if you'd like."

"I doubt that."

"Is that a challenge?"

McMurphy pushed Collins towards the village. "All of you, get moving. I didn't think I'd have to say this, but no one will be showing anyone anything."

"I don't know if this is important or not," Peter spoke. "But does anyone think it matters that there are big tire tracks going down the street?"

The soldiers looked, and he was right. Large truck tire tracks went down the main part of the street. From where they stood, they couldn't see where they led.

"We'll see what's going on first," McMurphy said. "Then split off."

The group remained silent and followed the captain down the street. Ryan and the rest of the civilians walked in the middle of the group, surrounded by the soldiers who formed a barrier between them and whatever was out there waiting for them. He suddenly felt comforted by the rifle he held in his hands. He heard voices from somewhere ahead, and his grip tightened. He looked around and saw the tension on the faces of the soldiers turn into confusion. Soon, Ryan understood why. He heard English words.

They turned a corner and saw the source of the voices, and tire tracks. A Red Cross tent was set up, and various volunteers skittered about carrying supplies from trucks to tables set up inside the tent.

"What the hell is this?" McMurphy said and turned to Shepero. "Did you hear anything about this?"

"Not a word," he answered. "What the hell are they doing here?"

"The West knows," Cam said simply.

"What are you talking about?" McMurphy asked.

Then it hit Maria. "The villages are getting support because of the attacks. Shepero, contact Kandahar, and back home. We need to know exactly what's being put out in the media." She looked around and found Cam's AIM. "Check the internet. I want every mention of the rogue attacks taken down, and keep monitoring it."

"Already started," it answered.

"Shepero," McMurphy added. "There's a film crew. Come with me. Collins, Kier, find out what the hell is going on and shut it down. Keep the civilians away from the cameras." He began to walk with Shepero but stopped briefly and swore as the cameras turned towards them. He looked over his shoulder and stared at

Maria for a moment. He glanced at Ryan and Cam before turning back to her. "On second thought, if we can't get rid of them, can we exploit the situation we have with you?"

Maria paused before realizing what he was asking. "Yeah, but people back home aren't going to be happy about it."

"Then spin it in a way that works best for them."

She grinned. She could do that. And if she couldn't, then Cam certainly could. "We'll go talk to them first," she said as the crew got closer. "Come on," she said to the others. She kept herself between the cameras and the civilians as she and Collins led them around to the tent.

Collins grabbed a volunteer who was nearly jogging with supplies. "Who's in charge?" He let the man go when he pointed to another man holding a tablet and examining piles of clothing. "Kier, come with me. The rest of you make sure the cameras don't get a good look at you." The two strode towards the tablet man. "What the hell is this?"

"What does it look like?" The man asked without a pause in his work.

"It looks like what's going to ruin our mission. How was this even approved and set up so quickly for just a few rural villages? There's no way you got approval for a joint peace support operation. You think you're helping people but you're just putting a target on their backs."

"Look, I'm just doing what I'm told."

"Then I guess you want more people to die."

The man looked up at Collins with an unimpressed look. "You're the ones with the guns, not us."

"You don't need guns to kill people," Maria added.

He sighed and set the tablet on the table. "Look, we heard there were people in the area who needed help after some attack, so we came. I don't see how that's ruining your mission. Maybe if there wasn't an attack in the first place, we wouldn't be in this situation."

"And the film crew?" She asked.

"Documentary on the 'secret war' going on in Afghanistan."

Maria groaned. "Next you'll be telling me there are AI rights activists here, too."

"What kind of attack do you think there was?" Collins asked as he stepped closer towards the man.

"We've heard a few things. Gas, bomb."

"Have you seen any victims?"

"None living."

"Do they look like they've been gassed, or bombed?" When the man didn't respond, he rolled his eyes. "Didn't think so."

"Do you know what happened the last time people found out about attacks of this nature?" Maria asked, stepping towards the man as Collins had.

That seemed to pique the man's interest. "There have been attacks like this before?"

"Two years ago. Do you know what happened to the people who knew the true cause of them?"

"You silenced them, I'm assuming."

"They were silenced by someone much worse than you could imagine. If this becomes known in the Western world, this person doesn't really care how many people have to die, just that they do. Do you really want to be part of spreading the word about something that will cause someone's death?"

The man paused for a moment. "And what exactly is your role in all of this?"

"We're ending the war. And we're stopping the S.O.Bs that are responsible. But we can't do that with this kind of activity going on. We're trying to draw as little attention to this area as possible," Maria explained. "Which means getting rid of the camera crew, and shutting down. Help the people you've seen here, but then you guys have to go. Tell your superiors whatever you want, but make sure more people don't get drawn into this than need be."

He looked at the camera crew which McMurphy and Shepero were attempting to speak with. "It's not like I can really control what they're doing. We agreed to let them film us, but they'd just look for something else if we don't let them continue."

Maria grinned. "I have something else for them. Can you get this shut down by the evening?" When he nodded, she returned it. "Good." She turned around and walked back to the civilians. "Cam, Ryan, come with me."

"What's going on?" Ryan asked.

She gave him a big smile. She took her helmet off and carried it under her arm. "We're going to give you guys a chance to boost the fanbase of Revolution."

Cam watched the camera crew for a moment, and he laughed. "This is gonna be good."

"Cam, can you give us a good enough show?" she asked.

"Do you even have to ask?"

She laughed with a shake of her head. "I guess not." She stopped when she reached McMurphy and Shepero, who were trying to cover the cameras. "Captain, I have something they may want to see."

McMurphy turned and gave her a small smile after a moment. He hid it quickly. "These guys are more interested in conspiracy theories than sports. I don't think they're going to talk to two athletes. Canadian athletes, no less. No offense, Cam."

The filmmakers suddenly turned towards the three. "Canadian athletes, in Afghanistan?" one asked. "Are you here with the charity workers? How did we miss you guys?"

Cam shook his head. "No, we're here with the military actually. But you guys probably don't even follow the CST. It was a good idea, Maria, but they're not interested."

The shorter man stepped forward, wagging his finger at them. "Wait, you guys look familiar. You said you're in the CST?"

"Yeah," Cam answered. "Ryan and I are on Revolution. Maria used to be with us as well, but she's in the Canadian Armed Forces now."

The short man swore. "You're Cam Tylar! What the hell are you guys doing in Afghanistan?"

"I got these guys to come for some extreme training," Maria answered with a smile. "I'll most likely be getting back into Scanning once my service is over, and I've learned a lot during my time as a soldier that I wanted to share with them."

"Wait, wait a minute," the first man said quickly as aimed the camera at them. "Can we do an interview with you guys?"

Cam looked at McMurphy and shrugged before answering. "Look, I love a good interview, believe me. But we're kind of here on the kindness of these soldiers. I don't know how an interview is going to affect their safety."

"Is there something they need to be afraid of, Captain?" The man asked McMurphy, likely still hoping to find out more about whatever conspiracy theory he believed in.

"The wars have been over for a while, but there are always going to be some people trying to cause trouble. We've been trying to make sure Cam and Ryan are safe by making them blend in. If Afghan people see us escorting civilians, our concern is that they'll believe we're taking hostages." McMurphy paused for a moment. "But it'd be nice to share our partnership with the CST to the people back home."

"So, the interview's fine?"

"I don't see why not. Just don't say our location."

The man grinned and looked around. "Great! How about around one of the relief tents?"

Maria shook her head. "We don't want to take away from what they're doing. Besides, we're not really involved with them right now." She glanced around. "Why not around our vehicles? Gives it a more military feel, and it gives us space to showcase the AIMs as well."

The three waited as the team set up their cameras around them, adjusting for the light. The soldiers milled around, somewhat interested in what was going on. Collins had a hard time understanding how this would make the situation any better, but even he had to admit that as long as word about the rogues didn't make it to the West, he didn't care what was filmed.

"I'm Phil, by the way," the short man introduced himself. "This is Stefan." He pointed to his film partner, who waved. "Ready? Okay." He paused until the red light came on above the camera. "Stefan and I came out to Afghanistan to see what it's really like for ourselves. We wanted to see the effects of the secret war on the civilians, but we found something very different, and very unexpected. We found two Canadian Scanning Tournament athletes, reunited with an ex-team-mate now in the Canadian Armed Forces."

He turned to the trio. "Cam Tylar, Ryan Hampton, and Lieutenant Maria Kier of Revolution. No offense to you guys, I'll get to you, but Maria, you haven't done an interview in three years. We have a lot of catching up to do."

She smiled politely. "I don't know about that. Depends how much you follow the CST."

Phil laughed. "I'll admit I'm a bandwagon guy. I follow the top teams."

"Which means you follow Revolution."

He laughed again. "Along with others. I'm sure you know what we're all dying to ask you."

"Yes, the gun is real."

"You were a Scanner," he continued without flinching. "And now you're a soldier. Explain how that even happened."

Maria smiled politely once more. "My father was a career soldier up until the day he died. I was in cadets until my final year of high school, and I only quit that when I was signed onto Revolution. I was only Scanning a year before I went pro, which most people don't know unless they look at my really old stats. So going back to the military lifestyle was a natural progression."

"It came at a good time then. I remember the comeback interview Cam did, and talked about your daughter."

She glanced at the soldiers and watched their faces. "It helped to have a clean break, yes. But I knew I would enlist at some point. Scanning gave me direction. It helped me figure out what my specialization would be. So now I work as an AIM Operations Technician. Which is how I ended up in Afghanistan. Every soldier has an AIM as a partner, so I travel to various bases and inspect them, put them through a few training situations, and basically use all the skills I acquired during my time with these guys." Maria looked at her team-mates with a fond smile. "And for some reason I dragged them both out here with me."

"So, okay, one of you explain what you guys are doing out here," Phil said.

Cam and Ryan looked at each other. Cam shrugged and answered the question. "The Army is giving us the opportunity to go through the ultimate training. We were given military scans for our AIMs to use to train them. And we were put through a pretty good training too."

Phil laughed. "They're treating you like soldiers."

"We had to," Maria answered. "We needed to make sure they'd be physically and mentally fit to go out on patrols with us. But these guys are top athletes. They passed the training with flying colours with scores even higher than some of the soldiers with us."

"To be a top team," Ryan said, finally finding his voice. "We have to be in top shape. We go through some pretty tough training at home year-round, so this was really just another day at work for us."

"You're saying anyone as long as they're athletic can go through military training."

"I said we're a top team," Ryan corrected in a tone Maria and Cam hadn't heard before. "And we went through a crash course of their basic training. What these guys do every day for their country is amazing, and I have the utmost respect for them, and Maria."

"Well, that's a nice sentiment, Ryan," Phil noted. "I'm sure it's strange for you two to see her in this element, but I hope it's been helping you with getting ready for the coming season."

Ryan nodded. "It definitely has. Being here has shown me, as I can't speak for Cam, the full extent to which I can use my AIM. When I first got here, I was training my AIM to be in desert climate in the form of a penguin." He laughed. "It was a pretty amusing sight, but being here in such a different atmosphere and environment is getting us both prepared, human and AIM, to make it to the top. We've been so close for so long, and I know this advantage is going to put us up to the level we want and deserve to be at."

"And Maria, how is it working with these two again?"

She grinned. "Are you kidding? I get to boss them around, and for once, Cam can't complain about it."

Phil laughed. "I'm sure he's been trying."

"Well, that goes without saying," she joked. "But in all honesty, it's been really nice. I've missed scanning with them, and being competitive on that level."

Phil nodded and looked around. "So, we have a nice open space here. Could you guys show us some things you've been training your AIMs with? If you're allowed to show us."

Cam grinned. "Normally we don't show people how we train. Athletes have to have some training secrets. But we could show you a few things. I'm actually pretty excited about the scans we're able to use. I'm sure Maria could give you a better idea about what's used, but the military typically uses scans of German shepherds. They're the same used for police K-9 units, but the training uploaded into the AIRC is a bit different to suit the situation, which is obvious." He pulled out his AIRC and flipped through a few screens before he chose the canine scan for his AIM.

"Most of the time we keep it in this form," he explained. "We've been trying to be as discreet as possible, and we don't necessarily want to draw attention to ourselves while we're here. We want to observe as much as possible. We're here because the soldiers are allowing it, so we're trying to respect that. And before you make any jokes, I'm trying to stay out of the way and keep my mouth shut. Which, yes, is very difficult for me."

He grinned when the others laughed. "Okay, so this is the basic form. It's not a huge change from what we're used to. We have other canine scans, so working with this one isn't so different. It's more the capabilities and the stats which, quite honestly, I'm jealous of. I wish I could use this scan in the tournament, but obviously I can't."

Ryan pulled out his AIRC and changed his AIM into the falcon. "They've shown us how to do a mock reconnaissance flight, so we have this scan of a Barbary falcon." He held out his fist and his AIM landed on it gently. "It's smaller than a peregrine falcon from back home, and a bit slower, but it's native to this region so it's built for this climate and weather.

"What Cam and I have been able to do is have our AIMs work together in these forms, looking for markers we've placed at specific coordinates. Much like a military exercise, but it's also very similar to many of the challenges we'll compete in during the duration of the tournament. Most of the time it's not just about how well Cam and I work together, or with Rick and Owen, but how our AIMs work together as well. They need to know to rely on each other's signals, and flight patterns," Ryan explained.

"They also need to watch for the slightest difference in activity," Cam continued. "That way, they work off each other. It's like if Ryan and I were sprinting to a finish line. I notice Ryan stumble slightly. I change how I run to accommodate for him. I need to be paying attention to if I need to offer myself as a crutch, or just to run slower in case he does end up needing more assistance. Most of the time, our AIMs do this automatically. But there's always room for improvement, and there's always another strategy we can use."

The filmmakers stayed with the three for a while longer, recording their AIMs as they shifted into various scans, and watched a mock training session. Satisfied they had thoroughly entertained the directors, the three re-joined the section as the filmmakers began to pack up their equipment.

McMurphy smiled. "Well, you got rid of them. At least the relief workers are doing something useful."

"I'd be interested to see how many people come looking for help," Maria wondered. "This might be good, actually. We wouldn't be as harsh looking if we're around people helping them."

"*We're* helping them," Collins snapped. "They have bandages, and splints. We're the ones getting rid of the source."

"And in the meantime," Cam started, stepping forward, "they're cleaning up your mess."

"My mess?"

"Cam," Maria warned harshly.

"When those AIMs were killing people, what were you doing?" Cam asked, ignoring Maria. "In the video footage I saw, I didn't see you fighting any of the AIMs or trying to get them under control."

Collins stepped up to Cam and looked him straight in the eyes. "You think I ran away?"

"You hid," he answered. "You hid while your men died."

McMurphy pulled the two apart. "It's called re-grouping. It's not like we've seen rogues before."

"Neither had Maria, but she shot the rogue she saw until it defaulted. You work with AIMs as part of your job. You should know how to default it or destroy it so the enemy can't get to it," Cam replied, still staring at Collins.

Maria sidled towards Ryan. "If this is how Cam and I were during your first season, I understand why we sucked during challenges," she whispered, to which he gave a small grin.

"The minute this mission is over, you watch your back," Collins growled at Cam. "You hear me?"

"Collins," McMurphy snapped. "That's enough. Do you hear me, Major?"

"McMurphy," Ellis called out. "More refugees."

The captain looked around and there were, in fact, a few people coming to see what was going on. Some were being immediately escorted to the medical section of the tent. "Let's check it out, but keep everything light. We'll get a better response if it looks like we're working with them. People have a hard time believing soldiers want to help unless there's something humanitarian going on."

Maria walked with Ryan, Sarah, and Ellis towards the tent. Their rifles were held gently in a relaxed position in an attempt to not look so intimidating. They walked around table, watching as people attempted to translate their problems from Pashto to English. She stopped suddenly, waved the other two to keep going, and stopped a young woman as she attempted to pass by. "This is going to sound like a strange question, but do you have any...feminine kits?"

The woman smiled lightly. "Didn't come prepared?"

Maria laughed. "No, not for me. I'm the only female soldier in this section, and I speak Pashto, so when there's a female we need to speak with, that's me. There are times they need things, from hygienic to tests. They can't buy them anywhere around here, and if they can, there's no way they can dispose of them, especially the tests, without being found out."

The woman thought for a moment and nodded. "I'm sure I could put together a few for you."

"Thanks." She paused. "We really are trying to help people, you know."

"I know," she answered as she put together a few items.

Maria nodded as if that was all that was needed to be said. She took the packages and quickly shoved them into the deep pockets of her pants. "Thanks again." She doubted she would ever have the chance to use them, but her last deployment, there was a young girl who she had needed to turn away. Maybe this time she could actually help. Even if it was just one person.

Then again, five weeks had gone by so quickly.

CHAPTER 14

Maria sat down next to Strong and flipped through her AIRC. "Has your AIM seen anything since the last group?"

He shook his head. "No. I'm not sure if that's a good thing or not."

"Definitely not a good thing," she noted. "The scouting group going to a village rather than a main Mjahdan site either means there is no main site, or they're extremely disorganized. Which means there are more rogues than just these four."

"What's going on now?" McMurphy asked as he sat down with the two around their makeshift fire. It was no use trying to hide their location anymore. They were being watched, and everyone in the area knew they were there when word got out the Red Cross had been there.

Maria motioned towards her AIM. "Do we have any idea how many AIMs were given to Mjahdan?"

McMurphy thought for a moment. "I'm sure I could find out, or get an idea. You're thinking that this is going to happen again?"

"It makes sense," Cam said from across the circle they had begun to form. "I doubt they would have stopped doing whatever they were doing when they contacted you guys. If they're as disorganized as we think they are, most of them probably don't even know about the rogues, or heard some version of the story. They are most definitely still using their original AIM units. But the main branch or whatever, they probably know now what's happening, and they're testing us. Which goes along with your hostage theory. They're testing us to not only see if we can get the AIMs back, but..." He paused, his voice trailing off slowly. "But who's going to do it."

Scanner.

"You know we're not going to let anything happen to any of you," McMurphy said. "Any of you. You hear me? We're all getting back, either alive or dead. We are not letting any of those insurgents get their hands on any of you."

"I wouldn't be so quick to speak for all of us," Collins said from behind them. He sat down with the rest of them, noticing their dark stares. "You want the element of surprise? We need to co-operate with them. They want a hostage, let them have a willing volunteer."

"Are you out of our mind?" Maria yelled as she stood, swearing at him. "We are not handing any of them over to a militia group."

Filsinger stood and held his hands out. "Honestly, Kier, at this point we need to be open to all options. If it makes Mjahdan feel comfortable, it gives us the chance to strike and take them down. If we have someone on the inside, we have an even better chance."

"You're talking about sending in a civilian," Maria snapped. "That's out of the question."

"It doesn't necessarily have to be one of them," he answered slowly.

"But it would only work if it was me."

Maria swung around to look at Cam, her heart dropping. "We are all going home, do you hear me?"

"Maria, Collins told me what was on the wall in that village," he said. His voice was calm.

Maria shot a glare at Collins, and before she could say anything, Cam continued.

"If we try sending anyone else, people are going to get hurt. They're looking at us. They want one of us." And she knew he wasn't referring to the whole group. Just the team. Her team.

Him.

"I quit the team to make sure I dealt with rogues. I gave up everything so people wouldn't get hurt. Now I find out there are more AIMs out there, just waiting to go rogue?" Cam made sure she was looking at him now. "If I can make sure more people don't get hurt, I'm doing this, Maria. You know I have to do this." His voice was so low near the end that it was almost a whisper.

"We're not making any decisions now," McMurphy interrupted and sat down next to Cam, who held his head in his hands. "And we're not asking anyone to do anything. But Filsinger is right. We need to look at all of our options, and whichever has the highest probability of success, we have to take it."

"And good riddance," Collins muttered.

"What the hell is wrong with you?" Shepero asked. "You're starting to sound like you're more robot than human yourself." He glanced over to Maria, who was at least being restrained by Ellis. Cam seemed to not have heard anything after he had spoken. But now all eyes were on Collins.

He sighed. "Fine. You want me to be a real person? You all want me to share?" He paused. "When I was deployed the first time, I was engaged. I know. Imagine me, getting down on one knee. Before I left, we found out she was pregnant. I came here a month later." He glanced at McMurphy. Only he knew this story, and only because he had been there when it all happened. "When I was able to go home for a visit six months in, I couldn't find her. We had a hard time getting in touch with each other, but she knew when I was coming home. No one would tell me where she was, and her clothes were gone from the house."

He cleared his throat and kicked his heel into the sand. "I was gone two years, and I had no idea if she was even alive. I came home, and my own family wouldn't speak to me. It was the typical hero's return. Found out eventually she had had an abortion. And got married the week before I came home from deployment."

Collins looked at Maria. "I'm sorry about your kid, I am. I'm not sorry for suggesting we leave someone behind, because it means that more people can survive this hell-hole and give the rest of us a chance to get home to whatever we have waiting there."

Everyone was silent for a few moments. What was to be said after someone shared something like that, and so unexpectedly? Maria looked back at him. "Knowing us women-folk, she would've put you into debt with a wedding."

Collins stared at her for a moment, and the rest of the group froze. He grinned, and then let out a laugh. "You're probably right. She had expensive taste. Oh, and you should've seen the dresses she kept saying she liked. How do you tell your fiancée that the dress she wants to wear on your wedding day looks like a big ball of stupid feathers?"

"Probably like that," McMurphy said with a smile.

Maria sat back as the American soldiers began to chat with each other, discussing the various ways women torture themselves for a dress they'll wear for one day. She was glad for the distraction and change of topic. The thought of Cam staying as a hostage…it was unthinkable for her. She'd much rather focus on hearing stories than anything else at the moment.

Collins had surprised her. Ryan was right. Sharing that, she knew, would have been hard for him. And it hadn't made him weak, or vulnerable. She didn't even pity him for what had happened. But it had made him real.

He had a story, they all did, and somehow each one had led them to the middle of the desert, chasing dangerous robots. Did this make her dislike him less? She was afraid of what the answer would be if she thought about it. It explained a lot. Unfortunately, it made him seem more and more like Cam, which definitely was a bad, if not confusing, thing.

"So, now that you've heard my sob story," Collins laughed. "What about you?" He turned back to Maria. He asked the question slowly, as if testing the waters after sharing his own story. "How does your husband handle you being here?" He remembered Ryan mentioning she was single, but there was a better way to get information. Go right to the source.

Maria shook her head quickly. "Oh, I'm not married. Never have been."

He raised an eyebrow. "He never stepped up when you were pregnant?"

"He didn't really have the chance to. She died before I could even tell him about her. He went his way, and I joined the army so there wasn't really anything to go back to. He's not really the marrying-type, anyway. I'm not the type to get married just because I was pregnant."

"Shondra and I didn't get married until after our son was born," McMurphy offered. "We were the same way. Didn't want to get married just because people thought we should. We'd been together ten years by then, and were planning on getting married but our son arrived and we figured there was no rush."

Cam leaned forward, putting his elbows on his knees. "Probably took the pressure off. You have enough with your job out here."

McMurphy smiled lightly, glad Cam was out from his coma. "It was nice, knowing what was in store for us," he agreed. "Well, I guess we don't need to ask about your wife," McMurphy said. "I already know you're not married. What happened there?" His mind was on the same line as Collins. He knew Maria and Cam had dated, and now he was beginning to make the connection between them both having a daughter die. It didn't hurt to hear both sides of the story.

He shook his head with a laugh. "We've heard enough sob stories for one night. Don't want Collins over there to break down in tears. Next thing you know he'll be saying he doesn't want any of us to leave because he loves us just so much."

"Oh come on," Collins joked. "This is a confidence circle. A healing circle." He laughed. "Seriously. You said you had a daughter. What happened with the mom?"

Cam shrugged and pulled the neck of his uniform jacket up to keep off the chill of the cold nighttime air. "We were together, and then we weren't. I took too long to grow up, and I didn't propose in time. By the time I got the courage, and the ring, to do it, she broke up with me." He ended quietly, his head down. "So, I went my way…she went hers."

Maria and Ryan's head both snapped up at the same time. Had he actually said that? Maria's eyes went wide, and she couldn't help but stare at him. All this time…all those fights, this was what he had been thinking? This was what he had been wanting?

Sarah nudged him with her arm. "Never took you to be so soft."

He smiled lightly. "Yeah, well, it's the healing circle."

"Feel healed?" Collins asked.

Cam shrugged again. "Depends what needs to be healed."

Collins gave him a soft look and leaned over, placing a hand over Cam's chest. "Your heart," he said gently, before laughing. For the first time, the laugh wasn't mocking, or sarcastic. It was a genuinely amused laugh. He looked up when Maria stood suddenly and stormed away. Instead of heading towards the bunk tent, she went to one of the Humvees, got in and slammed the door. "What's her problem? Jealous I made the move on you instead of her?"

He shook his head with a quick roll of the eyes. "You really think she'd be jealous to be with you?"

"So much for a healing circle," Collins muttered. He stood and began to walk towards the Humvee.

McMurphy leaned over to call after him. "What are you doing?"

He turned around to walk backwards. "Apparently I'm a nice guy now and feel the need to make people feel better."

"No hooking up!" McMurphy yelled. "I mean it!"

Collins waved him away and got into the Humvee. He put his hands up quickly when a handgun was pointed at his face. "Jesus, Kier, it's me." He grumbled and shoved the gun away from his face. "I just wanted to see if you're alright."

"Peachy," came her quick response.

They were silent for a few moments, but Collins heard slight sobs and he realized she was keeping it in while he was around. "Look, I'm sorry I've been such a jerk, and prick, pig, whatever else you want to call me. I have issues."

"You think?"

"You're a lot like her. Tanya," he added when she looked at him questioningly. "Annoyingly so, actually. You look like her, too."

"McMurphy mentioned that," Maria said softly. "You're a lot like my ex."

"Oh yeah?"

"Annoyingly so." She smiled briefly.

He watched her, noticing her face twitch as she fought to understand her emotions. What this had been triggered by, he had no idea. But McMurphy was right. They all needed to work together and be on the same page. If that meant making his soldiers happy by being nice, he'd have to do it. He leaned towards her slightly. "Tanya invited me to her anniversary party."

Her eyes widened as she looked at him. "You're kidding."

Collins shook his head. "Nope. The invitation mentioned it was a dry-party since, get this, she was pregnant. With their second child."

"Oh, God. Please tell me you didn't go."

He laughed. "No. I came here with you guys, instead."

"I'm flattered."

He smiled lightly, and while he had gotten her to cheer up slightly, he knew it wasn't addressing the main issue. "What exactly is it about Tylar that gets you so riled up? First you shoot him, you constantly put him in his place – and don't get me wrong, he needs to be put there – and now everything he says seems to piss you off. I'm going to have to step up my game if I'm going to stay the biggest prick out here."

Maria opened her mouth before there was a tap on Collins' window. She let out a sigh instead and looked forward as Collins let down the window. "What?"

Cam leaned against the vehicle slightly, trying to see her better in the dark. He looked at Collins warily. "Can we talk?" he asked her.

"I don't really have anything to say."

"Well, I do."

"I think you've already said more than enough," she replied with a quick glance in his direction. "You had no right to say any of that."

His eyes narrowed. "They asked me a question."

"And you drop that bomb on me?" She shook her head with disbelief and got out of the vehicle, leaving Collins behind. She started for the tents when Cam grabbed her arm to stop her. "Fine, they asked you a question. But you're the king of evasion. If you had wanted to continue to keep it a secret, you would have. You wanted to make a point."

"I didn't think it mattered if I said something or not. It was three years ago. I didn't think you'd care."

Maria wrenched her arm away. "You honestly thought I wouldn't care that you wanted to get married? That you had a ring and were going to propose?"

"Why would I think you would anymore?"

"What about what happened before we left?"

"Have you told Ryan?" He shook his head when she remained silent. "If you had wanted to leave him, you would have already. And not just because you were deployed. If you wanted to be with someone else more, you'd be with him, but you're not."

He turned away and took a few steps towards the tents before he stopped. "The thing is, Maria, you've always known we're not done. I convinced myself I don't want to be with you anymore, but I'm not too proud anymore to not take you back in a heartbeat. Not anymore. But you chose him."

"It's complicated now."

"How?" he snapped. "Because you felt bad and wanted one last time? Now you're feeling guilty?"

Collins stepped forward, putting himself between the two. He hadn't heard much of the conversation, but enough to pause it. "Look, I'm all for fighting, but not when it gets in the way of missions. We're going to an attack site tomorrow, and I need to know my people will have each other's back."

"I'll be fine," Maria muttered. She attempted to pass Collins, and when he stopped her, she gave him a small smile. "Thank you, for talking to me. Be careful, I may start thinking of you as a decent human being."

Collins watched as Maria walked away for a moment before turning his attention to Cam. He eyed him for a moment. It should have been obvious the two had hooked up at some point in their career, at least, that was what it sounded like when he caught the tail end of their conversation. "Is this going to be a problem?"

"Not yours."

Cam was the first one awake the next morning and put his portion of the equipment away. He hadn't gotten much sleep the night before, thinking about what Maria had said. He had tried to stay out of her relationship with Ryan, and had no idea what actually happened between them. The last time a complication had stopped

Maria starting a relationship with someone, there had been Lucy. He waited around the Humvees as the camp was quickly taken apart. He folded his arms as Maria made her way over to him. He took a quick glance around before he pulled her around to the far side of the wall of vehicles.

"You said it's complicated. You and Ryan getting back together," he stated simply. "I need you to actually say why."

She let out a sigh. She hadn't been able to do this before. And she had tried. Not as hard or as much as she should have, but it was better late than never. "I'm late." A blood test would have been more accurate, but there it was.

It took him a second to understand, but his face didn't change. "You were never really regular."

"Almost three weeks."

Cam wasn't sure how well he was doing at keeping his face blank, keeping the sound of his heart breaking within his chest. "That doesn't complicate getting back together with him."

"It does when it's not his," she said with her voice lowered. "Ryan and I…it's not his."

He examined her face, looking for any sign of…anything. But she kept her face blank, as he did. Better than getting burned. "Are you sure?"

"Am I sure I'm pregnant, or that it's not his?"

"Both."

"I mean, I don't have access to an ultrasound machine out here and I know I've never really been regular, but I think a cheap test I borrowed from the relief workers should still do the trick. But yes…I'm sure who the father is, Lucas."

Cam was silent for a moment. "You're pregnant." His face slowly broke out into a large smile. "You're pregnant."

She let herself smile hesitantly. "And for the record, I told you as soon as I found out."

He laughed happily and grabbed her into a large embrace, lifting her slightly from the ground. He let her go after a moment, and his smile faltered when she took a step back from him. "Sorry, I thought I was allowed to hug you."

"You can," she replied, but her forehead was furrowed. "I just...I didn't expect this kind of reaction from you."

Cam brought his face down to hers, locking her eyes with his. "Why wouldn't I be excited about being a dad?"

"You weren't last time." She glanced away to ignore his wince. "We both know that even if Lucy hadn't died, you would've run."

"You know I'm different now. It's not that I didn't want her. I did, Maria. But I didn't want her growing up with both of us hating each other. And with everything that was going on in the Underground at the time, no one was safe around me."

Maria looked back at him with a startled look. "You hated me?"

"No," he answered. "But you made your feelings pretty clear."

She stared at him. Had she hated him? There had been nothing to hate. Yes, he had chosen the Underground over her and she had been angry, furious even, about that. "Because I slept with Jack?"

"That, and everything else," Cam muttered.

Maria shook her head. "Cameron...if you thought for one second I knew how to stop loving you-" She spun around when a hand clapped her on the shoulder. She let out her breath when she saw Ellis. "Ready to go?"

"When you are, ma'am," he answered, his eyes flickering briefly towards Cam.

She nodded to dismiss him before she turned back to Cam. "You can't tell anyone. They'd send me back home no matter how much they need me."

Cam stepped forward again, his eyes narrowing. "You're serious? You actually want to stay out here? Maria, the baby-"

"Will be safe," she interrupted. "I'll be careful. With Lucy, I didn't know I was pregnant and pushed my body too hard. It was my fault, and I'm not going to let it happen again."

His face softened, then. "Maria..."

"I can't go home when you and Ryan are still out here."

"It wasn't your fault."

"Yes, it was. I was still drinking; I was training too hard." Maria backed away. "You said it yourself that it was my fault, and you were right. I took it all away from you. I didn't let you come to my appointments. I didn't let you even try to think of yourself as a dad. I didn't even tell you about her. I had to get the hospital to tell you." She fastened the chin strap of her helmet before she started for her vehicle. "Better mark your calendar. I just admitted you were right. Relish in that for a while," she called over her shoulder before she jumped into the Humvee.

Cam allowed himself to get shoved into the second vehicle, his mind still reeling. All this time she had blamed herself. He wondered what else she took the blame for. The state of their relationship? His inability to be open with her? The team's failure? He closed his eyes while the engine rumbled as they were carried towards the next village. All he knew was that this definitely did complicate things.

"When we get to the attack site, there are a few things we need to keep in mind," McMurphy called out through the headsets as they neared the village. "This site has been evacuated. From the recon it doesn't seem as though there are any survivors, but we need to be on the lookout for anything and everything. If we see anyone living, they need to be detained and questioned. No one goes anywhere alone. Tylar and Hampton will be looking for anything useful for their side of things: electronic signatures, or anything to do with the animals themselves. Strong, you'll accompany them to take a look at the bodies, see what you can determine from the trauma."

"And everyone," he added. "This is going to give us all a fresh reminder of why we're here, and why this needs to be dealt with soon. Let's leave our personal feelings aside, and figure out a way to get these AIMs under control."

Maria looked over at Ryan as McMurphy ended his announcement. "Are you going to be okay with this?"

Ryan looked out the window with a shrug. "Can it get much worse than what I've already seen?"

She let out a breath and turned away from him. This was a bad idea. His psych-eval can be damned. He's not ready for this. Her body jolted as the vehicle came to a stop. She jumped down and was immediately met with the scent of death. Blood was splattered along the base of the house next to them. A lonely hand sat in the middle of the doorway as though waving farewell to its life. She took in a deep breath and moved forward. She saw Ryan on the other side of the vehicle, his eyes wide open. *None of us are ready for this.*

Ryan gripped the rifle tight as he looked around. He jumped when Strong placed a hand on his shoulder. "Is it..." His voice trailed off as he searched for words. There were none.

"It's not always like this," the soldier said softly. "Humans kill differently. They have emotions, are fuelled by emotions. Animals...well, I'm sure you and Tylar know best what animals are like."

"This wasn't done by animals," Ryan whispered. "They're monsters." Suddenly, he understood. He was seeing the aftermath, but Maria had seen this happen in front of her. Collins and McMurphy, they had too. And Cam...

Cam swore as he came up next to them. "You see the pictures, but you never really know."

"You," Ryan started, but paused. "You've always known AIMs could do this. And you still worked with them, trained with them."

He looked at his team-mate and thought about his answer. "I had to. I needed to know everything I could about them." He swore again when he noticed more blood along the walls, dried streaks running down to the sand that had already been cleaned by the wind. "I tried to make sure this wouldn't happen. I gave up everything. Risked everything. I tried."

"Let's move out," Strong said, encouraging them to walk forward. "Looks like we have a lot of work to do."

Ryan nodded lightly and followed behind the soldier. He brought the bandana up from his neck and around his nose against the stench. "How long have they been left like this?"

"A few days, from what we've found," Strong replied. He knelt down next to the maimed body of a man and observed him while Ryan attempted to avoid looking directly at it. "Definitely killed by the AIM. No signs of human struggle or weapons."

Cam knelt down next to Strong and nodded in agreement. "Seems pretty consistent with tiger marks, but they're not usually this messy. That girl Kier was talking to, she said they were crazed.

They're probably starving, too. If all they're doing is making sure the others don't eat, it means none of them are."

"Hungry carnivores aren't happy ones."

He turned his attention back to Strong. "Ryan and I will send our AIMs around to see if they can pick up on any signatures. It's a long shot if the rogues have been gone for days, but it's worth a shot, at least." As the AIMs left their side, Cam noticed Shepero come up alongside them. "What'll happen to the bodies?"

"Once you guys get what you need, they'll move behind us and start to bury them," Strong answered. "They won't be able to give them a burial as their culture and religion dictates, but we can't just leave them out in the open longer than they already have been."

Ryan nodded lightly and looked around, wincing against the glare of the sun. "At least it's something." He followed the other two down the street and into the next white-washed building. They were greeted by overturned chairs and a young girl's body strewn atop a table. A wave swept over him and he had to rush outside, making it just in time to vomit on the street.

She looks like she's my sister's age, he thought to himself sadly, once he could think straight at all. *This is what Cam was trying to stop. I can see why he never quit the Underground. Owen has to know. He'd take back every harsh word.* It was then that he realized just how conflicted Maria must have been after she had found out about rogues. It made sense now, her confusion. She broke up with Cam for no reason. For a terrible reason, actually. Now that it was staring them all in the face, it was pretty difficult to disagree with Cam's decision to put his career in jeopardy.

He wiped his mouth with his sleeve and slowly went back inside. "Cam," Ryan started, averting his eyes from what he knew was in there. He waited until the man turned his attention from his AIRC to him. "How was this missed? How could no one have known that there were outdated AIMs here?"

"They did know," came the simple response. "Trevor probably had them killed pretty early on. The less people who knew, the better. For him, at least." He looked around and wiped his face as though it would wipe away the scene before them. "We tried so hard, Ryan. We thought we got them all. We thought we found every record, every manufactured unit." Cam looked out through the doorway, his eyes focused on something far away. "I have no idea how many more are out there. Not just in Afghanistan. We should've gotten them all…"

It took the group nearly three hours to go through every house. As Cam had predicted, there was little evidence that AIMs had been there, other than the corpses. Hanks squatted next to Maria as she finished covering the last grave with rocks. "That's the last, then?" he asked with a glance over his shoulder.

"Looks like it," she replied through gritted teeth. It had taken all of her self-control to keep her wits about her, to keep her emotions in check. So many children. "Was there anything worthwhile?"

"Found a few IEDs in the north end of the village, so those were taken care of." He shrugged. "Nothing that really implicated Mjahdan, which was probably planned."

She nodded and stood with her hands on her hips, looking around. They had taken the bodies, what was left of them, just outside of the village and was able to give each a separate grave. For those found within the same building, they put them together in a larger one with the assumption they were from the same family. They had agreed to cover the area with rocks and small boulders to keep predators away. Her eyes widened and she looked down at Hanks. "Wait, what did you say?"

"What?"

"You found IEDs?"

He stared at her for a moment before he swore and bolted up. "They're here. How did we miss that?"

"Cam," Maria called through her AIRC. "Get the AIMs out for recon, now! Collins, get the civilians to the vehicles. We've been set up." She turned back to Hanks. "Let's move!" Maria ran for their line of vehicles, and waited for Ryan to reach them. She looked around, her eyes scanning every building, every point on the horizon she could see. "Any report from the AIMs?" she called out to Cam when he got closer. She swore when he shook his head. She met eyes with Collins and she nodded. "We're good?"

"Time to fly," he said hurriedly and pushed Cam into the Humvee before him. He slammed the door behind him as the vehicle sped away, creating a sand cloud for the ones behind it. He gripped his rifle, his eyes locked outside the window. He swore to himself. "We should've seen this. We should've known other groups would be interested in you."

"I haven't changed my mind."

"Forget what I said before, Tylar," Collins said, waving him off. "This is bigger than we thought."

"Maria's pregnant."

Ellis and Shepero spun around from the front, their faces mimicking the shock on Collins' face. Ellis swore from the driver's seat.

"How do you know?" Collins asked. "And how the hell was she cleared to come?"

"You need to promise me you'll take care of her," Cam continued. "No matter what happens out there, you make sure she gets home."

He swore again. "Tylar-"

"Promise me. She's strong, and she can do it on her own, but she doesn't think she can."

It hit him then. He hesitated and looked out the front. "She'll get home." Collins met Cam's eyes. "I promise, Cam. They'll both get home." His attention was brought to the driver when the man pounded on the wheel. "What's going on?"

"Battery. Or something." Shepero looked over his shoulder. "We're not going anywhere, sir."

Collins swore as the vehicle came to a slow stop. He looked around the beige surroundings. He could not see anything around him besides sand hills and small mountains. He looked over his shoulder as though he could see the people in the vehicle behind him. "Truck one's dead."

"What?" came Maria's voice, McMurphy echoing. "Cam, have our AIMs found anything? Is anyone out there?"

"They haven't said anything, but something made the truck die," Collins replied. "Full tank of gas. It just stopped working. It couldn't have been an EMP, because the electronics are still going, for the most part at least."

"I would suggest continuing on your way," came a robotic voice from Cam's AIRC in the back of the convoy truck. "There are nearly twenty men to the east of you, just beyond the ridge."

Maria swore and fell back into the body of the truck from the gun house. She grabbed her rifle and cocked it. She closed her eyes for a moment, ignoring Ryan's stare. "Collins, what do you say?"

He looked around before closing his eyes, picturing his options. "McMurphy will take Tylar, Lim, and Hanks, and head north. There's a cave up in the base of the hill that gives a good view to the east. From what I saw back in Kandahar, Cam's a pretty good long-distance shot, so they'll be taking out the first wave. I'll take Hampton, Travato, Shepero, and Filsinger. We'll make a blockade here to defend ourselves. Kier, you, Ellis, and Strong go to the south and come up behind them. Pick off as many as you can."

Sarah began to tremble as she strapped her helmet on tightly. "There's...there's twenty of them. There's twelve of us. They outnumber us by eight. And we have four civilians. We're not soldiers."

Maria loaded her pockets with magazines fiercely, as she knew others began to do the same. "Well, at least you can do math. Collins, McMurphy?" She glanced at Ryan briefly. "You keep them safe, you hear me? If they die, there's no way we can get those AIMs back. Ellis, Strong, let's move." She jumped down from her vehicle. A hand grabbed her arm before she could run off and she saw Cam there.

"Have fun up there," she gave a forced smile. Of all the places to be, far away is best for him. *Thank you, Collins.* But Cam kept his grip on her, and Maria glanced over at Ryan who was keeping a watchful eye on them. "I'll be fine, Cam."

"You better be," he said in a low voice. "I don't want to lose another one." Cam ignored Ryan's stare and leaned close to her ear. "Please be safe." He stepped away and scrambled into McMurphy's vehicle before it sped away.

Cam lay on his stomach, his eye pressed into the sight of the long-distance rifle. His lips moved as he counted silently. Twenty men. Three AIMs. They seemed to be well-behaved AIMs, but of all people Cam knew that could change in an instant. "Once they get too close for us to do much good," Cam said to McMurphy without taking his attention away from the sight. "I want to get down there as quickly as possible. They have faulty AIMs with them. I'm too far away up here to be able to hack into their programming."

"If they go rogue while we're up here?" McMurphy asked, the second half of his question not needing to be voiced.

"You've seen what will happen already," Cam answered as he sat back onto his knees.

McMurphy nodded distractedly as Hanks readied himself, getting into position near the mouth of the cave. "Tylar, you're pretty safe up here. You don't need to man a gun. Shoot if shot at."

Cam paused and looked down the hill to the approaching group. "If it gives the people down there a better chance, and less enemies to face, then yes I do."

He could not argue with that. He looked down the hill, following Cam's gaze. "I know I said we each need to make this personal, but it can't get too personal, Cam." He smiled lightly when Cam whipped his head towards him. "If something happens, you can't blame yourself. You can't think that if you had just had one more shot, one more bullet, it'd be different."

Cam shook his head. "I won't." He laid back down, the uniform only slightly cushioning him against the hard dirt ground. "I don't miss."

Ryan held the rifle tight in front of his chest. He had his eyes closed as he leaned back against one of the vehicles, his lips moving in a silent prayer. There wasn't much of anything to make a blockade, but Collins was finishing up what they were able to make.

"The guys on the hill should be able to take out most of them," Sarah said quietly.

"Most. But as soon as that first shot goes..." Ryan paused. "They'll get maybe one or two."

"Collins, Shepero, and Hanks are all amazing soldiers. They'll take care of us," she continued. "We won't even have to shoot anyone."

He turned his head away from her once he realized she was only speaking to comfort herself. Would it be too much to ask for them to just...disappear? For us to disappear?

A shot fired.

Ryan's eyes snapped open and he kept himself pressed against the vehicle. He looked at his AIRC. "Do a quick recon. See what's going on out there." He met Collins' gaze. The soldier nodded at him, approving his decision.

"Keep the AIM out there," Collins said. "It looks like they have three AIMs with them."

"They do," Cam called out through their headsets. "I'm going to try to get down there as quickly as possible to dismantle them before-" He stopped and another shot echoed across the valley. "Before things get really bad."

Collins risked a look around the barricade. Two down. "Good job, Hanks. Get it down to even, and it'll be a walk in the park."

Another shot.

"Those were Tylar," came Hanks' voice. "This is me." Two more shots. "Now we're even. They'll be on you soon. Should be in range now. Kier, you guys are looking good."

Collins readied his rifle and looked at the other soldiers with him. The civilians were only supposed to fire if fired at, but he was willing to cover it if it meant they had a better shot at surviving. "Kier, are you three in position?"

"Ready when you are. Engage, and we'll give you a bit of a lead," she answered. "Try to draw them back towards you. Engage your AIMs to provide cover. If we can make them think we have rogues with us, it'll give us an advantage."

"Shouldn't be too hard." He looked at the civilians and he gave them his best reassuring smile. "Walk in the park. Keep your head down. If it gets too close, change positions. If you absolutely need to, shoot."

"We'll do what we can," Ryan said weakly.

Collins nodded. "Keep your AIM in recon. Travato, get your AIM out there and focused on the furthest person out there. Let's move!" he yelled before spinning out from behind the barricade, rifle firing.

Maria hunched down, waiting for the group of now frantic Mjahdan members to make their way towards the barricade. She looked up suddenly when she noticed a bird coming in for a landing. She watched it land beside her and shook itself, fluffing out its feather before the shaking turned into vibrations and ripples. The bird form morphed into the shape of a tiger, and it laid down next to Maria to keep itself hidden. Maria looked towards the direction of the cave. "What are you doing down here?" she asked Cam's AIM. "Where is he?"

"They'll be along shortly," it replied. "Lucas did well."

"Too well," she said softly. She had known he had it in him, to do what it took. He always had done that, after all. He had risked his relationship, and his career, for rogues. The next logical step was his life. At least he had been careful. That was something she had taken for granted. "What can you tell us?"

The tiger bobbed its head. "This is a magnificent scan. I have never felt this way. Such power."

Maria rolled her eyes. "Stay focused, would you? What can you tell us about what's going on?"

It yawned, showing off its large teeth. Not that anyone needed reminding. "The AIMs are in danger of disconnecting. They seem to have been poorly maintained, despite what Major Collins has claimed about the training Mjahdan had received."

"Can you do anything about it?"

"If Lucas cannot get here in time to disable them, I will engage them. Ryan has been made aware of the situation, and his AIM is prepared to join me. I advise against it, however. There is too great a risk of it joining the others."

Maria swore. "I knew it wasn't ready. Neither of them are."

"Lucas has a habit of pushing people."

"Who the hell is Lucas?" Strong asked.

She stared at the tiger for a moment, ignoring the soldier's question. "McMurphy, how are things on your end?"

"We're good to go," came the response.

"We're ready when you are, Kier," Collins called out, his voice muffled by the sound of gunfire.

"Fluffy, lead the rest of the AIMs. Keep them entertained and keep the insurgents occupied." Maria took a deep breath. The AIM put a large paw on her arm, nearly covering all of it. She looked into its eyes and swore she could see worry there. "Move out!" She leapt to her feet, Strong and Ellis close behind her. Immediately she was met with defensive stance of a tiger. She stopped; her heart stuck in her throat as the vision of Rebecca's body appeared at its feet.

"Kier! We need those AIMs intact," Cam called through their headset.

"I'll take care of it," his AIM said, stepping up beside. "Move, Maria."

She nodded and looked around, half expecting to see Cam somewhere nearby. He had always known her too well. With her rifle ready, she ran into the fray, not expecting it to be such mayhem with only a handful of people. She spotted Collins in hand-to-hand with an insurgent, and a second just behind. Without a thought, she fired and kept moving.

"I had it," Collins grunted as he threw the body to the ground.

"Where are the civilians?"

"Unless they've moved, they're fine."

Maria's eyes scanned the area. She took a shot as another man came at her. She flinched at the sounds of other guns, their echoes feeling as though they were shooting her. Dust and sand were kicked up everywhere, making it difficult to see much of anything clearly. But there, she saw him. Up against the side of the barricade, his rifle on the ground away from him, as he avoided the knife thrust of another insurgent.

She brought her rifle up as she noticed another man do the same, but aimed towards her. With a curse, Maria hit the ground with a thud as the sand exploded next to her head. She pushed herself to her knees and brought the rifle up and fired.

Ryan stumbled back as the man in front of him crumpled to the ground, his head torn apart by Maria's bullet. He looked at her quickly, his eyes wide as he finally saw her. He cringed as another shot was fired, and he turned to watch another man fall to the ground under the weight of Maria's aim.

She stood finally, only to be knocked to the ground. She struggled under the man's weight but managed to roll herself over to face the knife he held. Maria gripped her wrist with both hands, her arms shaking with the effort of holding the knife away from her throat. A shadow came from above, and suddenly the man was lying beside her with a bullet hole in temple. Her hands were still wrapped around the man's wrist when Cam pulled her to her feet, his uniform and face splattered with blood.

With a quick nod, he turned and kept his rifle up, looking for the next target. She watched him briefly before following suit, keeping Ryan behind her. "Get under cover," Maria called out to him. When she didn't receive a response, she turned to him quickly. He simply stood there in the open, staring at her. She looked around, panicky, until Collins ran over and pushed him down to the ground.

"Stop making our job difficult," Collins hissed. He turned his attention to Cam, his eyes scanning the surroundings. Their AIM partners had been useful in at least rounding up the insurgents, but could not do much more than that. Not that he wanted them to. Not after seeing their true power. "Tylar, how's it going with the hacking?"

Cam laughed. "Already done. You know, in between saving your life and Kier's. Ellis has them contained."

One last shot sounded, and Cam's AIM relaxed, sitting next to Maria. She looked down at it with surprise. As soon as it landed, it hadn't left her side. Something told her if it had been able to, it would have attacked all the people who were a danger to her. "Do you like me, or something?"

It looked up at her with what she considered a tiger grin. "I tolerate you more than I do Lucas, so perhaps I do. Have I not told you so previously?"

She smiled lightly, but it faded when she noticed Collins' grim look. She knew that look. She hated that look. "It was over so quickly." Maria paused. "Who?"

"Filsinger and Strong."

Maria took a step back. "Allen?" She looked around, looking for him to be standing next to her. "He was just right here."

McMurphy came up to her then and put a hand on her shoulder. "They were both good men, good soldiers."

Maria swore and flung her rifle to the ground, her helmet ripped off followed suit.

Everyone was silent for a moment. Ellis came forward finally with a container which held the deactivated AIMs. "I worked with him a few times. AIMOT business," he offered. He paused, then cracked a small smile. "He was actually kind of a jerk if he didn't like you. Made it pretty well known. Ran out on his girlfriend for her sister."

"Cousin," Maria corrected quietly.

"Isn't it bad luck to talk ill of the dead?" Shepero asked.

"If you don't want people speaking ill of you, don't do anything worth them bringing up against you," Collins suggested. "Let's move out. Clearly, we're not safe here."

"We're not safe anywhere," Shepero countered. "I got a message from Ghazni. They were ambushed this morning."

Collins swore and threw his helmet off. "What the hell for?"

He hesitated before stepping forward, handing him his AIRC. "Came through in Arabic."

Collins grabbed the device from him and read it, despite there being a translation. He swore again and handed it back. He looked at McMurphy, trying to find the answer in his comrade's face. For once, it'd be nice if just one thing was easy. "It's a warning. We have three days to make the exchange."

"Or else?" Sarah asked, finally stepping up from the hiding spot that had done so well.

He met Maria's eyes next, his anger mirrored which surprised him. A lot of things were surprising him. But not this.

"War."

CHAPTER 15

Shepero slammed the door of the Humvee closed. They arrived at their next checkpoint, which was now to be their last.

"Everything okay?" Peter asked, coming out from the other side.

"This was supposed to be easy." He smiled sardonically when he received a raised eyebrow. "Relatively. I've been on rescue missions, high profile missions. This...this is something else. We've lost three good men already, and we've barely faced the enemy. We haven't even found the stupid robots."

McMurphy joined them and motioned with his head towards the camp being set up. "Actually, Tylar thinks they found them. At least picked up their signature."

Shepero swore. "About time."

"It's not that easy," Peter said in defense. "We need to be within a certain range, and rogues have an altered electronic signature which itself is difficult to trace."

"Either way," McMurphy continued, "we're going to go through the new game plan." He began to follow Peter, but Shepero's hand on his arm stopped him. He looked around and sighed. "Collins says he knows, that he's on board."

"No one else knows?"

"They can't." He smiled grimly. "Element of surprise, right?"

"So, once we get in range," Collins started, "how easy is this going to be?"

"It'll take me less than five minutes," Cam answered.

He swore. "All of this for five minutes worth of work?"

"The actual deactivation isn't the hard part," Peter offered. "It's getting there, getting in range, and staying there. That's where you guys come in. Keep us safe, and we'll be fine. My concern is what happens after this. Getting these units back in an operational state is going to take more time than they're willing to give us."

Maria looked over at Ryan. He hadn't looked at her once since the ambush, which worried her. He hadn't really made eye contact with anyone at all. So soon after Johnson. Get him talking... "What about our AIMs? I know yours and Tylar's will be engaging the rogues directly, but how can we support you guys?"

After a moment of silence, Cam cleared his throat. "Keep them at bay. There's not much they can do, and we don't want the rogues to feel threatened. They're already going to be on edge, and likely starving. Well, they'll think they're starving. They're still robots, after all."

"And what exactly are your AIMs going to be doing, Hampton," she tried. More silence. "Ryan?" When he turned to look at her, her heart broke. His face was filled with anger, and disgust. A look similar to the one she wore when he told her of his hunting.

He held her eyes briefly before he stood. He opened his mouth as though to say something, but shook his head and began to walk away.

"Ryan," she called, following after him. "What's going on?"

He spun around on his heel. "What's going on?" he repeated through clenched teeth. "You killed them, Maria. They were alive, and then they weren't. And that was because of you."

She stopped as though she had walked into a wall. "What?"

"Did you even stop and think? You killed people, Maria."

She stared at him, blinking. When the weight of his words sunk in, her eyes narrowed. "I did my job."

"They're still dead."

"I saved your life."

"And who says my life is worth more than theirs?"

"I do! I say your life is worth more!"

"And who are you? You're a murderer," he spat.

At that, the rest of the soldiers stood and took a place beside Maria. McMurphy stepped forward. "I'd think very carefully about what you say, Ryan."

He kept his glare trained on Maria for a moment more before he turned and left, disappearing into the tent.

Collins turned his attention to Maria, who simply stared after Ryan. He put a hand on her shoulder, but took it away quickly. "He'll come around. He's a civilian. It's different for them."

She looked up at him with a shake of her head. "Is it? Is it really that different?" She jumped when Cam pushed past her and followed Ryan into the tent. She turned away then, but cast a quick look up at Collins once more. "The only difference between us and civilians is the uniform. And right now, they're wearing the same one as us," Maria said quietly before sitting back down around the fire.

Ryan only gave Cam a quick glance before turning his attention back to his AIRC. "I don't want to hear it," he muttered. Cam's fist connected with his jaw, and he found himself on the ground. Before he could get his bearing, he was punched again, and again. With a growl he attempted one in return, but it only landed him on his side.

"What the hell is wrong with you?" Cam yelled, standing up. When Ryan moved to stand, he kicked him back down and repeated his question.

"You saw what she did," Ryan said. He spat blood and wiped his mouth with a grimace.

"I saw her save your sorry ass. If I had known this was going to be your thanks, I would've taken you out myself!"

"Then do it."

Cam stared at him in response.

Ryan made his way to his feet finally and looked him square in the eye. "Just get me out of here, Cam. I don't blame you for bringing me here. I don't. It was my decision. But I don't know what I'm doing here. I don't know anyone. I can't do this."

He narrowed his gaze at the man, his team-mate. His friend. "You know Maria, and you know me."

"Do I?"

Cam mulled over the question as Ryan sat down on his cot with a wince. He watched as Ryan pushed away his AIM as it tried to give him its form of affection. It was so like his own AIM, but there was always the risk of it loving you one moment and killing you the next. "I don't know. But I hope so." He left Ryan sobbing on his cot.

Maria kept her eyes down as Hanks sat down next to her. She embraced the silence that followed, but it wouldn't last. Nothing ever did.

"You want to talk about it?" he asked. They hadn't spoken much since arriving in Afghanistan, but maybe that was best for this moment.

"Does anyone ever want to?" she replied. "What's there to talk about?"

"You killed eight men today."

The words hit her like a truck, but this time she managed to keep her gag reflex under control.

Hanks kept quiet for a moment as he watched her. "Have you said it yet?"

"Is that supposed to help?"

He gave a short laugh. "Nothing's supposed to help."

"He won't talk to me."

Leaning towards her, he asked, "who? Ryan?"

"I…I killed eight men. Two were on him. And I killed them. And now he won't speak to me."

"Collins was right, though. He'll get over it. Civilians aren't used to this."

Maria swore and looked at the soldier finally. "I'm not used to this. Eight men are dead because of me. I blink and I see them hit the ground. I see my bullet in their head. Every time someone dies in front of me, that doesn't get any easier."

"No. It doesn't," Hanks said simply. "But we come to expect people we know to die. Civilians don't. They think, even in this place, that they're the exception. That everything will be okay somehow, when you and I know that's a load of crap."

It was Maria's turn to laugh, but the sound was strange to her ears. "I'd like to be the exception. Just once. To just...have a husband, and kids running around in the yard. Maybe even a real dog rather than an AIM." She paused and gave her head a small shake. "You never realize how much you want something until you can't have it."

Hanks squeezed her shoulder and stood. "War makes us think about a lot."

She watched him leave before turning back to the fire raging before her. She didn't look up as Collins stood next to her. He stayed standing, and both remained silent. She appreciated the gesture, as foreign as she knew it was for him. War, death, it changed people. Changed how they acted, spoke, hated. Loved.

"The first person I killed was a woman." He sat down finally and threw a stone into the fire. "She was already dying. Bleeding to death from stepping on one of our landmines." He stared straight ahead, and Maria began to think he didn't even realize she was there. "So, I shot her. I still see her. They never stop haunting you."

"Can't say I'm looking forward to that."

"To be honest," Collins started. He looked at Maria then, but paused before he continued. "I'd rather be haunted by the dead than by the living." He turned away. "You and Hampton were together." He smiled, sensing Maria's surprise. "I may be blind to most things, but that outburst was the result of...something. But I can tell you it wasn't love."

"You don't know him."

"No. But I know what it's like to see someone haunted by the living. The woman you were when you met, the woman he fell in love with...she's dead. I saw you compete, you know. You looked familiar when I met you, but it wasn't until McMurphy forced me to watch Tylar's challenges that I realized how I knew you. You were a great athlete."

"Careful," Maria muttered. "You'll sound kind."

"You were a great athlete. Stop haunting him with that. You're a soldier now; a damn good one, too." He shrugged. "Not great. But pretty good. One shot each time. You may not think it, and Hampton probably doesn't want to think about it, but one shot means a lot. Less pain for them. Don't even know what happened." He stood when she did and grabbed her arm before she could walk away. "I mean it. If he can't see you differently, it's time you saw him differently, Maria."

She finally turned to leave but stopped when she saw Cam making his way towards them. "I think he does see me differently now. They both do." She made her way towards the far end of the camp, shoving past Cam before he could stop her.

Cam watched her walk by as he was joined by Collins. "She okay?"

"Are you?" Collins looked down at him. "Or are you going to evade my attempts of being a human?"

He laughed lightly with a shake of his head. "You know," he said after a moment. "I thought it'd be worse than this. You pull the trigger. You see the target go down. You know the two events are related, but somehow you look past that."

"When you have something to fight for."

He turned to look at the soldier. He clenched his jaw with a nod. "I meant what I said."

Collins nodded and patted him on the shoulder. "Then try to survive the next few days. I can't promise anything if you don't do that."

"I will."

Sarah rocked slowly back and forth on her cot, her eyes focused on a point on the wall of the tent. "I think he was out of line," she said off-handedly to no one in particular. "It's not like she's the only one who killed one of them. I'm not sure what he expected to happen."

Peter looked over to Ryan who seemed to be ignoring the conversation. Or trying to, at least. It appeared that Cam had already given him a good talking to. "How are you doing?"

She shrugged. "Expecting it doesn't make it easier to see. Easier to process, maybe. I just can't believe Strong and Filsinger are gone. Filsinger was so patient with us during training. Do you know what happens now?"

"They've been buried," Ellis said, sitting up on his cot to join the conversation. "We'll have to get them on our way back.

Kandahar won't get up here before we finish this. They have our coordinates, just in case."

Shepero strode into the tent and tossed his helmet onto the ground. "Gonna be a long day tomorrow. I suggest we get some sleep."

Ellis looked at the two civilians. "Have either of you seen Tylar deal with rogues before? He did it so quickly here I didn't even see it happen."

Sarah and Peter looked at each other briefly, and Peter nodded. "Yeah. He trained us with the newest upgrades. But we had a few of the outdated units still in storage. When we activated them...they were already rogue. One was in the form of a moose."

Shepero snorted. "How very Canadian."

Peter continued. "They're pretty powerful in their own right. Most of the others were in small forms: squirrels, rabbits, some birds. But one was a polar bear. I'd heard he had dealt with a Grizzly before, but I didn't see it. I saw this, though."

Shepero nodded towards Sarah. "Did you see it?"

She shook her head. "I work mostly on the computers, dealing with the coding of DNA for scans. Peter was the one working with the substance."

Hanks stepped into the tent followed by McMurphy. He looked around and found his cot for the night. "Are we having a party?"

"Apparently Tylar faced a rogue moose and polar bear at the same time."

McMurphy nodded with an impressed smile. "How very Canadian of him."

"His dad was American."

The group looked up to find Maria standing in the doorway. They watched her gaze travel across to Ryan before she sat down next to Sarah.

"From what I heard, the rabbit was relatively annoying," she said with a hesitant smile.

Peter laughed. "Mildly, yes. But he and his AIM dealt with it. Less than five minutes, like he said. For all ten units. The polar bear was not happy."

"They're generally not overly happy," Maria added thoughtfully. "Scanned one up in Churchill one season. Cam was so mad I got to it first. Wasn't so mad when we had to avoid being mauled."

"How does he do it?" McMurphy asked. "And how is it that only he knows how to do it?"

"I've done it once," she replied. "Don't ask me to repeat it," she added quickly. "It wasn't even fully rogue. I got it to deactivate in time."

"Still doesn't answer the question."

"His dad helped to create AIMs," she said with a shrug. "He's always known. Was taught as a kid to deal with it. You've seen, and heard, his AIM. He did start training more people. Spread the knowledge, that kind of thing. They're all dead now."

She noticed Ryan look over at her at that, but she looked away. "He has a lot to fight for, right now. I think we all do. I was nearly killed because of rogues. I don't know about you," she said as she stood. "But I'm willing to do whatever it takes to get rid of these rogues. And I'm not going to apologize for that." With nothing else more to be said, she left.

Cam stood quickly when he noticed Maria come towards the fire. Collins had gone off somewhere after their conversation. He didn't ask, nor did he want to know. "Hey, wait," he called out when she had turned back around.

She sighed and turned back around. She looked him over and after deciding he wasn't going to attack, she joined him by the fire, barely meeting his eyes. "How are you?"

He shrugged and looked around. "Fine. You?"

Maria simply looked at him. "You know me. Better than anyone else."

Without a word, Cam stepped towards her and pulled her close. He leaned his head down against hers and felt her breathe deep and slow. The type of breathing he knew she forced when she was worked up. "He still won't talk to you?" he said quietly.

"He doesn't love me," came her muffled response.

"What are you talking about? Ryan adores you. It's actually sickening. I mean, sure, he got a bit of a shock, but I think we all did. Collins doesn't think he cares about you, but I've seen you two together."

She shook her head against his chest. "He loves Maria Kier. He loves...the girl he watched on TV. He loves the Scanner he worked with, the one who was passionate against the Underground, and hunting. Who loves to ride horses and spend all her time outside. But I'm Lieutenant Kier, now. And he hates the woman who carries a rifle, who screams orders, who wears a uniform. He hates the woman who didn't hesitate to kill a man."

"It's impossible to hate you, Maria. Even trying, it can't be done."

She looked up at him then. "You tried to hate me?"

"I thought it'd make it easier to see you with him."

"Did it?"

He paused and shook his head. "Seeing you happy made it easier. Which was why it was so hard."

Maria took a step back to look up at him easier. "What do you mean?"

"You guys rarely fought, I know that much at least. But you weren't yourself with him."

"Is it so wrong for me to want to be a better person?"

"Only if it goes against who you are deep down." Cam smiled lightly. "You're the most passionate person I know. You never feel, or believe, things halfway. It's all or nothing for you. It's what I've always loved about you."

She copied his smile and shot a glance back at the tent. "You're the same way."

"Yes I am."

Maria looked up at him. The smile was gone and her face turned to stone. "You killed to save me."

"Yes I did. And I'd do it again."

She wrapped her arms around her to fight off the chilled dessert nighttime air. "Which was easier: saving me in Niagara Falls, or here?"

Cam thought for a moment. "Here. Surprisingly enough."

Maria nodded as she stuck her toe into the ground, creating a small hole. Not big enough to hide in, though. "Can we talk about something?"

He sat down and waited for her to do the same. "There're a few things to talk about, I'm guessing."

"You wanted to marry me."

Now it was Cam's turn to kick at the ground. His AIM sauntered up to them, and he waited for it to sit next to him. He remembered their last night in his house. The use of the past tense had never seemed so ominous than before that. "Is it that surprising to know I bought a ring?"

The AIM stood back up. "Perhaps this is something to be discussed in private. Would you like me to leave? Though, my presence has yet to stop either of you from saying, or doing, things in my presence."

Maria winced with embarrassment. "For the record, had I known you were sentient, I would've been a bit more discreet when we lived together."

"I know you would have been." It looked at Cam. "I was speaking to Lucas."

"Go then," Cam replied with a wave.

"Yes, master." The German shepherd trotted away, looking over its shoulder every once in a while before it reached the tent.

Maria waited for a moment before continuing the conversation. "It was more surprising because we never talked about it. It took me breaking things off with you before you realized you wanted a relationship. How could you have wanted to get married when we were so destructive by the end?"

"Because even at the worst of times, I'd rather fight with you than anyone else. When we were at our worst was when I knew how much I wanted to fight to make it work." He took a deep breath, and wondered how much she would hate him. "Whatever Ryan's problem is, you guys will work it out. Now you'll be able to be yourself around him." He dared to look at her. "He'll be a great dad."

Maria stared at him. "I'm sure he would, but you're the father." Her eyes narrowed. "You were so excited before. You said you'd be there. You said you wanted this," she said in a low voice.

"I do!" He leaned towards her and dared to take her hands in his. "Maria, I do. But we've been there before. And you can't make a decision without talking to Ryan about it first. I don't want to be with you just for the baby's sake. I want to be in a relationship with someone who wants me."

Cam looked down at their hands, somewhat surprised she hadn't pulled away from him. "But being out here...it's made me stop thinking about the future." He squeezed her hands to interrupt her. "You broke up with Ryan to focus on the mission. My part in this is coming up, and I need to focus on it. I need to be able to do it without hesitation, and knowing that Ryan is going to be a good dad helps."

"Cameron, what are you talking about?" she asked gently. "Whatever you think you need to do–"

"I love you," he said simply. "And I love this baby. And I want to be able to do whatever it takes to keep you both safe." He smiled and touched her cheek briefly. "Get some rest, would you?"

Maria looked away. She focused on the feel of his hand enveloping hers. How long had it been since she had felt content? She closed her eyes, knowing the answer. "You're my best friend, Cam, and the father of my child. Children." She smiled at him then. "I'm allowed to not want anything to happen to you. I'm allowed to think of some form of future with you, even if it's not what we thought." Nothing is ever what we think it is.

McMurphy handed the electronic tablet over to Ryan who looked it over. Maria watched as Cam and Ryan went over their final game plan with McMurphy before they headed out. The previous day Ryan's AIM had a confirmed sighting of the rogues and confirmed everything they didn't want to know.

"They're definitely working together?" Shepero asked her, leaving the other three to themselves.

She nodded in response as the last of the camp was taken apart and packed into a vehicle. "They're still not sure how, though. There's no traceable signal leading them, so they've ruled out Mjahdan interfering. At least directly." With a glance over her shoulder, she saw Peter approaching them.

Peter smiled at her. "You weren't invited to the meeting?"

Maria shrugged. "They'll update us when we're ready to leave. I'm surprised you're not involved. I'd have thought you had more to offer with the expert training Cam gave you in Boston."

He laughed at that. "Is that what he called it?"

"Well, wasn't it? I doubt you've had someone talk to you the way he talks to people," she said with a grin.

"That's true. It was quite an experience."

"You should've heard him with Ryan when he was first signed. He had never used an AIM before."

Peter nodded thoughtfully. "Yeah, I had heard that. How did that even work?"

"Cam's expert training."

He laughed again. "I don't think I got as in-depth training as Ryan. I've seen some of their challenges from the last season. Ryan's come a long way from someone with no AIM experience. And now seeing him out here. Quite the transformation."

Yes. Quite the transformation, and likely not for the better. "Well, what kind of training did Cam do with you? Did he show you how to handle rogues? I only caught part of the conversation last night with you guys."

"Nah. He said there wasn't much point, since he would deal with them." Peter shook his head. "Famous last words. Wish he had been a prophet. Not that this hasn't been...eye-opening, for lack of a better word. But I have no idea what good Sarah and I will do when it really comes down to it. If you ask me, he would've been better off trying to teach one of us, or Ryan, so we can at least be useful. One person shouldn't have all of the information."

She nodded, taking in his words. "He tried that."

"You mentioned that last night. What happened with all of that? What happens when he's gone?" He paused and held up his hands, sensing Maria begin an argument. "He's going to get old and die at some point. It happens to the best of us. But I'm serious. It's dangerous to be the only one with this information, with this skill. What's to stop Mjahdan, or someone else, from taking him out and that's that? No one else can deal with rogues, and a lot of people can get hurt."

"Because he's more than just his knowledge about rogues," Maria said slowly as the thoughts came together in her mind. "He created the programming. There are others who can do that, and as far as I know Dr. Baxter still has all of Cam's research and they're still utilising it."

Peter agreed. "He's been integrating all of it into our training modules in Boston, and I know it's being implemented in other labs across the States. Canada's going to be producing them too, soon. Two years, I think. It's so cost efficient now."

"That's my point. Cam's not only special because of the rogues. More people know how to create the new AIMs, or at least program them, that's true. But it's Cam who pioneered it. The way he understands them, connects with them is something people can't really be taught." Maria turned her attention to McMurphy and greeted him as though the conversation hadn't happened. "Are we ready to go, sir?"

McMurphy paused and looked at her. She had yet to address him as such. Actually, none of them had really been using their ranks or taking notice of the ranks of the other soldiers. Everyone had a part to play, and it seemed as though each was just as important. Maybe Collins took his a bit too far, though. "We're hoping to catch up with them tonight. We don't want to get too close." He looked at Cam and motioned towards him. "Maybe the animal guys should explain it to the rest of us. Animals act a bit different than humans. Robots acting like animals act different, too. Not sure that's much of a surprise."

Cam nodded and stepped forward as the group of those left surrounded him. Ten remained. No medic, and only two trained AIMOTs left. So far, the soldiers didn't seem to utilize their AIM units to the extent he had assumed, which was strange for him. He was so used to being in such a close partnership with his AIM, and he knew Maria and Ryan felt the same.

He wondered how much it had changed for Maria since being in the army. He hadn't noticed her use it much either, but while off-duty it was just like it used to be. He had seen her train with it, but hadn't seen the application. Not yet, at least. Though to be fair, during the scuffle he had been paying attention to other things. He vaguely remembered Maria giving an order for the AIMs. Everything happened so quickly.

"We know for sure the AIMs are working together. Not directly, and likely not happily, but this isn't unheard of in the animal kingdom either. If they knew their best chance of survival is moving with others, then they do it. But there's never much peace when food gets close. We need to make sure they don't think of us as food." He motioned towards his AIM and it transformed into a tiger once more. It shook itself, as though filling out the fur coat of the animal.

"I will accompany Cameron and Ryan," the AIM started, but then turned its attention to the soldiers. "Tylar and Hampton, for those who prefer last names. The practice of which is illogical, as Tylar could potentially be a first name, and the confusion would be quite unnecessary. Last names are also usually longer than given names, and the attempt to give an order to a soldier with an unfortunate family name-"

"Oh, just get on with it," Cam grumbled, but he smiled. He suppressed it quickly, but it had been there. He was glad the AIM was finding its voice around strangers. It had taken a while for it to open up around even Maria, but that had been like a flood gate.

"I will accompany both of them, and be as passive as possible. They will both mimic me, and the rogues will see that I am dominant over them. They will not bother with the humans, but I will most definitely give them some alarm. Tigers have strange rituals and courtesies, not seen in many other species. I will attempt to accept them into our group, but that may only work if they feel we can benefit them.

"We must assume that they are under the impression that they are starving. We must take advantage of that. While in range, Cameron will work on disabling the units. If at any point we need support, Ryan will have his AIM join us. This will be dangerous, as it will most definitely come across as aggressive and that is something that will not end well." He looked up at Cam, and stopped. It sat down and allowed Cam to continue.

He was glad the AIM stopped where it had. He still wasn't sure what would happen with Ryan's AIM. It could go both ways, and he knew that in the end, Maria had been right. It was a huge risk to have Ryan and his AIM there, but the benefit – if it worked – would outweigh the risk by far. "Once we get them deactivated, we're on a bit of a deadline."

"We have two days now," Collins offered.

But Cam shook his head. "No. Well, yes, I'm glad you can do math. But with AIMs that go rogue, there's a time limit on how long they can be disabled and still be usable afterwards. For some reason Mjahdan wants these units back along with the new ones. Can we get confirmation on why?"

"I highly doubt they would give us the real answer, even if we asked nicely," Collins grumbled.

"The programming," Ellis suggested. "They want the tactical assets. They were given training along with the units, but they've done more training since then and they want that in the new units as well."

Cam nodded slowly. "That's what I was thinking. The only problem with that is the training isn't just in the chip. It's not just a computer code. It's not a program. It's muscle memory."

"How can it be muscle memory when they don't have muscles?" Collins asked with a sneer.

Maria rolled her eyes. "They adapt. When they're in an animal form, they have muscles. Artificial, but they're there all the same. It's how Scanners train. Look at Tylar and Hampton's AIMs. Mine, even. Think we've ever had a Barbary falcon before? Or a Bengal tiger? But we've had similar scans, and it's because of those similarities that they're able to use those forms easier. That's because of muscle memory, not just because of computer memory. The computer remembers how the muscles feel."

"Which is why this isn't going to be a simple hand-over," Cam continued. He avoided looking at Maria. "The rogue units are going to have to be turned into the upgrades if they want to be used. Ideally, the easiest route would be to update their programming entirely in a way that keeps whatever training they have while maintaining contact with the unstable substance. If we can stabilize the material, that'd be even better."

They all paused for a moment, but it was Sarah who broke the silence. She had mostly been silent in the larger meetings, simply because of her civilian status and most of the time she had very little to say. But now… "You're saying that we need to update them, with no equipment? No lab, no new material to work with?"

"*We* don't have a lab." He let that sink in for a moment, and he finally caught Maria's eyes. "In theory, any of us can do it. If we can get more time from them, it'll help us, and them."

"The problem is that they're looking for any reason to go to war. They're prepared, and they have more weapons than we know and they know that, too," Collins said. He folded his arms across his chest and nodded, agreeing with himself. "So, what's the plan?"

"We do what they want," Cam said firmly. "We get the AIMs to them, both old and new, and we don't even bother telling them about the muscle memory until the end. Twenty-four hours won't do that much damage, and until we meet with them, I'll work on them with Travato and Lim's help. They have more practice with the actual substance, and I'm sure there's something we can do out here to them on a molecular level."

Peter laughed. "With what?"

"Our brains."

"You must think yourself a god if you think you can change something's molecular properties with your mind."

"And God said 'let there be light,'" Ryan said quietly.

Maria looked over at him briefly. At least he was in the same group as her today. He had moved to the far end of the tent just to get away from her the night before. Her only consolation seemed to have been that he had been quiet around everyone. The black eye and cut on his cheek and lip was disconcerting, and Cam had been silent on that. His knuckles spoke volumes. "No, I get it. It's possible. It's what happens when an AIM transforms, isn't it? There has to be something you can do with its properties without lab equipment."

"There is," Peter agreed with a small nod. "But the new AIMs have a completely different substance compound than the old. It won't handle the new programming."

"It can if I make it," Cam suggested.

"It took you five years to create the new programming and substance. Now you're saying we need to do it in twenty-four hours. You think you're that good?" Collins asked. For once, there was no sarcasm, no maliciousness. He asked the question everyone wanted to know the answer.

He looked him dead in the eye. "No, but I can start it, making it so that they have to let me finish it. This kind of programming...it'll take just as long to work out."

He didn't say it. Maria didn't need him to say it, but the underlying truth was there, screaming at each of them, screaming at her conscience.

Five years.

McMurphy nodded and clapped his hands together. "Alright, so we know what we have to do. We'll stay as support. If things get out of hand, or if they get too close to you and you don't have protection from your unit-"

"That's the other thing," Cam said slowly. "You can't shoot them to disable them. It disrupts their properties. They won't work the way Mjahdan expects them to once we give them back. We have to do it manually. All you can do is distract them. Get your AIMs into smaller forms, use them as bait to buy me some time, not that I'll need much of it, but if things get hairy or if they act outside of our parameters then get them away from me so I can regroup."

The group split up and headed for their vehicles. Maria stepped in front of Cam before he reached his, and she looked up at him. "I know you know what you're doing, but promise you won't do anything stupid."

"It'll be fine. I'm Cam Tylar, after all."

"Don't you remember? You're Lucas Tylar."

He smiled down at her before opening the door of the Humvee. "And always will be."

Cam groaned when there was a knock at the door. "If that's the crazy lady from downstairs one more time..."

Maria laughed and shoved him down onto the couch. "I'll handle her. Get the movie ready." She laughed again when he began muttering to himself. She opened the door and her smile faltered. "Hello?"

The young man's eyes widened and he looked up at the number on the door. "Sorry, wrong place. I think." He paused. "Wait, you're Maria Kier."

"Only a season and I already have fans?"

Cam came to her side, his eyes hard on the man. "Lost?"

Maria noticed a momentary look of recognition on the man's face before he nodded.

"Yeah, sorry." He gave another quick look at Maria before he started down the hall.

"I'm gonna make sure he doesn't bother anyone else," Cam growled and closed the door behind him. He strode down the hall, catching up to the man easily. With a quick movement he had the man pinned against the wall.

"Dude!"

"What the hell, Mark?" Cam's tone was low, which most found more threatening than when he yelled.

"I didn't think you guys were living together yet." Mark shoved him away and smiled lightly at an elderly woman who came out from her apartment. When she was onto the elevator he turned his attention back to Cam. "There's a situation."

Cam looked back down towards his door. "I can't just leave. Not after you just showed up."

"A rogue hurt Henk."

Cam swore. "What was he doing?"

"He thought he could control it, something about becoming too dependant on you or something."

He swore again and ran a hand through his hair. "And the rogue?"

"Contained, but it's going to have to be terminated if we don't get it under control."

He thought for a minute, but he knew it was an eventuality. "I'll be there in fifteen."

"Cam-"

"I said fifteen." Cam stormed back to his home with Maria and walked in, taking a deep breath.

She was sitting on the couch, already watching the movie. Of course, she always restarted it. She looked so comfortable, so content, so… Maria looked up when she noticed Cam return. She held up the remote to restart the movie. "I swear nothing was spoiled. Except this stupid movie has the twist in the beginning."

"I have to go."

Maria set the remote down, letting the movie continue while she stared at Cam. "What?"

"A friend of mine...he's in trouble."

She looked at the coffee table where his phone was, and had been sitting while he was in the hallway. "Cam-"

He grabbed his AIRC and his AIM immediately went to his side. "I promise you, I'll explain everything when I get home. Don't...don't wait up."

When he left, she noticed his phone still sitting on the coffee table.

And of course she waited up for him. She had pulled all-nighters plenty of times. That wasn't new. The new aspect was waiting for her boyfriend to come home from who knew where, helping a friend she didn't know, and had no way of contacting him. Even the tracker on his AIRC had been deactivated. And he always kept that on. Now that she thought about it, she assumed he always kept it on. She had never checked before.

She stared at the door, but barely noticed when Cam walked through. Maria shook herself and stood, waiting for him to take his shoes off. He looked as tired as she felt. And there were bruises on his arms. And a bandage wrapped around his arm.

"Cam, what the hell?"

Cam took a deep breath and his AIM made itself scarce. "Maria, I love you. So much."

"Cam, are you in trouble? What happened to you? Who was that guy last night?"

He closed his eyes. "He's a colleague."

Maria's eyebrows furrowed. "Colleague? He's a Scanner?"

"In the Underground."

She stared at him and he finally met her gaze. She wanted to laugh, but there was something in his voice. "I'm sorry. I don't think I heard you right."

"I'm in the Underground, Maria."

She looked around, looking for the hidden cameras. "No you're not. You wouldn't be that stupid."

"I joined just after my mom died, before I met you."

"You're not that stupid."

"Mark, the guy from last night, we joined together. He didn't know we were living together; I hadn't told anyone yet. No one will be by again. But someone got hurt last night, and I had to go."

All Maria could do was stare at him. "You're completely serious."

Cam paused. "Rick and Owen don't know."

Maria swore. "Cam, how could you? How could you?" She moved and opened the door. "Go, quit. Tell them you're done."

But he closed the door gently. "It's not that simple."

"What, they'll kill you if you do?"

"No. Maria, what you see on the news, all these laws? That has nothing to do with the Underground, with what we do."

"They, with what they do."

Cam put a hand on her arm but she pulled away. "They didn't think I should tell you, but you're too important to me to keep something like this from you."

"Am I important enough to quit for?" When he didn't respond she swore and stormed into their bedroom, swearing along the way.

"Maria, please."

She spun on her heel and stood in the doorway. "What? You just told me you choose them over me."

"Are you making me choose? Maria, come on. Do you want to know what I do? Because if you do, I'll tell you everything."

Maria stopped and thought for a minute. He had always been so closed off, so distant. She knew why now, at least. And he was willing to incriminate himself further. She looked him in the eyes, the desperation that was there...

"No. I don't want you to tell me anything." When he started to speak, she held up a hand. "The less I know, the better it is for the team. All I'd be able to tell officials is that yes, I knew you're part of the Underground but I didn't know in what capacity. That way Rick and Owen could at least have their stats and reputations intact."

Cam watched as she pulled a bag from their closet and began to fill it with clothes. "What are you doing?"

"I'm packing." She swore when he pulled the bag away and she snatched at it quickly. "Back off, Cam."

"So, you're just leaving? Without a conversation?" he yelled.

She threw the bag at him. "What do you want me to say? That I'm okay with this? That I don't care? Cam, this is against the law. You are breaking the law. If you get caught you will go to jail. I can go to jail."

He threw the bag back at her but she let it hit the ground. "You think I don't know that?"

"Let me be very clear." Maria took a few steps towards him, looking him directly in the eyes. "The only reason I'm not turning you in, is because of Rick and Owen. If you get caught, they go down too. But if you think for one second that I'm okay with you doing this, you're out of your mind."

"Oh, well thank you for your mercy," he growled sarcastically. "If you think this is how it's going to be, you lording this over my head and holding me hostage, then I'm done."

Maria stopped and sat on their bed slowly. "Lucas, I don't know what to do," she said, her voice barely above a whisper. "How could you do this?"

He stood there, staring at her. After a moment his temper levelled off and he sat beside her. "Do you trust me?"

"With my life."

"And I trust you with mine. I guess we'll have to go from there."

"Approaching perimeter," Maria's AIM called out and the convoy came to a stop. She jumped out of the Humvee and turned her attention to Cam as he exited the lead vehicle. "You guys ready for this?"

Cam looked over at Ryan who nodded. "Too late to go back now, even if we weren't." He put a hand on Ryan's shoulder to steady him. "You don't have to come with me. I can do this on my own."

"Will it be easier if I come with you?"

"For me, yes." He shot a glance towards Maria before he pulled his bandana over his mouth to cut against the wind-whipped sand. "Not sure if it's going to be so easy for her."

"Apparently there's a lot that comes easy to her," he muttered, but instantly regretted it when he felt a twinge of pain from the previous lesson.

"I'm not even going to justify that with a comment," Cam snapped. His AIM joined them in the form of the Bengal tiger and they began their walk into the range the rogues would be able to sense them. "You realize she's not the only one who killed people yesterday. You have a problem with what she did, but I…I killed people yesterday, too."

Ryan was silent for a moment while they walked. He knew the AIM was looking at him expectantly, but he ignored it. "It's different."

"How? You're not in love with me? I look like the type of person who finds it easy to take someone's life?"

"It just is."

"She's not an athlete anymore, Ryan. She's a soldier. She was put in a position that gave her two choices: let you die, or kill. She didn't need to be a soldier to have that happen. I was there two years ago." He paused, but continued when Ryan finally looked at him. "I hesitated. I thought I could talk Trevor down, get him to see reason. I didn't want anyone to get hurt, anyone else at least.

"And because I hesitated, Jack was killed. I swore that would never happen again. I'm not going to hesitate to save someone's life, and that's what happened. That's what she did. And if you thought she didn't have it in her to do that then you have no idea who she is to begin with. With someone with her amount of passion, how could you expect anything less from her?"

Ryan stopped when they were in visual range of the rogues. He stood there watching them for a moment with Cam beside him. They moved slowly, which gave credence to their starvation theory. But they saw it with their own eyes now: they were moving together. He looked at Cam finally, holding his AIRC tight in his hands. "You've always known her better than I do. I don't get it."

"It's not that hard."

"I hate to break up this intimate moment, but I'd like to remind you both that the radios are on," Collins said over their headsets.

"Rogues spotted," Cam said in response. "Stand by." He looked at his AIM, and then Ryan. "Are you both ready for this?"

His AIM nudged him, nearly knocking him over. "Whenever you are."

He nodded. "Right. Let's get moving, then. You know the drill, Fluffy."

"Can we please try another name? I am not opposed to Striker," it whined, if a robot could whine.

"Yeah," he replied as he began to busy himself with his AIRC. "Well, I am. We're almost in physical range." Using his peripheral vision, he walked with Ryan and 'Striker' closer towards the rogues. He had been in close range with large and dangerous animals before, but none with military training or programming. He had never had this much pressure before. "Ryan, are you following along?"

"I think so," Ryan answered and looked at his AIRC quickly. "This is what you did to my AIM in Toronto, right?"

"Basically." Cam scrolled through the various setting on his AIRC until he reached the in-depth computer coding. Most athletes didn't bother, mainly for the sole reason it was illegal to tamper with the programming. Not that any of them knew how to do it. Even the best computer hackers had little success, even before Cam's safety measures. He had done what he could to ensure rogues would never be a problem again, and he vowed to continue that.

With his AIM sentient, Cam had little need for his AIRC to communicate with it so it would be able to function while he used the electronic device to sync with the rogues. His forehead furrowed in concentration. There. They were close enough now that the rogues turned their attention towards them. Cam barely noticed as the rogues began to make their way to them slowly.

"We have incoming," Ryan said quietly, his eyes focused on the tigers. So far, they were making a beeline for them, the presence of another tiger they didn't recognize was all that kept them from attacking. The soldiers' AIMs morphed now and joined their group, which further deterred the rogues.

"Sync your AIRC with them," Cam said. His thumbs jabbed quickly along the touchscreen of his device. "They're resisting more than I've seen before. Probably because they've been stuck longer than I've dealt with." He looked up suddenly when Striker stood between him and the rogues. "We're nearly done."

A deep growl rose from the AIM's throat. "You will be, very shortly."

Ryan jumped when a rogue roared at them, its tail whipping back and forth as it began to walk to their side, now ignoring the other AIMs. The robots were unable to actually attack, and the rogues now seemed to realize that. "Cam, I've done all I can. You need to hurry up."

"Thank you," he muttered. "I need to deactivate you."

Striker turned to him quickly, keeping himself in front of Cam. "You cannot be serious. The risk is too-"

"There's no alternative. I need to have everything on these guys. These units have incredible firewalls. I have to reboot all of you."

"Cam, you can't be serious," Maria called over the headset. "There has to be another way. We'll get in there and give you more time."

"Honestly, Maria, I've let you do your job out here. Let me do mine." He looked at his AIM with apologetic eyes. "I know you hate this feeling."

He stepped back closer towards him. "Please do not do this, Lucas."

Cam kept his eyes on the rogues as he pressed his thumb down onto his device. He ignored his AIM as it morphed back into its default white-ish gel. His heart nearly stopped. The rogues didn't respond. He swore and flipped through his AIRC's screens as the rogues growled and moved around to his side.

"Cam," Ryan said in a hushed tone. "Something was supposed to happen."

"It will," he said hurriedly. "It will…give it a second…"

"Cam!" Maria screamed.

He threw himself to the ground as two of the tigers leapt at him. His AIRC flew from his hands, skirting across the dusty ground. He scrambled to his knees but was knocked to the side, batted like a toy by one of the rogues. He roared in pain, but was silenced by another roar. He looked above him as another AIM appeared, standing above him in the form of a Grizzly. It'd have no chance against three tigers, but all he needed was time.

Seven.

Cam bounced to his feet and grabbed his AIRC. A jump to the right. The paw's slash came away empty.

Six.

"Run!" he yelled to Ryan, pushing him back towards the others.

Five.

The Grizzly fell down on top of a rogue, its head shaking as another rogue jumped onto its back. Four more tigers came bounding towards them with a cloud of dust rising from behind them.

Four.

Ryan's AIM as the Grizzly looked around as though confused. It lifted its paw, stepping out from the gel it seemed to have stepped in. It shook off the other pile of gel from its back. It walked back towards Ryan who stood behind Cam, not quite sure where he had been going in the first place.

Cam looked around slowly. In a daze, he reactivated his AIM. He barely felt the ground when it hit him. The dark was so inviting. *At least it's not so hot.*

"He was an idiot to try that on his own."

"He's dealt with rogues before. What were we supposed to think?"

"Did no one think that military rogues might act a little different than AIMs used for stupid challenges?"

"They're all relatively the same, at their core."

"Obviously not. If he had been a second later-"

"But he wasn't," she said softly. "He did it. We have them. He wasn't a second later."

The group was silenced when a groan came from the cot.

Maria turned from Collins and sat down next to the cot and watched Cam's face, her face and eyes filled with concern. "He's had a bit of practice working with a time limit," she said with a small smile. "Would've been good to have a trained medic."

"I did what I could," Ellis said as he finished cleaning his hands. The ground where he stood was wet from where he had dumped the bloody water. "He's just lucky the rogue wasn't any closer. It would've ripped him in half. He'll be fine, though. It'll leave a nice scar, but he's not a stranger to those." He nodded down towards the man on the cot. "Nice bullet scar."

"That was courtesy of Trevor McCarthy," she replied, her eyes still focused down on him.

Collins swore. "No wonder the S.O.B stepped down."

"Don't pretend like you care, Collins. Lying doesn't become you."

"What happened to that healing circle?" Cam asked with closed eyes, and a small smirk. He opened his eyes slowly, his smirk turning into a genuine smile. "Hey gorgeous."

She punched him in the shoulder, and he let out a grunt. "What happened to not doing something stupid?"

"You're welcome." He tried to sit up, but he had to close his eyes. "Mind not spinning the tent?"

"I'd just try to relax," Ellis said. "You lost a bit of blood. It was superficial, but sometimes those are some of the worst."

Cam lay back down and put a hand to his forehead. "The rogues?"

"They're contained," Ellis answered. "Travato and Lim have been going through their coding, trying to get a head start on that idea you had. They think they may be able to manipulate the DNA codes, if not the actual material. They used a bunch of words that I'm pretty sure had no vowels, so I stopped listening." He looked at the others. "Let's just give him some space. We know he's okay now."

Maria stood and ran a hand through his hair, and he opened his eyes again. "Thank God." She followed the others outside the tent and stopped when she noticed Ryan hang back. She looked back at the tent before turning to him. "If you hadn't used your Grizzly scan… You saved his life back there."

"And no one had to die for me to do it." Ryan winced when she looked away. "Maria…"

"Is this how it's going to be from now on?"

He paused. "I don't want it to be. I don't know how to be around you. I don't know who I am around you."

She looked down at the ground and kicked at it. A recent habit, it seemed. She let out a deep breath and finally met his eyes. "Can we just…wait until we get back? I meant it when I said I can't have a boyfriend worrying about me. Can we just act like we're two people who haven't met before, and when we get home…we'll talk?"

"I don't know if I can." Ryan looked at his AIM, sitting affectionately at his feet. It looked up at him with judging eyes and he sighed. "I can try. I can't promise any heroic stunts."

Maria smiled and squeezed his shoulder. "You were already heroic. You saved his life. That counts. A lot."

He copied her smile, but his eyes were dull. "Probably more than I want it to count."

She took her hand away and started towards the rest of the group. She stopped after a few steps and turned back to him slowly. "Honestly…it does count more than it should. And I don't know how to make it not."

"I'm not sure if this is what they're looking for," Peter said. He handed an AIRC to Sarah, who looked thoughtfully down at the coding on the small screen. "But Cam's right. If we can change how the unit morphs, that might be enough."

"I love to hear those words."

The two looked over their shoulders to see Cam standing behind them. A small grin played on his lips but he winced when he took a step. "Good to see you walking," Sarah said. They made room for him to sit between them, and Sarah handed him the electronic device. "It won't change the substance itself, but we can change how the chip reacts to it. I've never been this far into the coding. You could spend years staring at it and still have questions."

"Only one year, actually," he muttered, his focus clearly not on the conversation. "But that's pretty much what I was thinking. It'll take us a good week just to change one unit, though. There are too many variables." Cam looked up when he heard the sound of boots on the ground. He stared up at Collins, who stared right back down at him. Once they were finished measuring, the men nodded at each other.

"Unfortunately, they declined our extension. It's tomorrow or nothing," Collins said. He folded his arms across his chest. "And they won't be happy about the state of the AIMs."

"If we tell them," Sarah pointed out. "We don't have to."

"And once they do, and the AIMs become useless, that's not going to end peacefully."

She shrugged. "You already said they're looking for an excuse to go to war. Seems to me that no matter what we do, there's going to be an attack at some point. They've already attacked a military base. How is that not a declaration?"

Collins waved it off. "That happens all the time. It's just for show. But we need to put on a better one to delay any war."

"And how exactly do we do that?"

He shrugged and turned away, heading back to the others. "We have a professional showman in the group. Ask him."

When they looked at Cam, he shrugged. "I may be fine throwing myself in front of a Bengal tiger, but armed men who want to declare war on my country? I don't have much experience with that."

"Well, good thing the soldiers are going to do the talking," Peter laughed.

"You don't believe that, do you? You know that Mjahdan will want to hear from one of us. From me," Cam said. "I'm the lead programmer."

"We can all talk to them." Sarah nodded. She shut down the AIRC in her hands and set it down beside her where they sat. "Come at them as a united front. From the sounds of it, they're looking to snag one of us. If we make it seem like each of us played a part it won't be so easy for them."

Cam remained silent as Sarah and Peter created their strategy. He only half listened, for most of it. He ran his hand over his side, feeling the bandages through his shirt. He smiled easily when his AIM trotted towards him as his usual golden retriever. "Hey, buddy." He ruffled the animal's head while it attempted to lick his face. "Where were you?"

"Exploring the perimeter," he replied. He sat down but his tail wagged back and forth to show his happiness. "There is quite a bit of tension within the camp. The soldiers are all on edge. Ryan has not spoken with anyone."

Cam swore and lowered his head. "Maria was right. I never should have brought him."

"He saved your life."

"And I ruined his." When the AIM was silent, Cam nodded. "For all the times I complain about your mouth, at least you've never lied to me. Kept things from me, maybe, but never lied."

"Am I to assume you have never lied to me?"

He shrugged. "Never needed to."

"Are you keeping something from me?"

Cam paused and stroked the animal's fur. "Remember when you said that you would stand by my children's side?"

"I also said I would stay by your side. Always."

He smiled and leaned down to him. "I know. You always have, even when I push you away. You're more determined than Maria ever was. But when it comes down to choosing between me and my children, you need to choose them. Take care of Maria."

It looked up at him and whined. It hid its face in his chest, careful to not disturb his wound. "You have set your mind on this?"

"I have to."

"Then I will do this last thing you command of me."

"It's not a command."

"I know."

CHAPTER 16

Maria smiled lightly as she sat down next to Cam later that evening. She shot a quick glance towards Sarah and Peter sitting a little away, both intently focused on prodding the gel of one of the rogues. She nodded down towards the AIRC in his hands. "Any luck?"

"Yeah. But we don't have enough time."

She mock gasped. "Are you telling me there's something Cameron Tylar can't do?"

A corner of his mouth twitched. "There's a lot I can't do."

"No. There's a lot you won't do. There's a difference."

"What I do, there's always a reason for it," he snapped.

Her face turned serious at the reprimand. "I know."

"Do you?"

"What's this about?" Maria leaned towards him to catch a look at his face. "Lucas. Talk to me."

"I'm done talking. I just want this job to be done."

"I'm not letting you drop this. Tell me what's going on," she snapped.

He stood suddenly, startling his AIM into a standing position as well. "When are you going to get it? It doesn't matter what you say. If I'm going to do something, I'm going to do it whether you like it or not."

"Is this going to be another one of your 'trust me, it'll be fine,' acts? Because those never usually work out well for either of us," Maria said, her eyes narrowed as she stood to look up at him. They had now drawn the attention of the other two civilians.

Cam rolled his eyes and held his arms out to the side. "Wake up, Maria. None of this has ever been about us. You think I did what I did in the Underground just for you? That I kept it up after Lucy because of you?"

"I'm not that self-important to think you'd do anything just for me," she hissed. "I'm not really that convinced I'm worth doing much for, and you know that."

He looked at her for a moment, silent, before he grabbed her by the wrist and pulled her towards the line of vehicles. He pulled her around behind them and quickly let her go. When he still remained silent, she folded her arms across her chest.

"Wow, you really meant you were done talking," she muttered. "Unfortunately, my telepathy skills are a bit rusty."

"What would you have said?"

"Right now? Probably anything to make this less awkward."

"If I had proposed."

She took a small step back, as if pushed by the shock of the question. "What?"

"What would your answer have been?"

She shook her head and looked around for an escape. "Cam, it was three years ago. You said it yourself that none of it matters anymore."

"Then it shouldn't matter if you tell me."

Maria stared at him, trying to read his face. He had always been so good at hiding behind his wall, that handsome mask that had fooled so many into thinking him unbreakable. But she had found that others saw as a mask was a patchwork veil, made up from all the broken promises he had heard growing up.

"Yes."

"And if I asked now?"

Her jaw nearly dropped and she took a full few steps away from him. "Cameron…"

He grinned his half grin, a secret behind his eyes. "Hypothetically. It's been three years. What would you say?"

"What does it matter?"

"Humour me."

"Cam," Maria breathed. "We haven't been together in over three years. We're different people now. We didn't work before."

"Exactly!" he exclaimed and stepped closer to her. "We're different people now, and I think that if all of this wasn't happening-"

"I'd still be with Ryan."

"We'd work now as these people."

She shook her head and took a step back. "Don't. Just don't. We need to focus on the mission. We're so close, Cam."

He stopped and put a hand on her shoulder. "Maria, I'm not asking you to marry me. I'm not even asking to get back together. I don't want to think about the future, not yet. I don't want to jinx anything. But I would like to know if our history, with our present, if that would be enough."

Maria avoided his gaze. Why was she hesitating? They were going to be parents again, together. They could be a family finally. He had wanted to marry her once, if he didn't still. But even now, working together again, they fought. It seemed to be what they did. Being friends was one thing, and they had done that well. Being team-mates wasn't working out so well. How were they going to be partners too? "We're a disaster, Cam."

He placed his hands on her arms as he forced her to look at him. "Yes, we're a disaster. But tell me your heart doesn't race in a hurricane, or in this God forsaken desert." Before she could respond, he pulled her close and pressed his lips against hers.

Without missing a beat, he felt her arms wrap around his neck. He took a few small steps forward, walking her backwards until he had her pinned against the side of the Humvee. Cam's hands slid down her sides until they found her hips. He pulled her even closer against him, his body flushing with desire for her.

"Cam."

He broke away from her lips quickly as they both looked to the side to find Ryan standing nearby.

"The AIMs are back," Ryan muttered.

"Ryan," Maria said softly.

But he shook his head. He turned and left, and Cam swore, shutting his eyes. He leaned his head against Maria's forehead. He cringed when he heard her swear as well.

"I'm sorry," Cam whispered.

"Ryan!" Maria called after him as he made his way to the tent. She followed him inside and stopped abruptly when he turned around to face her.

"So, that's it, then?" he asked.

"Ryan, it didn't mean anything like that."

"No? That kiss meant nothing? I'd hate to see one that did."

She shut her eyes. "I didn't mean that. I meant it nothing to us, you and me."

He let out a laugh, and Maria couldn't help but notice how much he sounded like Cam when he was angry. She remembered when she had first met him, how kind he had been. Hardly ever sarcastic, never swore. What had she turned him into? "You're telling me that when we get home, everything will go back to how it was before? That you only broke up with me while you were gone and you had every intention of getting back together?"

Maria paused, which she knew told Ryan the answer before she even spoke. "That had been the plan, yes."

"Until you killed a man in front of me, or until he kissed you?"

Another pause, and she swore she saw his heart break inside his chest. "No. Maybe." She let out a deep breath and looked around desperately as if the tent walls had the words she needed. "When I broke up with Cam, it was because I couldn't handle him having a second life, at first. Every day I wondered if that day would be the final straw, because I knew he'd never want to share his life with me. Our relationship had a deadline. I held off ending it for so long because I wanted to think he wanted more, even though he didn't. So, I slept with Jack, mostly because I thought Cam had cheated on me." Maria stopped and shook her head.

"I'm not even making any sense," she continued after a minute. She looked Ryan in the eyes. "I wanted to spend the rest of my life with him. And now I find out he had a ring, and that's a lot to take in, Ryan."

"If he were to ask you now," Ryan started slowly. "Would you say yes?"

"I don't know."

He shook his head and took a step towards her. "We both know, but you need to say it. Maria, you don't love me. We were together as long as you and Cam were, and you were ready to marry him."

"Stop," she said harshly. "Stop comparing two completely different relationships."

"You haven't been with him in three years, and if he were to ask you to marry him today, you'd say yes without even going back to dating first," Ryan continued as though she hadn't said a word.

"It's not that simple, Ryan."

"Why? If anything, us dating shouldn't have been so simple. You guys have a kid together. You've been through hell with Trevor together."

Maria stepped back at those words. "What did you say?"

He winced, realizing his mistake. "Cam told me everything. But," he continued quickly, seeing her face redden with either anger or embarrassment, or both. "He did it to make me feel better. It was after Johnson died. I made the mistake of having a pity party, so he told me how Jack actually died. How he listened to you die over the phone." Ryan shook his head with a small smile. "When I heard that, I had no idea how he managed to not take you away from me so he'd never lose you again."

"I don't want to give you up," was her only response.

He paused and took a step towards her. "Even if Cam proposed?" When she didn't answer except for a small shrug and a shake of her head, Ryan placed a hand on the side of her face. "Are you sure you don't love me?"

"No. But I think I'm sure you don't love me," Maria said simply.

He took his hand away with a small nod. "I did. But that woman isn't there anymore, is she?"

"I'm still the same, Ryan. I've changed, yes, but I never hid that. Lucy changed me. Nearly getting killed, twice, changed me. You changed me. Maybe you weren't paying attention, or you were just...trying to keep me as something familiar in your mind."

They were silent for a few moments, neither looking directly at each other. Finally, he backed away. "You were right to want to put things aside while you're here. None of us should be thinking about any of this right now."

"No."

"But, it's a conversation for later?"

Maria looked at him quickly. This was the most he had said to her, without yelling and without throwing insults, since the ambush. "Is that a conversation you even want to have?"

He shrugged. "We can at least keep it on the table. Who knows how all of this is going to end."

She nodded. She dreaded that conversation. It would be three years ago all over again. She was carrying Cam's child. Maria knew now that neither would leave her side, and Ryan wouldn't back down simply because of the baby. That is, if he could find it in him to be with her again. If she wanted to be with him, he would love the child as his own. But this time Cam wanted to be a family. He wasn't running away this time. "For later."

The next morning Collins shook his head as McMurphy went over the final stages of the mission. "This is not going to go over well with everyone. You know that, right?"

"Does it really matter?" Shepero asked. "This is what we rehearsed. There's no point changing it now. We all knew this was the best-case scenario, going into this."

"But is it best case?"

"It has to be."

McMurphy looked around, his eyes falling on the civilians. "There could be a better way, but we all know that there's more to this than only four rogue AIMs."

The three were silent for a moment as Maria strode by with Ellis, taking turns with an AIRC. McMurphy nodded after her. "I can see why she's where she is. I don't think most people bounce back the way she does, and has."

"It's our job to bounce back," Shepero muttered. "I know she's been through a lot, but it's our job."

"She's been through more than you realize, according to Tylar," McMurphy offered. "And our own records. After all of this, whether we're successful or not, she'll understand." He paused when Cam approached them, and nodded a greeting. "Are we good?"

"We're good," Cam answered without hesitation.

As Maria finished confirming her details with Ellis, she noticed Ryan off to the side and she watched him carefully. He checked his gear, patting himself down as though reassuring himself that his parachute would catch him when he fell. She saw the tension on his face and tried her best to keep her distance. When he finally noticed her, she was surprised that he did not turn away. She took the invitation and stepped towards him as the rest of the team prepared.

"Are you okay?"

He paused to think about his answer. "Better than I thought I would be. Everything seems...strangely calm. I mean," he looked around their surroundings, "the tension is a little suffocating. But I think for the first time since we got here, everyone knows their role, and that's all we can do." He kicked his toe into the ground when he caught Cam's eye briefly as he passed. "I don't even mind being in the dark. Seems to be a better place than wherever he is." He turned back to her finally and gave her a sad smile.

"I think everyone was right. I think the girl, the woman I loved was someone I held onto. I didn't let her change, not in my mind at least. I'm sorry you couldn't be yourself with me. I think…" His voice trailed off for a moment. "I think I don't even know who I am, or who I'm changing into. But I don't think I'm a Scanner. Or at the very least I can't go back like nothing happened here."

"Ryan," Maria started softly, "no one's expecting you to act like you're not a different person. You are a Scanner. That's who you are, deep down."

But he shook his head. "No. I don't think so. This, you, it's changed me. Shaken me to the core. I never thought it was possible to feel so...angry, and so much hate. I don't like this person. Frankly, I don't like a lot of people. Not anymore."

She opened her mouth to speak but Collins came up to them and clapped Ryan on the back.

"Let's get a move on. We're all set." Collins held Maria by the elbow as Ryan jogged towards the caravan. He lowered his head down to her. "Are you ready?"

"Are any of us?"

He stepped closer, keeping his grip on her arm. "I need to know you're okay to do this. However it goes down, I need to know you can do this."

She wrenched her arm back and glared up at him. "You're unbelievable. You'd never ask me that if I were a man. I'm not fragile because I'm a woman."

"I'm not saying you're fragile. But you are emotionally invested because you have two loved ones here and we're coming face to face with the enemy. And because you know Cam is in the most danger."

Maria stared up at him until she couldn't stand it anymore. She closed her eyes, remembering the feel of the blade against the skin of her forearms, how it seemed to release her every bad moment. When she opened her eyes, she nodded. "I shot him once to prove a point. I can do it again." She hoped.

"Don't say anything unless they bring it up," Collins reminded him.

"But we can't let them leave without knowing," Cam replied, his voice monotone. He stared out the window of the Humvee as the sandy landscape whipped by, barely flinching as the vehicle bounced over the uneven ground. "I'll be fine. If it comes down to it, you keep her safe."

"You know she hates me. She's not going to make it easy," Collins muttered.

Cam let himself smile. "She doesn't make anything easy."

"There are four vehicles at the rendezvous point," Cam's AIM spoke through the AIRC. "Five people, as far as I can tell. There are four more roughly two hundred metres away, likely as backup."

"Any AIMs with them?" Cam turned his attention to the console, looking at the live feed his AIM started.

"None active. They are all defaulted."

"Probably want a demonstration," Collins suggested.

"Well, they're not getting one." When he was given a questioning look, Cam continued. "Why would I show them how to fix their AIMs? Makes any of us useless. They'll know I can do my job when the AIMs we retrieved don't kill them. But that would make our lives a lot easier." He tapped on the screen of the AIRC, clearing it of the video feed. "Get back to us before we get there."

Fifteen minutes later, and with all the AIMs returned from their flight, the caravan came to a slow stop. Maria gripped her rifle. Through the front window she could see them: Mjahdan. What they had faced before in the ambush, those were nothing compared to the men who awaited them. Four vehicles of their own, impressive looking uniforms, impressive looking weapons, and stoic faces. She barely noticed when McMurphy put a hand on her arm. Her heart began to race and her hand began to involuntarily shake.

"Just breathe," he said. "Go through the steps. We give them the cases. We move out. That's it. We're back in the vehicles, and we leave." But they both knew that even if they did survive whatever this was going to be, they would never leave the desert. Not really. No one ever did.

With a short nod Maria followed the rest out of the vehicle, the soldiers forming a barrier between Mjahdan and the civilians. Everyone seemed to move so slowly. Maybe it was just her. She felt the ground beneath her shake, and she quickly met Cam's eyes. For that moment everything seemed to stabilise. She caught her breath just as he stepped in her path, the others moving ahead.

"Are you okay?" he asked in a hushed tone. When Maria nodded, he gave her a soft smile. "You're one of the strongest people I've ever known. My mom would have absolutely loved you, probably as much as I do."

"Nice pep talk," she muttered.

"I love you," he stated, so effortlessly.

She ignored the quick glances from the others, but was glad that Ryan at least pretended to be too far away to hear. "Yes." When Cam paused, trying to understand, she added, "I'd answer yes."

He smiled and squeezed her arm. But there was something behind his eyes, the same look Maria saw earlier. "Good."

"Get back in formation." Her face changed in an instant, and she focused on the job. That was all she could do. "Ellis, let's make this exchange."

Maria looked up from the cold dinner when Cam entered their home. She felt her anger rising, knowing he was going to have yet another excuse for this. She stood and began clearing the plates. "I'll put this away. I assume you've already had dinner since you're so late." She held up a hand before he could speak. "I don't want an apology, Cameron. Not again." When his arms went around her waist she tensed. "Cam."

"I love you."

She let out a sigh. "You said you were going to be home."

"I know. Things took longer than I thought."

The Underground. Again.

"I want to talk to you about something," he said. He took the plates from her hands and placed them on the counter.

The first thing she noticed was that he wouldn't meet her eyes. "What happened?"

"There's a lot about what I do in the Underground that I can't talk to you about. It kills me, keeping my life separate from you. And I know it hurts our relationship."

"What happened, Cam?"

He looked down at his AIM, always at his side. "I've been talking to someone, a... colleague, of sorts. She works on different things, but I can talk to her about anything."

Her heart fell. "Lucas, what did you do?"

"She came on to me, and-"

And shattered on the tiled kitchen floor.

"You..." Her hands were shaking.

"Maria-"

But she shook her head. "No. No more excuses." She shoved her feet into her shoes and grabbed the car keys, ignoring his protests as she slammed the door behind her.

* * *

Twenty minutes later Maria found herself looking around the bar. This was where he always came but she hadn't seen him yet. A deep laugh caught her attention. Her anger bolstered her resolve and she walked up to him, placing herself between him and his 'date.'

"Hey Jack."

His eyes widened. "Uh, hey Maria."

"Excuse me!" came a shrill voice from behind her.

Maria rolled her eyes and looked over her shoulder. "Sorry, here." She slid Jack's beer to the woman. "Drink that and be quiet for a minute." When she turned back to Jack his eyes were still wide with surprise.

"Hey, so what's going on?" he asked tentatively.

"Do you want to bring me back to your place?" She could see his mind racing, but his own resolve was set.

"Look, Maria, I may not like the guy, but Cam-"

"-and I are done."

Jack took the beer back from his date, downed it, and grabbed his coat. His eyes locked on Maria the entire time. "You can find your own way home, right...uh..."

"Brielle."

"Sure." He eyes always on Maria. "Let's go."

"Do you want to talk about it?"

Maria looked over at Jack with a small smile. "The sex?"

"You and Cam."

She rolled onto her back and stared at the ceiling. "Nope."

"Look, I'm more than happy to be rebound. But you and Cam...were you and Cam."

"Well, turns out it was Cam and someone else, too. So, there's that."

Jack sat up and turned towards her. "Wait, what?"

Maria closed her eyes and let out a small curse. "I know you guys aren't the best of friends, but would you mind not spreading that? It's one thing for him to cheat on me, but if it gets out it'll affect the entire team."

"Maria, he didn't cheat on you."

"Sorry, were you there?" she snapped.

He opened his mouth, and his hesitation got her attention. She swore and sat up with him. "Jack."

"Cam and I have a mutual friend. She's into him, told him so, came onto him...but he turned her down. Came crying to me about it unfortunately. 'Oh no, Cam Tylar doesn't want me'." When Maria didn't respond he watched her face. "I'm even more into revenge sex, but please tell me you and Cam are actually broken up."

"Oh God..." She pulled the sheet up and buried her face.

Jack swore and got out of the bed. "Are you kidding me? Are you kidding me, Maria?"

She heard him grabbing his clothes and dressing himself. What had she done? After a moment she looked up and saw him staring down at her with an unrecognizable look on his face. "Jack, I'm so sorry."

"You wanted something easy. You know how I feel about you, and you used me to get back at him," he said, his voice soft. "I hang out with some pretty crappy people, but I never, ever, expected this from you."

He sat down on the bed next to her and pulled her towards him as she began to sob. "I'll take you home in the morning. You'll talk to him and sort all of this out. In the future, tell people I seduced you with my wit and charm." When she began to cry harder, he stroked her hair, making sure she kept covered by the blanket. "Okay, yeah. Too soon."

The next morning, Maria opened the door to her home. She saw Cam pacing in the living room, his phone to his ear.

"I don't know where she went-" he said, his voice in a panic. When the door closed, he looked over hurriedly. "She just came in. Thanks, Rick." He hung up the phone and let it fall onto the couch. "Maria, thank God." He took a few steps toward her but stopped when she held up her hands. "Let me explain, please."

"All you ever do is explain," Maria said softly. "Explain, and excuses."

"I was being open with you; I want to be open with you." He slid his hand into his pocket. "None of this came out right. Please,

let me start over." He started to take something out from his pocket but stopped at her next words.

"I'm going to be gone for the next two days. When I get back, I don't want your things to be here," she explained slowly. "I'll buy you out of your half of the place, you can have the car if you want."

"Maria..."

"If you need more time, let me know. I'll be staying with a friend. I can let you know when I get there so you know I'm okay. I'm sorry I didn't call last night."

Cam stepped towards her again. "This is just a fight. We fight all the time." But this time she sounded so calm. So resolute.

"Cameron, neither of us have fought in a long time for what should really matter."

Then again, it had never felt quite like this before.

"You really want to do this?" He was angry now. "After everything."

She closed her eyes, and squeezed them briefly. "Please, I don't want this to be done while yelling. Because we'll think this is out of anger. Please just let me leave."

But he wanted to yell. He wanted to scream, and throw something, and grab her and never let go.

"Then leave. But you better be damn sure this is what you want."

Maria didn't respond as she opened the door and turned to leave. She paused. The picture of them in Cuba sat on the table next to the door. Smiling. Happy. She closed the door behind her and managed to control her breathing all the way back to Jack's car.

There was no going back from this. All their talk of always being there, taking one day at a time, trusting each other. That was over now, and she knew she'd have to live with her decision. They both would.

Ryan stood close to Shepero, letting the soldier's confidence and strength ease his nerves. His rifle felt unbearably heavy suddenly, but he didn't so much as fidget. He saw them: men who had ambushed their group, men who planted the IED that killed Johnson, the man Maria had killed to save his life. He blinked and realized Collins had already approached the insurgents standing before them.

With a nod from McMurphy, he greeted the men in Pashto. The one in front sported a thick mustache, reminiscent of pictures of old Cuban dictators. Different culture and race, but there was a resemblance. He waved dismissively as Collins continued to speak. "No need for a secret conversation. We all speak English. Do you have the creatures?"

Ellis and stepped forward with the disabled rogues in a large carrying case. Collins followed him with the new upgrades. Ellis waited for Collins to set down his cases before he spoke. "These ones are the ones which you lost. Undamaged. You're welcome, by the way."

The mustachioed man stepped aside for a shorter man to come forward. He took the case and busied himself with them along with various AIRCs. Within a few moments four tigers stood between the two groups, obediently awaiting orders. The two exchanged a few hushed words briefly.

When they were finished, Mr. Mustache smiled with a nod. "Impressive. You certainly have some talented soldiers. And the upgrades?" The shorter man answered in Pashto, and he held up his hands. "Apologies. They are in there as well. You can assure us that this will not be an issue again?"

Ellis pointed at the upgraded units with a nod. "Those will never turn against you. It's the same model we use."

"And what about the rest of our AIMs? What guarantee can you give that they will not go rogue?"

"They will go rogue," Ellis answered. "You need to know that having these reactivated is putting yourself, and everyone around you at risk of this happening again. You need to destroy them. All of them. You can input all of the training into the new upgraded units."

The man laughed and gestured towards the new units. "You have given us four replacements, and you want us to destroy all of the ones we already have? Destroy all of the work we have put into the ones we have now? Do you think we are idiots?"

Collins cleared his throat. "We'll get you in touch with the manufacturer so you can get a legitimate deal with them to receive the upgrade. That's all we can negotiate. It would be an exchange. You wouldn't need to buy anything."

"And you think the McCarthy Group will want to have it on paper that they have supplied us with these creatures? We want them from you."

It was at that point when Cam stepped up beside Maria, his eyes on the insurgents. In a lowered voice he asked her, "do you trust me?"

She turned her attention from the conversation about the AIM units. "With my life." That was when she saw it on his face. "Cam-"

"And I trust you with mine." He squeezed her arm quickly. "Bring me home." He pushed past the soldiers and stopped when he was beside Collins. "Do you seriously think they're going to just supply all of your AIM units and not make it legitimate?" Cam gave his arrogant laugh and eyed the man before him. "What, you're not happy enough with all the weapons the United States gives you?"

Collins shoved him backwards. "Get back in your place, Tylar," he growled.

The insurgent clapped his hands to get their attention. He smiled when they looked at him once more. "You have a better idea?"

Cam ignored Collins and gave a shrug. "You don't need to replace all of your units. At least, probably not. Most could just be tweaked and upgraded on their own."

"You expect us to use machines that will kill us? Your colleague is under the impression the old ones will kill us all."

"They won't after I'm done with them," Cam stated, folding his arms across his chest.

There was no shock on the man's face at Cam's offer. And Maria saw it then. This was it. This was the mission all along.

Scanner.

She felt herself take a small step forward, but when there was resistance she looked down. Cam's AIM stood in front of her in the form of the typical German shepherd. She could not even form the words. All she could do was watch her world be torn apart.

"You think you can do all of this work, fix our AIMs?" the man asked with a laugh. They all knew it was meant to goad Cam.

But despite the pounding in his chest, he had dealt with this before. Cam had looked into the eyes of a man ready to kill for his own purpose. He wasn't going to run away this time. "How many units do you have?"

"Two hundred." Mr. Mustache folded his arms over his chest to mirror Cam.

Cam shrugged. "Easy. That should only take me about six months. My colleague will assist."

Maria instinctively looked at Ryan, but her eyes widened in shock when Peter stepped up beside Cam. There were no words.
The man looked at Collins and McMurphy, and eyed Cam to size him up. After what felt like an eternity, the man nodded. "Good. Let's go."

Maria watched herself as though she was in a movie. She watched as she let herself allow Cam to walk away with the insurgents. She couldn't even feel her heart beating. Maybe she was dead. Maybe this was hell. Wherever she was, she watched as Cam so easily walked with the men to their vehicles, as though he had known them his whole life. There was no second glance, no look over his shoulder. In an instant, he was in their vehicle, followed close by Peter. The caravan hummed to life and rolled away.

It felt like an eternity. All of it. And everything was silent. Eventually she heard the muffled sounds of voices, and when she looked down, she noticed Cam's AIM still standing in front of her, an AIRC in its mouth. She took it from him silently as the sounds around her began to come back into focus.

"What just happened?" Sarah's shrill voice was the first to stand out.

"Clear out, everyone," McMurphy urged. "Now. Move!"
Maria felt herself ushered back into one of the Humvees, AIM close behind. The image of Cam climbing into the vehicle the only thing she could see.

CHAPTER 17

"He was the only one who could have made this work." The journey back to the Forward Operating Base had been quiet. McMurphy looked around at the group of them. Not a single person spoke. Now, back in relative safety, it was time the rest of them knew the remainder of the mission.

"Our hope was that this mission would also allow us to finally bring down Mjahdan, or at least learn their locations and strength," McMurphy continued. "While with them, Cam will be upgrading their current AIM units, while also linking them to our system. This will ultimately give us control over their AIMs, learn their tactics, and finally get the jump on them."

"And Peter?" Sarah asked quietly.

Collins looked at the woman. "He's our rear guard. He'll make sure Cam has enough time to finish what he needs to. He's our covert op. He has been given clearance to do what he judges will best keep himself and Cam alive. He'll also help however he can with the substance."

"All of their progress will be monitored live by a team of AIM technicians and a tactical team I don't even have the clearance to know the name of."

"What's the extraction plan?"

Collins paused when Maria finally spoke up. Her voice was monotone, and her eyes were dead. She hadn't made so much as a whisper of a sound since it had happened, hadn't really seemed to have looked at anything or seen anything. At least now she was participating. He cleared his voice and motioned to McMurphy.

"In six months, we will retrieve both Cam and Peter."

"How?"

Collins glanced at McMurphy and Shepero. "Unfortunately, that's classified."

"Bull," she said simply. "What's the extraction plan?"

"Kier-"

"Nathan," she said, standing up to stare him in the face. "How are you going to bring him home?" There was a desperation in her voice, but it didn't waver.

He put his hands on her shoulders and met her gaze directly. "Carefully. And alive. You have my word. You know you can't be there when we do." When she nodded, he squeezed her shoulder. "Go get some rest. We leave in two hours for Kandahar. You'll all go through debriefing before you return home."

"You're staying?"

"An extra week only. Make sure things take off on the right foot."

Maria looked at the ground with a wry smile. "You mean make sure Cam doesn't get himself killed in the first week?"

"Something like that. He's a pain in the ass, after all."

Ryan watched Maria as their vehicle shuttled them back across the desert. Her eyes were glued to the window, never really straying from it for more than a glance. He leaned to his left, towards McMurphy and gestured towards her. "How long do we need to stay in Kandahar? When can she go home?"

"We'll have our debriefing sessions, civilians and soldiers separate for the most part. We'll only come together when we need to do group reenactments," McMurphy started slowly.

"That's not what I asked." He shook his head. "Wait, reenactments?"

"Not exactly what you're thinking, but everyone goes through the events, one by one, everything that's happened. It helps everyone to focus on facts, helps ensure nothing gets exaggerated in our minds after the fact. Then we deal with what those events caused, the consequences."

Ryan shook his head. "When can she go home?"

"When we all go home. De-briefing usually takes about a week, but probably only five days for us to be honest. The mission is still technically ongoing but our part of it, yours especially, is done."

"He knew."

Ryan looked at Maria quickly, hearing her soft words. "What?"

"The bastard knew the entire time," she muttered. "You all knew." Without even moving her eyes from the window, Ryan knew she was referring to McMurphy, and even Collins in the other vehicle. "This was the plan all along. 'We're not going over to take down the militia. We're just going for the AIMs.' I should have known."

McMurphy leaned towards Maria. "He was given the option of not going, no one forced him."

"This goddamn job... As soon as you told him, there was never an option."

Ryan simply shook his head to the soldier while Maria continued to mutter under her breath. Five days didn't seem long enough for everyone to be ready to return home. Home. Canada. Back to where friends and family were waiting. His job as a Scanner, an athlete. But he wouldn't be going back; no one really seemed to return from the desert. For all he knew, the de-briefing would help get his mind clear, let him wrap his mind around the priorities this experience had created. But no one really seemed to return from the desert.

It had been nearly four hours since they arrived back to Kandahar. The soldiers were immediately pulled into a post-op brief which only took about half an hour. But Collins hadn't seen Maria since they were dismissed. He looked around and finally found McMurphy. "You haven't seen Kier, have you?"

He shook his head. "No. After the hot wash I sent her for her medical triage. I assume she's still there."

But Collins dismissed the idea. "I've already checked."

McMurphy raised an eyebrow. "You're suddenly curious about her." But even he couldn't deny that Maria was taking everything hard. Her answers during the brief sounded robotic. The way she described the events of their mission almost made it seem as though she already detached herself from everything.

He waved him off. "I told...I told Cam I'd watch out for her. We had a bonding moment, or whatever." He rolled his eyes. "Shut it. Just let me know if you find her."

After another ten minutes of looking, the last place he knew he hadn't tried was the washroom facilities. After calling out to make sure no one was in there, at least anyone who would answer, he stepped in. He was only slightly disappointed to find that the shower areas were identical to the men's. Somehow he had always thought the women's bathroom would be prettier, or frilly. And if his ex, or Maria, had known his thoughts, they would have both called him sexist and continue on a tirade. Just another affirmation that she was like his ex. Well, he knew he had similarities to Cam at least.

"Maria?" he called out, trying to sound inviting, or comforting. He wasn't sure it actually worked. There was no response. He looked into each stall as he made his way down the row slowly. The sound of metal scraping made him pause at the last shower stall. He stepped into the doorway and his jaw clenched.

She had turned off the shower by then, when she realized she wasn't going to go through with it. But she still sat in her soaking clothes on the floor of the shower, knife in front of her. She didn't look up when he sat down across from her on the wet floor.

"How was your shower?" he asked gently.

"Cold."

"Well, we're in a desert. Everything else here is hot." He paused, and then reached out for the knife.

She grabbed the handle before he could and pulled it towards her as though to hide it from him. "I can't..."

"You can't what?"

"Anything. I can't...I can't use this knife. I can't stay here. I can't go home."

"You can, you can go home, Maria."

But she shook her head violently. "You don't get it. He grounded me. He...he made me feel safe. He was my reminder I was back from war. I can't go home. He's here. I can't go home."

"Maria-"

"I'm pregnant, Nathan. How do I go home when he's here? I can't just leave him here."

Collins edged closer towards her and put his hands on her knees. "Maria, look at me." He waited and when she met his gaze, he saw then what Cam had been afraid of. "You need to trust him. He knows exactly what's at stake, and he knows exactly who's waiting for him. Cam didn't agree to do this just to have you sit on the floor of a shower. Or to use that knife on yourself and his unborn kid. We're going to get you cleaned up and dry. Have you gone for your triage yet?" When she shook her head, he continued. "Okay, so we'll take you there and work out some of what's going on in your head."

He took a risk and brushed her wet hair back from her face. "Then you're going to go home, tell your team what happened and what he's doing because they'll deserve to know. And in six months, Cam will be going through his own debriefing and coming home to you. And hopefully he won't think you got fat and ugly since you'll be what, eight months pregnant by then?"

Maria looked around, her eyes shifting as though seeing her surroundings for the first time. "I'm a mess," she stammered, either ignoring what he had said, she hadn't heard it, or she was not so subtly moving past it.

"Yes, you are." He got to his knees and helped her stand. "Let's get you cleaned up."

"Nathan?" She looked up at him. "You were right about me. I have no right to be here. Never have. And-" but she stopped when his hand covered her mouth.

"You talk too much, Kier. Now come on," he ordered and half carried her from the showers. He knew then what the next six months were going to entail, and he hoped he was up for the challenge.

CHAPTER 18

Maria was slightly surprised that Ryan had allowed her to sit next to him on the plane ride home. She wasn't entirely sure it wasn't from pity, or to make sure she was sane during the flight. He had been very cautious with her the past five days before they left Kandahar, and patient during her mild panic attack at the airport. It was the first time either of them had been around this many people since arriving, since everything had happened. But she was grateful at least that the debriefing period had taken five days.

Ryan and Sarah underwent multiple de-briefing sessions and medical appointments every few days to make sure they weren't showing any symptoms of shock. And the joint civilian debrief went extremely well with everyone adding in their perspectives of the events. No emotions. Just facts.

She could tell the sessions helped Ryan to work through everything that happened in a logical order. She also knew he had been warned about what he could and could not tell people once they returned home. But both he and Sarah were connected now with a counsellor to meet with. And Maria agreed to continue seeing her own therapist. Not that she had a choice in the end, but Nathan at least had seemed relieved by her decision.

But Maria and Ryan agreed she would be the one to tell Rick and Owen about Cam, what little they could say. It had been hard to keep the communication with them to a minimum, especially after they had asked to pick them up from the airport. She gave them the flight information but kept it at that. She knew it was cold, but it was all she could manage.

"I think I'm going to take the season off," Ryan said quietly.

Maria looked at him quickly, surprised both by his statement and him speaking in general. But it made sense. After a moment she nodded. "I think that's a good idea," she commented.

"Cam probably will too when he gets back," he continued. "He won't have missed much of the season, but I'm sure he'll need to work through things too."

She didn't respond this time, but closed her eyes instead and tried to sleep for the rest of the flight, dreading the reunion with her old team. It wasn't the first time she had gone through this, an awkward and sombre reunion. After Lucy and her year of radio silence, seeing Rick and Owen again had been difficult and humbling. But they had moved on from it. She wondered now if they would blame her if anything happened to Cam. She didn't wonder for long. She knew.

Rick waited with his dad at the arrivals area of the Toronto airport. He wasn't sure if Maria would be in uniform or not. He had seen clips online of soldiers coming home, their family greeting them at the airport, and the soldiers were usually in their uniform. He wasn't sure why it mattered, what she would be wearing. What any of them would be wearing. But the month had gone by slowly. The way Maria had spoken before they left it had seemed like it would take longer. Rick figured things must have gone well, or weren't as bad as they thought. At least they were home in time to celebrate Christmas.

Then another thought occurred to him. They could be coming home early because something happened. No. She had said specifically that "they" would be coming home today, on this flight. He was startled from his thoughts when Owen elbowed him gently and nodded towards the sliding doors.

Ryan came through first, and Rick was about to wave, but he noticed something. It was Ryan, but something was different. The way he walked, the way he looked around at the people beside him. Maria was close behind him, her face completely closed. He was used to that, though perhaps not quite to this extent. He continued looking, waiting. But when Ryan and Maria both reached him, his heart fell.

Owen put a hand on Rick's shoulder to steady himself, or to prepare Rick. When Maria finally met their eyes, they knew.

"What happened?" Owen was the one to find his voice first, but it was shaky and quiet.

She shifted the duffel bag on her shoulder. "Maybe we should sit down and talk."

"What happened to him, Maria?"

"He's still over there," she started slowly. She needed to be careful what she told them. If she couldn't be in Afghanistan keeping Cam safe, she would have to do it from this side of the world. "He...he's still finishing some work."

Rick swore, surprising all of them. "What the hell does that mean?"

"It means the group we dealt with needed someone to work on their AIMs, and he said he would do it."

"And you just *let him*?"

She closed her eyes and gripped the handle of her bag. "Cam knew exactly-"

"To hell with what he knew, or thought!" Rick screamed, gaining the attention of nearby security along with most people around them. "You were supposed to make sure all three of you came home. And why would they keep him alive, hm? Why won't they just kill him? Can you get him home then?"

Before Maria could respond, Striker stepped forward as the German shepherd. He had stayed back while the humans greeted each other, but this was too far. "They will keep him alive because they need him," he spoke. "Maria had no knowledge of the true nature of the mission or Cameron's intentions. I was not privy to the decision until the night before it happened."

Rick and Owen stared down at the AIM, jaws open in a loss for words.

Ryan shuffled a bit. "Oh yeah, Cam's AIM does that."

"Maria has been through enough, blames herself enough, that she does not need either of you to make her feel worse. You are both aware she suffers from PTSD. You are both aware that she has panic attacks. She has left someone very dear to her in the hands of people who can easily kill him. You are not allowed to make her feel little, or as though she let any of you down. Including you, Ryan."

The group of them were silent for a few moments, Rick and Owen both shocked and humbled by the AIM's chastisement. Finally, Maria reached down at stroked the top of Striker's head. He licked her hand in response. "I'll find my own way to Kingston," she mumbled.

But Owen put a hand on her shoulder. "How long is he there for?"

She flinched under his hand. "Six months."

He nodded and pulled her into an embrace. "Then in six months we'll pick him up from the airport. And you're not going to Kingston. You'll come home with us."

Maria didn't respond other than a quick shrug, but she still wouldn't meet the gaze of the rest of them. "There's a lot we can't talk about."

"We know."

She looked at Ryan, whose face was still clouded over. "And a lot we should talk about."

"We know."

The first twenty-nine days were the hardest for Maria. She had sat down with Rick and Owen individually and told them as much as she could about what happened. When she told them each what happened to Ryan, the IED incident, Striker once again had to step in to calm them. She had been surprised with Rick's outbursts. She expected it, but more from Owen to be completely honest. At the end of it all was when she told them the final detail, the thing that complicated every situation she could think of. Rick and Owen were conflicted, of course. Happy for her news, but there was the shadow of Cam's absence hanging over everyone.

She told Ryan last about the pregnancy, which turned out to be a good idea. He walked out and she hadn't heard from him since. The rest of the team hadn't heard from him either. That had been on day eleven. Day fifteen she moved into Cam's farmhouse. It was on day thirty-four that she learned about the agreement Cam had made.

The doorbell rang and she groaned as she got up from the couch. "How did I not know I was pregnant last time?" she muttered, feeling the nausea hit with every step. She opened the door without looking through the window first, and her jaw dropped.

"Hey, Kier."

"Collins?"

The man standing in her doorway looked vaguely familiar, but rather than a sandy, uniformed soldier there was a clean-cut, moderately handsome man in civilian clothing. He gave her a small smile and shrugged. "I was just in the neighbourhood."

She stood there staring at him for the briefest of moments. "You're from Pennsylvania."

"That's really all you have to say?" Nathan looked her over. "Well, you're not too fat yet, at least."

With a small shake of her head, she took the few steps towards him to close the distance and wrapped her arms around him, an embrace he returned. "What are you doing here, jerk?" she said into his chest.

"Oh, just checking in on the resident crazy lady." He pulled away and she led him inside. "I told Cam I'd make sure you were okay while he was gone. And I stayed in Afghanistan longer than I thought. I was there an extra three weeks going over logistical data." He paused. "They have me leading the recovery mission. We're getting him back at the five-month mark instead of the six."

She held her head. "Wait, what? Why have they moved it up?"

"Element of surprise. And Cam's making good progress."

At that her eyes widened. "You...you've heard from him? Is he alright?"

But Nathan shook his head. "We haven't heard from him personally. We can see each AIM unit he upgrades and brings onto our system." He lowered his face to hers. "He's doing it, and before long, you'll have him back. Mjahdan has even been pretty quiet, and some small factions have disbanded in the meantime. Things have calmed down over there."

"Can I...I want to be at a base. I want to watch."

He rubbed the back of his neck and finally looked around. He realized he didn't know Maria very well, but had the feeling he was in a man's house. "I don't know, Maria. You're way too close to this."

"I was part of that mission. I deserve to see it end, too. I get not being there in person for the recovery, but I need to see it through."

She had a point. "I'll see what I can do. We still have a few months to get that figured out. Now, in the meantime, I'm not planning on driving back to Pennsylvania tonight so, do you and your boyfriend have any beer?"

Maria watched as he walked into the living room and sat down on the couch. In her spot. "You know I'm single...ish. This...this is actually Cam's house. So don't blame me for the décor."

She looked around, trying to combine her two lives now, her life with Cam and yet seeing part of her military life in the same setting. Her eyes widened briefly when she realized he asked her a question. "Oh, yes, I have beer in the fridge." A thought hit her finally. "Wait, did you drive here?" When he shrugged, she paused. "That's a six-hour drive. Nathan-"

"Beer. Please. The healing circle can wait until I've had my beer."

"Yes, sir."

CHAPTER 19

Maria remembered the first time she had sat in a meeting room with high-ranking military officials. She was the only woman in the room, fresh out of Basic, and had to convince the group of them of her qualifications for her officer rank. With no university degree, she should have started at Private, but her work experience was what had given her the edge. Regardless, she stood out. Now as she sat in a similar meeting room, nearly six and a half months pregnant, she knew that despite what they had gathered there for, she was the focus. For now, at least.

It had taken Nathan a few weeks to convince the base in Ottawa to let her sit in, but recent developments made them open to the idea. Maria found out that Mjahdan had contacted the Kandahar base with a rendezvous proposal. The AIMs coming online were linking up less frequently now, which suggested there weren't many left. Mr. Moustache from their initial pass-off had bragged about having two hundred units. From the systems it looked as though close to that number had been linked.

This was good news, that they wanted the meeting. They could have simply sent Cam and Peter's bodies to the base. Or videos of them being killed. This meant they were trying to get on the army's good side. They wanted a show of peace. As the TV screens came to life, Maria wondered if Mjahdan was gearing up for something. If this was just to get Canada and America to either back off or turn a blind eye. She was willing to do both once Cam was home.

The screens were suddenly filled with bodycam feed and she felt her heart begin to race. "Comms, check," came Nathan's voice and Maria assumed he was the one wearing the camera.

"Loud and clear on this end," one of the senior officers in the room responded. Maria had been introduced to him, but she barely remembered getting to the base let alone the names of the soldiers around her. "You have clearance to go."

"Copy. Moving into position." The camera showed the recovery team moving down a dusty alleyway. Everything looked like it had been deserted long ago, scrap pieces of garbage fluttering on the wind as the only sign of life there. "The building is blocking all heat signatures. We're trying to tap into their electronics to get audio but those are being jammed. Informants confirmed a visual of Tylar and Lim escorted into the building." He paused. Maria noticed the pause. "Both healthy."

She let out a breath.

Cam looked around the dim room. For the past four months, he and Peter had been treated relatively well. They were never coerced or harassed. But the man he had come to call Joe, since none of them would tell him their real name, shoved him into the room with the butt of his gun. Cam rubbed his arm, shooting a glare at Joe. "Well, that was uncalled for."

A few more men stumbled into the room and spoke quickly with Joe. Cam looked up at Peter and gestured towards the others. "What's going on?"

But Peter shrugged. "They're speaking too fast. Something about needing to move, I think."

He was so close now. "Move? No. This is where they're getting us."

"If we need to move, they'll still find us. Something must be going on."

Cam shook his head. "No. I'm not waiting weeks for another meeting. I'm going home, now." He shoved Peter away when he tried to grab for him. "Hey." When they didn't respond, he shoved Joe. "Hey, I'm talking to you. We're not moving. I'm going outside."

"Cam!" Peter called out.

"No," he said simply. "I'm leaving. I did what you want. You have your new AIMs. I'm going home."

"On your command, Collins," the officer stated and sat back in his chair. He turned to the others and folded his arms. Like it was just an ordinary day at the office.

The building came into view. It wasn't large by any means, but Maria knew from their mission earlier that it was an abandoned Mjahdan holdout. Local government was talking about buying the building and converting it into a school. She smiled at the thought. Good things can come from the bad after all.

Cam grunted as he hit the floor, the air pushed from his lungs. He coughed as he stood slowly. "I've been through worse."

"Cam, enough!" Peter called out. The other men in the room began to speak quickly with each other, and two left the room. "Wait, compromised? Cam, I'm serious. They have to move us."

He groaned a bit and held his ribs. "What do you mean?" He turned on Joe again. "What's compromised?" A quick pop of Joe's rifle and Peter was down on the ground. Cam jumped back and swore. He felt calm. He thought he would feel different, looking down the barrel of a rifle.

Maria...

The team paused at the end of the alley and began to cross an open courtyard, moving towards an entrance. A voice yelling in Pashto came from the side off-camera accompanied by a high-pitched whistle. Maria watched as the building exploded, sending a cloud of dust and debris into the air.

The explosion rang through the room, and Maria could feel the walls around her shaking. She closed her eyes but she could still see the building tearing apart, could still feel the blast wave on her face, could smell the ash and dust tearing into her lungs. Her mind told her she could hear him screaming, but when she opened her eyes there was nothing. No sounds. Just a blurred video feed. No, it wasn't the feed. The tickle on her cheeks told her it was tears.

There was movement in the room around her; various people getting on phones, some opening up data pads to access other video feeds or satellite images. She didn't know which. Didn't care. He was in that building. He had been in that building. She put her hands on her stomach and felt the baby kick. She took a breath.

She could feel the texture of her shirt. It was soft. The material had started to pill. She could feel the raised bumps as she ran her hand across the material. It was striped. Black and white. The stripes were equal widths.

The room shook. The windows shattered. He screamed.

Maria put her hands on the table in front of her. It was brown and smooth. It was probably fake wood. She could see the grain and knots in the wood but she couldn't feel them. She tried with her finger nail to catch the grooves, but it was still smooth. She closed her eyes and saw the building still standing. She opened them again.

The building was gone.

Cam was gone.

'Bring me home.'

She felt the baby shift.

Cam was gone.

She put a hand on her chair's arm rest. It was black…

"Fall back! Move, move, move!" Nathan screamed at his team as the camera stayed on the wreckage. He was running backwards until the rest of the soldiers were behind him. And Maria could see all of it. All of the destruction.

"Can you confirm any survivors?" the senior officer asked. They had waited a few hours while the soldiers went through the rubble.

"No. We haven't found all the bodies," one of Nathan's soldiers responded. "But we've identified enough to know that Tylar and Lim were here, and can be classified as KIA." Another voice was heard, muffled. "We found Lim. Shot in the head."

A younger soldier stepped into the room. He looked around and saluted. "Sir," he addressed the senior officer. "There's a sat call for Lieutenant Kier."

She stood slowly, her face blank, not showing if she had actually heard the man or not. But she followed him anyway, and the video feed was shut down. She took the phone that was handed to her and she heard herself say, "Lieutenant Kier."

"Maria."

She closed her eyes and leaned against the wall. "Nathan. Are you alright?"

"I'm so sorry, Maria." The call was a surprise, but not as much as the waver in his voice. "I should have known it was going too well. We should have gone in and grabbed him when we had the chance."

"Are you alright?"

There was a pause. "I'm fine."

And then a silence.

"He told me to bring him home," she whispered. "I failed him. Oh God. He trusted me."

"Maria, no. Stop. You didn't fail him. I did. You..." There was a hitch in his voice, but Maria didn't hear it. "You brought the best part of him home. He wouldn't have wanted it any other way. He wanted you both to be safe. It's why he stayed. And he did it. Do you hear me? He did it," he reassured her. "He got us intel on other holdouts and weapons deals.

"Other militia groups have been reaching out, wanting to get rid of their old units. Cam had sent out footage of what could happen if they continue to use their current units. They basically came begging. Rogues are going to be a thing of the past. He did that."

Maria nodded, ignoring the fact that he couldn't see her. "I have a hard time believing it's over." *Just push through.*

"It's not," Nathan said forcefully. "This is, yes. But the world will keep on going around."

"Nathan."

"You don't need to say it yet."

She paused. "Cam's dead."

"I know."

"I thought...I thought I'd feel different." She took in a deep breath. "My dad died, you know. I...I remember falling to the floor. Cam catching me. And I sobbed. And the world literally fell away from under me. I don't feel that right now."

"What do you feel?"

"Numb." There it was again. "My baby kicking."

There was a sigh on the other end. "And I know you'll make sure that baby knows exactly the kind of man its father was. You'll tell his story, and hope the baby is less of an egotistical prick."

After another moment of static, she ended the call. There would be other calls to make, press releases to announce. Her tears and grief would come in time once she had a moment to breathe.

In time, she would learn to live in her new reality. But after all this, her horrible last year as a Scanner, after surviving Trevor McCarthy, this is what it came down to. It had all come down to this moment. People were safe. Finally. The AIMs Henk Baxter and Lucas Tylar Sr. pioneered were finally completed and being used around the world. Now the rest of it began.

Just one day at a time...

Six months later…

Maria sat on the damp grass, holding a sleeping baby. She put a hand on the stone in front of her, touching the engraved letters. Her breath caught in her throat.

“I wanted you to meet your son. Our son,” she finally managed to say. “He's perfect. Everything went well, I'm okay. Not back to work yet, of course, but I’m okay.” She paused, her hand sliding down and away from the stone. “I'm not…you were supposed to be here this time. You…”

She held their baby closer, trying not to wake him. Maria took in a slow, deep breath and held it briefly before letting it go.

Letting it all go.

“He's safe. I'm safe. Because of you. And I'll make sure…” Her tears flowed freely now, dropping down onto the baby's blanket. “He'll know. He'll know everything, Cam. About what you did, the man you were. How you saved us.”

Maria smiled lightly when the golden retriever beside her sniffed at the baby's head lovingly before resting its head back down on the grass in front of the headstone with a whimper. She closed her eyes and took in a few more deep breaths, counting backwards.

Seven.

Six.

Five.

Four.

ACKNOWLEDGMENTS

First, I thank God for the gifts He's given me, and the determination and courage to finally finish this novel.

My friends and family have been such an encouragement, even with the decade long wait to finally read this book. You've all supported me through so many ups and downs, and this book wouldn't be here without you.

To my beta readers, Samantha and Crystal, thank you for your invaluable feedback and for reading all three of my novels! And to all my previous beta readers, for being part of this journey.

And of course, thank you to all of my readers. Thank you for joining me and this group of characters from a futuristic sports team in Canada all the way to Afghanistan. Thank you for participating in my launch parties, for reviewing, for meeting me at book shows, and above all else thank you for reading.

I'm not quite ready to say goodbye to the world of Scanning. I make no promises, but while the stories of these characters are done, there are so much more I'd love to explore. And when/if that time comes, I hope you'll all join me there.

From the bottom of my heart, thank you.

ABOUT THE AUTHOR

Nichole Sotzek has a B.A Honours in Near Eastern Archaeology and Medieval Studies. A friend developed the idea for a novel as a child, and in 2010 the two began collaborating on 'Revealing the Revolution' until he gave her full control of the novel and concept a few months later. When she's not writing or reading, she spends most of her time outside, scanning.

'Finding the Impossible' is her third novel.

If you enjoyed reading 'Finding the Impossible' why not let people know? Leave a review on Goodreads and Amazon. Authors always love to hear what their readers think.

www.ingramcontent.com/pod-product-compliance
Lightning Source LLC
LaVergne TN
LVHW091112080826
845145LV00008B/1879

* 9 7 8 0 9 9 3 7 8 9 5 4 0 *